' 'Believe me when I te
investigation has ne
and extraordinary c

ELLERY QUEEN
in IPL Library of Crime Classics® editions:

The Drury Lane novels

TRAGEDY OF X

TRAGEDY OF Y

TRAGEDY OF Z*

DRURY LANE'S LAST CASE*

forthcoming

ELLERY QUEEN

THE TRAGEDY OF Y

INTERNATIONAL POLYGONICS, LTD.
NEW YORK CITY

THE TRAGEDY OF Y

Copyright© 1932 by Barnaby Ross. Copyright renewed 1959
by Barnaby Ross.
Reprinted with permission of the author's estate.
Cover: Copyright© 1986 by International Polygonics, Ltd.

Library of Congress Card Catalog No. 86-81917
ISBN 0-930330-53-6

Printed and manufactured in the United States of America
by Guinn Printing.
First IPL printing December 1986.
10 9 8 7 6 5 4 3 2 1

A Re-Open Letter
TO THE READER

Dear Reader:

In the event you read "The Tragedy of X" and failed to read its *Open Letter to the Reader,* or in the event you did *not* read "The Tragedy of X"—in which case you certainly failed to read its *Open Letter to the Reader*—let us explain for your benefit how it happens that Ellery Queen and Barnaby Ross are two and the same persons.

(All others may proceed directly to the story of "The Tragedy of Y.")

"The Tragedy of Y"—like the three other books in the *Drury Lane* tetralogy—was originally published under the author-pseudonym of Barnaby Ross.

This was at a time when certain works of fiction celebrating the exploits of that brash and intellectual young sleuth, *Mr. Ellery Queen,* were already staples in the bustling marts of mystery fiction.

Since *Mr. Ellery Queen,* the detective, was written about by a mysterious pair of authors known collectively as Ellery Queen, and since the new series celebrated the exploits of a different detective altogether—*Mr. Drury Lane*—the two young men who hid behind the Ellery Queen pseudonym felt that they should create a new pair of authors, so to speak . . . which they promptly did, and they christened themselves (or himself) Barnaby Ross.

A Re-Open Letter

Now if this explanation does not explain, it is because the English language is inadequate for the intricacies of the multiple identities involved.

Perhaps the whole stew will be more digestible if we simmer it down to this: We have been writing under the name of Ellery Queen for thirteen years; and at one period in our career we conceived a new fiction character and published him under a new author's name, Barnaby Ross, who lived and died only for the purpose of that conception.

Now the four books of the *Drury Lane*-Barnaby Ross cycle are being republished under our *real* fictitious name of Ellery Queen, by our Ellery Queen publisher; and we are very fond of them; and we are especially very fond of *Mr. Drury Lane;* and we vigorously trust that *you* will prove as fond of them and of him as we were and are and will remain.

On second thought, just plunge into "The Tragedy of Y" and devil take who wrote it.

"Ellery Queen"

New York
Spring, 1941

Scenes

PROLOGUE

Scene 1. The Morgue   3
    2. The Hatter House   14

ACT I

Scene 1. The Hamlet   29
    2. Louisa's Bedroom   47
    3. The Library   70
    4. Louisa's Bedroom   110
    5. The Laboratory   139
    6. The Hatter House   155

ACT II

Scene 1. The Laboratory   167
    2. The Garden   179
    3. The Library   187
    4. The Hamlet   199
    5. The Morgue   219
    6. Dr. Merriam's Office   224
    7. The Hatter House   233
    8. Barbara's Workroom   239
    9. The Laboratory   243

SCENES

ACT III

Scene 1. Police Headquarters		251
2. The Hamlet		258
3. The Morgue		269
4. Inspector Thumm's Office		272
5. The Hamlet		281
6. The Death-Room		286
7. The Laboratory		295
8. The Dining-Room		298

EPILOGUE   305
An Explanation in an Interlude

BEHIND THE SCENES   307

Characters

YORK HATTER, *a chemist*

EMILY HATTER, *his wife*

LOUISA CAMPION, *Emily's daughter by her first husband*

BARBARA HATTER, *a poet*

CONRAD HATTER, *a waster*

MARTHA HATTER, *his wife*

JACKIE HATTER, *their 13-year-old son*

BILLY HATTER, *their 4-year-old son*

JILL HATTER, *a hedonist*

EDGAR PERRY, *a tutor*

CAPTAIN TRIVETT, *a sea-dog*

CHESTER BIGELOW, *a lawyer*

JOHN GORMLY, *Conrad's partner*

DR. MERRIAM, *the family physician*

MISS SMITH, *a nurse*

MRS. ARBUCKLE, *cook and housekeeper*

GEORGE ARBUCKLE, *houseman and chauffeur*

VIRGINIA, *a maid*

DISTRICT ATTORNEY WALTER BRUNO

INSPECTOR THUMM

DR. SCHILLING, *Medical Examiner*

DR. INGALLS, *Chief Toxicologist, City of New York*

MR. DRURY LANE

QUACEY, *his familiar*

DROMIO, *his chauffeur*

FALSTAFF, *his major-domo*

Witnesses, Officers, Seamen, Reporters, Townsmen, etc.

Scene: NEW YORK CITY AND ENVIRONS

Time: THE PRESENT

A Dramatic Novel in Prologue, Three Acts, Epilogue, and Explanatory "Behind the Scenes."

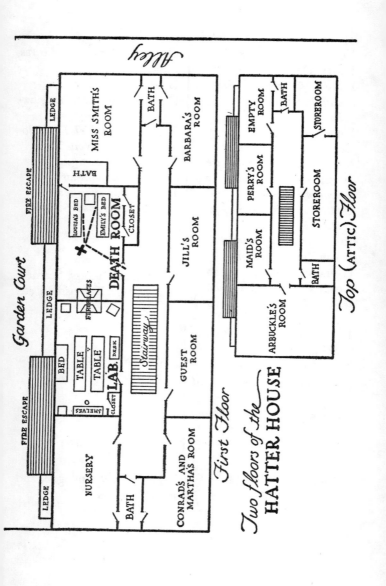

PROLOGUE

"Plays are like suppers . . . the prologue is the grace."

Scene 1

THE MORGUE. FEBRUARY 2. 9:30 P.M.

Ugly bulldog of a deep-sea trawler, the *Lavinia D* headed in from the long Atlantic swells on that interesting February afternoon, swam past Sandy Hook, snarled at Ft. Hancock, and pushed her way into the Lower Bay, foaming at the mouth and with her tail stuck straight out behind her. There was a poor seaman's catch in the hold, the dirty deck was a shambles, the raw Atlantic winds upset her stomach, and the crew cursed the captain, the sea, the fish, the graphite sky, and the barren shore of Staten Island to larboard. A bottle passed from hand to hand. Men shivered under spray-stung slickers.

A big fellow leaning on the rail disconsolately studying the flecked green swells stiffened all at once, eyes popping from a sea-red face, and yelled. The crew stared in the direction of his forefinger. A hundred yards away something small, something black, something unmistakably human and unmistakably dead was floating in the bay.

The crew jumped. "Hard a-port!" The man at the wheel leaned and swore.

PROLOGUE: SCENE I

The *Lavinia D* began a clumsy swing to larboard, creaking in all her joints. She circled the thing like the cautious animal she was, drawing nearer with every narrowing of her stalk. The crew, excited and happy, pawed the salt air with boathooks, eager to get at this queerest fish of the day's catch.

Fifteen minutes later it lay in a puddle of stinking seawater on the sloshy deck, limp and tattered and shapeless, but a man. A man who, from the ravished condition of his corpse, had been washed in the sea's deep vats for long weeks. The crew were silent now, standing with hands on hips, boots astride the deck. No one touched the body.

*   *   *

So, with the smell of fish and salt wind in his dead nostrils, York Hatter began his last journey. His bier was a dirty trawler, his pall-bearers rough unshaven men with scales clinging to their dungarees, his requiem the soft curses of sailors and the whistling of the wind through the Narrows.

The *Lavinia D* nudged her wet nose through the scummy water and tied up at a small slip near the Battery. Home with unpredicted cargo from the sea. Men leaped, the captain shouted himself hoarse, port officials nodded and looked briefly at the slick deck, telephones jangled in little Battery offices. And York Hatter lay quietly under a tarpaulin.

Not for long. An ambulance scurried up. Men in white took up the sopping burden. The dead march left the sea; and the dirge was made of clanging sirens. York Hatter was borne up lower Broadway to the Morgue.

His had been a curious, and until now mysterious, fate. On the twenty-first of December, four days before Christmas of the previous year, old Emily Hatter had reported her

The Tragedy of Y 5

husband missing from their house on Washington Square North in New York City. He had simply walked out of the red-bricked reliquary of the Hatter fortunes that morning, unattended, saying farewell to no one, and had vanished.

No trace of the old man's movements could be found. Old Mrs. Hatter could give no reason for her husband's disappearance. The Missing Persons Bureau offered the theory that Hatter had been kidnaped and was being held for ransom. This was effectually disproved when no word was received by the old man's wealthy family from the hypothetical abductors. Other theories were offered by the newspapers: he had been murdered, said one—anything was possible where the Hatters were concerned. The family denied this stubbornly; York Hatter had been an inoffensive little man, a quiet creature with few friends and, so far as could be discovered, no enemies. Another paper, perhaps on the strength of the curious and hectic history of the Hatter tribe, ventured the opinion that he had simply run away— away from his iron-jawed wife, his eccentric and trying children, his nerve-shattering household. This theory, too, went begging when the police pointed out that his personal bank account had been left untouched. It was from this fact also that the desperate surmise of a "mysterious woman in the case" died a-borning. And old Emily Hatter, furious at the suggestion, snapped that her husband was sixty-seven years old—hardly the time of life when a man leaves home, family, and fortune in pursuit of the amorous will-o'-the-wisp.

Throughout the five weeks of unremitting search the police had held to one theory—suicide. And for once, it appeared, the police were right.

*   *   *

6 PROLOGUE: SCENE I

Inspector Thumm of the New York Police Department, Homicide Squad, was fitting chaplain to York Hatter's rude funerary rites. He was big and ugly in everything: a hard gargoyle face, broken nose, smashed ears, big hands and feet on a big body. You would have supposed he was an old-time heavyweight prize-fighter; his knuckles were gnarled and broken from solid blows on crime. His head was gray and red: gray hair, slate eyes, sandstone face. He gave you the feeling of substance and dependability. He had a brain in his head. He was, as policemen go, forthright and honest. He had grown old in an all but hopeless fight.

This, now, was different. A disappearance, an unsuccessful search, the discovery of the fish-nibbled corpse. *And* plentiful hints to identification. All open and aboveboard, but there *had* been talk of murder and it was his duty, the Inspector felt, to settle the question for all time.

Dr. Schilling, the Medical Examiner of New York County, motioned to an assistant, and the nude body was lifted from the autopsy-table and restored to the wheel-table. Schilling's short fat Teuton body made obeisance before a marble sink; he washed his hands, disinfected them, wiped them thoroughly. When his fat little paws were dried to his satisfaction, he produced a much-bitten ivory toothpick and began thoughtfully to explore his teeth. The Inspector sighed; the job was done. When Dr. Schilling began to grope for cavities, the time had come for talk.

They walked together behind the wheel-table to the corpse depository of the Morgue. Neither said a word. York Hatter's body was dumped on a slab. The assistant turned inquiringly; into the niche? Dr. Schilling shook his head.

"Well, Doc?"

The Medical Examiner put away his toothpick. "Plain case, Thumm. The man died almost immediately after striking the water. Lungs show that."

THE TRAGEDY OF Y

"You mean he drowned right away?"

"*Nein*. He did not drown. He died of poisoning."

Inspector Thumm scowled at the slab. "Then it was murder, Doc, and we were wrong. The note might have been a plant."

Dr. Schilling's little eyes gleamed behind old-fashioned gold-rimmed spectacles. His dinky gray cloth hat stood in a grotesque peak on his bald head. "Thumm, you're ingenuous. Poisoning is not necessarily murder. . . . *Ja,* there are traces of prussic acid in his system. Then what? I say this man stood at the rail of a boat, swallowed prussic acid, and fell or jumped into the water. Salt water, mind you. Is that murder? Suicide, Thumm, and you were right."

The Inspector looked vindicated. "Great! Then he died just about as he hit the water—prussic acid killed him, eh? Swell."

Dr. Schilling leaned against the slab; his eyes fluttered sleepily. He was always sleepy. "Murder is improbable. There are no marks which might be ascribed to foul play. The few bone bruises and scrapings of the flesh—salt water is a preservative, or don't you know, you ignoramus?— were undoubtedly caused by the corpse colliding with undersea refuse. Plain bumps. The fish had a feast."

"Uh-huh. His face is unrecognizable, that's a fact." The man's clothing, lying on a chair nearby, was in rags, ripped and worried. "How is it we haven't found him before this? A body won't float five weeks, will it?"

"It is simple, childish. You blind men!" The Medical Examiner picked up a ragged wet overcoat, taken from the corpse, and pointed to a large rent in the fabric at the back. "Fish bite? Pah! This hole was made by something big and sharp. The body had been caught by a snag under water, Thumm. Tidal action or some other disturbance finally freed it; maybe the storm two days ago. No wonder you didn't find him for five weeks."

8   PROLOGUE: SCENE 1

"Then from the location of the body when found," said the Inspector thoughtfully, "it's easy enough to piece the story together. He swallowed poison, jumped overboard from, say, a Staten Island ferryboat, and floated out through the Narrows. . . . Where's the stuff from the body? I want to take another look."

Thumm and Schilling sauntered over to a table. A number of articles lay there: some papers so pulpy and shredded that nothing could be made of them; a brier pipe; a sodden box of matches; a key-ring; a sea-stained wallet containing paper money; a handful of miscellaneous coins. To one side lay a heavy signet-ring taken from the *annularis*, or ring finger, of the dead man's left hand; on the signet were the silver-etched initials *YH*.

But the Inspector was interested in only one salvaged object—a tobacco pouch. It was made of fish-skin and was waterproof; the tobacco was dry. Inside, safe from the salt water, a folded sheet of paper had been found. Thumm unfolded it for the second time; a message had been written in indelible ink in an almost mechanically perfect script, neat and clean as type.

The message consisted of one sentence:

Dec. 21, 19——.

To Whom It May Concern:

I am committing suicide in full possession of my faculties.   *York Hatter*

"Short and to the point," observed Dr. Schilling. "A man after my own heart. I am committing suicide. I am sane. Nothing more is required. A novel in one sentence, Thumm."

"Aw, stop, or I'll bust out crying," growled the Inspec-

The Tragedy of Y

tor. "Here comes the old lady. Notified her to come up and identify the body." He snatched a heavy sheet lying at the foot of the slab and flung it hastily over the body. Dr. Schilling uttered a Germanic guttural and stood aside, his eyes gleaming.

Into the mortuary trooped a silent company: a woman and three men. It was not necessary to wonder why the woman should be in advance of the men; this woman, you felt, would always take the lead, hold the reins, press the charge. She was old, old and hard as petrified wood. Her nose was a pirate's hook; her hair white, and her eyes dipped in ice, blue, and unwinking as a buzzard's. That chunky jaw would never waggle in surrender. . . . This was Mrs. Emily Hatter, familiar to two generations of newspaper readers as the "fabulously rich," the "eccentric," the "iron-willed beldame" of Washington Square. She was sixty-three, and looked ten years older. She wore clothes that were outmoded when Woodrow Wilson took oath of office.

She had eyes for nothing but the slab with its draped burden. Her approach from the door was a stalk, a judgment, a Fate. Someone behind her—Inspector Thumm noted that it was a tall, nervous, blond man strikingly in features like Mrs. Hatter—expostulated weakly; but she waded through the protest without pausing and, coming to the slab, raised the sheet and stared down at the torn, unrecognizable face with eyes that did not even flicker.

Inspector Thumm permitted her to indulge her emotionless fancy without interference. He watched her face for a moment, and then he turned to study the men who hovered by her side. The tall nervous blond—a man of thirty-two or so—he recognized as Conrad Hatter, only son of York and Emily Hatter. Conrad's face was predatory, like his mother's; but it was also weak, and dissipated, and in an

10 PROLOGUE: SCENE I

intangible way world-weary. He seemed ill; one quick glance at the dead face and he looked down at the floor, his right shoe beginning to dance.

By his side stood two old men, whom Thumm recognized from his original investigation of York Hatter's disappearance. One was the family physician, tall and gray, a man easily seventy, with thin sloping shoulders: Dr. Merriam. Dr. Merriam betrayed no squeamishness as he scrutinized the dead face; but he looked distinctly uncomfortable, a reaction the Inspector ascribed to his long acquaintance with the deceased. His companion was externally the queerest of the lot—an erect and salty figure, very lanky and attenuated. This was Captain Trivett, a retired ship's master and an old friend of the Hatters. Inspector Thumm saw with a sense of shocked discovery—he had never noticed it before! he thought with mortification—that where Captain Trivett's right leg should have been there was a leather-tipped pegleg protruding from the blue of his trouser. Trivett was making a great commotion over some obstruction in the depths of his throat.

He placed his old weatherpounded hand on Mrs. Hatter's arm in a deprecatory way. The old woman shook it off—a single flick of her rigid arm; Captain Trivett reddened and took a backward step.

For the first time she tore her gaze from the corpse. "Is this . . . ? I can't tell, Inspector Thumm."

Thumm took his hands from his overcoat pockets, cleared his throat. "No. Naturally you can't. Pretty much banged up, Mrs. Hatter. . . . Here! Have a look at the clothes and things."

The old woman nodded curtly; she betrayed only one sign of emotion as she followed Thumm to the chair on which the wet clothing was heaped—she licked her thin red lips like a cat after a feast. Dr. Merriam without a word

THE TRAGEDY OF Y

took her place by the slab, motioned Conrad Hatter and Captain Trivett away, and lifted the sheet from the corpse. Dr. Schilling watched him with professional skepticism.

"The clothing is York's. He was wearing these things the day he disappeared." Her voice, like her mouth, was tight and stubborn.

"And now, Mrs. Hatter, these personal items." The Inspector led her to the table. She picked up the signet-ring with slow claws; her frosty old eyes swept over the pipe, the wallet, the key-ring. . . .

"And this is his," she said dryly. "This ring. I gave it to him—— What's this?" She became excited all at once, snatched up the note, and encompassed its message in a glance. Then she was cold again, and nodded almost indifferently. "York's handwriting, beyond a doubt."

Conrad Hatter slouched over, his eyes shifting from object to object as if they could not find a resting-place. He, too, seemed excited by the dead man's message; he fumbled in an inner pocket and produced some papers as he muttered: "So it was suicide all the time. I didn't think he'd have the nerve. The old fool——"

"Samples of his handwriting?" snapped the Inspector all at once. He had for no apparent reason suddenly developed a temper.

The blond son handed the papers to Thumm. The Inspector, peevishly, bent over them. Mrs. Hatter, without another glance at either the corpse or her husband's effects, began to adjust her fur scarf about her scrawny throat.

"This is his fist, all right," growled the Inspector. "Okay. I guess that settles it." Nevertheless, he tucked both the message and the other handwriting specimens into his pocket. He glanced over at the slab. Dr. Merriam was just replacing the sheet. "What do you say, Doctor? You know what he looked like. Is this York Hatter?"

12   Prologue: Scene i

The old physician said, without looking at Thumm: "I should say yes. Yes."

"Man of over sixty," said Dr. Schilling unexpectedly. "Small hands and feet. Very old appendix stump. Operation, probably gallstones, some six or seven years ago. Does that check, Doctor?"

"Yes. I removed his appendix myself eighteen years ago. The other—biliary calculus of the hepatic ducts. Not a serious case. Robins of Johns Hopkins operated. . . . This is York Hatter."

The old woman said: "Conrad, make arrangements for the funeral. Private. A short announcement to the papers. No flowers. Do it at once." She began to walk toward the door. Captain Trivett looked uneasy and stumped after her. Conrad Hatter mumbled something that may have been acquiescence.

"Just a minute, Mrs. Hatter," said Inspector Thumm. She stopped and glared back at him. "Not so fast. Why did your husband kill himself?"

"I say, now——" began Conrad weakly.

"Conrad!" He retreated like a beaten dog. The old woman retraced her steps until she stood so close to the Inspector that he could sense the faintly sour exhalation of her breath. "What do you want?" she said in a clear acid voice. "Are you satisfied that my husband took his own life?"

Thumm was astonished. "Why—yes. Of course."

"Then the matter is closed. I want none of you bothering me again." And with a last malignant glance she went away. Captain Trivett seemed relieved and clumped after. Conrad gulped, looked sick, and followed. Dr. Merriam's thin shoulders sagged lower; and he, too, left without a word.

"Well, sir," said Dr. Schilling as the door closed behind

THE TRAGEDY OF Y

13

them, "that puts you in *your* place!" He chuckled. *"Gott, what a woman!"* He pushed the slab into the niche.

Inspector Thumm snarled helplessly and thundered to the door.

Outside a bright-eyed young man grasped his thick arm and began to walk with him. "Inspector! Howdy-do, hi-de-hi, and a good evening. What's this I hear—you've found Hatter's body?"

"The devil," growled Thumm.

"Yes," said the reporter cheerfully. "I just saw her stomping out. What a jaw! Like Dempsey's. . . . Listen, Inspector, you're here for no good reason, I know that. What's in the wind?"

"Nothing. Leggo my arm, you young baboon!"

"Nasty old temper, Inspector dear. . . . Shall I say suspicion of foul play?"

Thumm jammed his hands into his pockets and glared down at his inquisitor. "If you do," he said, "I'll break every bone in your body. Aren't you pests ever satisfied? It's suicide, damn it!"

"Methinks the Inspector doth protest——"

"Scram! Positive identification, I tell you. Now beat it, kid, before I kick you in the pants."

He strode down the steps of the Morgue and hailed a taxicab. The reporter watched him speculatively, the grin gone.

A man came running from Second Avenue, breathless. "Hey, Jack!" he shouted. "Anything new on the Hatters? See the old she-devil?"

Thumm's assailant shrugged, eying the Inspector's cab as it rolled away from the curb. "Maybe. Second question —yes, but nothing. Anyway, it makes a swell follow-up story. . . ." He sighed. "Well, murder or no murder, all I can say is—thank God for the Mad Hatters!"

Scene 2

THE HATTER HOUSE. SUNDAY, APRIL 10. 2:30 P.M.

The Mad Hatters. . . . Years before, during a period unusually full of Hatter news, an imaginative reporter, recalling his *Alice in Wonderland,* had so christened them. It was perhaps an unfortunate hyperbole. They were not one half so mad as the immortal Hatter, nor one quintillionth so delightful. They were—as their neighbors on the fading Square were prone to whisper—"nasty people." And, although they were one of the Square's oldest families, they never achieved the air of altogether belonging; always they were just an inch outside the pale of Greenwich Village's respectables.

The name took root and grew. One of them was always in the news. If it was not blond Conrad attempting to wreck a speakeasy in his constant cups, it was brilliant Barbara leading a new poetry cotillion, or holding levee under the lavish endearments of the literary critics. Or it was Jill, youngest of the three Hatter children; beautiful, perverse, sniffing sensation with avid nostrils. Once there had been the faint rumor of an excursion into the land of opium; occasionally the tale of a carousing week-end in the Adirondacks; always, with bimonthly monotony, there was the announcement of her "engagement" to some son of wealth . . . never, it was significant, to a son of family.

They were not only good copy, all of them, but queer copy. Weird, orgiastic, eccentric, unpredictable as they were, no one of them, however, surpassed the notorious achievements of their mother. Having spent her maidenhood more riotously than even her younger daughter Jill, she had plunged toward middle age as domineering, as iron-boned,

THE TRAGEDY OF Y

as irresistible as a Borgia. There was no "movement" beyond her social capacities, no market manipulation too intricate or perilous for her shrewd, hot, gambling blood. Several times it was whispered that she had badly burnt her fingers in the fires of Wall Street; that her immense personal fortune, inherited from a long line of rich and canny Dutch burghers, had dwindled like butter under the flame of her speculations. No one, not even her attorneys, knew the exact extent of her estate; and as the tabloid era sprang into being in post-war New York, she was constantly being referred to as "the richest woman in America"—a statement palpably untrue; and others accused her in print of being on the brink of penury, which was also pure fabrication.

From all of which—her family, her personal exploits, her background, her lurid history—old Emily Hatter was at once the bane and the delight of newspapermen. They disliked her, because she was a thoroughly disagreeable old witch; they loved her, because, as the editor of a great newspaper once said, "If it's Mrs. Hatter, it's news."

Before York Hatter's plunge into the chilly waters of the Lower Bay, it had been freely predicted that some day he would commit suicide. Flesh, they said—such honest flesh as clothed York Hatter—could stand so much, and no more. The man for almost four decades had been whipped like a hound and driven like a horse. Under the lashing whipcord of his wife's tongue he had shrunk into himself, lost his personality, become the specter of a man haunted in all his waking hours first by fear, then by desperation, and finally by hopelessness. His tragedy was that he, a normal human being with sensitivity and intelligence, was chained down in a lustful, unreasonable, vitriolic, lunatic environment.

PROLOGUE: SCENE 2

He had always been "Emily Hatter's husband"—at least since their nuptials thirty-seven years before, in furbelowed New York, when griffins were the last word in ornament and antimacassars were indispensable drawing-room accessories. From the day of their return to the Washington Square house—her house, of course—York Hatter knew his doom. He was young then, and perhaps he struggled against her strangling will, her rages, her mastery. Perhaps he reminded her that she had been divorced from her first husband, sober Tom Campion, under rather mysterious circumstances; that, in all good faith, she owed him, her second husband, a modicum of consideration and an abatement of that zigzag conduct which had been shocking New York since her débutante days. If he had, it sealed his fate; for Emily Hatter, who brooked no rebellion against her own commands, could not herself be commanded with impunity. It sealed his fate and ruined what promised to be a remarkable career.

York Hatter had been a chemist—young, poor, a scientific fledgling—but a research worker of whom earth-shaking things were predicted. At the time of his marriage he was experimenting with colloids, in a direction undreamed of by late-Victorian chemistry. Colloids, career, reputation withered under the assaults of his wife's fiery personality. The years dragged by; he became more and more morose, content finally merely to dawdle in the poor makeshift of a laboratory Emily permitted him to play with in his own quarters. He evolved into an all but hollow shell, piteously dependent on his rich wife's bounty (and religiously reminded of the fact), the father of her erratic brood but with no tighter rein over their arching necks than the family housemaid.

Barbara was the eldest of the Hatter children, and the

THE TRAGEDY OF Y 17

most nearly human of Emily's leaping blood. A spinster of thirty-six, tall, thin, faintly golden, she was the only one of the brood in whom the hereditary milk had not soured; she possessed a rich fund of love for all things alive and an extraordinary sympathy for nature which set her apart from the others. Of the three Hatter children she alone inherited the qualities of her father. At the same time she had not escaped the taint of abnormality which followed the steps of her mother like a musk-scented trail; except that in her case abnormality bordered on genius and gave vent to itself in poetry. She was already considered the foremost poetess of the times—a poetic anarchist, she was called in literary circles without opprobrium, a bohemian with a Promethean soul, an intellectual with a divine gift of song. Author of numerous volumes of enigmatic if coruscating verse, she had become with her sad, wise green eyes the Delphic oracle of New York's intelligentsia.

Barbara's younger brother Conrad had no such artistic weight to counterbalance his abnormality. He was his mother in trousers, a typical Hatter run wild. He had been the Peck's Bad Boy of three universities, thrown out of each in turn for reckless escapades as vicious as they were inane. Twice he had been dragged into the spotlight of the courts for breach of promise. Once he had run over and killed a pedestrian with his reckless roadster and had been saved only by the hasty and lavish bribes of his mother's attorneys. Innumerable times he had vented his Hatter spleen on peaceful bartenders when his strange blood became heated with liquor; he had in his time suffered a broken nose (carefully remodeled by a plastic surgeon), a cracked collar-bone, and welts and bruises uncountable.

But he, too, met the immovable barrier of his mother's will. The old lady hauled him out of the muck by the

18   PROLOGUE: SCENE 2

scruff of his neck and set him up in business with a sober, conscientious, and thoroughly praiseworthy young man named John Gormly. It had not kept Conrad away from the fleshpots; he returned often to wallow among them, depending upon Gormly's steadying hand for the preservation of their brokerage enterprise.

Somewhere in a comparatively sane moment Conrad had met and married an unfortunate young woman. Marriage, of course, did not check his mad career. Martha, his wife, a meek little woman of his own age, soon realized the extent of her misfortune. Compelled to live in the Hatter house dominated by the old woman, despised and ignored by her husband, her piquant face quickly grew a permanent expression of fright. Like York Hatter, her father-in-law, she was a lost soul in the Inferno.

Poor Martha could have expected little joy from her union with the quicksilverish Conrad; and what little she derived came from their two children, thirteen-year-old Jackie and four-year-old Billy . . . not an unmixed blessing, for Jackie was a wild, willful, and precocious youngster, a rampageous child with a wily brain and an inspired gift for inventing cruelties, who was a source of incessant trouble not only to his mother but to his aunts and grandparents as well. The tot, Billy, was inevitably imitative; and beaten Martha's thwarted existence became a grim battle to save them from the wreckage.

As for Jill Hatter . . . as Barbara said: "She's the eternal débutante. She lives only for sensation. Jill is the most vicious woman I have ever known—doubly vicious because she doesn't fulfill the promise of her beautiful lips and lecherous postures." Jill was twenty-five. "She's Calypso without the glamour, a thoroughly despicable creature." She experimented with men. And with what she constantly

THE TRAGEDY OF Y

referred to as "Life with a capital L." In a word, Jill was a worthy younger edition of her mother.

* * *

One would have said that this household was quite complete in its madness as it stood—the granite old witch at its head, haggard little York driven to suicide, the genius Barbara, the playboy Conrad, the wickedly pagan Jill, the cowed Martha, the two unhappy children. But it was not. For it housed one more, one so unusual, so tragically, gigantically pathetic that the vagaries of the others paled into normality beside her.

This was Louisa.

She called herself Louisa Campion because, while she was the daughter of Emily, her father was not York Hatter but Emily's first husband, Tom Campion. She was forty. She was small, plumpish, gently impervious to the bedlam about her. Mentally she was sound; of a docile temperament, patient, uncomplaining, a sweet good woman. Yet, surrounded by the notorious Hatters, far from being pushed into the background she was more than all of them the most widely known of the Hatter household. So much so that from the instant of her birth she became the instrument of a notoriety so deafening that repercussions of it had followed her resistlessly through all her dreary, fantastic life.

For, born of Emily and Tom Campion, Louisa had come into the world hopelessly blind and dumb, and with an incipient deafness which physicians said would grow more pronounced as she matured, and which would eventually leave her stone-deaf.

The medical profession had been mercilessly prophetic. On her eighteenth birthday—as a sort of birthday gift from the dark gods who seemed to rule her destiny—Louisa

PROLOGUE: SCENE 2

Campion suffered the final humiliation of total deafness.

To one less sturdily rooted, this affliction might well have proved fatal. For at that engrossing age in which other girls were discovering the passionate world, Louisa found herself stranded on a lonely planet of her own—a world without sound, image, or color; a world unexpressed and inexpressible. Hearing, her last strong bridge to life, lay behind her; the dark gods effectively burned it. There was no returning, and she faced a negation, a lack, a life sucked dry. As far as the primary senses were concerned, she might have been dead.

Yet clinging, timid, bewildered, all but helpless, something iron in her nature—perhaps the one beneficent heritage from her evil-dispensing mother—fortified her, so that she faced her hopeless world with equanimity born of a magnificent courage. If she understood why she had been so afflicted, she never indicated it; and certainly her relationship with the authoress of her misfortune was all that could be desired even between normal mother and daughter.

It was monstrously clear that the daughter's affliction lay at the door of the mother. It had been whispered at her birth that the father, Tom Campion, was at fault; that there was something evil in his blood which had taken toll of the child. But when Campion and the incredible Emily were divorced and Emily had remarried only to bear her own devil's litter of Mad Hatters, the world was assured that the fault had been the woman's. This was strengthened by the fact, it was thereupon recalled, that Campion had had a son by a previous marriage who was in all ways normal. The press forgot Campion, who died a few years after his divorce from Emily under mysterious circumstances; the son disappeared; and Emily, clutching the unfortunate York Hatter to her irresistible bosom, took the stunted

THE TRAGEDY OF Y 21

fruit of her first marriage to the ancestral house on Washington Square . . . a house which, after a generation of notoriety, was destined to be plunged into tragedy so stinging and mordant that all that had gone before might have been merely a weak prelude to the drama.

*   *   *

The bitter play began little more than two months after York Hatter's body had been fished out of the bay.

It began innocently enough. It was the custom of Mrs. Arbuckle, Mrs. Hatter's housekeeper and cook, to prepare an egg-nog for Louisa Campion each day after luncheon. The nog was pure swank on the part of the old lady; Louisa, aside from a rather weak heart, was in good physical health, and certainly at the age of forty, plump and soft, required few proteins in her diet. But Mrs. Hatter's insistence was not to be denied; Mrs. Arbuckle was a menial, and was incessantly being reminded of the fact; and Louisa, plastic enough in her mother's steel fingers, dutifully went each day after luncheon to the dining-room on the ground floor and sipped the maternal nectar. A custom of long standing, this, as it was important to note later. Mrs. Arbuckle, who would not dream of deviating from the old lady's commands by so much as a hair's breadth, always placed the tall glass on the southwest corner of the dining-room table, two inches from the edge —where Louisa would invariably find it, pick it up, and drain it each afternoon with as unhesitating assurance as if she could see.

On the day of the tragedy, or near-tragedy as it proved, a mild Sunday in April, everything proceeded normally . . . up to a certain point. At 2:20—Inspector Thumm later was careful to establish the precise time—Mrs. Arbuckle

PROLOGUE: SCENE 2

prepared the concoction in her kitchen at the back of the house (from ingredients which she defiantly produced during the police investigation), carried it herself on its accustomed tray to the dining-room, set it down on the table in the southwest corner, two inches from the edge, and—chore completed—left the dining-room and returned to the kitchen. No one, she testified, had been in the room when she entered, nor had anyone come in while she was setting the egg-nog down. So much, then, was clear.

It was a little more difficult to establish exactly what occurred thereafter; the testimony was not entirely sharp. It had been a period of excitement and no one's perceptions had been sufficiently objective to catch and fix the precise impression of positions, words, and events. It was approximately 2:30, Inspector Thumm determined rather unsatisfactorily, when Louisa came downstairs from her bedroom accompanied by the militant old lady bound for the dining-room and the egg-nog. They paused in the doorway. Barbara Hatter, the poetess, who had followed them downstairs, pressed close on their heels and looked, too; why, she could not afterward say, except that she sensed the vaguest feeling of something wrong. At the same moment Martha, Conrad's meek little wife, trudged wearily down the hall, coming from somewhere in the rear. Martha was saying in her lifeless voice: "Where's Jackie? He's been trampling the flowers in the garden again." She, too, stopped and craned in that split second of indecision in the doorway.

Coincidentally, a fifth person looked into the dining-room, eyes focused on the central figure. This was the one-legged old mariner, Captain Trivett, the Hatters' neighbor, who had accompanied the old lady and Conrad on the sad identification trip to the Morgue two months before. Captain Trivett appeared in the second of the two doorways to

THE TRAGEDY OF Y

the dining-room—a doorway looking not out upon the main corridor but upon the room adjacent to the dining-room, a library.

What met their eyes was not in itself disturbing. They saw, alone in the room, the undersized figure of the thirteen-year-old Jackie Hatter, Martha's elder son. He was holding the glass of egg-nog and looking at it. The old lady's harsh eyes grew harsher; she opened her mouth to say something. Jackie turned his head guiltily, all at once conscious of his audience; his gnomish face screwed up, a look of mischievous determination leaped into his wild eyes, and raising the glass to his lips he quickly gulped down a mouthful of the creamy liquid.

What followed was blurred. Instantly—and at the same moment as his grandmother darted forward and slapped the boy's hand viciously, screaming: "You *know* that's Aunt Louisa's, you filthy rascal! How many times has Grandma Emily *told* you not to steal her things!"—Jackie dropped the glass, a look of immense astonishment on his sharp little gamin face. The glass shattered on the floor, contents splashing far over the dining-room brick linoleum. Then, clapping his garden-grimed hands over his mouth, he began to scream hoarsely. Paralyzed as they all were, they somehow realized that it was not a peevish cry, but the result of genuine, burning pain.

Jackie's thin wiry body began to jerk, his hands twitched, he doubled up in agony, his breath came snorting, and his face turned a peculiar dusky hue. He sank, still shrieking, to the floor.

There was an answering shriek from the doorway; Martha flew in, her face bloodless, thudded to her knees, caught one horrified glimpse of the boy's contorted features, and fainted away.

24 PROLOGUE: SCENE 2

The screams had roused the house: Mrs. Arbuckle ran in, and George Arbuckle, her husband—the houseman and chauffeur; Virginia, the tall bony old housemaid; Conrad Hatter, disheveled and red-faced from early Sunday libations. Louisa, the afflicted, was forgotten; she stood helplessly in the doorway, pushed aside, bewildered. She seemed to recognize through a sixth sense that something was wrong, for she stumbled forward, her nostrils working, felt for her mother, and then began to pluck at the old lady's arm in a desperate way.

Mrs. Hatter, as might have been expected, was the first to recover from the shock of the boy's seizure and Martha's collapse. She leaped to his side, shoved the unconscious figure of Martha out of the way, took Jackie by the neck— his face was darkly purple now—and, forcing his stiffening jaws open, thrust her bony old finger down his throat. He gagged and vomited immediately.

Those agate eyes sparkled. "Arbuckle! 'Phone Dr. Merriam at once!" she shrilled. George Arbuckle ran hastily from the dining-room. Mrs. Hatter's eyes became grimmer; without the slightest squeamishness she repeated the first-aid treatment, and the boy responded again.

The rest of them, with the exception of Captain Trivett, seemed incapable of movement. They just gaped at the old lady and the squirming boy. But Captain Trivett, nodding approvingly at Mrs. Hatter's spartan measures, stumped around the room and sought out the deaf-dumb-and-blind woman. Louisa felt his touch on her soft shoulder, seemed to recognize him; and her hand crept into his and clung there.

But the most significant part of the drama was going on without being at the moment observed. For, unnoticed by anyone, a waddling spot-eared puppy—he was little Billy's

THE TRAGEDY OF Y

25

—had wandered into the dining-room. Seeing the splattered egg-nog on the linoleum, he yapped joyfully and scampered forward, burying his tiny nose in the liquid.

Suddenly Virginia, the maid, began to scream. She was pointing at the puppy.

He was threshing weakly on the floor. He shuddered, twitched a little. And then his four absurd legs became rigid. His belly heaved convulsively, once, and he lay still. It was evident that here was one puppy who would never lap egg-nog again.

* * *

Dr. Merriam, who lived in the neighborhood, arrived in five minutes. He wasted no time on the dazed Hatters, scarcely paid attention to them. The aged physician apparently knew his patients.

He took one look at the dead animal and at the retching, shuddering boy, and his lips compressed. "Upstairs at once. You, Conrad, help me up with him." Blond Conrad, a scared look in his now sober eyes, picked up his son and carried him out of the room, Dr. Merriam following quickly, already opening his medical bag.

Mechanically, Barbara Hatter dropped to her knees and began to chafe Martha's limp hands. Mrs. Hatter said nothing; the wrinkles on her face were hard as stone.

Jill Hatter, a sleepy look in her eyes, flounced into the room wrapped in a kimono. "What the devil's the matter now?" she yawned. "Saw old Sawbones going upstairs with Connie and the pest . . ." Her eyes widened and she stopped abruptly; she had spied the stiff puppy on the floor, the splashed egg-nog, unconscious Martha. "What . . . ?" No one noticed her; no one vouchsafed a reply. She sank into a chair, staring at the colorless face of her sister-in-law.

A tall, stout middle-aged woman in crisp white came

26 PROLOGUE: SCENE 2

in—Miss Smith, Louisa's nurse, who had been reading, she later told Inspector Thumm, in her bedroom upstairs. She took in the situation in a glance, and something like fright invaded her honest features. She looked from Mrs. Hatter, who stood like granite, to Louisa, who was trembling by Captain Trivett's side; then she sighed and, shooing Barbara away, knelt and with professional bruskness began to minister to the unconscious woman.

No one uttered a syllable. Together, as if moved by a common impulse, they turned their heads and regarded the old lady uneasily. But Mrs. Hatter's face was inscrutable; she had placed her arm about the quivering shoulders of Louisa and was watching Miss Smith's deft movements over Martha without expression.

After a century they stirred. They could hear Dr. Merriam's heavy tread descending the stairs. He came in slowly, set down his bag, glanced at Martha, who was beginning to revive under Miss Smith's ministrations, nodded, and turned to Mrs. Hatter.

"Jackie is out of danger, Mrs. Hatter," he said in a quiet voice. "Thanks to you. Fine presence of mind. He didn't swallow enough to kill him, but the prompt vomiting undoubtedly prevented a serious illness. He'll be all right."

Mrs. Hatter nodded manorially; then she jerked her head back and transfixed the old physician with frigid interest. She had caught something deadly in his tone. But Dr. Merriam turned away, and examined the dead puppy, and sniffed at the liquid on the floor, and finally scooped some of it into a little vial from his bag, stoppered the vial, and stowed it away. He rose and whispered something into Miss Smith's ear. The nurse nodded and left the room; they could hear her plodding upstairs to the nursery, where Jackie lay moaning on his bed.

THE TRAGEDY OF Y

Then Dr. Merriam bent over Martha, helped her to her feet, reassured her in a steady voice—all with the surrounding silence of the tomb—and the meek little woman, a strange expression distinctly not meek on her face, tottered from the dining-room and followed Miss Smith upstairs to the nursery. She passed her husband on the way up; neither said a word. Conrad lurched into the room and sat down.

As if she had been awaiting this, as if Conrad's entrance had been a signal, old Mrs. Hatter pounded on the table. It startled them all, all except Louisa, who crept deeper into the curve of the old lady's arm.

"Now!" cried Mrs. Hatter. "By Heaven, now we can get to the bottom of this. Dr. Merriam, what was it in that egg-nog that made the whelp sick?"

Dr. Merriam murmured: "Strychnine."

"Poison, eh? I thought so, from the dog." Mrs. Hatter seemed to rise inches higher; she glared about at her household. "I'll get to the bottom of this, you ungrateful devils!" Barbara sighed faintly; she placed her long delicate fingers on the back of a chair and leaned her weight on it. Her mother spoke acidly, in freezing tones. "That egg-nog was Louisa's. Louisa drinks a glass every day at the same time in the same place. All of you know this. Whoever poured poison in that drink between the time Mrs. Arbuckle placed it on the dining-room table and the time that rascal of a youngster came in and snatched up the glass, *knew* that Louisa would drink it!"

"Mother," said Barbara, "please."

"Keep quiet! Jackie's greed saved Louisa's life and almost took his own. My poor Louisa's safe, but the fact remains that someone tried to poison her." Mrs. Hatter clutched the deaf-dumb-and-blind woman to her breast; Louisa was

28 PROLOGUE: SCENE 2

making little whimpering, formless sounds. "There, there, darling," the old lady said in a soothing voice, as if Louisa could hear; she stroked the woman's hair. Then her voice rose in another piercing screech. *"Who poisoned that eggnog?"*

Jill sniffled. "Don't be so melodramatic, mother."

Conrad said weakly: "You're talking nonsense, mother. Who of us would dream of——?"

"Who? All of you! You all hate the very sight of her! My poor afflicted Lou . . ." Her arms tightened about Louisa. "Well?" she snarled, her old frame vibrating with passion. "Speak up! Who did it?"

Dr. Merriam said: "Mrs. Hatter."

Her rage drained off instantly; suspicion sprang into her eyes. "When I want your opinion, Merriam, I'll ask for it. Keep out of this!"

"That," said Dr. Merriam coldly, "I'm afraid is impossible."

Her eyes narrowed. "Just what do you mean?"

"I mean," replied Dr. Merriam, "that my duty comes first. This is a criminal case, Mrs. Hatter, and I have no choice."

He walked slowly to a corner of the room where an extension telephone stood on a cabinet.

The old woman gasped, her face becoming as purple as Jackie's had been. Throwing off Louisa, she darted forward and, grasping Dr. Merriam's shoulder, began to shake him violently. "No, you don't!" she shouted. "Oh, no, you don't, you infernal meddler! Make this public, will you? More publicity, more—— Don't touch that, Merriam! I'll——"

Heedless of the old woman's frenzied clutch on his arm, the imprecations rattling about his gray head, Dr. Merriam calmly picked up the telephone.

And called Police Headquarters.

ACT I

*"For murder, though it have no tongue, will speak
With most miraculous organ."*

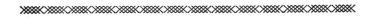

Scene 1

THE HAMLET. SUNDAY, APRIL 17. 12:30 P.M.

In the beginning, mused Inspector Thumm, God created the heaven and the earth, and a mighty good job He made of it, too, especially when He came to the Hudson River, some miles from the metropolis, in Westchester County.

The good Inspector was scarcely in either a religious or an æsthetic mood, since he was perforce supporting on his broad shoulders a particularly weighty Old Man of official responsibility; but even he, occupied as he was with mundane thoughts, could not long remain insensible to the beauty of his surroundings.

His car was toiling up a narrow winding road, straight up, up to the sky, it seemed, with an intricate faery vision ahead of battlements, ramparts, spires framed in green foliage and topped by blue-and-white clouds; and for contrast, the scintillant trickle of the Hudson, blue wrinkles studded with the white dots of pigmy boats, far below. The air that the Inspector sucked into the bellows of his lungs was sprinkled with wood and pine-needles and flowers and sweet dust, the noon sun was shining powerfully, and an

ACT I: SCENE 1

ice-tinged April breeze riffled his gray hair. It made a man glad to be alive, reflected the Inspector sententiously as he wrestled with an unexpected angle in the road, crime or no crime. This was his half-dozenth visit to The Hamlet, incredible residence of Mr. Drury Lane, he thought, and the damned place snuggled under your skin more and more each time.

He snorted to a stop before the familiar little bridge, the outpost of Mr. Drury Lane's estate, and waved rather boyishly at its sentinel, a ruddy little old man wreathed in smiles who pulled at his ancient forelock.

"Hi!" shouted Thumm. "Mr. Lane home this fine Sunday?"

"Yes, sir," piped the bridgemaster. "Yes, *sir*. Go right on through, Inspector. Mr. Drury says you're always to be admitted. Right this way!" He scampered to the bridge, tugged at a creaky gate, swung it back, and bobbed the Inspector's car across the quaint little wooden trestle.

The Inspector sighed for sheer content and stepped on the accelerator. Damned nice day, by God!

This was familiar terrain—this perfect gravel road, this wild greening copse, and suddenly, with the impact of a fanciful dream, this clearing before the castle. The castle was the pinnacle not only of the steep cliffs that thundered hundreds of feet down to the Hudson, but also of Mr. Drury Lane's aspirations. Its conception had been howled down by critics of the modern age; its architecture had been sniffed at by young men freshly out of the Massachusetts Institute of Technology, whose drawing-boards supported mile-high steel spires and solid concrete fastnesses; its author had been variously derided as "an old fogy," "an anachronism," "a strutting mummer"—this last from a bitter-keen fellow of the new school of dramatic criticism, to

THE TRAGEDY OF Y

31

whom any playwright earlier than Eugene O'Neill and any actor antedating Leslie Howard were "punk," *"Wiener-schnitzel,"* "archaic," and "bellywash."

Yet—there it was, with its sprawling cultivated gardens, its precise yew trees, its Elizabethan village of gabled cottages, cobbles, side lanes, its moat and drawbridge, and above all the buttressed stone immensity of the castle itself. It was a suety segment sliced out of the sixteenth century, a chunk of old England, something out of Shakespeare . . . the inevitable setting for an old gentleman living quietly among the relics of his fruity past. A past which not even his harshest critics could deny had been generously dedicated to the perpetuation of the immortal dramas, dedicated with something very like genius to a service in the theater which had brought him great fortune, great fame, and privately an immeasurable happiness.

This then was the native habitat of Mr. Drury Lane, retired emperor of thespians. And no matter how those busy fools in the City chose to regard it, Inspector Thumm observed to himself, as another old man swung open the massive iron door in the high stone wall surrounding the estate, this *was* peace, and it *was* pretty, and it *was* a relief from the dizzying atmosphere of New York.

He slammed on his foot-brake suddenly, and his car squealed to a stop. Twenty feet to his left there was an astonishing apparition. A tulip garden in the center of which grinned a stone Ariel spouting water . . . but it was the creature whose brown gnarled hand splashed in the fountain basin that fascinated him. The Inspector never overcame, in all the months of his acquaintanceship with Mr. Drury Lane and his establishment, a feeling of quaint unreality when he saw this gnome of an old man. The splasher was tiny, and brown, and wrinkly, and bald, and

32 ACT I: SCENE 1

bewhiskered, and on his elfin back there was a knobby hump—the entire unbelievable creature swathed in a leather apron, like the caricature of a blacksmith.

The ancient hunchback looked up, and his small brilliant eyes sparkled.

"Hey, there, Quacey!" yelled the Inspector. "What you doing?"

Quacey, who was the chief memento out of Mr. Drury Lane's past—his wig-maker and make-up man for forty years—placed tiny hands on crooked little hips. "I am observing a goldfish," he said gravely, in the clipped and creaking tones of advanced age. "You're a stranger here, Inspector Thumm!"

Thumm heaved himself out of the car and stretched with yawning arms. "Guess I am. How's the old man?"

Quacey's hand darted forth like a snake and came up dripping from the water with a wiggling little thing. "Pretty colors," he observed, smacking his leathery lips. "You mean Mr. Drury? Well, very well." He started suddenly, and looked aggrieved. "Old man? He's younger than you, Inspector Thumm, and you know it. He's sixty, is Mr. Drury, but he could outrun you like a—like a rabbit, and he swam four solid miles in that—brr!—ice-cold lake back yonder this morning. Could you do that?"

"Well, maybe not," said the Inspector with a grin, carefully skirting the tulip-bed in his path. "Where is he?"

The goldfish lost his courage, and of a sudden his squirmings decreased alarmingly. Almost with regret the hunchback threw him back into the fountain. "Behind the privets. They're clipping 'em. Great one he is for prettiness; Mr. Drury, I mean. These gardeners love——"

But the Inspector, chuckling, strode past the old man—not without caressing that grotesque hump, however, in passing, for Inspector Thumm was an eminently practical

THE TRAGEDY OF Y

33

man. Quacey guffawed, and dipped both fists of talons into the water.

Thumm parted a mathematically clipped privet, from behind which came a busy snicking and snipping and the deep pleasant tones of Lane's unusual voice. He stepped through, and grinned at a tall slender man in corduroys surrounded by a bevy of gardeners.

"Mr. Drury Lane himself, *in* person," announced the Inspector, extending an enormous palm. "Well, well! Don't you ever get older?"

"Inspector!" cried Lane in a delighted voice. "A nice surprise. Heavens, I'm glad to see you!" He dropped a heavy shears and gripped Thumm's hand. "How did you find me? People generally wander about The Hamlet for hours before coming upon the lord and master."

"Quacey," said the Inspector, dropping hungrily to the brilliant grass. "Ah-h! This is good! He's back a way there at the fountain."

"Tormenting the goldfish, I'll warrant," chuckled Lane. He doubled up like a lean spring and sat down by the Inspector's side. "Inspector, you're getting heavier," he said critically, eying Thumm's bulging bulk. "You should exercise more. I should say you've put on ten pounds since I last saw you."

"I should say you were damned right," grumbled Thumm. "Sorry I can't return the compliment. You look fit as a fiddle."

He eyed his companion with something suspiciously like affection. Lane was tall and spare and, somehow, vibrant. Except for the mat of pure white hair worn low on the neck, he might have been forty rather than sixty: his severely classical features were utterly unlined and youthful. In his gray-green eyes, so sharp and deep, there was certainly no trace of old age. His throat, revealed by the laid-

34 ACT I: SCENE I

back collar of his white shirt, was sturdy and muscular and bronzed. His face, so serene and immobile, yet so capable of sudden mobility, was the face of a strong man in his prime. Even his voice, powerful, resonant, and yet a flicking rapier under the necessities of expression—the voice that had rung almost sensually in the ears of multitudes of audiences —belied his lightly carried years. He was in the ensemble altogether an extraordinary figure.

"Something," remarked Mr. Drury Lane with a twinkle, "something not entirely social inspired that long journey from the City, Inspector. An elementary deduction, since you've neglected me all winter—in fact, ever since the culmination of the Longstreet affair.* What's buzzing in that busy brain of yours?" His penetrating eyes were fixed on the Inspector's lips. The actor was stone-deaf, a late development which had forced his retirement from the theater. With his uncanny ability to adapt himself to new situations, he had promptly taught himself the art of lip-reading, in which he had become so proficient that most persons with whom he came in contact remained unaware of his affliction.

Thumm looked sheepish. "I wouldn't say that. I wouldn't say that exactly, Mr. Lane. . . . But it's a fact that there's a little something going on in New York which has us buffaloed. Thought you might want to try your hand at it, sort of."

"A crime," said the actor thoughtfully. "Not this business of the Hatters?"

The Inspector brightened. "Then you've been reading the papers about it! Yes, it's these nutty Hatters. Attempted

---

*Reference to the murder of Harley Longstreet, the crime which instituted the investigation pursued by Inspector Thumm and Mr. Drury Lane in *The Tragedy of X* (IPL Library of Crime Classics, 1986).—The Editor.

THE TRAGEDY OF Y 35

poisoning of the old lady's daughter by her first marriage —this Louisa Campion."

"The woman who is deaf, dumb, and blind." Lane looked grave. "She interests me particularly, Inspector. A remarkable example of man's capacity for rising above mere physical handicaps. . . . And, of course, you've been unsuccessful."

"Yup," said the Inspector grumpily, wresting a fistful of grass from the sod. The gentle beauty of his surroundings seemed all at once to have lost its savor for him. "Absolutely stymied. Not a lead to work on."

Lane eyed him keenly. "I've read everything the newspapers reported," he said, "although probably details have been garbled and the entire story has not been told. Nevertheless, I know something about the family, the affair of the poisoned egg-nog, the child's nearly tragic greed—all the superficial facts." He sprang to his feet. "Have you had luncheon, Inspector?"

Thumm scratched his blue jaws. "Well . . . I'm not very hungry. . . ."

"Nonsense!" Lane grasped Thumm's beefy arm and heaved. To his astonishment the Inspector found himself half-lifted from the grass. "Come along and don't be an ass. We'll have a bite of something and discuss your problem over a mug of cold beer. You like beer, of course?"

Thumm scrambled to his feet and looked thirsty. "I wouldn't say I like it, but I wouldn't say I don't. . . ."

"I thought so. You're all alike. Cautious but willing. It might also be possible to persuade Falstaff, my little major-domo, to serve a drop or two of, let us say, Three-Star Martel. . . ."

"No!" said the Inspector enthusiastically. "Now, by God, you're talking, Mr. Lane!"

36 ACT I: SCENE 1

Mr. Drury Lane sauntered along the bulb-bordered path and observed with an inward chuckle that his guest's eyes were beginning to pop.

They were approaching through the trees the feudal village surrounding the castle. Its low red roofs and cobbled street, its narrow walks, its peaks and gables, were utterly charming. The Inspector blinked rather dazedly. It was only when he saw several men and women dressed in twentieth-century garments that he began to feel easier. Although he had visited The Hamlet a number of times, this was his introduction to the village.

They paused outside a low brown structure with mullioned windows and a swinging sign outside. "You've heard of the Mermaid Tavern, that rendezvous of Shakespeare, Ben Jonson, Raleigh, Francis Beaumont, and the rest?"

"Seems to me I have," said the Inspector wonderingly. "In London, where the boys used to hang out and throw parties."

"Precisely. In Bread Street, Cheapside—near Friday Street. And there's as quaint a collection of names as you'll find in a world of Sundays. This," continued Mr. Drury Lane, with a polite bow, "is an honest replica of that imperishable tavern, Inspector. Let's go in."

Inspector Thumm grinned. The beam-ceilinged room was filled with smoke, chattering, and smelt of good strong ale. He nodded approvingly. "If this is the sort of thing the boys of three-four hundred years ago went in for, Mr. Lane, me for it. Ummm!"

An astonishingly rubicund and pot-bellied little man, swathed in a spotless white apron tied high around the barrel of his waist, bustled forward to greet them.

"You remember Falstaff, my matchless Falstaff?" asked Lane, patting the little old man's bald pate.

THE TRAGEDY OF Y

"Indeed I do!"

Falstaff—Falstaff!—bowed and grinned. "The big mug, Mr. Drury?"

"Yes, and another for Inspector Thumm, and a bottle of brandy. *And* something good to eat. Come along, Inspector."

He led the way through the crowded room, nodding and smiling at the noisy diners. They found an unoccupied corner and seated themselves at a long, pew-like settle. Falstaff, more the innkeeper than ever, supervised the preparation of a savory luncheon, and served it himself. The Inspector heaved a huge sigh and buried his ugly nose in a foaming mug.

"Now, Inspector," said the actor, when Thumm had masticated his last mouthful and paid a last visit to the brandy bottle, "tell me something about your problem."

"That's the trouble," complained the Inspector. "There's precious little to tell. If you've read the papers you know darned near as much as I do. You've read about the old lady's husband committing suicide a couple of months ago, too?"

"Yes. The newspapers were naturally full of York Hatter's defection. Tell me what happened when you arrived on the scene."

"Well," said Thumm, slumping against the high walnut back of the settle, "the first thing I did was try to fix the exact time when the strychnine must have been slipped into the egg-nog. The cook and housekeeper, Mrs. Arbuckle, had set the glass on the dining-room table at about 2:25, and it was between five and ten minutes later, as near as I can figure it, that Mrs. Hatter came in with the deaf-dumb-and-blind woman to find that little hellion, Jackie, swigging the drink intended for his aunt. Not much there, hey?"

38 ACT I: SCENE 1

"No," said Lane. "From the surrounding circumstances, as I believe you pointed out to the reporters, any number of people had opportunity to poison the drink. Have you questioned the child to determine exactly when he came into the dining-room?"

"Sure, but you know kids. What could you expect? He said he'd gone in there just before his grandmother and his Aunt Louisa popped in on him. And we haven't been able to establish who might have sneaked into the dining-room before the kid."

"I see. Has the child fully recovered?"

Inspector Thumm snorted. "And how! Take more than a swig of poison to kill *him*. What a kid! The kind of brat you feel like choking to death. 'Course he didn't *want* to steal the egg-nog—oh no, of course not! He doesn't know *why* he drank it. Said: 'Gran'ma Em'ly scared me, and I just swallowed it.' Just like that. Too bad he didn't swallow a little more, I say."

"I'll wager you weren't exactly a Little Lord Fauntleroy yourself when you were a child, Inspector," chuckled Lane. "What was the disposition physically of the others during the approximate period when the egg-nog must have been poisoned? The papers weren't clear."

"Well, sir, in a mess, as you might expect. This sea-captain, Trivett—he'd been right in the next room, the library, reading a newspaper. But he didn't hear anything, he says. Then Jill Hatter—*she* was in her bedroom upstairs, half awake, in bed. At half-past two, mind you!"

"The young lady was probably out the night before," observed Lane dryly, "on what is professionally known, I believe, as a bender. Rather a pagan, I gather. The others?"

Thumm enveloped his brandy glass in a glance full of gloom. "Well, this Louisa woman—the queer one—gener-

THE TRAGEDY OF Y

39

ally takes a nap after lunch. She and her old lady occupy the same bedroom upstairs. Anyway, Mrs. Hatter, who'd been out in the garden making it miserable for somebody, went up, woke Louisa, and just at half-past two they came downstairs together, bound for the egg-nog. The skirt-chaser, Conrad—the kid's old man—he'd been wandering up and down the alley on the east side of the house, smoking. Had a bad headache—hangover, most likely—and wanted a breath of air, he says. The gal who writes poetry, Barbara Hatter—she's a big shot, I understand, and the only human one of the bunch, Mr. Lane, just a nice young lady with brains—she'd been writing in her workroom upstairs. Miss Smith, Louisa's nurse, whose bedroom is next door to Louisa's, overlooking the alley on the east—she'd been in *her* room, she says, reading the Sunday newspapers."

"And the others?"

"Small fry. There's this Mrs. Arbuckle, the housekeeper—she was in the kitchen at the back, cleaning up after lunch with the maid Virginia. George Arbuckle, Mrs. Arbuckle's husband, was in the garage at the back shining up the car. And that's about all. Sort of hopeless, isn't it?"

Lane nodded; his eyes were fixed immovably on the Inspector's lips. "Your one-legged Captain Trivett," he said finally. "An interesting character. Just where does he fit into the puzzle, Inspector? What was he doing in the house at two-thirty of a Sunday?"

"Oh, him," grunted Thumm. "He's an ex-sea-captain. Been living next door to the Hatters for a good many years —bought the place on his retirement. We've looked him up, don't worry. Got plenty of jack—he'd been to sea with his own freighting vessel for thirty years. Forced to retire after a bad storm on the South Atlantic. Big sea came over and

40 ACT I: SCENE 1

swept him off his feet—busted his leg in a couple of places. First mate did a rotten job, and when they made port they had to amputate. He's a rather salty old guy."

"But you haven't answered my question, Inspector," said Lane gently. "How did he happen to be in the house?"

"Give me a chance, can't you?" growled Thumm. "Excuse me. I was feeling grand until you reminded me of this business. . . . Trivett's always coming into the Hatter house. They say he was the only real friend York Hatter had—two pretty lonesome old codgers brought together, I suppose, by their mutual loneliness. Trivett took Hatter's disappearance and suicide pretty hard, I understand. But he didn't stop his visits. You see, he sort of shines up to this Louisa Campion—maybe because she's such a sweet uncomplaining sort with a terrible affliction, and him with a leg gone."

"Very likely. Physical deficiencies do bring people together. Then the good Captain was merely waiting to pay his respects to Louisa Campion?"

"That's the ticket. Calls on her every day. They get along fine, and even that old she-devil approves—only too glad there's someone who pays attention to the deaf-mute—God knows the others don't much. He came in around two o'clock; Mrs. Arbuckle told him Louisa was upstairs, napping, and he went into the library to wait for her."

"How do they communicate, Inspector? After all, the poor woman can't hear, see, or speak."

"Oh, they've worked it out some way," grumbled the Inspector. "She didn't get deaf, you know, until she was eighteen, and in the meantime they taught her lots of things. Mostly, though, Captain Trivett sits and holds her hand. She likes him a lot."

"Pitiful business! Now, Inspector, the poison itself. Have

THE TRAGEDY OF Y   41

you attempted to track down the source of the strychnine?"

Thumm grinned sourly. "No luck. We grabbed that lead right from the start. Naturally. But it stacks up this way. You see, this bird York Hatter never really lost his love for chemistry—big pumpkins as a chemical research worker in his young days, I understand. He'd rigged up a laboratory in his bedroom. Used to spend whole days up there."

"His personal escape from a distasteful environment. Quite so. And the strychnine came from that laboratory?"

Thumm shrugged. "I'd say so. Even there, though, we got into trouble. Ever since Hatter's fade-out the old lady's kept the laboratory locked. Strict orders; no one was to go in there. Sort of monument to his memory, or something. She wanted to preserve it in exactly the same condition that Hatter left it—especially two months ago when his body was found and it was definitely known that he was dead. See? Only one key, and she had it all the time. No other entrances to the lab—windows barred with iron. Well, as soon as I heard about the lab, I scooted up there for a look around, and——"

"You got the key from Mrs. Hatter?"

"Yes."

"She has had it in her possession all the time, you're certain?"

"That's what she claims. Anyway, we found strychnine tablets there in a bottle on a bunch of shelves Hatter had built. So we figured the poison came from that bottle— easier to drop a tablet into the egg-nog than to carry around a powder or a liquid. But how in hell did he get into the lab?"

Lane did not reply at once. He crooked a long, pale muscular finger at Falstaff. "Fill the mugs. . . . A rhetorical question, Inspector. Windows barred with iron—Hatter

ACT I: SCENE 1

must have been inordinately jealous of his one avenue of escape—door locked, and the only key constantly in Mrs. Hatter's possession. Hmm. . . . Not necessarily demanding a fantastic explanation. There are such things as wax impressions."

"Sure," snarled Thumm, "and didn't we think of *that*. Way I figure it, Mr. Lane, there are three possible explanations. First: the poisoner may have stolen the strychnine from the laboratory *before* York Hatter's disappearance, when the room was open and accessible to anybody, and saved the poison till last Sunday. . . ."

"Ingenious," commented Lane. "Go on, Inspector."

"Second, someone took a wax impression of the lock, as you suggest, had a key made, and so gained entrance to the lab and got the poison shortly before the attempted crime."

"Or *long* before, Inspector. Yes?"

"Or third, the poison was secured from an outside source altogether." Thumm accepted a brimming, spumy mug from Falstaff's hand, and drained it thirstily. "Swell," he said in a gurgly voice. "I mean the beer. Well, we've done what we could. The key theory—followed it up— general search of all locksmith and hardware stores . . . nothing doing yet. Outside source—we're checking up on that, also with no success to date. And that's how it stands today."

Lane drummed reflectively on the table. The room was thinning; they were almost alone in the Mermaid. "And has it occurred to you," he said after a silence, "that the egg-nog might have been poisoned *before* Mrs. Arbuckle carried it into the dining-room?"

"Holy Mother of God, Mr. Lane," growled the Inspector, "what do you think I am? Sure it occurred to me. Exam-

The Tragedy of Y

43

ined the kitchen, but there wasn't a sign of the strychnine or poisoner. It's true, though, that Mrs. Arbuckle had left it on the kitchen table for a couple of minutes and had gone into the pantry for something. The maid Virginia had gone into the drawing-room a minute before to dust it. So someone might have sneaked into the kitchen and poisoned the drink while Mrs. Arbuckle wasn't looking."

"I begin to appreciate your perplexity," said Lane with a rueful smile. "And to share in it, Inspector. There was no one else in the Hatter house that Sunday afternoon?"

"Not a soul that I've been able to discover. But the front door was unlocked, and anyone might have slipped into the house and out without being seen. That business of the daily egg-nog in the dining-room at half-past two is known to all the acquaintances of the Hatters."

"I understand that someone of the household was not in the house at the time of the poisoning—Edgar Perry, the private tutor of Conrad Hatter's two children. Have you checked up on him?"

"Absolutely. Perry has his Sundays off, and last Sunday morning he took a long walk, he says, through Central Park—spent the day by himself. Didn't get back to the house until late afternoon, when I was already there."

"How did he take the news of the attempted poisoning?"

"Seemed surprised and, I think, kind of worried when he learned about it. Couldn't offer any explanation."

"We seem," observed Mr. Drury Lane, the smile gone from his carved features, a frown between his eyes, "to be pushing farther into the fog. And motive? The crux of the situation may lie there."

Inspector Thumm groaned unashamedly, as a strong man with his strength balked might groan. "Every damned one of 'em might have had motive. The Hatter bunch are

ACT I: SCENE I

nuts—crazy as loons, the caboodle of 'em, excepting maybe the poetess, Barbara, and even she's screwy in her own way, only her screwiness is poetry. You see, Mrs. Hatter's whole life is wrapped up in this deaf-dumb-and-blind daughter of hers. Watches over her like a mama tiger. Sleeps in the same room, practically feeds her, helps her dress—devotes her life to making Louisa's as bearable as possible. Only thing in the old hell-cat that's human."

"And, of course, the other children are jealous," murmured Lane with a flicker in his lamp-eyes. "They would be. Passionate, wild, and with the instinct to violence unrestrained by any moral consideration. . . . Yes. I begin to see the possibilities."

"I've been seeing 'em for a week," snapped the Inspector. "The old lady's attentions to Louisa are so persistent that her other children are damned sore, jealous. Not that it's any matter of sweetness and light and 'I love you, mummy dear!'" The Inspector smiled wickedly. "I doubt if it's love. It's just pride and a sort of cussedness. And then, as far as Louisa is concerned—well, remember that she isn't their sister, Mr. Lane, but their half-sister."

"It makes a considerable difference," agreed Lane.

"It makes all the difference in the world. For instance, Jill, the youngest, won't have a thing to do with Louisa, claims her presence is a pall over the house and that none of her friends like to come there, because Louisa makes everybody feel uncomfortable with her peculiar ways. Peculiar ways! She can't help it, but that doesn't make a particle of difference to Jill. Not *her*. I wish she were my daughter." Thumm's hand descended with a swish on his thigh. "Conrad feels the same way—constantly bickering with his mother to have Louisa shipped off to some institution where she'll be out of the way. Claims she prevents them from

The Tragedy of Y

45

leading normal lives. Normal!" sneered the Inspector. "That bird's idea of normal living is a case of hooch under the table and a Follies girl on each knee."

"And Barbara Hatter?"

"Now that's something else again." Inspector Thumm seemed to have developed a passion for the poetess, for he consulted his beer, licked his chops, and replied in a very warm tone after Lane's questioning glance: "What I mean —she's a fine girl, Mr. Lane. Sensible. I won't say she loves the deaf-mute, but from all I've fished out of 'em Barbara pities her, tries to help her get some interest in life—what you'd expect a real woman with a heart in her to do."

"Miss Hatter has evidently made a conquest," said Lane, rising. "Come along, Inspector, for a breath of air."

Thumm struggled to his feet, loosened his belt, and preceded his host into the quaint little street. They strolled back toward the gardens. Lane was sunk in thought, his eyes cloudy and his mouth a tight line. Thumm clumped along rather morosely.

"Conrad and his wife don't get on very well, I take it," said Lane at last, dropping on a rustic bench. "Sit down, Inspector."

Thumm obeyed, limply, like a man tired of thinking. "They don't. Lead a cat-and-dog life. She told me that she was going to take her two kids out of 'this awful house' as soon as she could—got all excited, she did. . . . Found out something interesting about her from Miss Smith, Louisa's nurse. Couple of weeks ago Martha and the old lady had a scrap. Seems Mrs. Hatter was slapping the kids around, and Martha got all worked up. Called her mother-in-law an 'evil old witch,' damned her for an interfering old busybody, and said she wished the old lady were dead —you know how women are when they get excited. Any-

46 ACT I: SCENE 1

way, it developed into almost a hair-pulling match. Miss Smith got the kids out of the room—both of 'em were scared stiff. . . . Martha's meek as a lamb, you understand, but bad when she's riled. I sort of feel sorry for her; she's living in a nut-factory. I wouldn't want my kids growing up in such an environment, I'll tell you that."

"And Mrs. Hatter is a wealthy woman," mused Lane, as if he had not caught the import of Thumm's story. "Possibly a money motive in the background. . . ." He was growing gloomier with each passing moment.

They sat in silence. It was cool in the gardens; from the little village came the sound of laughter. The Inspector folded his arms on his chest, watching Lane's face. What he saw there evidently dissatisfied him, for he growled: "Well, what's the verdict, Mr. Lane? See any light?"

Mr. Drury Lane sighed, smiled faintly, and shook his head. "Unfortunately I'm not a superman, Inspector."

"You mean you——?"

"I mean I haven't the vaguest notion of the answer. Who poisoned the egg-nog? Not even a workable theory. Facts, facts—insufficient for an exclusive hypothesis."

Thumm looked sad. He had both expected and feared this. "Any recommendations?"

Lane shrugged. "Only one warning. Once a poisoner always a poisoner. There will be, beyond any doubt, another attempt on Louisa Campion's life. Not immediately, of course. But some day, when the poisoner thinks he is safe. . . ."

"We'll do all we can to prevent it," said the Inspector in a none too confident voice.

The old actor rose suddenly to his lean height, and Thumm looked up at him in astonishment. Lane's face was expressionless—an infallible sign that an idea was shouting in his brain. "Inspector. I understand that Dr. Merriam took

THE TRAGEDY OF Y

47

a sample of the poisoned egg-nog from the pool of it on the dining-room linoleum?" Thumm wagged his head, eying his host curiously. "And did the Medical Examiner analyze the sample?"

The Inspector relaxed. "Oh," he said. "That. Yes, I had Doc Schilling test it in the City laboratory."

"Did Dr. Schilling report the result of his analysis?"

"Here, here!" said the Inspector. "What's eating you? Nothing mysterious about it, Mr. Lane. Sure he reported the result."

"Did he say whether the amount of poison in the egg-nog was *a lethal dose?*"

The Inspector snorted. "Lethal? You bet your boots it was lethal. Enough in that drink, Doc said, to kill half a dozen people."

The moment passed; Lane's face resumed its normal pleasant expression, slightly tinged now with disappointment; and the Inspector read failure in the gray-green eyes. "Then all I can suggest—a poor reward for your long hot journey, Inspector!" said Mr. Drury Lane, "is that you watch the Mad Hatters very closely indeed."

Scene 2

LOUISA'S BEDROOM. SUNDAY, JUNE 5. 10 A.M.

It will be observed that from the beginning the Hatter case struck a leisurely note. This was no business of crime following hotly on the heels of crime, a swift series of events, a rapid pounding of the fatal hammer. It was slow, slow, almost indolent in its pace, and because of its very slowness

48 ACT I: SCENE 2

there was something remorseless about it, like the march of Jagannath.

In a way, this tardy evolution of events seemed significant, although at the time no one, including Mr. Drury Lane, came within guessing distance of the truth. York Hatter's disappearance in December, the discovery of his dead body in February, the attempt to poison the deaf-and-dumb-and-blind woman in April, and then, a very little less than two months later, on a sunny Sunday morning in June . . .

Lane, snug and cloistered in his castellated retreat up the Hudson, had forgotten the Hatter case and Inspector Thumm's visit. The papers had gradually dropped their copious interest in the poisoning attempt, until finally the entire incident was omitted from the news. Despite Inspector Thumm's best efforts nothing further had been uncovered which in the slightest degree pointed to any single person as the poisoner. The excitement subsiding, the police subsided as well.

Until June the fifth.

Mr. Drury Lane was apprised of it by telephone. He had been lying outstretched on the bare battlements of the castle, sunning his nude body, when old Quacey stumbled up the curving turret stairs, his gnome's face purple with exertion.

"Inspector Thumm!" he wheezed. "On the telephone, Mr. Drury! He—he . . ."

Lane sat up in alarm. "What is it, Quacey?"

"He says," panted the ancient, "something has happened at the Hatter house!"

Lane wriggled his brown body forward and squatted on his lean haunches. "So it's come at last," he said slowly. "When? Who? What did the Inspector say?"

Quacey wiped his dripping forehead. "He didn't say. He

THE TRAGEDY OF Y

49

was excited, the Inspector was. He yelled at me. I was never so put out in my whole——"

"Quacey!" Lane rose. "Talk quickly."

· "Yes, Mr. Drury. If you want to look things over, he says, come down to the Hatter house at once, he says. Washington Square North. Everything will be held for you. But hurry, he says!"

Lane had already bounded down the turret stairs.

Two hours later, piloted by that perpetually grinning young man whom Lane called Dromio—it was a conceit of his to rename his familiars out of Shakespeare—Lane's black Lincoln limousine was dodging in and out of heavy traffic on lower Fifth Avenue. As they slid across the car-tracks at Eighth Street, Lane could see a farflung crowd of people massed in Washington Square Park, belabored by police and obstructing the motor highway beneath the Arch. Two motorcycle policemen stopped Dromio. "No passing this way!" one of them yelled. "Turn around and detour!"

A fat red-faced sergeant ran up. "Mr. Lane's car? Inspector Thumm said to pass you through the lines. Okay, boys. Official."

Dromio crawled around the corner into Waverly Place. Police lines had been established, cutting off the entire north side of the Square between Fifth Avenue and Macdougal Street. The walks in the Park across the street were jammed with onlookers; reporters and cameramen were scurrying about like ants. Police and heavy-footed plainclothesmen were everywhere.

The vortex of the disturbance was apparent at once, and Dromio brought the limousine to a stop before it. It was a three-story box-like structure of bright red brick, an old-fashioned house of obvious antiquity—a relic of the Square's horsy days, with wide windows heavily curtained, a frieze

ACT I: SCENE 2

of a cornice at the roof, and a high white stone stoop with an iron handrail running up each side; at the head of which, on the landing, were two cast-iron lionesses green with age. The stoop was thickly populated by detectives. The wide white-paneled door stood open, disclosing from the sidewalk a small vestibule.

Lane descended from his limousine rather sadly. He was dressed in a cool linen suit, a leghorn hat, white shoes, and he carried a rattan stick. He stared up at the landing, sighed, and then began to climb the stone steps. A man popped his head out of the vestibule.

"Mr. Lane? Right this way. Inspector Thumm's waiting for you."

The Inspector himself—his face a study in crimson surliness—met Lane inside. It was a hushed interior: a long cool hall, wide and deep, flanked by closed doors. In the center of the corridor there was an old-fashioned walnut stairway leading to the upper floors. And, in contrast to the swirling street, the inside of the house was as quiet as a tomb. No one was about—not even, so far as Lane could see, police.

"Well," said Thumm in a tragic voice, "it's come." For once he seemed at a loss for words; "it's come" seemed to represent the ultimate boundary of comment.

"Louisa Campion?" asked Lane. It seemed a futile question. How could it be anyone but Louisa Campion, when an attempt on her life had been made two months before?

Inspector Thumm growled: "No."

Lane's astonishment was almost comical. "Not Louisa Campion!" he exclaimed. "Then who . . . ?"

"The old lady. Murdered!"

*　　*　　*

They faced each other there in the cool hall, eye to eye, and saw no consolation in each other's features. "Mrs. Hat-

THE TRAGEDY OF Y   51

ter," repeated Lane for the third time. "That's strange, Inspector. Almost as if someone has murderous intentions against the Hatters as a family, rather than against an individual."

Thumm moved impatiently toward the staircase. "You think so?"

"I was merely thinking aloud," said Lane a little stiffly. "Evidently you don't agree with me." They began to mount the stairs side by side.

The Inspector plodded upward, as if in pain. "I don't disagree either. I just don't know what the devil to think."

"Poison?"

"No. At least it doesn't look that way. But you'll see for yourself."

At the head of the stairs they paused. Lane's glance sharpened. They stood in a long corridor. On all sides were closed doors, and before each door stood a policeman.

"Bedrooms, Inspector?"

Thumm grunted and began to skirt the wooden railing of the stairhead. He stopped short, tensing, and Lane collided with him. For a chunky officer leaning against a door at the northwest corner of the corridor suddenly said: "Ouf!" and staggered backwards as the door behind him was yanked open.

The Inspector relaxed. "There go those damned kids again," he snarled. "Hogan, for God's sake, can't you see that the brats *stay* in the nursery?"

"Yes, sor," panted Hogan, who was having his difficulties. A small boy, shouting and whooping, had shot between the officer's meaty legs and was scrambling down the hall with earnest determination. Hogan regained his balance only to be upset again by an even smaller boy, no more than a toddler, who scurried between the inviting legs and shouted and whooped in gleeful imitation of the first. The

52   ACT I: SCENE 2

officer dashed forward, followed by a harassed-looking woman who shrieked: "Jackie! Billy! Oh, you children— you *know* you mustn't!"

"Martha Hatter?" whispered Lane. She was rather a pretty woman, but there were crow's-feet around her eyes and her freshness had been washed out. Thumm nodded, grimly watching the mêlée.

Hogan valiantly grappled with Jackie, the thirteen-year-old boy; Jackie, from his yells, wanted to observe what was going on, it appeared; he screamed and kicked at the officer's legs, to that gentleman's painful embarrassment. Martha Hatter snatched up the toddler who, following his brother's example, was directing wild but energetic kicks at Hogan's ankles; and in a flurry of arms, legs, red faces, and disheveled hair all four combatants disappeared into the nursery. From the screams ripping through the door, it was evident that the scene of the battle had merely been transferred.

"And that," said Inspector Thumm bitterly, "is a sample of this combination nut-and-charnel house. Those little devils have been making our lives one long hell. . . . Here we are, Mr. Lane."

                    *   *   *

Directly opposite the head of the stairway there was a door, not five feet from an angle in the corridor wall toward the east. This door stood slightly ajar. Thumm swung it open soberly enough and stepped aside. Lane paused in the doorway, the glitter of the manhunt in his eyes.

The room was almost square: a bedroom. There were two oriel-windows opposite the door across the room, overlooking the garden which lay at the north, or rear, of the house. A door on the eastern wall near the windows led to a private bathroom, Thumm explained. The hall doorway in which Lane and Thumm stood was at the left side

THE TRAGEDY OF Y

of the bedroom's corridor wall; at the right side, Lane observed, there was a long deep closet, which explained why the corridor narrowed at the head of the staircase outside, for the extra space consumed by the closet continued along the rest of the corridor toward the east, where there was another room.

From where Lane stood he could see two beds—of the twin-bed variety—set with their backs to the right-hand wall, and separated from each other by a large night-table with two feet of leeway on either side. The nearer bed sported a small bed light, attached to the headboard; there was no lamp on the farther bed. On the left-hand wall, toward the center and directly opposite the beds, there was a vast old-fashioned stone fireplace, with a look of disuse about it despite the set of fire-irons hanging on a rack nearby.

These observations were instinctive and instantaneous. For Lane, after one quick glance about at the general disposition of the furniture, brought his eyes back to the beds.

"Deader than a last year's mackerel," grunted Inspector Thumm, leaning against the jamb. "Take a good look. Pretty, ain't she?"

On the bed nearer the door—the bed with the attached lamp—lay Mrs. Hatter. Thumm's cynical comment was scarcely necessary; the old lady, lying in a contorted position amid a helter-skelter of bedclothes, her glassy eyes wide open, her face suffused and ropy-veined and purplish, was the least lifelike object imaginable. There were some extremely peculiar markings on her forehead—bloody marks reaching up into her wild straw-gray hair.

Lane squinted at them, looked puzzled, and then turned his attention to the other bed. It was empty, a tumbled pile of clean bedclothes.

"Louisa Campion's?"

54   ACT I: SCENE 2

Thumm nodded. "That's where the deaf-dumb-and-blind woman sleeps, but she's been removed from this room. She was found here on the floor early this morning, unconscious."

Lane's silky white brows went up. "Attacked?"

"I don't think so. Tell you all about it later. She's in the next room—Miss Smith's room. The nurse is taking care of her."

"Then Miss Campion is all right?"

Thumm grinned owlishly. "Funny, hey? You'd suppose that whoever's on a bender in this house would go for her, judging from past performances. But she's okay, and it's the old lady who got it."

There was a step in the corridor behind them, and both men turned quickly. Lane's face brightened. "Mr. Bruno! This is a pleasure."

They shook hands warmly. Walter Bruno, District Attorney of New York County, was a sturdy, ascetic-faced man of middle height wearing rimless eyeglasses. He looked tired. "Glad to see you, Mr. Lane. We don't seem to meet except when somebody's been yanked into hell."

"Your fault entirely. Like Inspector Thumm, you've neglected me all winter. Have you been here long?"

"A half hour. What do you think of it?"

"Nothing yet." The actor's eyes kept roving about the death-room. "What happened exactly?"

The District Attorney slumped against the jamb. "I've just seen the Campion woman. Pitiful thing. The body was found at six o'clock this morning by Miss Smith—she's in the room next door, overlooking both the garden at the rear and the alley to the east. . . ."

"Geography, Mr. Bruno?" murmured Lane.

Bruno shrugged. "It may be important. Anyway, Louisa

The Tragedy of Y

is a pretty early riser, and Miss Smith generally gets up at six to come in here and see if she wants anything. She discovered Mrs. Hatter exactly as you now see her, in bed; but Louisa was lying on the floor, roughly between her own bed and the fireplace there, her head toward the fireplace and her feet just about in the space between the twin beds. Here, I'll show you." He started forward into the room, but Lane placed a hand on his arm.

"I think I can visualize it," he said. "I rather think, too, that the less we walk about on the floor the better off we'll be. Please continue."

Bruno regarded him curiously. "Oh, you mean these footprints! Well, Miss Smith saw at once that the old woman was dead, and she thought Louisa was dead, too. So she screamed, being a woman after all, and her screams aroused Barbara and Conrad Hatter. They ran in, took in the situation at a glance, and without touching anything——"

"You're positive of that?"

"Well, they were all checks on each other, so we've got to believe them.—Without touching anything they ascertained that Mrs. Hatter was dead. She was already stiff, in fact. Louisa, however, they discovered to be merely unconscious; they carried her from this room into Miss Smith's. Conrad telephoned Dr. Merriam, the family physician, and the police; and no one was permitted to come in here."

"Merriam pronounced Mrs. Hatter dead, and then went into the nurse's room," added Thumm, "to look after the deaf-mute. He's still in there. We haven't been able to talk to her yet."

Lane nodded thoughtfully. "Just exactly how was Miss Campion found? Even more exactly than you've indicated, Mr. Bruno?"

"She was found stretched out, her face down. The

56 ACT I: SCENE 2

doctor says she fainted. There's a bump on her forehead, and Merriam's theory is that in fainting she struck her forehead against the floor, which didn't help any. She's conscious now, but sort of dazed. It's a question whether she knows what's happened to her mother, because Merriam won't permit us to inform her yet."

"Has the corpse been examined?"

"Except for Merriam's original examination, which was superficial, I understand," said Bruno, and Thumm nodded, "no. We're waiting for the Medical Examiner. Schilling's notoriously slow."

Lane sighed. Then he turned with decision to face into the room again, looking down. His eyes were fixed on the short-cropped green rug which covered the entire floor of the bedroom. From where he stood he saw a number of whitish, powdery heel-and-toe marks, widely separated. They seemed to proceed from the region between the two beds, although this was not visible to Lane in his position. The toe marks were pointed toward the hall door, and were most clearly impressed on the solid green of the rug just beyond the foot of the dead woman's bed, fading out as they approached the door.

Lane walked into the room, circling the line of prints. He paused opposite the space between the two beds, so that he could examine that area. The footprints, he now saw, led from a thickly scattered cloud of a white powder which dusted the green rug between the beds. The source of the powder did not long remain a mystery. A large circular cardboard box of white talcum powder, now almost empty, lay near the foot of Louisa Campion's bed—bath powder, from the inscription on the carton. The entire stretch of carpeting between the beds was generously dusted with the talcum.

The Tragedy of Y

Carefully avoiding the footmarks and the powder, Lane edged between the two beds for a clearer view of the night-table and the floor. It was apparent at once that the box of talcum had been lying on the edge of the night-table, for there were white smudges and traces of dusty film on the table's top, and a circular ring of powder in one corner indicated where the box must have been lying before it fell from the table. A few inches behind the circular ring there was a fresh dent in the wood of the table, as if a sharp edge had struck it with force.

"I should say," Lane commented, "that the box was rather loosely covered, and the lid fell off as the box was overturned." He stooped and picked up from the floor at the foot of the night-table a powder-box lid. "You've seen all this, of course?" Thumm and Bruno nodded wearily.

On the white cardboard top near the rim were several thin parallel lines. The lines were red. Lane looked up inquiringly.

"Blood," said the Inspector.

Where the blood lines were, the top was crumpled, as if the object which had left the lines had struck forcibly and smashed the lid's edge as well. Lane nodded.

"No doubt about this, gentlemen," he said. "Obviously the powder-box was swept from the table by a blow, which left its mark on the table top and the lid, and landed on the rug near the foot of Miss Campion's bed, scattering the talcum as the cover dropped off."

He replaced the crumpled top where he had found it, eyes restless. There were so many things to see.

He chose to examine the footprints first. In the thickest mass of strewn powder between the beds there was a number of toemarks about four inches apart, leading from the head of the dead woman's bed roughly parallel to the bed

58 ACT I: SCENE 2

and toward the foot, in the general direction of the fire-place wall. Almost at the edge of the powder-splotched area there were two prints of shoe-toes clearly defined in the heavy talcum; from this point the direction veered around the foot of the dead woman's bed heading for the door, heels and toes plainly marked thenceforward; and the steps, from the distance between the prints, considerably length-ened.

"Proving basically," murmured Lane, "that whoever left the footprints began to run as he rounded the bed."

The running footsteps were made only on the unpowdered rug—made by the powder clinging to the soles of the runner's shoes.

"Superficially, Inspector," observed Lane, looking up, "I should say you are playing in luck. These are a man's foot-prints."

"Maybe we are, and maybe we aren't," grunted Thumm. "Somehow I don't like the look of these prints. Too damned easy! Anyway, we've been able to take their measure from several of the clearer prints, and they're size $7\frac{1}{2}$, 8, or $8\frac{1}{2}$, narrow-toed, worn heels on both shoes. My men are searching the house now for just such a pair."

"It may be quite simple, after all," remarked Lane. He turned back to the space between the feet of the beds. "I take it, then, that Miss Campion was found lying near the foot of her bed, at the edge of the powdered area, almost on the spot where the man's prints change direction?"

"That's right. She's left some of her own prints in the powder, too, you'll notice."

Lane nodded; in the talcum leading up to the spot where Louisa Campion had fallen were a woman's barefoot prints. The nude prints began at the point to the side of the deaf-mute's bed where the covers had been thrown back, and hugged the side of her bed going toward the foot.

THE TRAGEDY OF Y

"No doubt about it, I suppose?"

"Not the slightest," replied Bruno. "They've been positively identified as hers. Easy enough to reconstruct that part of it. She evidently crept out of bed and stole along the side toward the foot. And there something happened that caused her to faint."

Mr. Drury Lane's brow was furrowed; something seemed to disturb him. He walked cautiously to the head of Mrs. Hatter's bed and leaned over for a close scrutiny of the dead woman. The peculiar markings on her forehead which he had noticed before held his attention for some time. They were composed of a number of deep thin vertical lines, varying in length, parallel, and slightly scraped toward one side—in the direction of the night-table. The marks did not extend the entire depth of the forehead; they commenced halfway between eyebrows and hairline, rising into the stiff gray hair.

Blood had oozed out of these queer lines. Lane's eyes strayed as if for confirmation to the carpet beneath the night-table; and he nodded.

There, lying on the floor half under the table, string-side up, was a battered old mandolin.

He stooped for a closer view—and turned to regard his two colleagues. District Attorney Bruno was smiling sourly. "You've found it," he said. "The weapon."

"Yes," said Lane in a low voice. "So it is. You can see the blood on the lower part of the steel strings." One of the strings had snapped and all were rusty, as if they had not been played on for a long time; but the scarlet tinge of fresh blood was unmistakable.

Lane picked up the mandolin, observing as he did so that it had been lying on the fallen talcum powder: there were distinct impressions in the powder where the mandolin had lain. On examination, he saw, too, that there was a fresh abrasion on one edge at the lower portion of the instrument, an abrasion suspiciously like the dent in the table top.

"Now, isn't that one lulu of a murder weapon, Mr. Lane?" asked Inspector Thumm in snarling tones. "A mandolin, by God!" He shook his head as if to ask what in the world crime was coming to. "They'll be using lilies next."

"Quaint, very quaint," observed Lane dryly. "So the ubiquitous Mrs. Hatter was bashed over the forehead with the face of a mandolin. . . . The significant part of the affair, gentlemen, is not so much the choice of weapon as the fact that it was scarcely sufficient, I should say, judging from the depths of the marks, to have caused death of itself. Yes, very quaint indeed. . . . We could use Dr. Schilling at the moment."

He replaced the mandolin on the rug exactly where he had found it, and turned his attention to the night-table again. He saw nothing very sinister: a bowl of fruit (at the side nearer the deaf-dumb-and-blind woman's bed), a clock, the marks of the overturned powder-box, two heavy book-ends enclosing an old Bible, and a vase of wilting flowers.

In the fruit-bowl were an apple, a banana, a bunch of early grapes, an orange, and three pears.

* * *

Dr. Leo Schilling, Chief Medical Examiner of New York County, was hardly an emotional man. The multitudinous array of corpses which dotted his official career like markers —the bodies of suicides, murder victims, unidentified dead, experimental cadavers, drug addicts, and of all those others who met, were overcome by, or plunged into death under suspicious circumstances—had naturally rather calloused him. He despised the word "squeamish" and his nerves

THE TRAGEDY OF Y

were as tough as his scalpel-wielding fingers. His associates often suspected that beneath the chitinous shell of his official exterior beat a gentle heart; no one, however, had ever proved it.

He marched into Mrs. Emily Hatter's last resting-place, nodded absently to the District Attorney, grunted at Thumm, chirped something indistinguishable to Mr. Drury Lane, flashed a comprehensive look about the bedroom, duly noted the whitish footprints on the rug, and threw his bag on the bed—where, to Mr. Drury Lane's horror, it landed with a hollow thud on the old woman's stiff dead legs.

"Walk over the footprints?" snapped Dr. Schilling.

"Yes," said the Inspector, "everything's been photographed. And let me tell you, Doc, you might try to make a little better time after this. It's a good two and a half hours since I sent word——"

"Es ist eine alte Geschichte, doch bleibt sie immer neu," grinned the tubby doctor. "It's an old story, as Heine doesn't say so inelegantly, yet it's always new. . . . Keep your shirt on, Inspector. These dead ladies have a lot of patience."

He pulled down the front of his cloth hat—he was as bald as a hen's egg and rather sensitive about it—pottered around the bed, stepped all over the powder marks with indifference, and went to work.

The grin faded from his fat little face, and his eyes became intent behind his old-fashioned gold spectacles. Lane observed him screw up his blubbery lips at the vertical markings on the dead woman's forehead, and nodded at his instant glance down at the mandolin. Then he very carefully grasped the gray head between his little muscular hands and began to part the hair, feeling swiftly about the skull. Something was wrong, it was evident, for his face

62 ACT I: SCENE 2

set like concrete and, throwing back the tumbled covers, he commenced a minute examination of the body.

They watched him in silence. The good Medical Examiner was becoming more and more puzzled, that much was apparent; he muttered: *"Der Teufel!"* several times, wagged his head, sucked his lips, hummed a little drinking-song. . . . Suddenly he swung about on them.

"Where is this woman's personal physician?"

Inspector Thumm left the bedroom and two minutes later returned, followed by Dr. Merriam. The two physicians saluted each other formally, like duelists, Dr. Merriam in his stately way rounded the bed, and together they bent over the corpse, pulling up the thin nightgown, talking in low tones as they examined the body. Meanwhile stout Miss Smith, Louisa Campion's nurse, had hurried into the room, snatched up the bowl of fruit from the night-table, and hurried out again.

Thumm, Bruno, and Lane watched without speaking.

The doctors straightened up at last, and Merriam's fine old face betrayed a certain emotional disquietude. The Medical Examiner jerked his cloth hat lower over his beaded forehead.

"What's the verdict, Doc?" asked the District Attorney.

Dr. Schilling grimaced. "This woman did not die from the actual concussion of the blow." Mr. Drury Lane nodded in a pleased way. "Dr. Merriam and I agree that the blow itself was not sufficient to do more than stun her."

"Well then," growled Inspector Thumm, "what the hell did kill her?"

"Ach, Inspector, you always anticipate," said Dr. Schilling irritably. "What are you worried about? The mandolin caused her death, although indirectly. *Ja.* How? By giving her a severe nervous shock. Why? Because she was old—

THE TRAGEDY OF Y 63

sixty-three—and Dr. Merriam says she was a bad cardiac. *Nicht wahr, Herr Doktor?*"

"Oh," said the Inspector, looking relieved. "I get it. Somebody socked her over the head, the shock of the blow made her bum heart go blooey, and she died. According to that, she might actually have died in her sleep!"

"I think not," said Mr. Drury Lane. "On the contrary, Inspector, far from being asleep, she was very wide awake indeed." The two physicians nodded together. "On three counts. The first: please observe that her eyes are open, wide, staring, horrified. Consciousness, Inspector . . . The second: you will note that there is a most unique expression on her face." The term was mild; Emily Hatter's dead old features were contorted with an extraordinary pain and an intense astonishment. "Even the hands are half-clenched, clawing . . . Third: a bit more subtle."

Lane went to the bedside and pointed at the blood marks of the mandolin strings on the cold forehead. "The position of these marks definitely proves that Mrs. Hatter was sitting up in bed when she was struck!"

"How do you figure that?" demanded Inspector Thumm.

"Why, very simply. Had she been asleep when she was struck—that is, lying down and, from her general position, lying flat on her back besides—the marks of the steel strings would show not only at the top of her forehead but at the bottom also, and on the nose, and perhaps even on the lips. Since the marks are confined to the top, she must have been either in a sitting or a semi-sitting position. But if that's the case, the immediate conclusion is that she was awake as well."

"Very clever, sir," said Dr. Merriam; he was standing rigid, and his long white fingers were nervousl" intertwining.

64   ACT I: SCENE 2

"Really elementary. At what time, Dr. Schilling, do you estimate Mrs. Hatter died?"

Dr. Schilling plucked his ivory toothpick from a vest pocket and began to worry the crevices between his teeth. "Dead six hours. That is, she died just about four o'clock this morning."

Lane nodded. "It may be important, Doctor, to know exactly where the murderer was standing when he struck Mrs. Hatter. Can you make a definite statement on that point?"

Dr. Schilling squinted reflectively at the bed. "I believe I can. The murderer stood between the two beds—*not* on the far side of the old woman's bed. From the position of the body and the slant of the blood-lines on her forehead. Eh, Dr. Merriam?"

The old physician started. "Ah—I quite agree," he said hastily.

Inspector Thumm scraped his heavy jaw with irritation. "This blasted business of the mandolin . . . Disturbs me, somehow. The point is, rotten heart or no rotten heart, *could* a wallop from a mandolin have killed her? I mean—after all, if a man's intending to commit murder, even if he picks a funny weapon he'll pick one that'll do the trick."

"*Ja*, no doubt about the possibilities, Thumm," said the Medical Examiner. "A blow of great force from so comparatively light a weapon as a mandolin could kill a woman of Mrs. Hatter's physical condition and advanced age. But the blow here was rather feeble."

"There are no other marks of violence on the body?" asked Lane.

"No."

"How about poison?" demanded the District Attorney. "Any signs?"

The Tragedy of Y

"There are no signs," replied Dr. Schilling carefully. "On the other hand—yes, I shall perform an autopsy. At once."

"You can bet your German boots you will," retorted Inspector Thumm. "Just to make sure nobody's slinging poison around here again. I don't figure this case at all. First somebody tries to poison the deaf-mute, and now somebody bumps off the old she-devil. I'm going to take a look around for signs of poison."

Bruno's sharp eyes glittered. "This is murder, of course, even if the blow itself wasn't the direct cause of death—but merely the shock of the blow. One thing is sure: there was intent to kill."

"Then why such a light blow, Mr. Bruno?" asked Lane dryly. The District Attorney shrugged. "And why," continued the old actor, "this perfectly insane choice of a weapon?—a mandolin! If it was the murderer's purpose to kill Mrs. Hatter by a blow on the head, why did he select a mandolin when here *in this very room there are several heavier weapons?*"

"By God, I never thought of that," muttered Thumm, as Lane pointed to the rack of fire-irons hanging by the fireplace, and to the massive bookends on the night-table beside the bed.

Lane took a short turn about the room, hands clasped loosely behind his back. Dr. Schilling was beginning to show signs of impatience; Dr. Merriam still stood stiffly, like a soldier on inspection; the District Attorney and Thumm looked more and more disturbed.

"And by the way," murmured Lane at last, "did the mandolin come from the bedroom here?"

"No," replied the Inspector. "From a glass case in the library downstairs. The old lady preserved it that way after York Hatter's suicide—another one of her widow's bou-

66 ACT I: SCENE 2

quets. It belonged to Hatter . . . Say, come to think
of it——"

Mr. Drury Lane's hand had shot up in a peremptory
command for silence, his eyes narrowing. Dr. Schilling was
drawing the bedclothes back over the dead woman. And,
in pulling them taut, a small object, which glittered in the
rays of the sun spearing through the windows, fell from a
fold of the bedcover to the powdered rug.

Lane darted forward and snatched it from the floor.

It was an empty hypodermic.

They pressed about him, keenly alive to the significance
of the discovery. Lane, holding the hypodermic carefully
by the tip of the plunger, sniffed the stained needle, then
held the instrument up to the light.

Dr. Schilling unceremoniously took the hypodermic from
Lane's hand and retired to one of the windows with Dr.
Merriam.

"Empty syringe," muttered the Medical Examiner.
"What's this number 6 on it? That sediment in the barrel
might be—might be . . ."

"Yes?" asked Lane eagerly.

Dr. Schilling shrugged. "I'll have to analyze."

"No hypodermic marks on the body?" persisted Lane.

"No."

And suddenly, as if he had been shot, Lane straightened,
his eyes flashed gray-green. . . . Thumm's jaw dropped.
For Mr. Drury Lane, his face working with intense excitement, had dashed for the door, shouting: "The nurse—
the room——"

They streamed after.

* * *

Miss Smith's bedroom adjoined the death-chamber. A
placid enough sight met their eyes as they plunged in.

THE TRAGEDY OF Y 67

On a bed, her blind eyes open, her plump body at rest, lay Louisa Campion. And sitting on a chair by her side, smoothing the deaf-mute's forehead, was the stout elderly nurse. Louisa was mechanically plucking grapes from a cluster in her hand and munching them without appetite. On a table near the bed lay the bowl of fruit Miss Smith had taken from the death-room only a few moments before.

Mr. Drury Lane wasted no words. He hurled himself across the room and tore the grapes from Louisa's hand—a rapacious movement which caused Miss Smith to jump to her feet with a squeal of fright, and the deaf-dumb-and-blind woman to jerk upright in bed, her lips writhing, an expression of curdled fear on her usually blank features. She began to whimper in a horribly animal way, her hand groping for Miss Smith's, and clutching it quickly. Her shivering skin was alive with apprehension; her arms had instantly become covered with goose flesh.

"How many did she eat?" snapped Lane.

The nurse was pale. "How you startled me! A—a handful."

"Dr. Merriam! Dr. Schilling! Is she all right?" demanded Lane.

Dr. Merriam hurried to the bed; the moment the woman felt his touch on her forehead she stopped whimpering.

He said slowly: "She seems perfectly well."

Mr. Drury Lane dabbed at his forehead with a handkerchief; his fingers were noticeably trembling. "I was afraid we should be too late," he said a little hoarsely.

Inspector Thumm doubled up his mallets of fists and strode forward, glaring down at the fruit-bowl. "Poison, hey?"

They all looked at the bowl. Lying innocently before

68   ACT I: SCENE 2

them were the apple, the banana, the orange, and the three pears.

"Yes," said Lane. His deep voice was quiet. "I'm sure of it. And the facts being what they are, gentlemen, the entire complexion of the case has . . . altered."

"Just what——" began Bruno in bewilderment. Lane waved his hand absently, as if he did not care to expand his statement at the moment; he was studying Louisa Campion. She had quieted under Dr. Merriam's stroking fingers and lay there limply. Forty years of thwarted living had left little impress on her smooth features. In a way she was almost attractive: her nose was tiny and tilted; her lips were delicately curved.

"Poor creature," muttered Lane. "I wonder what she's thinking. . . ." His eyes sharpened as he turned to the nurse. "A few moments ago you took this bowl of fruit from the night-table in the next room," he said. "Is fruit customarily kept in that room?"

"Yes, sir," replied Miss Smith nervously. "Louisa is immensely fond of fruit. There's always a bowl of it on the night-table in there."

"Has Miss Campion a special preference in fruits?"

"Well, no. She likes them all in season."

"I see." Lane seemed puzzled by something; he began to speak, changed his mind, bit his lips, and then hung his head in thought. "And Mrs. Hatter?" he said finally. "Did she ever eat fruit from that bowl?"

"Just once in a while."

"Not regularly?"

"No, sir."

"And did Mrs. Hatter like all kinds of fruit, too, Miss Smith?" He put the questions quietly, but Bruno and Thumm caught the note of import in his voice.

THE TRAGEDY OF Y 69

Miss Smith also caught it; she said slowly: "Now, that's queer, that question. No, sir, Mrs. Hatter had one pet aversion in fruit; she detested pears—hadn't eaten them in years."

"Ah," said Mr. Drury Lane. "Splendid. And did everyone in the household know of this aversion, Miss Smith?"

"Oh, yes. It's been a family joke for years."

Mr. Drury Lane seemed content. He nodded several times, favored Miss Smith with a friendly glance, and then, going to the table near the nurse's bed, looked down at the fruit-bowl from Louisa Campion's room.

"She detested pears," he murmured. "Observe that, Inspector. I daresay a closer scrutiny of the pears is called for."

Two of the three pears in the bowl were perfect fruit—golden, mellow, firm. The third . . . Lane turned it curiously in his fingers. It was marred by decay; its rind was brown in spots; and each spot was soft, squashy. Lane uttered a little exclamation and brought the pear to within three inches of his right eye.

"As I thought," he muttered. He turned to Dr. Schilling with a little gesture of triumph. "Here you are, Doctor," he said, handing the Medical Examiner the three pears. "You'll find the prick of a needle in the skin of the spoiled pear, unless I'm very much mistaken."

"Poisoned!" exclaimed Thumm and Bruno together.

"It's unwise to anticipate, but—I think so. Yes . . . To make sure, Doctor, analyze all three. Let me know, when you ascertain the nature of the poison, if the decay in the spoiled pear was caused by the presence of poison, or if the pear decayed before the poison was injected."

"*Jawohl,*" said Dr. Schilling, and he trundled out of the room bearing the three pieces of fruit as if they were precious.

70 ACT I: SCENE 3

Inspector Thumm drawled: "There's something screwy ... I mean, if there's poison in the pear, and the old lady didn't eat pears——"

"Then the murder of Mrs. Hatter was probably an accident, never planned at all—and the poisoned pear was meant for this poor woman!" concluded Bruno.

"Right, right!" cried the Inspector. "Right, Bruno! The murderer sneaked in, jabbed the hypo into the pear, and then the old lady woke up—see? Maybe even recognized the poisoner—remember that look on her face. So what? Wham! She gets it on the head with the mandolin, and it's curtains for her."

"Yes, and now we're getting somewhere. The poisoned pear is undoubtedly the work of the same one who poisoned the egg-nog two months ago."

Mr. Drury Lane said nothing. There was a faint perplexity between his brows. Miss Smith seemed bewildered. As for Louisa Campion, ignorant of the fact that the law had just decided that for the second time she had been the victim of an attack against her life—as for Louisa Campion, she clung to Dr. Merriam's fingers with a tenacity born of darkness and desperation.

Scene 3

The Library. Sunday, June 5. 11:10 A.M.

There was an interlude. Men prowled about, someone with a preoccupied air reported to Inspector Thumm that no fingerprints were to be found on either the hypodermic syringe or the mandolin, and Dr. Schilling fussed about, superintending the removal of the body.

THE TRAGEDY OF Y   71

In all the bustle of tramping Morgue attendants, Mr. Drury Lane stood quiet and thoughtful, for the most part searching the blank face of Louisa Campion as if for a solution to the riddle. He barely heard District Attorney Bruno's comment that, since no fingerprints had been discovered anywhere, the murderer must have worn gloves.

Finally something like order was restored, Dr. Schilling departed with his corpse, and the Inspector shut the door of Miss Smith's room. Mr. Drury Lane said at once: "Has Miss Campion been told?"

Miss Smith shook her head, and Dr. Merriam said: "I thought it best to wait until——"

"There is no danger to her health now?"

Dr. Merriam pursed his thin lips. "It will be a shock. She has a weak heart. But most of the excitement has subsided, and since she must be told eventually . . ."

"How does one communicate with her?"

Silently Miss Smith went to the bed, rummaged under a pillow, and straightened up holding a queer apparatus. It consisted of a flat grooved board, resembling remotely an abacus, and a large box. She removed the lid of the box; it contained a great number of small metal blocks, like dominoes, each of which had a projecting piece at the back which slipped into the grooves of the board. The faces of the blocks themselves were studded with raised dots, rather large, arranged in peculiar and varying patterns on the metal.

"Braille?" asked Lane.

"Yes," sighed Miss Smith. "Each block represents a different letter of the alphabet in Braille. The apparatus was especially constructed for Louisa. . . . She takes it with her everywhere she goes."

To assist the uninitiate in reading this "written" language

ACT I: SCENE 3

of the blind, each block had painted on its surface, in addition to the raised dots, a flat white English letter—the translation from Braille of the letter represented by the block.

"Ingenious," remarked Lane. "If you don't mind, Miss Smith . . ." He pushed the nurse gently aside, took up the board and pieces, and looked down at Louisa Campion.

It was, they all felt, a fateful moment. What would this blighted, unusual creature reveal? That she already sensed the prevailing tension was apparent. Her white beautiful fingers were in constant motion—she had slipped her hand out of Dr. Merriam's a moment before—and Lane with a little shiver realized that those waving fingers were like the antennæ of a bug, oscillating with intelligence, clamoring for enlightenment. Her head was jerking from side to side anxiously, quickly, heightening the insectivorous resemblance. Her pupils were large, but dull and glazed—blind eyes. In this moment, when all attention was riveted upon her, one forgot that externally she presented a plain, if pleasant, appearance—she was rather plump, no more than four inches above five feet in height, with luxuriant brown hair and a healthy complexion. It was the odd features that impressed them—the piscine eyes, the still, blank, almost lifeless features, the quivering fingers. . . .

"She looks all worked up," muttered Inspector Thumm. "Watch her fingers go. They give me the willies."

Miss Smith shook her head. "That—that's not nervousness. She's talking, asking questions."

"Talking!" exclaimed the District Attorney.

"Of course," said Lane. "The manual deaf-and-dumb language, Mr. Bruno. What is she signaling so frantically, Miss Smith?"

The stout nurse collapsed in her chair suddenly. "I—this

The Tragedy of Y

73

is beginning to get me," she said in a hoarse voice. "She's saying, over and over: 'What is the matter? What is the matter? Where is mother? Why do you not answer? What is the matter? Where is mother?'"

Mr. Drury Lane sighed in the hush that followed, and took the woman's hands in his own strong ones. They struggled wildly; and then they went limp and her nostrils quivered, as if she were trying to scent him. It was weird. Something in Lane's touch must have reassured her, or perhaps in the faint aura common to all animals and to which most human beings are insensible; for she relaxed, slipped her fingers out of his. . . .

What is the matter. Where is mother. Who are you.

Lane, swiftly selecting pieces from the box of blocks, arranged a series of words; he placed the board in Louisa's lap and her hands clutched it eagerly. Her fingers fluttered over the metal blocks.

"I am a friend," read Lane's message. "I want to help you. I have something unpleasant to tell you. You must be brave."

She made a gurgling sound in her throat, piteous, wrenching; Inspector Thumm winced and half turned away. Dr. Merriam was turned to stone behind her. Then Louisa Campion drew a deep breath and her hands began to flow again.

Miss Smith wearily translated.

Yes. Yes. I am brave. What is the matter.

Lane's fingers dipping into the box, rearranging letters, constructing new words. . . . There was a palpable silence in the room.

"Your life is an epic of bravery. Keep it so. There has been a great tragedy. Your mother was murdered during the night."

ACT I: SCENE 3

The flashing hands made one convulsive movement over the board. It fell from her lap, scattering little metal blocks over the floor. She had fainted.

* * *

"Oh, get out, all of you!" shouted Dr. Merriam as they all started forward with eyes full of pity. "Miss Smith and I will handle this."

They stopped and watched him lift her limp body from the chair with an effort of his old muscles.

They hurried uneasily to the door.

"I hold you responsible for Miss Campion," muttered Inspector Thumm to the physician. "Don't leave her even for a moment."

"I won't be responsible for anything if you don't get out!"

They obeyed, Lane going last. He shut the door softly and stood thinking for a long moment. Then he placed his fingers on his temples in a curious gesture of fatigue, shook his head, dropped his hands, and followed the District Attorney and Inspector Thumm downstairs.

* * *

The Hatter library downstairs adjoined the dining-room. It was old and redolent of leather. It was composed chiefly of books on science and poetry. It had a well-used air and housed well-worn furniture. It was a most comfortable room, and Lane sank into an armchair with a sigh of approval.

Thumm and Bruno sat down, too, and the three men looked at each other without speaking. The house was quiet; only the Inspector's stertorous breathing was audible.

"Well, boys," he said finally, "it's a puzzler."

"An interesting puzzler at any rate, Inspector," said Lane.

The Tragedy of Y

75

He burrowed deeper into the armchair and stretched his long legs. "By the way," he murmured, "does Louisa Campion know that two months ago someone attempted her life?"

"No. No sense in telling her. It's tough enough for her as it is."

"Yes, of course." Lane mused for a moment. "It would be cruel," he agreed. He rose suddenly and crossed the room to examine a pedestal-like affair supporting a glass case. The case was empty. "This, I suppose, is the case in which the mandolin is kept."

Thumm nodded. "And," he said grimly, "no fingerprints."

"You know," said District Attorney Bruno, "this business of the poisoned pear—if it is poisoned—simplifies matters enormously."

"Sticking to the pear, eh? At least we know it's Louisa he's after," growled Thumm. "Well, let's get going."

He rose and went to the door leading out into the corridor. "Hey, Mosher," he called. "Get Barbara Hatter down here for a talk."

Lane strolled back to the armchair.

* * *

Barbara Hatter was infinitely more pleasing in appearance than her published photographs indicated. The natural sharpness of etching in the photographs accentuated her thin features; in life, while thin, they were womanly soft, with a purely physical handsomeness which Kurt, the well-known photographer, chose to disregard in his interpretation of her more ethereal qualities. She was very tall and regal; frankly in her thirties. She moved with grace, almost with rhythm. And she gave the impression of an inner

ACT I: SCENE 3

glow, a fire which faintly illuminated her exterior and gave warmth to every gesture. Barbara Hatter, the poetess, one felt, was not only a woman of intellect but an unusual creature of delicate passions as well.

She nodded to Inspector Thumm and bowed to the District Attorney. Her fine eyes widened at sight of Lane. "Mr. Lane!" she said in her deep calm voice. "Are you probing into the cesspool of our private lives, too?"

Lane blushed. "I am rebuked, Miss Hatter. Unfortunately, I'm of a curious disposition." He shrugged. "Won't you sit down? There are some questions." He did not seem surprised that she had known his face and called him by name at first meeting; people were doing that continually.

She sat down, her full eyebrows quizzically arched, and looked about at the inquisition. "Well," she said with a little sigh, "I'm ready if you are. Fire away."

"Miss Hatter," began the Inspector abruptly, "tell me what you know about last night."

"Very little, Inspector. I came in at about two o'clock in the morning—I had been attending a dull party at the home of my publisher. The gentlemen present forgot their manners, or the liquor was slightly too much for them; at any rate, I came home alone. Everything was quiet. My room, as you know, is to the front, overlooking the Park, across the hall from—from mother's. I can positively assure you that all bedroom doors on the floor upstairs were closed. . . . I was tired, and went to bed at once. I slept until six this morning, when I was awakened by Miss Smith's screams. That's really all."

"Hmm," said the Inspector, frowning.

"I agree," said Barbara with a tired smile, "that the recital isn't particularly brilliant."

She turned her head to glance at Mr. Drury Lane, as if

The Tragedy of Y

expecting a question from him. It came, but it seemed to astonish her, for her eyes narrowed and she stared hard at him. He said: "Miss Hatter, when you and your brother Conrad ran into your mother's bedroom this morning did either of you walk between the two beds?"

"No, Mr. Lane," she replied evenly. "We saw at once that mother was dead. In lifting Louisa from the floor we skirted the footprints leading to the door and avoided going between the beds."

"You're positive your brother didn't?"

"Quite."

District Attorney Bruno got to his feet, flexed the aching muscles of his thighs, and began to pace up and down before her. She waited patiently. "Miss Hatter, I'll speak frankly. You're a woman of far more than average intelligence, and certainly you must be aware of the—ah—abnormalities of certain members of your family. Being aware of it, you must also deplore it. . . . I'm asking you to cast aside for the moment any consideration of family loyalty." He paused at the calm unwinking expression on her face. He must have felt the futility of the question, because he resumed hastily: "Naturally, you don't have to answer if you don't want to. But if you have any explanation for the attempted poisoning two months ago and last night's murder, we're anxious, of course, to hear it."

"My dear Mr. Bruno," said Barbara, "what do you mean? Are you insinuating that I know who murdered my mother?"

"No, no—just a theory, some attempt to clear the atmosphere . . ."

"I have no theory whatever." She stared down at her long white fingers. "It's common knowledge, Mr. Bruno, that in her own way my mother was an insufferable tyrant.

ACT I: SCENE 3

I suppose many people at one time or another have had the impulse to do her violence. But murder . . ." She shivered. "I don't know. It seems incredible. The taking of human life——"

"Oh," said Inspector Thumm quietly, "then you're convinced somebody *wanted* to kill your mother?"

She was startled, and looked up with a flash of her eyes. "Whatever are you driving at, Inspector? Naturally I assume that if she was murdered it was someone's intention to . . . Oh!" She stopped short and grasped the seat of her chair. "You don't mean it was—it was a ghastly *mistake?*"

"That's just what the Inspector does mean, Miss Hatter," said Bruno. "We're convinced that your mother was killed by accident—on the impulse of the moment. We feel sure that the murderer's purpose in going into that bedroom was not to do away with your mother, but with your half-sister Louisa!"

"And why," put in Mr. Drury Lane in gentle tones before she could recover her composure, "why should anyone want to harm that poor afflicted creature upstairs, Miss Hatter?"

Barbara put her hand to her eyes suddenly and shaded them. She sat still. When she took her hand away, they saw that her face was haggard. "Poor Louisa," she murmured. "Poor Louisa." She stared unseeingly at the pedestal across the room. "Her empty, cruel life. Always the victim." Her lips compressed and she regarded them with a fierce intensity. "As you said, Mr. Bruno, ties of family— *my* family—should be put aside. No one who could dream of hurting that helpless creature deserves a grain of consideration. I must tell you, Mr. Lane," she continued, turning her earnest eyes his way, "that with the exception of

THE TRAGEDY OF Y   79

my mother and myself, my family has always hated Louisa. *Hated* her." Her voice burned. "The essential cruelty of humanity. The impulse to step on a crippled insect. . . . Oh, it's too hideous."

"Yes, yes," said the District Attorney, watching her keenly. "Is it true that everything belonging to York Hatter was taboo in this house?"

She cupped her chin. "Yes," she murmured. "My mother respected my father's memory much more assiduously than she respected my father." She fell silent, thinking over perhaps a wealth of unpleasant recollections, for her expression was sad and slightly bitter. "Mother tried to make up for a lifetime of tyranny after father's death by making us all bow to his memory. Consecrated, everything that belonged to him. I think that in the past few months she came to realize . . ." She did not finish, but brooded at the floor.

Inspector Thumm pounded up and down. "We're not getting anywhere. Why did your father commit suicide?"

Pain passed over her face. "Why?" she repeated tonelessly. "Why does any man commit suicide whose only interest in life has been stolen from him, smothered, leaving him spiritually a pariah?" Something resentful and spirited and at the same time hurt crept into her voice. "Poor father was dominated all his life. It wasn't his own; he had nothing to say in his own house. His children disobeyed him, disregarded him. Cruel . . . And yet—people are so queer—mother had a soft spot in her heart for him. I understand he was a rather handsome man when they met. I think she dominated him because she considered he needed stiffening. Everyone weaker than herself, she thought, needed stiffening." She sighed. "Instead of bracing him up, it broke his back. He became a recluse, almost a

80   ACT I: SCENE 3

haunt. Except for that quaint old darling next door, Captain Trivett, father had no friends. And even the Captain wasn't able to shake him out of his apathy. I'm rambling . . ."

"On the contrary, Miss Hatter," said Lane softly, "you're intelligently discussing very essential matters. Was Mrs. Hatter's taboo on your father's mandolin and laboratory respected?"

"One always respected mother's commands, Mr. Lane," replied Barbara in a low voice. "I can swear that no one even dreamed of touching that mandolin or going into the laboratory. . . . No, that's inane. Someone did. Oh——"

"When did you last see the mandolin in the glass case over there?" demanded the Inspector.

"Yesterday afternoon."

"Is it," asked Bruno with a flicker of eagerness, as if he had just had an inspiration, "the only musical instrument in the house?"

Lane glanced at him sharply, and Barbara looked surprised. "Yes, so it is," she replied. "Although what significance . . . I suppose it's none of my business. We're not a musical family. Mother's favorite composer was Sousa, and father's mandolin was a relic of his university days. . . . There used to be a grand piano—one of those ornate affairs, all scrolly and gilt, of the rococo 'nineties—but mother had it thrown out several years ago. She became resentful——"

"Resentful?" Bruno was puzzled.

"You see, Louisa couldn't enjoy it."

Bruno frowned. Inspector Thumm's big hand scrabbled about in his pocket and emerged holding a key. "Recognize this?"

She studied it obediently. "It's a Yale key, isn't it? I can't

THE TRAGEDY OF Y

81

say I do. They all look so much alike, you know. . . ."

"Well," grumbled Thumm, "it's the key to your father's laboratory. Found it in your mother's effects."

"Oh, yes."

"Do you know if this is the only key to that room?"

"I believe so. I know that mother had it in her possession ever since the news of father's suicide."

Thumm returned the key to his pocket. "That checks with what I've been told. We'll have to look into that laboratory."

"Were you a frequent visitor to your father's laboratory, Miss Hatter?" asked Bruno curiously.

Animation possessed her face. "Indeed I was, Mr. Bruno. I was one of the worshipers at the shrine of father's scientific gods. His experiments fascinated me, although I could never understand them. I often spent an hour with him upstairs. He was happiest at those times—he lived most intensely then." She looked thoughtful. "Martha—my sister-in-law, you know—also was sympathetic to father; she sometimes watched him, too. And, of course, Captain Trivett. The others——"

"So you don't know anything about chemistry," asserted the Inspector in a disagreeable voice.

She smiled. "Come, come, Inspector. Poison? Anyone can read labels, you know. No, I'm hardly a student of chemistry."

"From all I hear," remarked Mr. Drury Lane, with what the Inspector irritably considered irrelevance, "what you lack in scientific ability you make up for in poetic genius, Miss Hatter. You present an interesting picture, you and Mr. Hatter: Euterpe seated at the feet of Scientia. . . ."

"Horsefeathers," said Inspector Thumm distinctly.

82   Act I: Scene 3

"Oh, no doubt," replied Lane, smiling. "At the same time my remark is actuated by more than a desire to show off my classical knowledge, Inspector. . . . What I was getting at is this, Miss Hatter: did Scientia ever sit at the feet of Euterpe?"

"I'd like to have that translated into United States," growled the Inspector. "I want to know the question, too."

"Mr. Lane means to ask," said Barbara with a dab of color in her cheeks, "whether father took as much interest in my work as I did in his. The answer, Mr. Lane, is yes. Father always had the most passionate admiration—not, I'm afraid, so much for my poetry as for my material success. He often puzzled over my verse. . . ."

"As I have, Miss Hatter," said Lane with a little bow. "Did Mr. Hatter ever try to write?"

She made a *moue* of dismissal. "Hardly. He did try his hand at fiction once, but I don't believe anything came of it. He could never apply himself to anything for very long—except, of course, his eternal experiments with retorts and burners and chemicals."

"Well," said the Inspector belligerently, "if *that's* over, I'd like to get back to business. We haven't all day, Mr. Lane. . . . Were you the last one in last night, Miss Hatter?"

"I really can't say. I'd forgotten my house key—we all have a personal key—and so I rang the night bell in the vestibule. The night bell communicates directly with the Arbuckles' rooms on the attic floor, and George Arbuckle pottered downstairs after five minutes or so to let me in. I went upstairs at once. Arbuckle remained behind. . . . So I can't say whether I was the last one in or not. Perhaps Arbuckle knows."

"How'd it happen that you didn't have your key? Mislaid? Lost?"

The Tragedy of Y

"You're so transparent, Inspector," said Barbara, sighing. "No, it was not mislaid, not lost, not stolen. I'd merely forgotten it, as I said. It was in another purse in my room; I looked before retiring."

"Can you think of anything else?" the Inspector demanded of Bruno after a little silence.

The District Attorney shook his head.

"You, Mr. Lane?"

"After the way you squelched me, Inspector," replied Lane with a rueful grin, "no."

Thumm clucked what might have been apology, and said: "Then that's all, Miss Hatter. Please don't leave the house."

"No," said Barbara Hatter wearily. "Of course not."

She rose and left the room.

Thumm held the door open and watched her retreat. "There," he muttered, "no matter how I may've talked to her, goes a damned fine woman. Well," he said, squaring his shoulders, "we may as well tackle the lunatics. Mosher, get those Arbuckles down here for a gabfest."

The detective tramped off. Thumm closed the door, hooked his thumb in a belt loop, and sat down.

"Lunatics?" repeated Bruno. "The Arbuckles struck me as normal."

"Hell, no," snarled the Inspector. "That's just the way they *look*. Inside they're crazy. They must be crazy." He ground his molars. "Anybody who lives in this house must be crazy. I'm beginning to feel crazy myself."

* * *

The Arbuckles were tall strong people of middle age; they looked more like brother and sister than husband and wife. Both had coarse features and pebble-grained skins in

84 ACT I: SCENE 3

which the pores were large and oily: peasants, both of them, with generations of thick blood and stolid brains behind them—and both of them dour and unsmiling, as if the pervading spirit of this house had crushed them.

Mrs. Arbuckle was nervous. "I went to bed last night at eleven o'clock," she said. "With George here—my husband. We're peaceable people; we don't know anything about this."

The Inspector grunted. "Slept till morning, both of you?"

"No," said the woman. "About two o'clock in the morning the night bell rang. George got up, put on his pants and shirt, and went downstairs." The Inspector nodded gloomily; he had, perhaps, expected a lie. "He came back upstairs in about ten minutes, and he said: 'Barbara—she forgot her key.'" Mrs. Arbuckle sniffed. "And then we went back to bed and didn't know a thing else till morning."

George Arbuckle's shaggy head bobbed slowly. "That's right," he said. "God's truth. We don't know a thing about this."

"You speak when you're spoken to," said Thumm. "Now——"

"Mrs. Arbuckle," said Lane unexpectedly. She surveyed him with feminine curiosity—this female with a mustache. "Can you tell us if fruit was left on the night-table in Mrs. Hatter's room every day?"

"I can. Louisa Campion loves it. Yes," said Mrs. Arbuckle.

"There is a bowl of fruit upstairs now. When was it purchased?"

"Yesterday. I always keep the bowl full of fresh fruit. Mrs. Hatter wanted it that way."

"Miss Campion is fond of all varieties of fruit?"

"Yes. She——"

The Tragedy of Y

"Sir," said Inspector Thumm grimly.

"Yes, sir."

"Mrs. Hatter also?"

"Well . . . so-so. She did hate pears. Never ate 'em. Folks in the house used to make fun of her about it."

Mr. Drury Lane glanced significantly at Inspector Thumm and the District Attorney. "Now, Mrs. Arbuckle," he continued in a genial tone, "where do you buy your fruit?"

"At Sutton's on University Place. Delivered fresh every day."

"And does anyone except Miss Campion eat this fruit?"

Mrs. Arbuckle reared her square head and stared. "What kind of a question is that? Sure the others eat fruit. I always take some off the order for the family."

"Hmm. Did anyone eat a pear from the batch delivered yesterday?"

The housekeeper's face became dark with suspicion; this harping on fruit, it appeared, was getting on her nerves. "Yes!" she flared. "Yes! Yes . . ."

"Sir," said the Inspector.

"Yes . . . sir. I ate one myself, I did, and what of it?——"

"Nothing, Mrs. Arbuckle, I assure you," said Lane in a soothing voice. "You ate one of the pears. No one else did?"

"The br—the children, Jackie and Billy, had a pear apiece," she muttered, mollified. "*And* a banana, too—they eat like fury."

"And no ill effects," remarked the District Attorney. "That's something, anyway."

"When was yesterday's fruit brought to Miss Campion's room?" asked Lane in the same soothing tone.

86 ACT I: SCENE 3

"In the afternoon. After lunch—sir."

"All the fruit was fresh and new?"

"Yes. Yes, sir. A couple of pieces were in the bowl from day before yesterday, but I took those out," said Mrs. Arbuckle, "and put in fresh ones. Louisa is very fussy about her food and drink, she is. Fruit especially. She won't eat fruit at all that's overripe or, you know, touched."

Mr. Drury Lane started; he began to say something, gulped it down, and became very still. The woman stared dully at him; her husband, shuffling his feet by her side, scratched his jaw and looked uncomfortable. The Inspector and Bruno seemed puzzled by Lane's reaction; they watched him closely.

"You're certain of that?"

"Sure as I'm alive, I am."

Lane sighed. "How many pears did you put into the fruit-bowl yesterday afternoon, Mrs. Arbuckle?"

"Two."

"What!" exclaimed the Inspector. "Why, we found—!" He looked at Bruno, and Bruno looked at Lane.

"You know," muttered the District Attorney, "that's downright queer, Mr. Lane."

Lane's voice rolled on imperturbably. "You would swear to that, Mrs. Arbuckle?"

"Swear? What for? There were two, I say. I ought to know."

"Certainly you should. Did you take the bowl upstairs yourself?"

"I always do."

Lane smiled, looked thoughtful, and sat down with a little wave of the hand.

"Here, you, Arbuckle," growled the Inspector. "Was Barbara Hatter the last one in last night?"

THE TRAGEDY OF Y 87

The chauffeur-houseman quivered perceptibly at being directly addressed. He wet his lips. "Uh—uh—I don't know, sir. After I let Miss Hatter in, I just stayed downstairs long enough to sort of make my rounds—see that all the doors and windows were locked. I locked the front door myself, and then went back upstairs to bed. So I can't say who came in and who didn't."

"How about the basement?"

"That ain't used," replied Arbuckle with more assurance. "It's been shut down and boarded up back and front for years."

"So," said the Inspector. He went to the door, stuck his head out, and yelled: "Pinkussohn!"

A detective said hoarsely: "Yes, Chief?"

"Downstairs to the basement. Have a look around."

The Inspector closed the door and came back. District Attorney Bruno was asking Arbuckle: "Why were you so careful to check up on the doors and windows at two o'clock in the morning?"

Arbuckle grinned apologetically. "Habit of mine, sir. Mrs. Hatter was always tellin' me to be careful about that, because Miss Campion—she's afraid of burglars. I'd done it before goin' to bed, but I thought I'd do it again to make sure."

"Were they all closed and locked at two a.m.?" demanded Thumm.

"Yes, sir. Tighter'n a drum."

"How long have you people been working here?"

"Eight years," said Mrs. Arbuckle, "come this past Lent."

"Well," grunted Thumm, "I guess that's all. Anything else, Mr. Lane?"

The actor was sprawled in the armchair, eyes fixed on the housekeeper and her husband. "Mr. Arbuckle, Mrs.

88 ACT I: SCENE 3

Arbuckle," he said. "Have you found the Hatters a difficult family to work for?"

George Arbuckle became almost animated. "Difficult, you say?" He snorted. "I'll tell the world, sir. Batty, they are, all of 'em."

"It's hard pleasing 'em," said Mrs. Arbuckle darkly.

"Then why," asked Lane in a pleasant voice, "have you people persisted in working for them for eight years?"

"Oh, that!" replied Mrs. Arbuckle, in the tone of one who considers the question irrelevant. "Nothing mysterious about *that*. The pay is good—very good, and that's why we've stuck. Who wouldn't?"

Lane seemed disappointed. "Do either of you recall yesterday seeing the mandolin in the glass case yonder?"

Mr. and Mrs. Arbuckle looked at each other, and both shook their heads. "Can't remember," said Arbuckle.

"Thank you," said Mr. Drury Lane, and the Arbuckles were sent packing by the Inspector.

* * *

The housemaid, Virginia—no one thought of asking her last name—was a tall bony spinster with a horsy face. She was wringing her hands and on the verge of tears. She had worked for the Hatters for five years. She liked her job. She loved her job. The pay . . . Oh, sir, I went to bed so early last night. . . .

She had heard nothing, she had seen nothing, and she knew nothing.

So she was peremptorily excused.

* * *

Pinkussohn, the detective, lounged in with disgust written all over his big face. "Nothing doin' in the basement,

THE TRAGEDY OF Y 89

Chief. Looks as if it hasn't been entered for years—dust an inch thick all——"

"An inch?" echoed the Inspector disagreeably.

"Well, maybe less. Doors and windows not touched. No footprints anywhere in the muck."

"Get out of the habit of exaggerating," growled the Inspector. "Some day you're going to make a damned big mountain out of a damned small molehill, and it's going to be serious. Okay, Pink." As the detective disappeared through the doorway a policeman came in and saluted. "Well," snapped Thumm, "what do you want?"

"Two men outside," said the officer. "Want to come in. Say they're the family lawyer and one of 'em the partner or something of this here Conrad Hatter. Let 'em in, Inspector?"

"You dope," snarled the Inspector, "I've been looking for those birds all morning. Sure!"

Drama, and something of comedy, entered the library with the two newcomers. Alone together, although richly contrasting types, they might have been friends; with the presence of Jill Hatter, however, all possibility of amicability fled. Jill, beautiful, keen, her face already touched beneath the eyes and in the lines around her nose and mouth with the brush of high living, had evidently encountered the men in the hall; she came in with them, between them, clinging to a masculine arm to right and left, gazing sadly at them, turning from one to the other, accepting their hasty fragments of condolence with a lifting breast and drooping lips. . . .

Lane, Thumm, Bruno watched the tableau silently. This young woman was the essence of coquetry, that much was apparent at a glance. There was in every subtle movement of her body the suggestion of sex, and a half-promise of

90 ACT I: SCENE 3

delight. She was using the two men like foils, one against the other, playing them off, making them clash unconsciously, utilizing the tragedy of her mother's death with a cold fixity of purpose to draw them closer to her and in opposition to each other. Altogether, Mr. Drury Lane decided grimly, a female to be wary of.

At the same time Jill Hatter was frightened. Her masterful handling of the two men was accomplished more by habit than momentary design. Tall, full-figured, almost Junoesque—and frightened. Her eyes were red with sleeplessness and fear. . . . Suddenly, as if for the first time conscious of her audience, she released her men's arms with a pout and began to powder her nose. The first time . . . Her eyes had seen everything from the instant she stepped over the threshold. Frightened . . .

The men came to themselves, too, and their faces stiffened into formal lines. Two men could scarcely have been more different. Chester Bigelow, the family attorney, was a man of good height, but by the side of John Gormly, Conrad Hatter's business partner, he seemed puny. Bigelow was dark, with a small black mustache and blue-black jaws; Gormly was fair, with straw-colored hair and reddish bristles beneath the hastily shaven skin of his face. Bigelow was brisk, gleaming, rapid in his movements; Gormly was slow and deliberate. There was something shrewd, almost sly, in the lawyer's intelligent features; whereas Gormly was earnest and sober-faced. And the tall blond man was young—ten years younger than his rival at the very least.

"You wanted to talk to me, Inspector Thumm?" asked Jill in a small helpless voice.

"Not right now I didn't," said Thumm, "but as long as you're here . . . Sit down, you men." He introduced Jill, Bigelow, and Gormly to the District Attorney and Drury Lane. Jill collapsed in a chair and contrived to look as small

The Tragedy of Y

and helpless as her voice sounded. Lawyer and broker preferred to stand, rather nervously. "Now, Miss Hatter, where were you last night?"

She turned to look up at John Gormly, slowly. "I was out with John—Mr. Gormly."

"Details."

"We went to theater, and then to a midnight party somewhere."

"What time did you get home?"

"Very early, Inspector . . . five this morning."

John Gormly flushed, and Chester Bigelow made an impatient, instantly checked movement with his right foot. His precise little teeth showed in a smile.

"Did Gormly take you home? Eh, Gormly?"

The broker began to speak, but Jill interrupted plaintively: "Oh, no, Inspector. It was—well, rather embarrassing." She looked demurely down at the rug. "You see, I'd got pie-eyed about one o'clock in the morning. I'd quarreled with Mr. Gormly then—he thought he ought to constitute himself a Committee of One on Moral Turpitude, you see . . ."

"Jill—" said Gormly. He was as red as his cravat.

"So Mr. Gormly left me flat. Actually! I mean to say, he was in the most beastly rage," continued Jill in a sweet voice, "and then—well, I don't remember anything after that except drinking some rotten gin and having a high old time with somebody fat and sweaty. I do remember walking the streets in my evening things, singing at the top of my voice. . . ."

"Go on," said the Inspector grimly.

"A policeman stopped me and put me in a cab. The nicest young man! Big and strong and with crinkly brown hair. . . ."

"I know the force," said the Inspector. "Go on!"

Act I: Scene 3

"I was soberer when I got home; it was dawning. So nice and fresh in the Square, Inspector—I love the dawn. . . ."

"I don't doubt you've seen many of 'em. Go on, Miss Hatter. We can't waste all day."

John Gormly's face threatened to burst. He stormed in his throat, clenched his fists, and began to traverse the rug. Bigelow's expression was enigmatic.

"And that's all, Inspector," said Jill, dropping her eyes.

"Is it?" Thumm's muscles swelled his coat sleeves; he was mighty in his contempt. "All right, Miss Hatter. Answer some questions. Was the front door locked when you got home?"

"Let me see. . . . I believe it was. Yes! It took me a few minutes to manipulate the damned key."

"Did you hear or see anything off-color when you got to your bedroom upstairs?"

"Off-color? Inspector, I'm *shocked*."

"You know what I mean," snarled the Inspector. "Funny. Peculiar. Something that attracted your attention."

"Oh! No, Inspector."

"Did you notice whether the door to your mother's bedroom was open or closed?"

"It was closed. I went into my room, tore my things off, and dropped off to sleep. I didn't awaken until the fuss this morning."

"That's enough. All right, Gormly. Where'd you go when you left Miss Hatter flat at one in the morning?"

Avoiding Jill's innocently inquiring gaze, Gormly muttered: "I walked downtown. The party was on Seventy-sixth Street. Walked for hours. I live at Seventh Avenue and Fifteenth Street, and I got home—I don't know. It was growing light."

"Hmm. How long have you and Hatter been partners?"

The Tragedy of Y 93

"Three years."

"How long have you known the Hatters?"

"Ever since my college days. Conrad and I were room-mates, and I got to know his family then."

"I remember the first time I saw you, John," volunteered Jill softly. "I was the littlest girl. Were you nice, or were you nice?"

"None of that blarney," growled the Inspector. "Step aside, Gormly. Bigelow, I understand your firm has been handling all of Mrs. Hatter's legal business. Did the old lady have any business enemies?"

The lawyer replied politely: "You know as well as I do, Inspector, that Mrs. Hatter was a—hmm!—a rather peculiar woman. Unorthodox in every way. Enemies? Certainly. All Wall Street operators have enemies. But I shouldn't go so far as to say—no, decidedly not—that anyone hated her enough to commit murder."

"That's a help. Then what's your idea about this business?"

"Sad, very sad," said Bigelow, pursing his lips. *"Very* sad. And, do you know, I haven't the faintest notion about it. Not the faintest." He paused, and added hastily, "Nor of who might have tried to poison Miss Campion two months ago, as I think I told you then."

The District Attorney stirred impatiently. "Come, Inspector, we're getting nowhere. Mr. Bigelow, is there a will?"

"Certainly."

"Anything unusual about it?"

"Yes and no. I——"

They all turned at a tap on the door. The Inspector strode heavily across the room and opened the door two inches. "Oh, Mosher," he said. "What is it?"

ACT I: SCENE 3

Big Mosher's voice touched rumbling bass undertones. The Inspector said: "No!" in a very affirmative voice. He chuckled suddenly and slammed the door in Mosher's face. Then he went to District Attorney Bruno's side, whispered something; and Bruno's face became a study in self-control.

"Ah—Mr. Bigelow," said Bruno, "when do you intend formally to read the will to Mrs. Hatter's heirs?"

"Tuesday at two o'clock, after the funeral."

"Good. We'll hear the details then. I think that's all for——"

"One moment, Mr. Bruno," said Mr. Drury Lane in a peaceful voice.

"Of course."

Lane turned to Jill Hatter. "When did you last see the mandolin that is usually kept in this room, Miss Hatter?"

"Mandolin? Last night after dinner—just before I left the house with John."

"And when were you last in your father's laboratory?"

"York's smellery?" Jill shrugged her pretty shoulders. "Months ago. Yes, a good many months ago. Never did like the place, and York didn't like to have me there, either. You know—father and daughter respecting each other's privacy, and all that sort of bunk."

"Quite so," said Lane, unsmiling. "And have you visited the laboratory upstairs since the disappearance of Mr. Hatter?"

"No."

He bowed—the tiniest ghost of a bow. "Thank you."

"That's all," snapped Inspector Thumm.

The two men and the girl left the room with alacrity. Outside in the corridor Chester Bigelow caught Jill's elbow persuasively, and she smiled up at him. John Gormly, scowling, watched them saunter into the drawing-room. He

THE TRAGEDY OF Y   95

stood hesitating a moment, then began rather uncertainly to parade up and down the hall, followed by the indifferent eyes of several lounging detectives.

The three men in the library looked at each other. Words seemed unnecessary. Inspector Thumm went to the door and sent a detective to fetch Louisa Campion's nurse.

*   *   *

Miss Smith's examination, with total unexpectedness, developed a number of interesting points. The buxom nurse had subdued her feminine frailties under the mantle of her profession, and was very brisk, very official, in her early replies.

Had she seen the mandolin in the case the day before? She did not recall.

She was, with the late Mrs. Hatter, the most frequent visitor to Louisa Campion's bedroom? Yes.

Did she recall the mandolin ever having been in Louisa's room for any reason whatsoever?—this was Mr. Drury Lane's question. No; it had been in the case ever since York Hatter's disappearance and so far as she knew had never been removed for any reason at all.

Lane: "Did anyone beside Mrs. Hatter ever eat fruit from Mrs. Campion's bowl?"

Miss Smith: "Oh, no. Louisa's room is shunned by the rest of the family, sir, and none of them would dream, after Mrs. Hatter forbade it, of taking *anything* belonging to Louisa . . . poor creature. Of course, occasionally the children would sneak in and steal an apple or so, but this doesn't happen often, because Mrs. Hatter was very *stern* with the children, and the last time it happened, about three weeks ago, she whipped Jackie and scolded Billy, and there was a fuss, and Jackie screamed his young head off as

96   ACT I: SCENE 3

usual, and his mother had another of the usual quarrels about Mrs. Hatter striking the child; and it was rather awful. It wasn't the first time; Mrs. Hatter—that's Martha, I mean—Martha is meek as anything usually, but she's fierce when her mother-instinct is aroused, and she and Mrs. Hatter—that is, her mother-in-law—were continually quarreling about the right to discipline Martha's children. . . . Oh, I'm sorry, sir, I *do* go on."

"No, no, Miss Smith, we're vitally interested."

District Attorney Bruno: "The fruit, Mr. Lane, the fruit. Miss Smith, did you notice the fruit-bowl on the night-table last night?"

Miss Smith: "Yes, sir."

"Did it contain exactly the same fruit it contains today?"

"I think so, sir."

Inspector Thumm: "When did you last see Mrs. Hatter?"

Miss Smith (beginning to show nervousness): "Last night at about eleven-thirty."

"Tell us all about it."

"Mrs. Hatter generally attended to Louisa's before-bed wants herself, but I went in for a last look about and found Louisa already in her bed. I patted her cheek and used the board to ask her if she wanted anything before I turned in. She said no—I mean, she told me she didn't by the sign-language."

"We understand all that. Go on."

"Then I asked her if she wanted any fruit, and I turned to the fruit-bowl. She said no."

Lane (slowly): "Then you did observe the fruit?"

"Oh, yes."

"How many pears were there?"

Miss Smith (her piggish eyes filling with alarm): "Oh! There were only *two* there last night, and this morning there were *three!* I didn't recall before . . ."

The Tragedy of Y

97

"You're positive, Miss Smith? This is of vital importance."

Miss Smith (eagerly): "Yes, sir. There were two. I'll swear to it."

"Was one of the pears *spoiled?*"

"Spoiled? No, sir. Both were ripe and fresh-looking."

"Ah! Thank you, Miss Smith."

Inspector Thumm (grumpily): "What has this to— All right, Miss Smith. What was Mrs. Hatter doing all this time?"

"She was dressed in an old wrapper and was about to go to bed. She just—well, you know what women do before they go to bed."

"You bet I do. I'm a married man. How did the old lady act?"

"Snappy, grumpy—but nothing unusual. She'd just taken a bath, and in fact seemed in better spirits—for her, I mean—than usual."

"Then that was how the box of bath powder happened to be on the table!"

"No, sir. The powder-box is always on the table. Louisa, poor thing, loves nice smells, and she likes the odor of talcum—she's always powdering herself."

"Did you notice the box on the table?"

"Yes, sir."

"Was it open?"

"No, sir, the lid was on."

"Tight?"

"Well, no, as I recall; it was on sort of loose."

Mr. Drury Lane nodded and smiled very agreeably, and Inspector Thumm acknowledged this minor victory with a surly bob of his head.

District Attorney Bruno: "Miss Smith, are you a registered nurse?"

ACT I: SCENE 3

"Yes, sir."

"How long have you been in Mrs. Hatter's employ?"

"Four years. Oh, I know it's an unheard-of time to be on one case, but I was getting older, the salary was tempting, and I didn't like knocking about—it's an easy job, sir, and besides I've grown *very* fond of Louisa, poor soul—she has *so* little to live for. Actually, my nursing talents aren't used much here. I've been more a companion to Louisa than a nurse. I generally stay with her in the daytime, while Mrs. Hatter took care of her at night."

"Please be a little less verbose, Miss Smith. After you left the bedroom last night, what did you do?"

"I went to my own room next door and retired."

"Did you hear anything during the night?"

Miss Smith (blushing): "No, sir. I—I'm a heavy sleeper."

Inspector Thumm (eying Miss Smith's figure critically): "That's the word, all right. Any idea who might have wanted to poison this deaf-mute patient of yours, Miss Smith?"

Miss Smith (blinking rapidly): "No. Oh, no!"

"Did you know York Hatter well?"

Miss Smith (with relief): "Yes, sir. He was a quiet little man, and henpecked by Mrs. Hatter."

"Are you familiar with his chemical research work?"

"A bit. He seemed to feel that my being a nurse—you know—linked us in some way."

"Were you ever in his laboratory?"

"A few times. Once he invited me in to watch him experiment with a serum on a bunch of guinea-pigs—injected them, he did. Very interesting and educational. I remember a big doctor I once——"

Lane: "I suppose your nursing-kit includes a hypodermic syringe?"

THE TRAGEDY OF Y   99

"Yes, sir, two of them. One for large injections and one for small injections."

"Are you still in possession of both of them? One couldn't have been stolen from your kit?"

"No, sir! Just a few minutes ago I looked into my kit, because I saw that the hypo was found in Louisa's room—Dr. Schilling, is his name?—he was carrying it when he came into the room—and I thought maybe someone *had* stolen one of mine. But both were in my kit."

"Have you any notion where the syringe found in Mrs. Hatter's room might have come from?"

"Well, I know there are a number of them in the laboratory upstairs. . . ."

Inspector Thumm and District Attorney Bruno (together): "Ah!"

". . . because Mr. Hatter used them in his experiments."

"How many did he have?"

"I really don't know. But he kept a card index of everything in his laboratory in a steel cabinet there, and you may find a record of the number of hypos still in the cabinet."

*   *   *

"Come in, Mr. Perry," said Inspector Thumm, in the cajoling tone of a hungry spider. "Come in. We want to talk to you."

Edgar Perry hesitated in the doorway. He was, one felt instantly, the type of man who would always hesitate before taking action. Tall and slender—a man in his mid-forties—he was every inch the student. The face, closely shaven and bluish, was ascetic, sensitive, fine. He looked rather younger than his age; an illusion created, Mr. Drury Lane noted, chiefly by the brilliance and depth of his eyes.

ACT I: SCENE 3

He came in slowly and sat down in the chair the Inspector indicated.

"This is the children's tutor, I gather?" inquired Lane, smiling pleasantly at Perry.

"Yes. Yes," said Perry in a husky voice. "Er—what was it you wanted of me, Inspector Thumm?"

"Just a little talk," replied the Inspector. "Nothing special."

They all sat down and stared at each other. Perry was nervous; he kept moistening his lips and, for the most part, examining the rug at his feet when he realized the accusing nature of the glances directed toward him. . . .

Yes, he knew the mandolin was never to be touched.

No, he had never been in York Hatter's laboratory. He had no particular bent for science, and besides Mrs. Hatter's command was strict. He had assumed his duties in the Hatter household in the week after the preceding New Year's; the former tutor of Conrad Hatter's children had resigned after an argument with Martha, for she had protested strenuously when she had caught him whipping the boy Jackie one day for having tried to drown a cat in the bathtub.

"And do *you* get along with the brats?" asked the Inspector sternly.

"Oh, quite. Yes. I manage very nicely," murmured Perry. "Although they *are* difficult at times. I've worked out a system"—he smiled apologetically—"one of rewards and punishments, and it has been fairly successful."

"You find this a pretty tough place to work, I'll bet," said the Inspector, not very subtly.

"Sometimes," confessed Perry with a trace of animation. "The youngsters have a tendency to run wild, and I'm afraid—this is in no sense a criticism, please understand!—

THE TRAGEDY OF Y

I'm afraid that their parents aren't the best of disciplinarians."

"Especially the kids' old man," remarked Thumm.

"Well—perhaps he is not the best example for his children," said Perry. "I do find it trying at times, but I need the—the money, and the salary is excellent. Several times," he went on in a burst of confidence, "I'll confess I've been tempted to resign, but—" He stopped in confusion, startled, it seemed, at his own temerity.

"But what, Mr. Perry?" asked Lane encouragingly.

"The household, while hectic, has its compensations," he replied, clearing his throat. "I mean—there's Miss Hatter— Miss Barbara Hatter, I should say. For whom I have—for whose really remarkable poetry I have the most profound admiration."

"Ah," said Lane. "An academic reverence. What is your idea, Mr. Perry, about the odd things that have been occurring in this house?"

Perry flushed, but his voice grew firmer. "I have no explanation, sir. But one thing I am morally certain of: Barbara Hatter, no matter how the others may be involved, would never stoop to the ignominy of—of crime. She's too fine, too splendid a person, too sane, too sweet. . . ."

"It's nice of you to say so," remarked the District Attorney gravely. "I'm sure she'd be pleased. Now, Mr. Perry, how often are you away from the house—of course, you live in?"

"Yes. In a room on the third floor—the attic floor. I rarely take an extended leave from my duties; I had a short vacation, in fact, only once—five days in April. Otherwise Sundays are my own, and generally I spend them by myself away from the house."

"Always by yourself?"

ACT I: SCENE 3

Perry bit his lip. "Perhaps that's not strictly true. Miss Hatter several times has been kind enough to—to go out with me."

"I see. Where were you last night?"

"I retired early to my own room and read for an hour. Then I went to sleep. I might say," he added, "that I was entirely unaware of anything wrong until this morning."

"Naturally."

There was a silence. Perry wriggled in his chair. Grimness flared in the Inspector's eye. . . . Does he know that Louisa Campion loves fruit and always has a bowl of it on her night-table? He looked bewildered—yes, but what of it? Does he know whether Mrs. Hatter had preferences in fruits? Blankness—a shrug. And again a silence.

Mr. Drury Lane's tone was friendly. "You say you first came to this house early in January, Mr. Perry. Then you never met York Hatter, I take it?"

"No. I've heard very little about him, and what I know I've learned chiefly from Bar—from Miss Hatter."

"Do you recall the attempt to poison Miss Campion two months ago?"

"Yes, yes. A ghastly thing. The house was in an uproar when I returned that afternoon. I was naturally shocked."

"How well do you know Miss Campion?"

Perry's voice lifted, and his eyes brightened. "Rather well, sir. Rather well! Altogether a remarkable person. Of course, my interest in her is purely objective—she's an extraordinary problem in education. She has learned to know me, and trust me, I'm sure."

Lane was thoughtful. "You said a moment ago that you're not interested in science, Mr. Perry. I assume, then, that you haven't much of a scientific education. You're unfamiliar, for example, with pathology?"

The Tragedy of Y   103

Thumm and Bruno exchanged puzzled glances. But Perry nodded in a frigid way. "I see clearly what you're driving at. It is your theory, I suppose, that there must be some fundamental pathological condition in the background of the Hatter family to account for their aberrations?"

"Bravo, Mr. Perry!" smiled Lane. "And do you agree with me?"

The tutor said stiffly: "I am neither a physician nor a psychologist. They're—abnormal, I admit; but that is as far as I care to go."

Thumm heaved himself to his feet. "Let's get this over with. How'd you get the job?"

"Mr. Conrad Hatter had advertised for a tutor. I presented myself with a number of others, and was fortunate enough to be selected."

"Oh, then you had references?"

"Yes," said Perry. "Yes. Yes, indeed."

"Still got 'em?"

"Yes . . . yes."

"I want to see them."

Perry blinked, then rose and quickly left the library.

"There's something doing," said the Inspector the instant the door closed behind Perry. "Something big at last. This is just goin' through the motions, Bruno!"

"What on earth are you talking about, Inspector?" asked Lane, smiling. "Do you mean Perry? I confess that aside from certain infallible indications of romance, I can't——"

"No, I don't mean Perry. Wait and see."

Perry returned with a long envelope. The Inspector extracted a sheet of heavy paper from the envelope and hastily looked it over. It was a short letter of recommendation, stating that Mr. Edgar Perry had satisfactorily performed his duties as private tutor to the undersigned's

104   ACT I: SCENE 3

children, and had left for no reason of incompetence. The note was signed *James Liggett* and bore a Park Avenue address.

"Okay," said Thumm a little absently, returning the letter. "Just keep available, Mr. Perry. That's all for now."

Perry sighed with relief, stuffed the letter into his pocket, and hurried out of the library.

"Now," said the Inspector, rubbing his huge palms together, "now for the dirty work." He went to the door. "Pink! Get Conrad Hatter in here."

* * *

All the long conversations, all the tedious questions, all the fog and doubt and uncertainty seemed pointed toward this. Actually, it was not so; but it seemed so, and even Mr. Drury Lane felt a quickening of the pulse at the exultation in Inspector Thumm's voice.

The incident of the male Hatter, however, began with as little fanfare as had the others. Conrad Hatter came in quietly—a tall and fidgeting man with harsh features deeply stamped. He was holding his emotions in check, it appeared; he walked carefully, like a blind man treading on eggs, and he held his head stiffly, with the unnaturalness of a paralytic. His forehead was wet.

He had no sooner sat down, however, when the illusion of peace was violently shattered. The library door banged open, there was a scuffle in the corridor, and Jackie Hatter came bounding in, yelping in his small-boy's conception of the Indian call, and herding the diminutive figure of his toddling brother Billy before him. Jackie's dirty right hand gripped a toy tomahawk, and Billy's hands were tightly if inexpertly tied behind his proudly stiff back.

Inspector Thumm gawped.

The whirlwind came at their heels. Martha Hatter, her

THE TRAGEDY OF Y

tired face drawn and harried, flew into the library after the two children. None of the three paid the least attention to the room's occupants. She caught Jackie behind Lane's chair and slapped his face with vigor. The boy dropped his tomahawk, which had been swishing dangerously close to little Billy's skull and, throwing back his head, began to howl.

"Jackie! You terrible child!" she cried stridently. "I'll teach you to play that way with Billy!"

Billy promptly began to cry.

"Here, for God's sake," snarled the Inspector, "can't you take care of your children, Mrs. Hatter? Keep 'em out of here!"

Mrs. Arbuckle, the housekeeper, puffed into the room at the tail of the chase. Hogan, the unfortunate policeman, lumbered behind her. Jackie had one wild glimpse of his persecutors before they closed in on him. He kicked Hogan's leg almost with pleasure. For a moment nothing could be seen but flying arms and red faces.

Conrad Hatter half rose from his chair, self-control shattered. Hate burned in his pale eyes. "Take the damn' brats out of here, you fool!" he said in a quivering voice to his wife. She started, dropped Billy's arm, flushed to her hair, and looked around with conscious, frightened eyes. Mrs. Arbuckle and Hogan managed to get the two boys out of the room.

"Well!" said the District Attorney, lighting a cigarette with shaking fingers. "I sincerely hope there's no more of *that*. . . . Might's well allow Mrs. Hatter to remain, Inspector."

Thumm hesitated. Lane rose unexpectedly with pity in his eyes. "Here, Mrs. Hatter," he said gently. "Sit down, and calm yourself. There is no need for fright. We don't intend to hurt you, my dear."

ACT I: SCENE 3

She sank into the chair, her face drained of color, staring at her husband's cold profile. Conrad seemed to have regretted his outburst; his head was lowered now, and he was muttering to himself. Lane retired quietly to a corner.

A point of valuable information came out at once. Both husband and wife had noticed the mandolin in its glass case the evening before. But Conrad was able to establish the essential fact: he had got home past midnight, at 1:30 a.m., to be exact. He had stopped in the library downstairs to get a night-cap. "There's a well-stocked cabinet of liquor in this room," he explained calmly, pointing to a boule cellaret nearby. It was at this time that he had noticed the mandolin in its case, quite as it had been for months.

Inspector Thumm nodded with satisfaction. "Swell," he remarked to Bruno. "That helps us fix the layout. Whoever took the mandolin out of the case probably did so just before committing the murder. Where were you last night, Mr. Hatter?"

"Oh," he replied, "out. Business."

Martha Hatter's pale lips tightened; she kept her eyes steadily on her husband's face. He did not look at her.

"Out on business at one in the morning," said the Inspector judiciously. "Well, I don't blame you. Wha'd' you do when you left the library?"

"Look here!" shouted Conrad so suddenly that the Inspector's eyes narrowed and his teeth stuck out in a fighting grin. The man's neck was knotty with passion. "What the hell are you trying to hint at? I said 'out on business,' damn you, and I *meant* out on business!"

Thumm was still; then he relaxed and said genially: "Sure you mean it. Well, where'd you go from here, Mr. Hatter?"

"Upstairs to bed," mumbled Conrad, his rage subsiding

The Tragedy of Y 107

as quickly as it had come. "My wife was sleeping. I heard nothing all night. Tanked up—I slept like a dead one."

Thumm was very solicitous: it was "Yes, Mr. Hatter," and "Thank you, Mr. Hatter," in the sweetest of voices. The District Attorney repressed a chuckle and Lane looked at the Inspector with amused curiosity. The spider again, he thought—a rather obvious spider, to be sure, and a most susceptible fly.

Conrad seated himself, and Thumm turned to Martha. Her story was brief: She had put the children to bed in the nursery at ten o'clock, and had gone out for a walk through the Park. She had returned a little before eleven, and soon after had gone to bed. No, she had not heard her husband come in; they occupied twin beds, and she had slept the sleep of the dead, for the children's antics during the day had worn her out.

The Inspector proceeded in leisurely fashion now; his impatience of the previous interviews had quite disappeared. Now he seemed content to ask routine questions and receive uninformative replies in the most generous spirit. Neither, it seemed, had entered the laboratory since its sealing by Mrs. Hatter. Both were well acquainted with the household custom of the daily fruit-bowl on Louisa's night-table, and with old Mrs. Hatter's aversion to pears.

But the virus in Conrad Hatter's blood could not long be denied. The Inspector asked some inconsequential question concerning York Hatter. Conrad looked disturbed, but shrugged.

"My old man? A queer duck. Half nutty. Nothing much to him."

Martha sucked in her breath and flashed a baleful look at her husband. "The poor soul was just hounded to his death, Conrad Hatter, and you didn't lift a finger to save him!"

108 ACT I: SCENE 3

That strange rage gripped him again; it puffed into hot life on the instant, the cords of his neck swelling like hoods. "Keep out of this! This is my affair, you rotten slut!"

There was a stunned silence. Even the Inspector was shocked, and growled deep in his throat. District Attorney Bruno said with cold emphasis: "You'll do well to moderate your language, Hatter. It's rather *my* affair, and the affair of Inspector Thumm. Sit down!" he said sharply, and Conrad, blinking, sat down. "Now," continued Bruno, "talk to us, Hatter. Have you any explanation for the attempts to take the life of your half-sister, Louisa Campion?"

"Attempts? Wha' d'ya mean?"

"Yes, attempts. The murder of your mother was an accident, we're convinced. The real object of last night's visit was to poison a pear intended for Miss Campion!"

Conrad's mouth opened stupidly. Martha rubbed her weary eyes, as if this were the crowning tragedy. When she dropped her hands, her face glowered with loathing and horror.

"Louisa . . ." muttered Conrad. "An accident . . . I—I don't know what to . . . I really don't know."

Mr. Drury Lane sighed.

*   *   *

The moment had come.

Inspector Thumm made for the library door so suddenly that Martha Hatter clutched her breast. He halted at the door and turned to say: "You were one of the first to see the body and your mother's room this morning—you, your sister Barbara, and Miss Smith."

"Yes," said Conrad slowly.

"Did you notice the marks of footprints made by talcum powder on the green rug?"

The Tragedy of Y

"Dimly. I was excited."

"Excited, hey?" Inspector Thumm teetered on his toes. "So you noticed the footprints. Well, well. Hold everything." He yanked the door open and yelled: "Mosher!"

The big detective who had whispered to Thumm during the examination of Jill Hatter, Bigelow, and Gormly tramped obediently in the room. He was breathing hard, and holding his left hand behind his back.

"You say," remarked Inspector Thumm, carefully shutting the door, "that you dimly noticed the footprints?"

Suspicion, fear, and that instantaneous anger suffused Conrad's face. He leaped to his feet, shouting: "Yes, I said!"

"Swell," replied Thumm, grinning. "Mosher, my lad, show the gentleman what the boys have found."

Detective Mosher whipped his left hand into view with the dexterity of a prestidigitator. Lane nodded sadly—it was as he had supposed. In Mosher's hand was a pair of shoes . . . a pair of white canvas oxfords, obviously a man's despite the pointed toes. The shoes were grimy, yellowed, worn with age.

Conrad remained staring; Martha had risen, clutching the arm of her chair, white and drawn.

"Ever see these before?" asked Thumm jovially.

"I— Yes. That's an old pair of my shoes," stammered Conrad.

"Where d'ye keep them, Mr. Hatter?"

"Why—in the clothes closet in my bedroom upstairs."

"When did you last wear 'em?"

"Last summer." Conrad turned slowly to his wife. "I thought," he said in a strangled voice, "I told you to throw them out, Martha."

Martha moistened her white lips. "I forgot."

"Now, now, Mr. Hatter," said the Inspector, "don't be

110 ACT I: SCENE 4

going into one of your tantrums again. Pay attention . . .
Do you know why I'm showing you these shoes of yours?"

"I— No."

"You don't? Then I'll tell you." Thumm stepped forward
and all the assumed friendliness left his face. "It might
interest you to know, Hatter, that the soles and heels of
this pair of *your* shoes fit exactly into the footprints your
mother's murderer left on the rug upstairs!"

Martha uttered a weak cry and put the back of her hand
to her mouth at once, as if she had been indiscreet. Conrad
blinked—a habit of his, thought Lane; he was growing
befuddled; whatever intelligence he might once have had
was dying of alcoholism. . . .

"What of it?" whispered Conrad. "That's not the only
pair of shoes in the world of that size and shape——"

"True," growled Thumm, "but it's the only pair in this
house, Hatter, that not only exactly fits the murderer's
footprints, but that also has grains of the same powder as
was spilled upstairs stuck to its soles and heels!"

Scene 4

LOUISA'S BEDROOM. SUNDAY, JUNE 5. 12:50 P.M.

"Do you really think . . . ?" began the District Attorney
doubtfully when the Inspector had packed Conrad Hatter,
moving like a man in a dream, off to his room under guard.

"I'm going to quit thinking," snapped Thumm, "and go
into action. These shoes, now—pretty conclusive, I'd say!"

"Ah—Inspector," said Mr. Drury Lane. He came forward
and took the dirty white canvas shoes from Thumm's hand.
"Please."

THE TRAGEDY OF Y

He examined the shoes. They were run down at the heel, old and worn. There was a small hole in the sole of the left shoe. "Does this shoe match the left footprints on the rug?"

"Sure," grinned the Inspector. "When Mosher told me what the boys found in Hatter's closet, I had 'em check up on the print."

"But surely," said Lane, "you don't intend to let it go at that?"

"What do you mean?" demanded Thumm.

"Well, Inspector," replied Lane, weighing the right shoe thoughtfully, "it seems to me that you will have to have this one analyzed."

"Hey? Analyzed?"

"Look here." Lane held up the right shoe. At the front, on the toecap, there were splattered stains, as of some liquid.

"Hmm," muttered the Inspector. "You think . . . ?"

Lane smiled broadly. "I don't think, Inspector, in this case—I, too, suggest action. If I were you I should send this shoe to Dr. Schilling at once for an examination of the stains. It's possible that they were made by the same liquid that filled the hypodermic. If so . . ." He shrugged. "Confirmation that the poisoner wore the shoes, in which case it will look bad for Mr. Hatter, I'm afraid."

There was the merest suggestion of mockery in Lane's tone, and Thumm looked at him sharply. But Lane's face was sober.

"Mr. Lane's right," said Bruno.

The Inspector hesitated, then took the shoes from Lane and, going to the door, beckoned a detective.

"Schilling. Pronto," he said.

The detective nodded and took the shoes away.

ACT I: SCENE 4

It was precisely at this moment that the stout figure of Miss Smith appeared in the doorway.

"Louisa feels much better now, Inspector," she said shrilly. "Dr. Merriam says it will be all right to see her. She has something she wants to tell you."

* * *

On the way upstairs to Louisa Campion's bedroom, District Attorney Bruno muttered: "What the devil can she have to tell us?"

The Inspector grunted. "Some queer notion, I suppose. After all, she's a lousy witness. What a case! A murder with a live witness, by God, and she has to be deaf-dumb-and-blind. Might's well have been dead last night for all the good her testimony will do."

"I shouldn't be so positive about that, Inspector," murmured Lane, trotting up the stairs. "Miss Campion isn't a total loss. There are *five* senses, you know."

"Yes, but . . ." Thumm's lips moved silently and Lane, able to read them, was amused to see that he was cataloguing the five senses and having, for the moment, a hard time of it.

The District Attorney said thoughtfully: "Of course, it might be something. If she can tag it onto this Conrad chap . . . After all, she must have been awake in the approximate period of the crime—her bare footprints in the powder tend to show that—it's even probable from the spot where she fainted and the criminal's footprints facing it that she might have tou——"

"An excellent point, Mr. Bruno," said Lane dryly.

The door to the bedroom, across the corridor from the stairhead, now stood open. The three men went in.

The removal of the dead body had done something to

The Tragedy of Y

113

the room, despite the fact that the whitish footprints still showed on the rug and the bedclothes were still tumbled. There was an air of cheerfulness about it; the sun streamed in, and motes danced in its shafts.

Louisa Campion sat in a rocking chair on the farther side of her own bed, her face blank as usual, her head cocked, however, in a peculiar position—as if she were straining her dead ears to hear. She rocked with slow rhythm. Dr. Merriam was there, hands clasped behind his back, looking out of a window into the garden below. Miss Smith stood at the other window in a defensive attitude. And, leaning over Louisa's chair patting her cheek gently, was Captain Trivett, the neighborly mariner, his red bristly face grave with concern.

They straightened up at the entrance of the three men; all except Louisa, who ceased her steady rocking the instant Captain Trivett's corrugated hand stopped patting her face. Louisa's head instinctively jerked toward the doorway; her large blind eyes remained expressionless, but a look of intelligence, almost eagerness, captured the plain pleasant features, and her fingers began to wriggle.

"Hello, Captain," said the Inspector. "Sorry to meet you again under such circumstances. Hmm! Captain Trivett—District Attorney Bruno, Mr. Lane."

"Glad to meet ye," said the Captain, in a hoarse deep-sea voice. "This is the most horrible thing I've—I just heard th' news, and I come over to see if—if—Louisa was all shipshape."

"Sure, she's all right," said Thumm heartily. "Brave little woman, she is." He patted her cheek. She shrank back with the lightning recoil of an insect. Her fingers twirled dizzily.

Who. Who.

114   ACT I: SCENE 4

Miss Smith sighed and, bending over the board with its domino-like pieces in Louisa's lap, spelled out: "The police."

Louisa's head nodded slowly, and her soft body stiffened. There were deep circles under her eyes. Her fingers moved again.

I have something to tell that may be important.

"She looks serious enough," muttered Thumm. He arranged the pieces on the board to read: "Tell us the story. Tell us everything. No matter how slight."

Louisa Campion nodded again as her fingers flew over the metal dots, and a startling expression of grimness touched her lips. She raised her hands and began.

*   *   *

The story Louisa told through the medium of Miss Smith was as follows: She and Mrs. Hatter had retired to their bedroom the night before at half-past ten. Louisa had undressed and her mother had tucked her into bed. She had crept into bed at fifteen minutes to eleven; she knew the exact time because she had asked her mother with her fingers what hour it was.

With Louisa propped up on her pillow, knees high and the Braille board resting upon them, Mrs. Hatter had informed her that she meant to take a bath. Louisa did not communicate with her mother again for about three-quarters of an hour, she estimated; at which time Mrs. Hatter returned from the bathroom (she supposed) and began to conduct another little conversation by means of the Braille pieces. Despite the fact that the conversation was inconsequential—mother and daughter discussed the problem of new summer clothes for Louisa—she had felt uneasy. . . .

The Tragedy of Y

(At this point Mr. Drury Lane gently interrupted the flow of the woman's story to spell out on the board: "Why did you feel uneasy?"

She shook her head in a piteously troubled way, and her fingers quivered.

I do not know. It was just a feeling.

Lane pressed her arm softly, in reply.)

During this amiable little conversation about a summer wardrobe, it appeared, Mrs. Hatter was powdering herself, the result of her bath. Louisa knew because she had smelled the powder, which she and her mother both used and which always stood ready on the night-table between the twin beds.

It was at this time that Miss Smith had entered the bedroom. She knew, because she had felt Miss Smith's touch on her brow, and because Miss Smith had asked her if she wanted any fruit. She had signaled no.

(Lane stopped Louisa's story by engaging her fingers. "Miss Smith, when you entered the bedroom, was Mrs. Hatter still powdering herself?"

Miss Smith: "No, sir, she'd just finished, I imagine, because she was getting into her nightgown, and the powder-box with its lid loosely on, as I said before, was on the table. I saw the streaks of talcum on her body."

Lane: "Did you notice whether talcum had fallen on the rug between these beds?"

Miss Smith: "The rug was clean.")

Louisa went on.

It was only a few minutes after Miss Smith left—although Louisa did not know the exact time—that Mrs. Hatter went to bed, after bidding her daughter good-night

ACT I: SCENE 4

in the customary way. Louisa was certain that her mother
had actually got into bed, for a moment later, moved by
an inexplicable impulse, she had crept out of her own bed
and kissed her mother again, the old lady patting her cheek
fondly in reassurance. Then Louisa had returned to her
bed and composed herself for sleep.

(Inspector Thumm interrupted: "Did your mother tell you
anything last night that showed she was afraid of something?"
No. She seemed gentle and calm, as always with me.
"What happened then?" Thumm spelled out.
Louisa shuddered and her hands began to tremble. Dr. Merriam watched her anxiously. "Perhaps you'd better wait a moment, Inspector. She's a little upset."
Captain Trivett patted her head, and she reached up quickly
to grasp his hand and squeeze it. The old man reddened, with-
drawing his hand after a moment. Louisa seemed comforted,
however, and resumed with a rapid rhythm and a compressed
mouth that indicated the strain she was under and the iron
determination to proceed.)

She slept fitfully, having always been a poor sleeper,
night and day being the same to her. She had no idea how
much time elapsed. But suddenly—it was hours, of course—
she found herself wide awake, wrapped in her smothering
mantle of silence, but straining with all her senses. What
awakened her she did not know, but she *knew* that something was wrong, *felt* something alien in the room, very
near, near her bed. . . .

("What was it more exactly?" inquired District Attorney
Bruno.
Her fingers fluttered.
I do not know. I cannot explain.

The Tragedy of Y   117

Dr. Merriam braced his tall figure and sighed. "Perhaps I should explain that Louisa has always been slightly psychic, a natural development from her frustrated sensory condition. Her intuitive faculty, some sixth sense, has always been abnormally active. I've no doubt this is a result of her completely thwarted senses of sight and hearing."

"I think we understand," said Mr. Drury Lane softly.

Dr. Merriam nodded. "It may have been no more than a vibration, the aura of a moving body, the feel of footsteps attacking the always alert sixth sense of this unfortunate woman.")

The deaf-dumb-and-blind woman went on with a rush. . . . She was awake. Whoever it was near the bed, she felt, had no right to be there. She had experienced once more a queer formless emotion that at rare intervals stirred her—the convulsive desire to give voice, to scream. . . .

(She opened her pretty mouth and emitted a choked mewing sound, so utterly alien to any normal human sound that they all felt suddenly chilled. It was rather horrible—the spectacle of that plump little woman, so quiet and plain, giving voice to a distorted cry of animal fright.)

She closed her mouth and proceeded as if nothing had happened.

Naturally, she went on, she could hear nothing, since she had lived in a soundless world since she was eighteen; but the intuition of something wrong persisted. And then, striking her remaining senses with the shock of a physical blow, she smelled the bath powder again. This was so strange, so unforeseen, so seemingly causeless that she felt more alarmed than before. The talcum! Could it possibly be mother? And yet—no, she knew it was not her mother;

118 ACT I: SCENE 4

her aroused instinct of fear told her that. It was someone—
someone *dangerous*.

She made up her mind in that whirling instant to creep
out of bed, to get as far from the menace as she could. The
impulse to flee was hot within her. . . .

(Lane grasped her fingers gently. She stopped. He went to
the bed, Louisa's bed, and tested it with one hand. The spring
squeaked in protest, and he nodded.

"Noisy," he said. "Undoubtedly, the marauder heard Miss
Campion get out of bed.")

He pressed her arm, and she continued.

She had slipped off on the side to her mother's bed.
Barefooted on the rug, she had crept along her bed toward
its foot. Near the foot she had straightened up and extended her arm.

Suddenly she rose from the rocking chair, her face working, and with sure steps went around her bed. She evidently felt that her powers of description were inadequate,
and that illustration would make her story clearer. With
remarkable gravity—like a child engrossed in a game—she
lay down fully clothed as she was on the bed, and then
began to enact in dumb-show her movements of that early
dark morning. She sat up noiselessly, a look of immense
concentration on her face, head cocked in that peculiar and
deceptive listening attitude. Then she swung her legs to the
floor, the bed spring creaking, slipped off the bed, and began to creep along its side doubled over, one hand feeling
its way along the mattress. Almost at the footboard she
straightened up, turned so that her back was toward her
own bed and she was facing her mother's squarely, and put
out her right hand. . . .

THE TRAGEDY OF Y 119

(They watched in a palpable silence. She was living over that horrible moment, and something of the strain and fear of it came to them dimly through her mute absorption. Lane was scarcely breathing; his eyes were almost shut, and what was visible glittered; they were fixed on Louisa. . . .

Her right arm was stretched rigidly before her in the familiar blindman's gesture, as unbending as a steel bar and exactly parallel to the floor. Lane's glance dropped sharply to the spot on the rug directly below the tips of her extended fingers.)

Louisa sighed, relaxed, and her arm dropped heavily to her side. Then she began to speak with her hands again, Miss Smith breathlessly interpreting.

A moment after Louisa had stretched out her right arm, something brushed her fingertips. Brushed by—she had felt a nose, and then a face . . . a cheek, really, as the face moved by her stiff fingers. . . .

("A nose and cheek!" exclaimed the Inspector. "God, what luck! Here—let me talk to her——"

Lane said: "Now, Inspector, there's no reason to become excited. If you'll pardon me, I'd like to have Miss Campion repeat what she has just illustrated for us."

He got the board and made her understand what he wanted. She passed her hand wearily across her forehead, but nodded and went back to the bed. They watched more intently than before.

The result was uncanny. In every movement, in every inclination of head and body, in every gesture of her arms, her second illustration was an exact repetition of her first!

"Oh, splendid!' murmured Lane. "This is fortunate, gentlemen. Miss Campion, in common with other blind people, has a photographic memory for physical movements. It helps—it helps considerably. Considerably."

They were puzzled—what helped considerably? He did not

120 ACT I: SCENE 4

enlighten them, but it was apparent from the extraordinary expression on his face that an all but overwhelming thought had struck him—something so clearly remarkable that even he, trained as he was by a lifetime in the theater to control his facial muscles, could not conceal his reaction to the mental discovery.

"I don't see . . ." began District Attorney Bruno in a troubled way.

Lane's features ironed themselves out magically, and he said in a smooth voice: "I fear I've been melodramatic. Please observe Miss Campion's resting position. She stands precisely where she stood in the early hours this morning—her shoes fit almost to the inch in the bare prints near the foot of her bed. What do we see opposite her position, facing her? The arrested marks of the murderer's shoes. Obviously, then, the murderer must have stood in the thick of the talcum-strewn area at the instant of contact with Miss Campion's fingers— for on this spot the two shoe-toe marks are clearest, as if the murderer momentarily froze to the spot when he felt those ghostly fingers out of the darkness."

Inspector Thumm scratched his heavy jaw. "All right, but what's so marvelous about that? That's the way we've been figuring it all along. I don't see . . . A second ago you seemed——"

"I suggest," said Mr. Drury Lane quickly, "that Miss Campion proceed."

"Here, here, wait a minute," said the Inspector. "Not so fast, Mr. Lane. I think I see what struck you." He wheeled on Bruno. "You know, Bruno, from the position of this woman's arms when she touched the murderer's cheek we'll be able to establish the murderer's *height!*" He glared triumphantly at Lane.

The District Attorney's face darkened. "A good stunt," he said incisively, "if you can do it. But you can't."

"Why not?"

THE TRAGEDY OF Y   121

"Come, come, gentlemen," said Lane impatiently, "let's get on. . . ."

"Just a moment, Mr. Lane," said Bruno in cold tones. "Look here, Thumm. You say we can reconstruct the murderer's height from the fact that Miss Campion's arm was outstretched and that she touched the murderer's cheek. Yes, certainly—if the murderer was standing erect when she touched him!"

"Well, but . . ."

"As a matter of fact," continued Bruno briskly, "we have every reason to assume that, far from being erect, the murderer was *crouching* when Miss Campion touched him. From the trail of footprints it's evident that he had just left the head of Mrs. Hatter's bed after killing her and was on his way out of the room. He may have heard, as Mr. Lane suggested, the creaking of Miss Campion's bed. He would, therefore, be in a hurry—the instinct to stoop, to crouch would operate instantaneously." He smiled faintly. "So there's your problem, Thumm. How are you ever going to determine the extent of our murderer's crouch? For you would have to know exactly before you could figure his height."

"All right, all right," said Thumm, flushing. "Don't rub it in." He cocked a sour eye at Lane. "But if I know Mr. Lane, something just hit him like a ton of bricks. If it isn't the murderer's height, what the devil is it?"

"Really, Inspector," murmured Lane, "you make me blush for my art. Did I actually give you that impression?" He squeezed Louisa's arm, and at once she proceeded with her story.)

Things had happened in a flashing instant. The shock, the materialization out of eternal darkness of a solid body, the flesh-and-blood reality of her formless fears, had made her feel faint. She realized with horror that her senses were deserting her, and she felt her knees buckle under her. She was still slightly conscious as she fell; but she must have

122 ACT I: SCENE 4

fallen with more force than she realized, for her head struck the floor hard and she remembered nothing more until she was being revived in the early morning. . . .

* * *

Her fingers stilled, her arms dropped, and with sagging shoulders she returned to the rocking chair. Captain Trivett once more began to pat her cheek. She rested it against his hand, wearily.

Mr. Drury Lane looked at his two companions with an inquiring eye. Both men seemed puzzled. He sighed and went to Louisa's chair.

"You have omitted something. What *kind* of cheek was it that your fingers felt?"

Something like astonishment banished the weariness for a moment. As plainly as if she had spoken, they read in her features: "Why, I mentioned that, didn't I?" And then her fingers flew, and Miss Smith translated with a tremor in her voice.

It was a smooth soft cheek.

If a bombshell had exploded behind him, Inspector Thumm could not have acted with more stupefaction. His big jaw hung loose, and his eyes goggled at the still fingers of Louisa Campion as if he could not believe his eyes—or his ears. District Attorney Bruno remained staring incredulously at the nurse.

"Are you sure, Miss Smith, that you've translated correctly?" asked Bruno with difficulty.

"That's just what—what she said, sir," replied Miss Smith nervously.

Inspector Thumm shook his head like a prize-fighter shaking off the effects of a hard blow—his habitual reaction to surprise—and glared down at Louisa. "Smooth and soft!"

THE TRAGEDY OF Y   123

he cried. "Impossible. Why, Conrad Hatter's cheek——"

"Then it wasn't Conrad Hatter's cheek," said Mr. Drury Lane softly. "Why proceed on preconceptions? After all, if Miss Campion's testimony is credible, we must rearrange our data. We know that Conrad's shoes were worn by the marauder last night, but it is fallacious to assume, as you and Mr. Bruno did, that merely because Hatter's shoes were worn, Hatter wore them."

"You're perfectly right, as usual," muttered Bruno. "Thumm——"

But Thumm, like the human bulldog he was, refused to discard a solution so readily. He ground his teeth and snarled at Miss Smith: "Use those damned dominoes and ask her if she's sure, and how smooth it was. Go ahead!"

Miss Smith, frightened, obeyed. Louisa eagerly ran her fingers over the board. She nodded immediately, and her hands spoke once more.

A very smooth soft cheek. I am not mistaken.

"Well, she seems positive enough," muttered the Inspector. "Ask her, you, if it couldn't have been her half-brother Conrad's cheek."

No. Impossible. It was not a man's cheek, I am certain.

"All right," said the Inspector. "That settles that. After all, we've got to take her word for it. So it wasn't Conrad, and it wasn't a man. That makes it a woman, by God. At least we've made up our minds on that!"

"She must have worn Conrad Hatter's shoes to leave a false trail," remarked the District Attorney. "That means the powder was upset on the rug deliberately. Whoever it was knew the shoes would leave prints, and that we would look for the pair which matched exactly."

"You think so, Mr. Bruno?" asked Lane. The District Attorney scowled. "No, I am not being facetious or smart,"

Act I: Scene 4

Lane went on in a worried tone. "There is something preposterously peculiar about all this."

"What's peculiar about it?" demanded Thumm. "Open and shut, as Bruno explained it, seems to me."

"Still open, Inspector, I'm sorry to say, and far from shut." Lane manipulated the metal Braille letters, spelling out the message: "Could that cheek you felt by any chance have been your mother's?"

The reply flashed in protest:

No. No. No. Mother had a wrinkled face. Wrinkled. This was smooth. Smooth.

Lane smiled sadly. There was the feeling of undistorted truth in everything this amazing creature communicated. Thumm was pacing the floor with elephantine strides, and Bruno looked thoughtful. Captain Trivett, Dr. Merriam, Miss Smith stood quite still.

Decision came into Lane's face. He arranged the pieces again. "Think hard. Do you recall anything—anything—else?"

She hesitated when she had read the message, and rested her head against the back support of the rocker. Her head moved from side to side—a slow and grudging negative, as if something tottered on the brink of remembrance, something which refused to fall.

"There *is* something," murmured Lane with a trace of excitement, as he studied that blank face. "It needs prompting!"

"But what, for God's sake?" cried Thumm. "We've learned as much as we could possibly hope for. . . ."

"No," said Lane. "We have not." He paused, and then continued slowly: "We are dealing with a human witness two of whose five senses are atrophied. The only contacts this witness makes with the outer world are taste, touch,

THE TRAGEDY OF Y

and smell. Any reactions this witness may have had through these three remaining senses are our only possible clues."

"I never thought of it in that way," said Bruno thoughtfully. "And, to be sure, she's already provided one clue through her sense of touch. Maybe——"

"Exactly, Mr. Bruno. To hope for a clue from her sense of taste is, of course, futile. But smell! We have every reason to believe. . . . If she were an animal, a dog, for example, with the ability to communicate sensory impressions, how simple it would be! Yet something of such a strange condition exists. Her olfactory nerves are probably hypersensitive. . . ."

"You are," said Dr. Merriam in a low voice, "perfectly correct, Mr. Lane. There has been much dispute in the medical profession about the problem of compensatory sense impressionism. But Louisa Campion is a remarkable answer to the argument. The nerves at the tips of her fingers, the taste-buds in her tongue, the olfactories in her nose are acutely developed."

"Very pretty," said the Inspector, "but I——"

"Patience," said Lane. "We may be on the track of something extraordinary. We are discussing smell. Already she has testified to the odor of the talcum when it was upset—certainly not a normal sensitivity. It's barely possible . . ." He stooped swiftly and rearranged the metal pieces on the Braille board. "Smell. Did you smell anything aside from powder? Think. Smell."

Slowly, as her fingers traversed the dots on the board, something both triumphant and puzzled came into her face, and her nostrils flared wildly. That she was struggling with a recollection was apparent; that the recollection was tugging, tugging . . . Then the light dawned over her,

126 ACT I: SCENE 4

and she uttered another of those thrilling animal cries which seemed to break from her spontaneously when she was aroused. Her fingers rippled into motion.

Miss Smith's mouth dropped open as she stared at those intelligent digits. "It's hard to believe she knows what she's saying. . . ."

"Yes?" exclaimed the District Attorney with a shrill excitement.

"Why, do you know," continued the nurse in the same stupefied voice, "she says that in the instant she touched the face, and as she fell fainting, she smelled . . ."

"Come, come!" cried Mr. Drury Lane, his eyes glittering, fixed on Miss Smith's fat lips as she paused. "What did she smell?"

Miss Smith giggled nervously. "Well—something like ice cream, or cake!"

* * *

For a moment they stared at the nurse, and she stared back. Even Dr. Merriam and Captain Trivett seemed astounded. The District Attorney repeated the words mutely, as if he could not believe his ears. And Thumm scowled a terrifying scowl.

The tense smile left Lane's face. He was plainly nonplused. "Ice cream or cake," he repeated slowly. "Strange, very strange."

The Inspector broke into an ugly laugh. "There you are," he said. "Not only is she deaf-dumb-and-blind, by God, but she's inherited the nuttiness of her mama's family as well. Ice cream or cake! Hell and damnation. This is a farce."

"Please Inspector . . . It may not be so insane as it sounds. Why should she think of ice cream *or* cake? There is hardly anything in common between the two except a cer-

THE TRAGEDY OF Y 127

tain pleasantness of odor. It may be—yes, I believe it may
be much saner than you think."

He moved the metal letters. "You say ice cream or cake.
Hard to believe. Perhaps face powder, cold cream."

A pause, as her fingers searched the board.

*No. Not a woman's face powder, or cold cream. It was—
well, like cake or ice cream, only stronger.*

"Not definite enough. It was a sweet scent, was it not?"

Yes. Sweet. Piercing sweet.

"Piercing sweet," muttered Lane. "Piercing sweet." He
shook his head and formed another question. "Perhaps
from a flower?"

Perhaps . . .

She hesitated, and her nose wrinkled as she bent her will
to recapture that hours-old odor.

*Yes. One kind of flower. An orchid, a rare variety. Cap-
tain Trivett gave it to me. But I am not sure. . . .*

Captain Trivett's old eyes blinked; they were a sharp
blue, but they were bewildered now. His weatherbeaten
face turned the color of old saddle leather as their eyes
focused upon him.

"Well, Captain?" demanded Thumm. "Can you lend a
hand?"

Captain Trivett's rusty voice cracked. "She remembers,
bedad! Lemme see, now . . . 'Twas nigh on seven year'
ago. Friend o' mine—Cap Corcoran of th' freighter *Trini-
dad*—hauled it up with him from South America. . . ."

"Seven years ago!" exclaimed the District Attorney.
"That's a long time to remember one odor."

"Louisa's a mighty remark'ble little lady," said the Captain, blinking again.

"Orchid," mused Lane. "It grows stranger. What variety
was it, Captain, do you recall?"

128 ACT I: SCENE 4

The old seaman's hulking bony shoulders twitched. "Never did know," he said, with the tonal charm of a rusty old winch. "Somethin' rare."

"Hmm." Lane turned to the board again. "Just that one variety of orchid, no other?"

Yes. I love flowers and never forget the odor of a blossom. That was the only time I had ever smelled such an orchid.

"The great horticultural mystery," remarked Lane, with an effort at lightness. But his eyes were humorless and he kept tapping the floor with one foot. They watched him with a species of helpless fatigue.

And suddenly he brightened, and smacked his forehead. "Of course! I neglected the most obvious question!" and became busy once more with the little metal letters.

The message spelled out: "You say 'ice cream.' What kind of ice cream? Chocolate? Strawberry? Banana? Walnut?"

That at last the right note had been struck was so apparent that even Inspector Thumm, whose temper was far from friendly, glanced at Lane with admiration. For the moment Louisa discovered through the medium of her fingertips what Lane was asking, her face lighted up, she nodded brightly as a bird, several times, and replied at once in the sign language:

I know now. Not strawberry, not chocolate, not banana, not walnut. Vanilla! Vanilla! Vanilla!

She was sitting pertly on the edge of the rocker, her blind eyes veiled, but her face begging for commendation. Captain Trivett furtively smoothed her hair.

"Vanilla!" they exclaimed together.

The fingers flew on.

Vanilla. Not necessarily ice cream or cake or orchids or anything else definite. Just vanilla. I am positive. Positive.

THE TRAGEDY OF Y   129

Lane sighed, and the frown between his eyes deepened. Louisa's fingers were moving so rapidly now that Miss Smith had a difficult time translating; she was forced to make Louisa repeat the finger-motions. Something soft came into the nurse's eyes as she turned to the others.

Please. Does that help. I want to help. I must help. Does it, does it help.

"Lady," said the Inspector grimly, as he strode to the door of the bedroom, "you bet your sweet life it helps."

Dr. Merriam bent over Louisa, who was trembling, and put his hand on her wrist. He nodded, patted her cheek, and stood back again. Captain Trivett, for no conceivable reason, looked proud.

Thumm opened the door and yelled: "Pink! Mosher! Somebody! Get that housekeeper up here right away!"

*   *   *

Mrs. Arbuckle was inclined at first to be truculent. The initial shock of having her household overrun by police had passed off. She puffed up the stairs grasping her skirts with both hands, rested on the landing, muttering rebelliously to herself; and then she barged into the death-room with a frank glare for the Inspector.

"Well! What d'you want of me now?" she demanded.

The Inspector wasted no time. "What did you bake yesterday?"

"Bake? For goodness' sake!" They faced each other like two bantams. "What d'you want to know for?"

"Ha!" said Thumm fiercely. "Evading the question, eh? Did you bake yesterday or didn't you?"

Mrs. Arbuckle sniffed. "I can't see . . . No, I did not."

"You did not. Hmm." He thrust his jaw two inches closer. "Do you use vanilla in your kitchen?"

ACT I: SCENE 4

Mrs. Arbuckle stared at him as if he were demented. "Vanilla? Of all things! Certainly I use vanilla. What kind of pantry do you think I keep, anyway?"

"You use vanilla," said Thumm judiciously. He turned to the District Attorney and winked. "She uses vanilla, Bruno. . . . All right, Mrs. Arbuckle. Did you use any of it for any purpose at all—yesterday?" He rubbed his hands.

Mrs. Arbuckle flounced to the door. "I won't stand here and be made a fool of, I'll tell you that," she snapped. "I'm going downstairs where I don't have to answer crazy questions."

"Mrs. Arbuckle!" thundered the Inspector.

She halted uncertainly and looked around. They were all staring very seriously indeed in her direction. "Well . . . no." She added with a weak recurrence of temper: "Say, are you trying to tell me how to run my house?"

"Pipe down," said Thumm pleasantly. "Don't get nasty. Have you got vanilla in your pantry or kitchen now?"

"Ye-es. A brand-new bottle. I ran out of it three days ago, so I ordered a new bottle from Sutton's. I haven't had time to open it yet."

"But how is that possible, Mrs. Arbuckle?" asked Lane gently. "According to my information you prepare an egg-nog for Miss Campion every day."

"What's that got to do with it?"

"Egg-nogs, when I was a boy, Mrs. Arbuckle, contained *vanilla.*"

Thumm started forward, surprised. Mrs. Arbuckle tossed her head. "And what does that prove, pray? You'll find grated nutmeg in *mine*. Is that a crime, too?"

Thumm stuck his head into the hall. "Pink!"

"Yep."

"Go on downstairs with the housekeeper. Bring up everything that smells vanilla." Thumm jerked his thumb toward

THE TRAGEDY OF Y

the door. "Get going, Mrs. Arbuckle, and make it snappy."

No one said anything while they waited. Thumm whistled a hideous tune and strolled about, hands behind his back. Bruno's thoughts were far away; he seemed bored. Louisa sat quietly, and behind her stood the motionless figures of Miss Smith, Dr. Merriam, and Captain Trivett. Lane looked out of a window at the deserted garden.

Ten minutes later Mrs. Arbuckle and her escort plodded up the stairs. Pinkussohn was carrying a small flat bottle wrapped in paper.

"There's a lot of smells down there, fancy and assorted," grinned the detective, "but nothin' besides this bottle of vanilla smells vanilla. Didn't open it, Chief."

Thumm took the bottle from Pinkussohn. It was labeled VANILLA EXTRACT, and its seal and wrapper were intact. He passed it to Bruno, who examined it indifferently, and returned it. Lane did not move from the window.

"Wha'd you do with the old bottle, Mrs. Arbuckle?" asked Thumm.

"Threw it out in the garbage three days ago," the housekeeper replied shortly.

"It was empty then?"

"Yes."

"Did you ever find any of it missing while the bottle still had vanilla in it?"

"How on earth should I know? Do you think I count every drop?"

"I wouldn't be surprised," retorted the Inspector. He tore off the wrapper and seal, uncorked the bottle, and held it up to his nose. A strong odor of vanilla slowly permeated the air in the bedroom; there could be no doubt of the authenticity of this bottle. It was full and quite untampered with.

Louisa Campion stirred, her nostrils dilating. She sniffed

132 ACT I: SCENE 4

aloud, and turned her head toward the bottle across the room, like a bee scenting honey from afar. Her fingers sprang into life.

"She says that's it—that smell!" cried Miss Smith excitedly.

"Does she indeed?" murmured Mr. Drury Lane, who had wheeled and was watching the nurse's lips. He strode forward and arranged a message on the board. "As strongly as you smell it now?"

Not quite. Fainter last night.

Lane nodded rather hopelessly. "Is there any ice cream in the house, Mrs. Arbuckle?"

"No, sir."

"Was there yesterday?"

"No, sir. None all week."

"Utterly incomprehensible," said Lane. His eyes were as brilliantly thoughtful as ever, his face as young and fresh, but there was something weary about him, as if he were exhausted from thinking. "Inspector, it might be wise to have everyone in the house assembled here immediately. In the meantime, Mrs. Arbuckle, if you will be so gracious, please collect and bring to this room all the cake and candy in the house."

"Pink," growled Inspector Thumm, "you go along—just in case."

* * *

The room filled up. Everyone was there—Barbara, Jill, Conrad, Martha, George Arbuckle, Virginia the housemaid, Edgar Perry, even Chester Bigelow and John Gormly, both of whom had doggedly remained on the premises. Conrad seemed dazed, and kept glancing stupidly at the policeman by his side. The others had an expectant air. . . . Inspector Thumm hesitated, and then stepped back out of the way.

THE TRAGEDY OF Y 133

He and District Attorney Bruno looked on gloomily.

Lane stood still, waiting.

The children, as usual, had pounced in with their elders. They were noisy and ran whooping about the room. For once no one paid attention to their antics.

Mrs. Arbuckle and Pinkussohn staggered in under a mountain of cake and candy-boxes. Everyone looked astonished. Mrs. Arbuckle deposited her load on Louisa's bed and wiped her scrawny neck with a handkerchief. Pinkussohn, with an expression of profound disgust, dumped his armful on a chair and walked out.

"Have any of you ladies and gentlemen cake or candy in your personal quarters?" inquired Lane gravely.

Jill Hatter said: "I have. I always have."

"Will you please fetch it, Miss Hatter."

Jill went soberly enough from the room and returned a moment later with a large rectangular box, on which the words: "Five pounds," could be detected. At the sight of this gargantuan packet of sweets John Gormly's fair skin turned the color of brick. He grinned feebly and shuffled his feet.

Under their wondering eyes Mr. Drury Lane proceeded about a curious business. He collected all the boxes of candy in a pile on the chair, and opened them one by one. There were five—one of peanut brittle, one of fruit-filled chocolates, one of hard candy, one of hard-centered chocolates, and Jill's which, opened, presented a delectable array of expensive *glacéd* nuts and fruits.

Lane selected pieces at random from all five boxes, nibbled thoughtfully at several, and then fed sample pieces to Louisa Campion. The sturdy youngster, Billy, looked on with hungry eyes; and Jackie, subdued by this mysterious procedure, stood on one leg and stared with fascination.

ACT I: SCENE 4

134

Louisa Campion shook her head.

No. Not any of this. Not candy. I was wrong. Vanilla!

"Either these confections are made without vanilla," observed Lane, "or the vanilla content is so slight that it makes no difference appreciable to the taste." He said to Mrs. Arbuckle: "These cakes, Mrs. Arbuckle. Which of these did you bake yourself?"

Haughtily she pointed to three.

"Did you use vanilla in them?"

"I did not."

"The others were purchased?"

"Yes, sir."

Lane fed small pieces of each bought cake to the deaf-dumb-and-blind woman. She shook her head again, emphatically.

Miss Smith sighed and watched Louisa's fingers.

No. I do not smell the vanilla.

Lane tossed the cakes back on the bed and stood musing in desperation. "Er—what's all this rigmarole about?" asked Bigelow, the lawyer, with a trace of amusement.

"I'm sorry." Lane turned absently. "Miss Campion was face to face last night with Mrs. Hatter's murderer. She is positive that at the moment of contact she detected a pronounced odor of vanilla, presumably emanating from the person or vicinity of the murderer. Naturally, we're trying to solve this minor mystery—which may lead to a major discovery and ultimate success."

"Vanilla!" repeated Barbara Hatter with amazement. "Scarcely credible, Mr. Lane. And yet Louisa is uncanny in her sensory memories. I'm sure——"

"She's daffy," said Jill distinctly. "She makes things up half the time. Too much imagination."

"Jill," said Barbara.

The Tragedy of Y 135

Jill tossed her head, but fell silent.

They might have known. There was the confused sound of scrambling feet, and they wheeled in some alarm to see Jackie Hatter, his undersized little body agile as a monkey's, diving into Louisa's bed, his hands scrabbling for the candy-boxes. Little Billy squealed with delight and dived after. They began with frantic haste to stuff their mouths with candy.

Martha pounced on them, crying hysterically: "Jackie! Good heavens, you'll cram yourself *sick*. . . . Billy! Stop that this instant, or mother will spank you *hard!*" She shook them and slapped sticky candy out of their clawing fingers.

Billy looked defiant, even as he dropped his handful. "Want candy like Unka John gimme yest'day!" he screamed.

"What's this?" roared Inspector Thumm, darting forward. He tilted Billy's determined little chin roughly, and growled: "What candy did Unka John give you yesterday?"

Thumm even in his pleasant moments was scarcely a gentleman to inspire confidence in little boys; and when he scowled, as he did now, he was positively terrifying. Billy stared up at the smashed nose for one fascinated instant, and then, wriggling out of the Inspector's grasp, he buried his tiny head in his mother's skirt and howled.

"Very diplomatic, I must say, Inspector," remarked Lane, pushing Thumm out of the way. "You'd frighten a Sergeant of Marines with those tactics. . . . Here, son," he said, squatting down by Billy's side and squeezing his shoulder reassuringly, "don't take on so. No one is going to hurt you."

Thumm snorted. But in two minutes Billy was in Lane's arms, smiling through his tears, and Lane was conducting

136 ACT I: SCENE 4

a conversation with him anent the relative delights of candy, toys, worms, and cowboys-'n'-Indians. Billy grew very confidential; this was a nice man. Unka John had brought candy for Billy. When? Yest'day.

"For me, too!" shouted Jackie, tugging at Lane's coat.

"Indeed. What kind of candy was it, Billy?"

"Licorice!" shouted Jackie.

"Lic'rish," lisped Billy. "Big bags."

Lane set the boy down and looked at John Gormly. Gormly was fretfully rubbing the back of his neck. "Is this true, Mr. Gormly?"

"Of course, it's true!" said Gormly with irritation. "You're not suggesting the candy was poisoned, I hope? I was calling on Miss Hatter—I brought her that five-pound box there—and, knowing how fond the boys are of licorice, I brought some for them. That's all."

"I'm suggesting nothing, Mr. Gormly," replied Lane mildly. "And it means nothing, for licorice hasn't a vanilla odor. At the same time one cannot be too careful. Why must you people spring to the defensive at the simplest questions?" He stooped over Billy again. "Did anyone else give you candy yesterday, Billy?"

Billy stared; this question was a trifle beyond his comprehension. Jackie planted his thin legs squarely on the rug and said shrilly: "Why don't you ask *me*? *I* can tell you."

"Very well, Master Jackie. I ask you."

"No. Nobody did. Only Uncle John."

"Fine." Lane pressed a handful of chocolates into each child's grimy fist and sent them off with their mother. "That's all, Inspector," he said.

Thumm waved the company out of the bedroom.

Lane observed that Edgar Perry, the tutor, managed furtively to slip into step beside Barbara: the two began

The Tragedy of Y 137

to converse in low voices as they descended the stairs.

Thumm was restless; undecided; and at the last moment, as Conrad Hatter was crossing the threshold in custody of the policeman, Thumm said: "Hatter! Wait a minute."

Conrad nervously returned. "What is it—what is it now?" The man was in a funk; all his former belligerence had deserted him; he seemed anxious to please.

"Let Miss Campion feel your face."

"Feel my *face . . . !*"

"Oh, I say," objected Bruno, "you know, Thumm, what she——"

"I don't give two hoots in hell," said Thumm doggedly. "I want to make sure. Miss Smith, tell her to feel Mr. Hatter's cheek."

The nurse silently obeyed. Louisa looked expectant. Conrad, pale and tense, leaned over her rocker and Miss Smith placed Louisa's hand on his clean-shaven, almost beardless face. She drew it swiftly down, up, and down again; and shook her head.

Her fingers flew. Miss Smith said: "She says it was much softer than that. A woman's, she says. Not Mr. Hatter's."

Conrad straightened up, utterly bewildered. Thumm shook his head. "Okay," he said in deep disgruntlement. "You may go anywhere in the house, Hatter, but don't leave it. You, officer, stay with him."

Conrad trudged out, followed by the policeman. Thumm said: "Well, Mr. Lane, it's a grand mess, isn't it?" and looked around for the actor.

Lane had disappeared.

*   *   *

The magic, however, was catholic. Lane had slipped out of the bedroom with a fixed purpose; a simple errand, it

138 ACT I: SCENE 4

would seem—the mere pursuit of an odor. He wandered from room to room, from floor to floor, going through bedrooms, bathrooms, empty rooms, the storerooms—he omitted nothing. His chiseled nose was on the alert. He smelled everything he could lay hands on; perfumes, cosmetics, vases of flowers, even women's scented undergarments. Finally, he went downstairs and into the garden, where he spent fifteen minutes in olfactory contemplation of its many flowers.

The whole affair, as somehow he had known it would be, proved entirely vain. Nowhere did he sniff anything which might possess the "piercing sweet" vanilla odor Louisa Campion had smelled.

When he rejoined Thumm and Bruno in the death-room upstairs, Dr. Merriam had gone, and Captain Trivett was holding mute communication with Louisa by means of the Braille pieces. The two investigators were dejected.

"Where you been?" asked Thumm.

"Following the tail of a scent."

"Didn't know scents had tails. Haw!" No one laughed, and Thumm scratched his jaw sheepishly. "Nothing doing, I suppose?"

Lane shook his head.

"Well, I'm not surprised. There's nothing anywhere. The house was searched from top to bottom anyway this morning, and we haven't found a solitary thing that might be important."

"It's beginning to look," remarked the District Attorney, "as if we had another white elephant on our hands."

"Maybe, maybe," said Thumm. "But I'm going to take a look at that laboratory next door after lunch. I was in there two months ago, and it's just possible that . . ."

"Ah yes, the laboratory," said Mr. Drury Lane morosely.

Scene 5

THE LABORATORY. SUNDAY, JUNE 5. 2:30 P.M.

Mrs. Arbuckle, still in the truculent mood, served Inspector Thumm, District Attorney Bruno, and Mr. Drury Lane a hazardous luncheon downstairs in the dining-room. The meal was for the most part silent and permeated with the odor of gloom. The prevailing mood was punctuated by Mrs. Arbuckle's heavy shoes clumping in and out of the dining-room, and the clumsy thumps of dishes on the table, set there by the rawboned maid, Virginia.

The conversation was desultory. At one point it was dominated by Mrs. Arbuckle, who was bitterly complaining aloud, to no one in particular, about the mess her kitchen was in. . . . It seemed that numerous gentlemen of the police were eating their heads off at the back of the house. But not even Inspector Thumm bridled at her tone; he was too absorbed in chewing a leathery chop and an even tougher thought.

"All right," said Bruno after a silence of five minutes, and *à propos* of nothing, "it's Louisa the woman is after—we'll say woman, since that cheek business could hardly be more conclusive. Murder of the old lady wasn't intended. She was battered over the head in the murderer's panic when she awakened during the poisoning period. But who? I can't see a streak of light in that direction."

"And what the hell does this vanilla business mean?" growled Thumm, throwing down knife and fork in disgust.

"Yes . . . Queer. I have the feeling that once we solve that problem, we'll be close to the truth."

139

Act I: Scene 5

"Hmm," said Mr. Drury Lane, chewing powerfully.

"Conrad Hatter," muttered the Inspector. "If it weren't for that cheek testimony . . ."

"Forget it," said Bruno. "Someone's trying to frame him."

A detective strolled in bearing a sealed envelope. "Messenger from Dr. Schilling just brought this, Chief."

"Ah!" said Lane, dropping knife and fork. "The report. Read it aloud, Inspector."

Thumm tore open the envelope. "Let's see. On the poison business. He says:

> Dear Thumm:
> The spoiled pear contains considerably more than a lethal dose of liquefied bichloride of mercury. One bite of the pear would have caused death.
> In answer to Mr. Lane's question: No, decay in this pear was not caused by the poison; the pear was already in a rotten condition when the poison was injected.
> The other two pears are free from poison.
> The empty hypodermic found on the bed contained the same poison. I should say, from the amount of bichloride found in the pear and from the estimated bichloride content in the hypo, that it was from this syringe that the pear was poisoned.
> There is a minor difference; I think I may say it is made up by the stains on the white shoe you sent over. The splatters are of bichloride of mercury. Probably some dripped and splashed on the shoe tip during the injection of the pear. The stains are of recent origin.
> Autopsy report on the cadaver will be forthcoming late tonight or tomorrow morning. But from preliminary examination I am certain the post-mortem results will show no signs of poisoning whatsoever and will confirm original opinion on cause of death.
>
> SCHILLING

The Tragedy of Y   141

All of which checks," muttered Thumm. "Well, that clarifies the shoe business and the poisoned-pear theory. Bichloride of mercury, hey? Seems to me . . . Let's go on up to that laboratory."

Mr. Drury Lane was content to pull a long face and remain silent. The three men left their coffee half finished, scraped their chairs back, and quit the room. As they went out they met Mrs. Arbuckle, grim and unsmiling, bearing a tray on which stood a glass of yellow creamy fluid. Lane consulted his wrist-watch; it was two-thirty exactly.

On the way upstairs Lane took the letter from the Inspector's hand and painstakingly read it. He returned it without comment.

The bedroom floor was quiet. For a moment they stood at the head of the stairs. Then the door of Miss Smith's room opened, and the nurse appeared leading Louisa Campion—despite the tragedy, despite the disruption of the household, custom remained, and the deaf-dumb-and-blind woman made her way past the three men down the stairs, bound for the dining-room and the daily egg-nog. None of the three said anything. It had been arranged that Louisa was to stay and sleep in Miss Smith's room until further notice. . . . Captain Trivett and Dr. Merriam had left the house long before.

The burly form of Mosher, Thumm's man, was propped against the closet wall of the death-room. Mosher, smoking quietly, yet on the alert, had a clear view of the doors leading into all the rooms on the floor.

The Inspector yelled down: "Pink!"

Detective Pinkussohn came running up the stairs.

"You and Mosher are on duty at this floor, get me? Relieve each other. Nobody's to go into the old lady's bedroom. Otherwise don't bother anybody; just keep your eyes peeled."

142   ACT I: SCENE 5

Pinkussohn nodded and went downstairs again.

The Inspector fished in his vest pocket and produced a Yale key. It was the key to York Hatter's laboratory which he had found in the effects of the dead woman. He hefted it thoughtfully in his hand, then rounded the stairhead and made for the laboratory door, followed by Bruno and Lane.

He did not unlock the door at once. Instead, he squatted on his hams and squinted into the small keyhole. He grunted, took a tiny wire probe from one of his inexhaustible pockets, and inserted it into the hole. He scraped it through, and through again, and began a rotary motion. Finally, satisfied, he withdrew the probe and examined it.

It was clean.

He got to his feet, put away the wire, and looked puzzled. "Funny," he said. "Thought sure we'd find signs of wax in this lock. Would confirm the idea that someone made a wax impression of the keyhole and had a duplicate key whittled out. But there's no wax."

"It's not so important," said Bruno. "Either a wax impression was made and the keyhole cleaned out, or else Mrs. Hatter's key was 'borrowed' temporarily by the poisoner, a duplicate made, and the original returned without her knowledge. In any event, we'll never know, now that the old woman is dead."

"Come, come, Inspector," said Lane impatiently. "This is getting us nowhere. Open the door."

Thumm jabbed the key into the hole. It fitted snugly, but he had difficulty turning it over; the mechanism was rusty, as if it had not been used for a long time. He dashed a drop of perspiration from the tip of his nose and twisted hard. With a squeak the lock surrendered; something clicked; and Thumm, grasping the handle of the door,

The Tragedy of Y

143

pushed. It squealed protest, like the lock—rusty door hinges as well.

As the door swung open, and the Inspector began to cross the threshold, Lane put his hand on the big man's arm.

"Well?" said Thumm.

Lane pointed to the floor just inside the room. It was uncovered hardwood, and it was coated with an even layer of dust. He stooped and ran his finger along the floor; it came up smudged. "No sign of *this* entrance having been used by your marauder, Inspector," he said. "The dust is undisturbed, and from its thickness must be many weeks old."

"Wasn't that way when I saw it two months ago—not so much, anyhow," said Thumm, looking uncomfortable. "Couldn't have jumped it, either. There's a good six feet between the door and the disturbed area. Funny!"

They stood side by side in the doorway and examined the room without going in. As the Inspector had said, the entire space before the door was untrampled; the dust lay like dun-colored velvet. Some six feet from the door, however, the dust was in a state of confusion. Feet had made their marks there, and as far into the room as they could see. But the feet had also been most careful to scuff out every clear print. The condition of the dust was as remarkable: hundreds of steps, evidently, and not a single identifiable print!

"Damned careful, whoever it was," said Thumm. "Just a minute. I want to see if there isn't one print, anyway, around the tables there that we can photograph."

He tramped in, callously planting his own Number Twelves in the unviolated dust, and began to snoop around the trampled areas. His face grew black as he peered into

144   ACT I: SCENE 5

shadowy places. "Simply unbelievable!" he grumbled. "Not a clear footprint. Well, come in—you can't do any harm to *this* floor."

The District Attorney stepped inquisitively into the laboratory, but Lane stood still on the threshold and examined the room from where he was. The doorway in which he stood was the only one to the room. The room was of similar shape to the death-room next door, on the east. Two windows, like the windows of the death-room, were on the wall opposite the corridor wall, overlooking the garden at the rear. But, unlike the windows of the adjoining room, these were barred with thick solid stanchions of iron, no more than three inches of daylight between them.

Between the windows there was a white iron bedstead, simple and severe; in the angle made by the west and garden walls, near the west window, there was a dresser. Both articles of furniture were made up, but dusty.

Immediately to the right of the hall door there was an old battered rolltop desk and in the corner a small steel filing cabinet; to the left a clothes closet. On the west wall, extending for fully half the wall-space, Lane saw a sturdily built series of shelves holding an army of bottles and jars. The shelves rested flush on a floor closet as their base, and the floor closet's wide low doors were closed.

At right angles to these shelves were two rectangular work-tables, scarred and massive, covered with dusty retorts, racks of test-tubes, Bunsen burners, water-taps, electrical apparatus of unfamiliar design—a collection of chemical equipment which even to Lane's inexperienced eye seemed very complete. The two tables were parallel to each other, with a space between them wide enough to have

The Tragedy of Y 145

permitted the scientist to work on either table by merely swinging about.

On the east wall, directly across from the shelves and at right angles to the tables, there was a large fireplace exactly like the fireplace in the death-room next door. And at the rear of the laboratory, on the east wall between bed and fireplace, stood a small rough work-bench pitted and burned by chemicals. A few chairs stood untidily about; a three-legged stool with a circular seat stood directly before the floor closet beneath the middle shelves.

* * *

Mr. Drury Lane stepped in, closed the door, and crossed the room. Everywhere he stepped beyond the six-foot space of unmarked dust there were signs of the scuffed footprints. That someone had been frequenting the laboratory since York Hatter's death and Inspector Thumm's first investigation immediately thereafter was self-evident. And even more plain, from the condition of the dust and the absence of even one clear footprint, was it that the marauder had deliberately erased with scrapings of the feet every well-defined print.

"This is the result of more than one visit," ejaculated the Inspector. "But how'd she get in?"

He went to the windows, grasped the bars, and tugged with all his strength. They were immovable, imbedded in concrete. Thumm carefully examined the concrete and the bars themselves, on the lorn hope that several might be false with some device for unlocking. But this, too, proved fruitless, and he examined the sill and the ledge outside the windows. The ledge, however, which was wide enough to permit passage to an agile person, showed no sign of foot-

Act I: Scene 5

prints; nor was the dust on the sills in the least degree disturbed. Thumm shook his head.

He left the windows and walked over to the fireplace, in front of which—as in the rest of the room—many scuffed footprints were visible. He regarded the fireplace thoughtfully. It was real enough, although in a comparatively clean condition. He hesitated, then doubled his bulky figure and stooped to poke his head into the fireplace.

Growling with satisfaction, he quickly withdrew his head.

"What is it? What's up there?" asked Bruno.

"Dumb not to have thought of it before!" cried the Inspector. "Why, you can see the sky when you look up that chimney! And there are old spikes stuck into the brick for footholds—probably a hangover from the days of chimney-sweeps. I'll bet a dollar this is the way . . ." His face fell.

"Our *lady* entered the laboratory, Inspector?" inquired Lane gently. "Your face is too honest to disguise your thoughts. You were going to say that our hypothetical female poisoner entered via the chimney. Rather far-fetched, Inspector. Although, it's true, a male *accomplice* might have used this means of entry."

"The gals nowadays can do anything men do," said Thumm. "At the same time, that's an idea. There might be two of 'em in on this thing, at that." He stared at Bruno. "By God, that would let Conrad Hatter in on it again! Louisa Campion may have touched a woman's face, but it was Conrad Hatter who smashed Mrs. Hatter on the noodle and left those footprints!"

"And that," said the District Attorney, "is precisely what I had in mind, Thumm, the instant Mr. Lane suggested an accomplice. Yes, I think we're getting somewhere. . . ."

The Tragedy of Y 147

"Gentlemen, gentlemen," said Lane, "don't put words into my mouth, please. I suggested nothing. I merely pointed out a logical possibility. Ah—Inspector, is the chimney wide enough to permit a male adult to descend from the roof?"

"D'you think I— Say, take a look at it yourself, Mr. Lane. You're no cripple," said Thumm in a disagreeable voice.

"Inspector, I'll take your word for it."

"Sure, it's wide enough! I could do it myself, and my shoulders aren't exactly what you'd call skimpy."

Lane nodded, and in leisurely fashion strolled to the west wall for an examination of the shelves. There were five, one under another; and each of the five widths of shelving had been subdivided by partitions into three sections, making fifteen separate sections in all.

Nor was this the only sign of York Hatter's neat mind. For all the bottles and jars on the shelves were of uniform size, the bottles were of the same width as the jars, and all bore uniform labels. The labels were precisely hand-lettered in indelible ink with the names of the containers' contents, many bearing an additional strip of red paper marked POISON; and each descriptive label showed, besides the name of the chemical and in some cases its chemical symbol, a number.

"An orderly mind," observed Lane.

"Yes," said Bruno, "but it doesn't mean a thing."

Lane shrugged. "Perhaps not."

It was apparent, as he scrutinized the shelves, that all the containers were arranged in strictly numerical order, Bottle #1 standing at the extreme upper left of the topmost left-hand section, Bottle #2 next to #1, Jar #3 next to Bottle #2, and so on. The shelves were

148 ACT I: SCENE 5

full—there were no gaping spaces; obviously, the shelves' full complement of chemicals was displayed before them. There were twenty containers to each section of shelving, three hundred in all.

"Ah," said Lane. "Here's something interesting." He pointed to a bottle almost in the center of the first section of the top shelf. It was marked:

$$\# 9$$
$$C_{21}H_{22}N_2O_2$$
$$(\text{Strychnin})$$

POISON

and bore the red POISON tab. This bottle contained white tablets of a crystalline composition, and was only half full. But it was not the bottle itself in which Lane seemed interested; it was the dust at the base of the bottle. The dust had been disturbed, and it seemed certain that the bottle of strychnine had been removed from the shelf recently.

"Wasn't strychnine the poison in the egg-nog?" Lane asked.

"Sure," said Thumm. "I told you we'd found strychnine here in our investigation of the lab after that attempt a couple of months ago."

"The bottle was standing exactly where we see it now?"
"Yes."

"Had the dust of the shelf where the bottle stands been disturbed, as it is now?"

Thumm pushed forward and looked at the pressed dust with a scowl. "Yep. Just that way. Wasn't so much dust, but enough to make me remember it. I was careful to put

THE TRAGEDY OF Y

the bottle back, after looking at it, in the identical spot where I found it."

Lane turned back to the shelf. His eyes dropped to the shelf below the topmost one. On the lower part of the shelf's edge directly below Bottle #69, there was a curious oval smudge, as of a dirty or dusty fingertip. The label on this bottle read:

$$\# 69$$
$$HNO_3$$
$$(\text{Nitric Acid})$$

POISON

and contained a colorless liquid.

"Queer," said Lane to himself in a surprised voice. "Do you remember this smudge below the nitric acid bottle, Inspector?"

Thumm squinted. "Yes. Certainly do. It was there two months ago."

"Mmm. Fingerprints on the nitric acid bottle?"

"No. Whoever used it wore gloves. Although it's true that we haven't found traces of nitric acid being used. Maybe Hatter used it in an experiment while he was wearing rubber gloves."

"Which fails," said Lane dryly, "to explain the smudge."

He let his eye travel along the shelves.

"Bichloride of mercury?" asked the District Attorney. "If we can find some of it here—and with Schilling's report that it was in the pear . . ."

"A well-stocked laboratory, I must say," observed Lane. "Here it is, Mr. Bruno."

He pointed out a bottle on the central, or third, shelf

150 ACT I: SCENE 5

in the right-hand section. It was the eighth container in that section; and its label read:

168

BICHLORIDE OF MERCURY

POISON

The bottle was not quite full of the liquefied poison. The dust rimming it on the shelf had been disturbed. Thumm plucked the bottle out by the neck and looked it over minutely. "No fingerprints. Gloves again." He shook the bottle, scowled, and replaced it on the shelf. "Here's where the bichloride in the pear came from, all right. What a set-up for a poisoner! All the ammunition in the world just for the taking."

"Mm," said Bruno. "What was that poison Schilling said was in Hatter's vitals when they fished him out of the Lower Bay?"

"Prussic acid," replied Lane. "And here it is." The poison which York Hatter had swallowed just before jumping overboard was in Bottle # 57, on the top shelf, in the right-hand section. It was, like the others they had examined, plainly marked POISON. A considerable quantity of the colorless fluid was missing; and on the glass Inspector Thumm pointed out several fingerprints. The dust in which the bottle stood had not been disturbed.

"The fingerprints are York Hatter's. We checked them in the original investigation of the first poisoning attempt against the Campion woman."

"But how," inquired Lane mildly, "did you secure samples of Hatter's prints, Inspector? He was buried by

The Tragedy of Y   151

that time, and I don't suppose you were able to ink his fingers when you had him in the Morgue."

"You don't miss a trick, do you?" said Thumm with a grin. "No, we didn't have a record of his prints from the body itself, because the flesh of his fingers was so eaten away that the loops and whorls were gone. We had to come up here and dust the furniture, looking for prints. We found plenty, and they checked with the prints on the prussic acid bottle."

"On the furniture, eh?" murmured Lane. "Quite so. I asked a stupid question, Inspector."

"Undoubtedly Hatter filled a vial from this prussic, or hydrocyanic acid—as Schilling calls it—from Bottle # 57," said Bruno, "and then went out to poison and drown himself. The bottle hasn't been touched since."

Mr. Drury Lane seemed fascinated by the shelves. He looked and looked. He retreated and surveyed the fifteen sections for a long time. Twice his glance returned to the smudge mark on the edge of the shelf on which Bottle # 69—nitric acid—stood. He moved nearer and ran his eye along all the edges. His face brightened very soon: there was another oval smudge, similar to the first, on the edge of the second shelf, central section, under Bottle # 90, which was marked Sulphuric Acid.

"Two smudges," he said thoughtfully, but there was a gleam in the gray-green eyes that had not been there before. "Inspector, was this second smudge here when you first examined the laboratory?"

"That?" Thumm peered. "No. What the deuce of it?"

"I should think, Inspector," remarked Lane without rancor, "that anything here now which was not here two months ago would be of interest." He lifted the bottle from its place with care, observing that the ring of dust in

ACT I: SCENE 5

which it stood was sharp and clean in outline. His glance raised instantly, and the exultation left his face. Worry, a look of doubt, replaced it; he stood in silent indecision for a moment, then shrugged and turned away.

He roamed about the room for a while, disconsolate, his gloom deepening with every step. As if the shelving were a magnet drawing him, eventually, however, he found himself back before it. He looked down at the floor closet on which the five lengths of triple shelving rested. Then he opened the two low wide doors and peered inside. . . . Nothing of interest: cartons, tins, packets of chemicals, test-tubes, tube-racks, a small electric refrigerator, various scattered electrical equipment, innumerable miscellaneous chemical supplies. He banged the closet doors shut with a little mutter of impatience at his own uncertainty.

Finally he crossed over to look at the rolltop desk near the door. The top was drawn down, and he tried it. It began to roll up.

"You might have this looked into, Inspector," he suggested.

Thumm snorted. "Was looked into, Mr. Lane. We opened it and examined it at the time Hatter's body was found off Sandy Hook. Not a thing in there that might interest us in this case. It's full of personal and scientific papers and books, and some of Hatter's chemical notes—experiments, I guess."

Lane rolled the top up and looked about. The interior of the desk was in confusion.

"Just the way I left it," said the Inspector.

With a shrug Lane shut the desk and went to the nearby steel filing cabinet. "That's been looked into, too," said Thumm patiently; but Lane, pulling open the steel drawer which was unlocked, rummaged about until he found a

THE TRAGEDY OF Y 153

small card index, placed neatly behind folders containing bulky sheafs of experimental data.

"Oh, yes, that hypo," muttered the District Attorney.

Lane nodded. "The index records twelve hypodermic syringes, Mr. Bruno. I wonder . . . Here they are." He dropped the index and seized a large leather case lying at the rear of the drawer. Bruno and Thumm craned over his shoulders.

In the lid of the case, stamped in gold, were the letters *YH.*

Lane opened the case. Inside, neatly ranged in grooves on a field of purple velvet, lay eleven hypodermics of assorted sizes. One of the grooves was empty.

"Damn it," said Thumm, "Schilling's got that hypo."

"I scarcely think," said Lane, "that it's necessary to send for it, Inspector. You remember there was a number, 6, on the hypodermic we found in Mrs. Hatter's bed? Another example of York Hatter's methodical mind."

He touched the empty groove with his fingernail. All the grooves bore little strips of black linen, each strip containing a printed white number. The hypodermics were ranged in numerical order. The empty groove was marked with a 6.

"And the size of the groove," he went on, "if I recall correctly, corresponds with the size of the syringe. Yes, it was from this case that the hypodermic later filled with bichloride of mercury came. And here," he concluded, stooping and straightening up with a small leather case, "if I'm not mistaken, is a case full of needles. . . . Yes. One needle is missing, for the index lists eighteen, and there are only seventeen here. Well!" He sighed, returned both cases to the rear of the drawer, and rather listlessly rummaged through the folders. Notes, experiments, data

154   ACT I: SCENE 5

recorded for the future. . . . One folder in a separate compartment was empty.

He closed the cabinet drawer. Thumm, somewhere behind him, exclaimed aloud, and Bruno's immediate movement in the Inspector's direction caused Lane to wheel quickly. Thumm was kneeling in the dust, almost invisible behind one of the heavy work-tables.

"What is it?" cried Bruno, as he and Lane rounded the table. "Find something?"

"Well," grunted Thumm, standing up, "it looked like a mystery for a moment, but it isn't any more. Look here." Their eyes followed his pointing fingers, and they saw what had caused him to exclaim. Between the two work-tables, nearer the fireplace than the shelves, there were three neat round little spots imprinted in the dust of the floor. They were arranged in a triangle, equidistant from each other. Lane saw, by closer scrutiny, that the spots themselves were dusty, but merely a film compared with the thick dust surrounding them. "Simple. Thought at first it might be something important. But it's only the stool."

"Ah, yes," said Lane reflectively. "I'd forgotten. The stool."

The Inspector plucked the little tri-legged stool which stood before the middle sections from the floor, and set it down so that its legs exactly covered the dust spots. "There you are. As simple as that. Stool originally stood here, but was moved, that's all."

"Nothing there," said Bruno, disappointed.

"Not a thing."

But Lane seemed pleased in a dark fashion, and he eyed the seat of the stool with familiarity, as if he had examined it before when he had stood before the shelves. The stool

THE TRAGEDY OF Y   155

too was dusty, but its seat was scratched and smudged, the dust gone in spots and not in others.

"Ah—Inspector," murmured Lane. "When you investigated the laboratory two months ago, was the stool where it is now? I mean, has it been handled or moved since the time of the first investigation?"

"I'll be damned if I know."

"I think," said Lane mildly, turning away, "that's all."

"I'm glad you're satisfied," grunted the District Attorney. "I can't make head or tail of it."

Mr. Drury Lane did not reply. He shook hands absently with Bruno and Thumm, murmured something about getting back to The Hamlet, and left the laboratory. His face was tired and his shoulders sagged a little as he descended the stairs, retrieved his hat and stick from the foyer, and walked out of the house.

The Inspector muttered: "He looks as much up in the air about this thing as I am," sent a detective up to the roof to guard the entrance to the chimney, locked the door of the laboratory, bade farewell to the District Attorney (who with a hopeless air left the house to return to his clamoring office), and himself stamped downstairs.

Detective Pinkussohn was standing on the first floor juggling a dejected thumb as the Inspector went down.

Scene 6

THE HATTER HOUSE. MONDAY, JUNE 6. 2 A.M.

With the departure of Drury Lane and Bruno, Inspector Thumm lost much of his nastiness. Became, in fact, almost

156 ACT I: SCENE 6

humanly lonely. The general feeling of defeat which filled
him, the recollection of Lane's worried face and Bruno's
despairing one, were not conducive to a merry spirit—a
state of being rare in Thumm even at the jolliest of times.
He sighed repeatedly, lolled in a big easy-chair smoking
a cigar he found in a humidor in the library, received
negative reports periodically from his men, watched the
spiritless wanderings of the Hatters about the house; in a
word, disported himself like a very busy man who suddenly finds that he has nothing to do.

The house preserved its unusual quiet, a condition accentuated sporadically by the shrill shouts of Jackie and Billy,
who were playing in the nursery upstairs. Once John
Gormly, who had been restlessly pacing the garden walk
at the rear, came in search of the Inspector; the tall blond
young man was in a temper, and he wanted to talk to
Conrad Hatter, and the damned cop upstairs wouldn't let
him into Hatter's room, by George, and what was Inspector Thumm going to do about it? Inspector Thumm
drooped one eyelid cautiously, inspected the tip of his
cigar, and said viciously that he was going to do nothing
about it, by God; Hatter was confined to his room, and
he was going to stay there; and for all the Inspector cared,
Mr. Gormly could go to hell.

Mr. Gormly grew properly red and was about to utter
some hotly indiscreet rejoinder when Jill Hatter and Attorney Bigelow strolled into the library. Gormly bit his
tongue. Jill and Bigelow were speaking in confidential
tones; they were at the moment evidently on the most
delightfully intimate terms. Mr. Gormly's eyes flashed fire,
and without waiting for the Inspector's permission he
dashed out of the room and out of the house, striking
Bigelow's shoulder *en route* with his big hand—a fare-

The Tragedy of Y

well salute hardly calculated to please Bigelow, who stopped short in the middle of a tender sentence and said: "Ouf!" very earnestly.

Jill cried: "Why, the—the dismal brute!" in a surprised voice, and Inspector Thumm grunted to himself.

Five minutes later Bigelow, his ardor dampened, took his leave of Jill, who seemed suddenly peevish; reiterated to the Inspector his intention to read Mrs. Hatter's last will and testament to the assembled heirs on Tuesday after the funeral; and hastily left the house.

Jill sniffed and smoothed her frock. Then she caught the Inspector's eye, smiled devastatingly, and swished out of the library and upstairs.

The day passed drearily. Mrs. Arbuckle furnished a respite from the business of doing nothing by becoming involved in a wordy altercation with one of the detectives on duty. Jackie ran in whooping some time later, halted abruptly at sight of the Inspector, looked mildly abashed, and whooped out again. Once Barbara Hatter passed like a lovely wraith, accompanied by the tall grave figure of Edgar Perry, the tutor. They were deep in conversation.

Thumm sighed and sighed and wished he were dead. The telephone rang. He answered it. District Attorney Bruno . . . Anything? Nothing. He hung up and chewed on the remains of the cigar. After a while he jammed his hat on his head, got to his feet, and strode out of the library to the vestibule door. "Going, Chief?" asked a detective. Thumm considered this, then shook his head and returned to the library to wait—for what, he had not the slightest idea.

He went to the boule cellaret and took out a flat brown bottle. Something like pleasure overcame the gloom as he pulled out the cork and raised the bottle to his lips. It

158   ACT I: SCENE 6

gurgled long and satisfactorily. Finally he put the bottle
on the table beside him, closed the cellaret, and sat down
with a sigh.

At five o'clock in the afternoon the telephone bell trilled
again. It was Dr. Schilling, the Medical Examiner, this
time, and the Inspector's jaundiced eye brightened. Well,
well, Doc?

"Finished the job," croaked Dr. Schilling, in a voice
dripping with fatigue. "Original cause of death still stands.
Gott sei dank! The blow on the forehead from the mandolin was not sufficient to kill her, although it probably
stunned her. Shock gripped the heart and, *pfui!* out. Probably also a preliminary moment of intense excitement,
Herr Inspektor, contributed to the cardiac collapse. Good-
by, damn you."

Thumm flung the receiver back on its hook and sulked.

At seven a dull meal was served in the dining-room next
door. The Inspector, still grimly hanging on, dined with
the Hatters. Conrad was silent and flushed—he had been
drinking heavily all afternoon; he kept his eyes on his
plate, chewed vaguely, and rose to return to his temporary
cell long before the end of the meal, a policeman doggedly
following. Martha was subdued; the Inspector saw the
anguish in her tired eyes, the horror when she looked at
her husband, the love and determination when she turned
to the two children, who squirmed and made noise quite
as usual, and had to be reprimanded for their manners
every two minutes. Barbara kept up a low-voiced conversation with Edgar Perry, who seemed a new man: his eyes
were shining, and he talked contemporary poetry with the
poetess as if *vers moderne* were the chief passion of his
life. Jill contented herself with stabbing at her food and
being sullen. Mrs. Arbuckle presided over the serving,

THE TRAGEDY OF Y 159

like a sour-faced watchwoman; Virginia, the maid, banged dishes and stamped about.

Over all brooded Thumm, who watched them with impartial suspicion. He was the last to leave the table.

After dinner old Captain Trivett, thumping along on his wooden leg, came in; he greeted Thumm politely and at once went upstairs to Miss Smith's room, where the nurse was supervising Louisa Campion's lonely dinner. Captain Trivett remained there for half an hour. Then he came down and quietly went away.

The evening dragged on, and then the night. Conrad staggered into the library, glared at the Inspector, and devoted himself to a solitary orgy of drinking. Martha Hatter tucked the two children into bed in the nursery and shut herself up in her bedroom. Jill had disappeared into her room, since she was forbidden to leave the house. Barbara Hatter was writing upstairs. After a while Perry came into the library and asked if he was wanted further that night; he was tired, he said, and, if he might be excused, he should like to retire. Thumm waved gloomily, and the tutor went upstairs to his attic-floor bedroom.

Gradually, even the small sounds died away. Thumm sank deeper and deeper into a lethargy of despair; he did not even come to life when Conrad lurched out of the library and stumbled upstairs. At 11:30 one of the Inspector's men came in and sat down wearily.

"Well?" Thumm yawned cavernously.

"Nothing doing on the key. Boys've been trying to trace that duplicate you said might've been made. Not a sign in any locksmith's or hardware store. We've covered the City."

"Oh!" Thumm blinked. "That's out, anyway. I know how she got in. Go home, Frank, and get some sleep."

160 ACT I: SCENE 6

The detective went away. Promptly at midnight, the Inspector heaved his bulky body out of the armchair and went upstairs. Detective Pinkussohn was still juggling his thumb, as if he had not stopped all day. "Anything doing, Pink?"

"Nope."

"Go on home. Mosher just came in to relieve you."

Detective Pinkussohn obeyed with something less than reluctance. In fact, he scrambled downstairs and almost upset Detective Mosher, who was plodding up. Mosher saluted and took Pinkussohn's place on the bedroom floor.

The Inspector pounded up to the attic floor. Everything was quiet; all doors were closed; there was a light in the Arbuckles' rooms, which suddenly went out as the Inspector stood there. Then he climbed up the attic stairs, opened the trapdoor, and stepped out on the roof. A pinpoint of fire near the center of the black roof vanished instantly. Thumm heard a stealthy step and said, wearily: "It's all right, Johnny. Anything stirring?"

A man materialized by the Inspector's side. "Hell, no. This is a swell detail you put me on, Inspector. Not a soul's been up here all day."

"Stick it for another couple of minutes. I'll send Krause up to relieve you. Be back here in the morning."

The Inspector lifted the trapdoor and went downstairs again. He sent a man up. Then he trudged into the library, groaned his way into the armchair, ruefully eyed the empty brown bottle, put out the lamp on the table, hung his hat on his nose, and went to sleep.

* * *

The Inspector never quite knew when he was first aware of something wrong. He remembered shifting uneasily in

THE TRAGEDY OF Y

his sleep, easing a leg which had gone to sleep, and wriggling deeper into the sofa cushions of the armchair. At what time this occurred he had no idea. It might have been one o'clock in the morning.

But of one thing he was certain. Promptly at two, as if a clock had struck in his ear, he jerked awake, his hat falling from his nose to the floor, and sat up in an intense, strained, quivering attitude. Something had awakened him, but he did not know what it was. A sound, a fall, a cry? He sat like listening stone.

And then it came again, a faraway, hoarse, and excited cry in a man's voice: "FIRE!"

The Inspector sprang out of the chair as if it had been cushioned with pins, and dashed out into the corridor. There was a small nightlight burning, and in its feeble rays he could see curling wisps of smoke drifting down the stairs. Detective Mosher crouched at the head of the staircase, yelling at the top of his voice. The whole house was permeated with the acrid odor of smoky fire.

The Inspector did not pause to ask questions. He scrambled up the padded staircase and flung himself around the landing upstairs. Thick yellow smoke was pouring out of the cracks of the door leading to York Hatter's laboratory.

"Turn in the fire alarm, Mosher!" screamed Thumm, and fumbled frantically for the key. Mosher stumbled down the stairs, pushing three detectives, who had been on duty around the house, out of his way. The Inspector, cursing steadily, jabbed the key into the keyhole, twisted, tore open the door—and slammed it shut instantly as a burst of evil-smelling greasy smoke and tongues of flame licked out at him. His face was working; he stood uncertainly for a moment, looking from side to side like a trapped animal.

ACT I: SCENE 6

Heads were popping out of doorways; fright was on every face; his ears were besieged with coughed and trembling questions.

"Fire extinguisher! Where the hell is it?" roared Thumm.

Barbara Hatter hurried into the corridor. "Good heavens! . . . There isn't any, Inspector . . . Martha—the children!"

The hall became a smoky inferno filled with scurrying figures. The flames were beginning to show at the cracks of the laboratory door. Martha Hatter in a silk nightgown screamed and ran for the nursery, emerging a moment later with the two boys, Billy shrieking with fear and Jackie, for once cowed, clinging to his mother's hand. They all disappeared down the staircase.

"Everybody out! Out!" thundered Thumm. "Don't stop for anything! Those chemicals—explosion—" His voice was drowned in answering screams; Jill Hatter scrambled by, her face white and pinched; Conrad Hatter pushed her out of his way and stumbled down the stairs; Edgar Perry, in pajamas, dashed down from the attic floor and caught Barbara as she sank, overcome by the fumes, to the floor. Heaving her to his shoulder, he carried her downstairs. Everyone was gasping and coughing; eyes streamed bitter tears.

The detective Thumm had stationed on the roof came pounding down, herding the Arbuckles and Virginia before him. Faintly, as in a dream, the Inspector, coughing, choking, crying, flinging buckets of water at the closed door, heard the wail of sirens. . . .

It was hot close work. Screaming brakes heralded the arrival of the engines; firemen began to attach hose-lines and to haul them through the alley alongside the house to the garden in the rear. Flames were streaking out of the iron-barred windows; ladders were telescoped upward;

THE TRAGEDY OF Y   163

axes smashed in what glass had not melted, and streams of water were directed through the bars into the room. . . .

Thumm, disheveled, blackened, gory-eyed, stood on the sidewalk outside the house as firemen lurched by dragging hose-lines upstairs, and took count of the shivering, flimsily clad people beside him. They were all there. No . . . they weren't!

The Inspector's face became a gargoyle of pain and horror. He ran up the stairs, into the house, dashed upward, made for the bedroom floor, stumbled all the way over wet hose. Upstairs he went directly to Miss Smith's room, Detective Mosher at his heels.

He kicked open the door and burst into the nurse's room. Miss Smith in a billowy nightgown, like a white hilly landscape, lay unconscious on the floor; and Louisa Campion, with the look of a wild animal at bay, bewildered, shuddering, crouched over her, nostrils oscillating with the acrid unpleasantness of the fumes.

With difficulty Thumm and Mosher managed to get the two women out of the house. . . .

Just, it seemed, in time. For as they stumbled down the stone steps outside, from behind, from above, came a dull blare—a flash like the detonation of a cannon struck out at the rear, out of the laboratory windows. There was the appalling thunder of an explosion, an instant of stunned silence, and then the hoarse screams of firemen caught in the blast. . . .

The inevitable had happened. Some chemical in the laboratory, licked by fire, had exploded.

The huddled group shivering on the sidewalk stared stupidly at the house.

An ambulance clanged. A stretcher went in and out of the house. A fireman had been injured.

*　*　*

164   Act I: Scene 6

Two hours later the fire was out. The false dawn was just breaking as the last engine snorted away. The Hatters and other members of the household, who had been taken into Captain Trivett's brick next door, climbed wearily back into the singed old mansion. The Captain himself, in dressing gown and pajamas, his pegleg striking hollowly against the pavement, assisted a revived Miss Smith in taking care of Louisa Campion, who was in her helpless way dumbly terrified, oddly hysterical. Dr. Merriam, roused by telephone, had appeared and was busy supplying sedatives.

The laboratory upstairs was a shambles. The door had been blown out by the blast; the iron bars of the windows had been loosened in their sockets. Most of the bottles on the shelves had been smashed and broken, and strewed the wet floor. The bed, dresser, and desk had been badly burned, and most of the glass of retorts, test-tubes, and electrical equipment had fused. The rest of the floor had suffered, strangely enough, little damage.

Thumm, red-eyed, his face an iron gray mask, assembled the occupants of the house downstairs in the library and sitting-room. Detectives everywhere were on guard. There was no jesting now, no tolerance of temperament or rebellion. For the most part they sat subdued, the women even quieter than the men, and watched each other dumbly.

The Inspector went to the telephone. He called Police Headquarters. He spoke to District Attorney Bruno. He engaged in a grim conversation with Police Commissioner Burbage. Then he put in a long-distance call for The Hamlet, Lanecliff, N. Y.

There was some trouble with the connection. Thumm waited with, for him, remarkable patience. When finally

The Tragedy of Y

he heard the peevish quavering of old Quacey, Drury Lane's humpbacked familiar, he related in crisp detail the events of the night. Lane, prevented by his deafness from personally conversing over the telephone, stood by Quacey's side and heard the story, bit by bit, from Quacey's lips as the Inspector transmitted it over the wire.

"Mr. Drury says," squeaked the ancient hunchback when Thumm had finished, "do you know how the fire started."

"No. Tell him the chimney exit on the roof was under observation every second, the windows were locked on the inside and not tampered with, and the door to the laboratory was under my man Mosher's eye all night."

The Inspector heard Quacey's shrill repetition of the message, and the deep faraway tones of Lane's voice. "He says are you sure, Inspector?"

"My God, of course I'm sure! That's what puzzles me so much. How the hell did the firebug get in to start the fire?"

There was a silence after Quacey repeated this; and the Inspector, waiting, strained his ears. Then Quacey said: "Mr. Drury wants to know if anyone tried to get into the laboratory after the fire and the explosion."

"No," snarled Thumm. "I was on the watch for that."

"Then he says to station somebody *in* the room right away," shrilled Quacey, "besides the fireman who'll be there. Mr. Drury will be down in the morning. He's sure now that he knows how it was done, he says . . ."

"Oh, he is, is he?" said the Inspector fretfully. "Then he's a better man than I am.—Say! Ask him if he expected this fire!"

An interlude. And Quacey reported: "No, he says. No, he didn't. It's absolutely a surprise to him. He can't understand it."

ACT I: SCENE 6

"Thank goodness there's something stumps him," growled Thumm. "All right—tell him to be early."

And as he was about to hang up the receiver, he heard, very clearly, Lane's voice muttering—muttering!—to Quacey: "It must be. Everything points to it. . . . And yet, Quacey, it's impossible!"

ACT II

*"I have shot mine arrow o'er the house
And hurt my brother."*

Scene 1

THE LABORATORY. MONDAY, JUNE 6. 9:20 A.M.

Mr. Drury Lane stood in the center of the wrecked laboratory, his sharp eyes roving. Inspector Thumm had managed to wash the soot and grime from his face and to brush his wrinkled suit; but his eyes were sleepy and bloodshot, and he was in a bearish mood. Detective Mosher had been relieved; the shambling Pinkussohn sat on a salvaged chair amiably conversing with a fireman.

The shelves still clung to the wall, but they were soggy and smoke-blackened. Except for a scattering of miraculously unbroken bottles on the lower shelves, the sections were denuded; and their smashed freight had littered the filthy floor in thousands of tiny glass pieces. Their contents had been carefully disposed of.

"Chemical Squad cleaned up the dangerous chemicals," said Thumm. "The first firemen on the scene were bawled out plenty by the Deputy Chief. Seems like some chemicals feed on water, or something, when they're burning, and there might have been a bad time here—worse than actually happened. As it is, it was damned lucky the fire was

168 ACT II: SCENE I

checked when it was. Even though Hatter had specially reinforced walls built in the laboratory, the whole house might have gone up."

"Well, there it is," growled the Inspector. "We've been taken over like a bunch of amateurs. Quacey said over the 'phone that you know how the firebug got in. How? I'll admit it's a mystery to me."

"No," said Mr. Drury Lane. "Not half so subtle, Inspector. I believe the answer is ludicrously simple. Look here—could the incendiary have entered the laboratory through the one door here?"

"Of course not. Mosher—one of my most reliable men—swears that no one even came near it all last night."

"I believe him. The door, then, is clearly eliminated as a means of ingress. Now, the windows. They are iron-barred; and the bars, as you yourself pointed out yesterday when we examined the room, are quite genuine. It is logically conceivable that, despite the bars, the incendiary by creeping along the ledge outside and opening a window, could have thrown a piece of burning waste into the room and so started the fire. . . ."

"I told you that's impossible," said the Inspector tartly. "The windows were locked on the inside. No signs of jimmying, and the glass of both was unshattered when the firemen got here, before the explosion. So the windows are out."

"Precisely. I was merely presenting every possible theory. Then the windows as an avenue of ingress are eliminated. What is left?"

"The chimney," said Thumm, "but that's out. One of my men was parked up on the roof all day yesterday, so that no one could have sneaked into the chimney and stayed

THE TRAGEDY OF Y 169

there until the night-time. And then he was relieved about midnight by another of my men, who says not a soul came up to the roof. So there you are."

"And there I am," chuckled Lane. "You think you have me. Three known modes of entry, all three guarded. And yet the incendiary managed not only to get in, Inspector, but to get out as well. . . . Now let me ask you a question. Have you had these walls examined?"

"Ah," said Thumm instantly. "So that's what you had in mind! Sliding panel stuff." He grinned, and then scowled. "Nothing doing, Mr. Lane. The walls and floors and ceiling are as solid as Gibraltar. I've seen to *that*."

"Mmm," replied Lane with a twinkle in the gray-green of his eyes. "That's excellent, Inspector, excellent! It banishes the last doubt from my mind."

Thumm stared. "Why, you're talking through your hat! That makes it just about impossible!"

"No," smiled Lane. "Not at all. Since neither the door nor the windows by any stretch of the imagination could have afforded entrance to the incendiary, and since walls, floor, and ceiling are solid—only one possibility remains, and therefore that possibility becomes certainty."

Thumm's eyebrows screwed down over his eyelids. "You mean the chimney? But I can't——"

"Not the chimney, Inspector." Lane became grave. "You forget that there are two major parts to such an apparatus: the chimney stack and the fireplace itself. You see what I mean?"

"No, I don't. Sure the fireplace opens out into this room. But how are you going to get into the fireplace unless you shinny down the stack?"

"Precisely what I asked myself." Lane strolled over to

ACT II: SCENE 1

the fireplace. "And, unless your men are lying, unless there *is* a sliding panel of some sort in this room, then without even examining this fireplace I can tell you its secret."

"Secret?"

"Do you recall what room adjoins this on the fireplace wall?"

"Why, the Campion woman's room, where the murder was committed."

"Exactly. And do you recall what lies on the other side of this fireplace in Miss Campion's room?"

The Inspector's jaw dropped. He stared at Lane for an instant and then darted forward. "The *other* fireplace!" he cried. "By God, another opening exactly behind this one!"

He bent low and scuttled beneath the mantel to the rear wall of the fireplace. He straightened up inside, his head and shoulders disappearing from view. Lane heard his heavy breathing, the sounds of a scraping hand, and then a muffled exclamation. "Cripes, yes!" shouted Thumm. "Both fireplaces use the same stack! This brick wall here doesn't go all the way up—it ends about six feet from the floor!"

Mr. Drury Lane sighed. It had not been necessary even to soil his clothes.

*   *   *

The Inspector was keen on the scent now, his whole demeanor transformed. He clapped Lane on the back, grinned all over his ugly face, roared orders to his men, kicked Pinkussohn out of the chair, and gave a cigar to the fireman.

"Sure!" he bellowed, his hands dirty and his eyes shining, "that's the answer—a cinch!"

The secret of the fireplace was simplicity itself. The fireplace in the laboratory and the fireplace in Louisa Cam-

THE TRAGEDY OF Y

pion's room backed each other up—fireplace to fireplace on opposite sides of the same wall. Not only did the same chimney serve both, but there was only one dividing wall between—a thick structure of hardened firebrick about six feet high, its top therefore invisible from the interior of either room, since the mantels of both fireplaces were only four feet from the floor. Above the six-foot dividing wall the chimney orifices merged into one, forming a large vent through which the smoke of both fireplaces ascended to the roof.

"Clear, clear enough," said the Inspector gleefully. "This means anybody could have got into the lab at any time—either from the inside of the house by climbing over the dividing wall from the death-room, or from the outside by coming down from the roof, using those hand- and foot-holds on the inside of the chimney. Last night it must have been through Louisa's room. No wonder Mosher didn't see anyone go into the lab from the hall, or my man from the roof!"

"True," said Lane. "And your visitor escaped by the same route, of course. Have you considered, Inspector, how our mysterious incendiary got into Miss Campion's room, however, in the first place, in order to be able to go through the fireplace into the laboratory? Mosher had that door under observation all night as well, you know."

Thumm's face fell. "Didn't think that of that. There must be— Sure! The ledge outside, or the fire-escapes!"

They went to the shattered windows and looked out. A two-foot ledge ran outside the windows of the entire bedroom floor at the rear; it would obviously provide passage for a daring creeper from or to any room on the garden side of the house. Two fire-escapes, long and narrow, had landings outside the bedroom floor. One provided egress

172 ACT II: SCENE 1

from the laboratory and the nursery, and the other from the death-room and Miss Smith's room. Both fire-escapes ran past windows from the attic floor down to the ground of the garden below.

Lane glanced at Thumm, and they shook their heads together.

The two men left the laboratory and went into the death-room. They tried the windows; they were unlocked and slid up easily.

They returned to the laboratory and Pinkussohn produced a chair from somewhere. Lane sat down, crossed his legs, and sighed. "The story is plain, Inspector, as I see you've also surmised. Virtually everyone could have entered the laboratory last night providing he knew the secret of the double fireplace."

Thumm nodded without enthusiasm. "Anybody, inside or out."

"So it would appear. Have you questioned the movements of your little cast, Inspector?"

"Uh-huh. But what good does it do? You don't think for a moment the firebug would give himself away, do you?" The Inspector chewed savagely on a filched cigar. "Anybody on the attic floor could have done it, no matter what the pack of 'em testified. And as far as the first floor here is concerned, with the exception of Jill and Barbara Hatter everybody had access to the ledge and fire-escapes. And though Conrad and his wife are at the front of the floor, either one of them had access to the fire-escapes and ledge at the rear by going through the nursery past the sleeping kids. And they wouldn't have to go out into the corridor to be spied on by Mosher, because they can get from their bedroom into the nursery through that connecting bathroom between the two rooms. So there you are."

The Tragedy of Y 173

"What have they to say for themselves?"

"Well, they've got no alibis for each other. Conrad says he went upstairs about eleven-thirty. That's true enough, because I myself saw him leave the library around that time and Mosher says he saw him, too, going into his bedroom. Says he went to sleep. Martha Hatter was in her room all evening, but she says she dropped off to sleep and didn't hear her husband come in."

"And the Misses Hatter?"

"They're clear—couldn't have done it, anyway."

"Indeed?" murmured Lane. "But what do they say?"

"Jill wandered out into the garden, and returned to her own room about one o'clock; Mosher confirms this. Barbara retired early, about eleven. Neither woman was seen leaving her room. . . . Mosher saw no suspicious activity of any kind; no one opened a door or left a bedroom as far as Mosher remembers—and he's got a good memory. Trained him myself."

"Of course," remarked Lane slyly, "we may be completely wrong in our analysis. The fire may have started through spontaneous combustion, you know."

"I wish I could believe that," replied Thumm glumly. "But the experts of the Fire Department looked over the lab after the fire and came to the conclusion that the fire'd been started by human agency. Yes, sir. Somebody'd struck matches and ignited something between the bed and the work-table nearer the windows. Found the matches—ordinary house matches, they are, like the ones in the kitchen downstairs."

"And the explosion?"

"That wasn't an accident, either," said the Inspector grimly. "The chem guys found the remains of a shattered bottle on one of the work-tables—a bottle of stuff they

174   ACT II: SCENE 1

called carbon bisulphide. It's highly explosive, they say, when it's exposed to heat. Of course, it might have been there all the time—left by York Hatter, maybe, before he disappeared—but I don't remember a bottle on the tables, do you?"

"No. Did it come from one of the shelves?"

"Uh-huh—scrap of glass with part of the regular label was found."

"Obviously, then, your conjecture cannot be true. York Hatter could not have left the bottle of carbon bisulphide on the table, because it was one of the regulation bottles, as you say, and I distinctly recall that the full complement of containers was on the shelves; there was not an empty space anywhere. No, someone deliberately took the bottle from a section of the shelving and placed it on the table, knowing that eventually it would explode."

"Well," said Thumm, "that's something. At least whoever we're battling's come out in the open. Let's go downstairs, Mr. Lane. . . . I've got an idea."

*   *   *

They descended to the ground floor and the Inspector sent for Mrs. Arbuckle. The housekeeper, it was to be observed the instant she appeared in the library, had quite surrendered her bellicosity. The fire seemed to have unnerved her and burned out much of the starch in her Amazonian make-up.

"You want me, Inspector Thumm?" she asked in an uncertain voice.

"Yes. Who takes care of the laundry in the house?"

"Laundry? I—I do. I sort it out each week into separate bundles and send it to a hand-laundry on Eighth Street."

"Good! Now listen carefully. Do you remember in the

THE TRAGEDY OF Y

past few months anybody's linen being in a specially dirty condition? You know—grimy, full of soot or coal dust? Also scraped, maybe, scratched or torn?"

Lane said: "Permit me to congratulate you, Inspector. An inspired thought!"

"Thanks," said Thumm dryly. "I get 'em sometimes—mostly when you're not around. You take something out of me. . . . Well, Mrs. Arbuckle?"

She said in a frightened way: "No, sir—no."

"Funny," muttered Thumm.

"Perhaps not," remarked Lane. "How long is it since there have been fires in the fireplaces upstairs, Mrs. Arbuckle?"

"I—I don't know. I never heard of any being made."

Thumm beckoned a detective: "Get that nurse in here."

Miss Smith, it appeared, was in the garden tenderly caring for her shaken charge. She came in, smiling nervously. The fireplaces in the laboratory and Louisa's room?

"Mrs. Hatter never used hers," said Miss Smith, "at least since I've been here. Mr. Hatter didn't use his, either, as far as I know. It's been years, I suppose. . . . In the wintertime a cover is put over the chimney opening on the roof to keep out the draft, and it's taken off in the summer."

"Lucky break for *her,*" grunted the Inspector with dark subtlety. "Didn't get a spot of coal dust on her clothes—if there was dust, she brushed it off or it wasn't enough to attract attention. . . . What are you looking at, Miss Smith? That's all!"

Miss Smith gasped and beat a hasty retreat, wabbling her jelly breasts like a fat old cow.

"You're constantly referring to our quarry, Inspector," said Lane, "as 'she.' Doesn't it strike you as incongruous that a woman should come down a chimney or climb over

176 ACT II: SCENE 1

a six-foot brick wall—as I think I suggested before?"

"Listen, Mr. Lane," replied Thumm in desperation. "I don't know what strikes me and what doesn't. I thought maybe we'd get something on somebody by tracing dirty clothes. Now that's out. So what?"

"But you haven't answered my objection, Inspector," smiled Lane.

"Well, then, it was an accomplice! A male accomplice. Hell, I don't know," said Thumm disconsolately. "But that isn't what's bothering me right this minute." Cunning crept into his tired eyes. "*Why the fire at all?* Eh, Mr. Lane? Have you thought of that?"

"My dear Inspector," said Mr. Drury Lane abruptly, "if we knew that, we should probably know everything. That problem agitated me from the moment you telephoned The Hamlet."

"What do you think?"

"I think this." Lane rose and began to stride up and down the library. "Was the fire planned in order to *destroy* something in the laboratory?" He shrugged. "But the laboratory had already been looked over by the police, and the incendiary must have known this. Was it something that we missed in our examination yesterday? Was it something too big for the incendiary to have carried away with him, and that had to be destroyed in consequence?" He shrugged again. "I confess that I'm entirely at sea on the point. Somehow, it doesn't ring true—any one of the possibilities."

"Sounds flukey, all right," confessed the Inspector. "Might have been a blind, Mr. Lane, hey?"

"But, my dear fellow," cried Lane, "why? Why a blind? If it was a blind, it was to divert attention from something else that was scheduled to happen—a *divertissement*, a *ruse*

THE TRAGEDY OF Y   177

de guerre, a feint attack. But nothing did happen, so far as we know!" He shook his head. "Logic reminds me, strictly speaking, that it's possible the fire-setter was prevented at the last moment, after igniting the laboratory, from carrying out his hypothetical design. Perhaps the fire took hold too quickly. Perhaps last-minute funk overcame him. . . . I don't know, Inspector, I really don't."

Thumm sucked at his protruding lip for a long time, deep in thought, as Lane continued the incessant patrol. "I have it!" said the Inspector, jumping to his feet. "The fire and explosion were planned *to cover up the theft of more poison!*"

"Don't excite yourself, Inspector," said Lane wearily. "I thought of that and discarded it some time ago. How could the poisoner expect the police to have inventoried every dram of chemical in the laboratory? A vial of anything might have been stolen last night and no one would have been the wiser. Certainly a fire and explosion would have been unnecessary. Besides, the poisoner has frequented the laboratory in the past, to judge from the myriad footprints in the dust. If he had foresight—and he must have, for the crimes so far have been uncanny in some respects— he would have laid up a supply of poison at a time when he had unhindered access to the laboratory, obviating the necessity of making dangerous and superfluous trips to it at a time when it was under strict observation. . . . No, Inspector, it's not that. It's something utterly different, so utterly different that it transcends the bounds of common sense." He paused. "Almost," he continued slowly, "almost as if there were no reason. . . ."

"Nuts," agreed Thumm with a scowl. "That's what comes of investigating a crime in which all the suspects are daffy. Reason! Motive! Logic!" He threw up his hands.

178 ACT II: SCENE 1

"Bah!" he said. "I almost wish the Commissioner would take me off this assignment."

They sauntered into the hall, and Lane accepted his hat and stick from George Arbuckle, the houseman, who hovered by with a pitiful eagerness to please strikingly similar to his wife's new self-abasement.

"There is one thing, Inspector, before I go," remarked Lane as they paused in the vestibule, "that I should like to warn you against. That is the possibility of another poisoning attempt."

Thumm nodded. "I've thought of that."

"Good. After all, we're dealing with a poisoner who twice has been unsuccessful. We must expect—and thwart —a third attempt."

"I'll get somebody from Doc Schilling's office down here to test all the food and drink before it's served," said Thumm. "There's one fellow down there Schilling uses on jobs like this—smart young doctor by the name of Dubin. Nothing'll get by *him*. I'll station him in the kitchen, where he'll be at the source. Well"—he stuck out his hand—"good-by, Mr. Lane."

Lane took his hand. "Good-by, Inspector."

He half turned away, and then turned back. They looked at each other with questions in their eyes. Finally Lane said, with painful distinctness: "By the way, Inspector, I think I owe it to you and to Mr. Bruno to present my views of certain aspects . . ."

"Yes?" said the Inspector eagerly, his face brightening.

Lane waved his stick in a negative. "After the will-reading tomorrow, I think, will be the best time. Good-by. Luck!"

Turning sharply on his heel, he left the house.

Scene 2

The Garden. Monday, June 6. 4 p.m.

Had Inspector Thumm been a psychologist, or even had his mind been less occupied, the Mad Hatters might have afforded him a fascinating study that day. Since they were forbidden to leave the house, they wandered about like lost souls, restlessly picking up things and putting them down, flashing looks of hatred at each other, avoiding each other whenever possible. Jill and Conrad were at each other's throats all day, squabbling over trifles, clashing at the least provocation, saying biting things in deadly cold voices that had not even the merit of quick temper to excuse them. Martha kept her children about her skirts, scolding and slapping them almost stolidly, awakening in every nerve only when Conrad Hatter lurched by; and then sending such fierce glances toward his pale pinched face that even her children took notice and asked questions.

The Inspector grew more irritable the longer he thought over the remarkable indecisiveness of all his clues. The feeling that Drury Lane had something tangible in mind, and the wonder as to its possible nature, irked him. And yet Lane had seemed oddly disturbed, uncertain, in a peculiar way apprehensive. The Inspector could not understand it. Twice during the afternoon he started for the telephone to call The Hamlet, and each time he stopped with his hand on the instrument, aware at the last moment that he had nothing to ask, and certainly nothing to say.

The odd chimney passageway gradually took hold of his imagination, and he forgot Lane. He went upstairs to the laboratory and himself scaled the dividing firebrick wall,

180   ACT II: SCENE 2

to prove to his own satisfaction that it was possible for a grown man to pass from the one room to the other by means of the fireplaces without extraordinary effort. . . . Yes, even his own mammoth shoulders negotiated the chimney space easily.

He crawled back into the laboratory and sent Pinkussohn to gather the clan.

They straggled in one by one, scarcely exhibiting interest in this fresh inquisition. The rapidity of events and the shock of the fire had dulled their capacities for a surprise. When they were all assembled the Inspector launched into a series of general questions, the point of which no one apparently foresaw. They replied mechanically and, as far as Thumm could tell, truthfully. When he came to the matter of the chimney passageway, subtly broaching it without revealing its existence, he was convinced that either the culprit was a remarkable actor or that they were all telling the truth. He had hoped to trap someone in a web of lies; he had even anticipated someone else inadvertently revealing the lie from some untapped source of recollection. But when the Inspector had finished, he knew little more than he had known before.

The tribe trooped out when he dismissed them; and Thumm sank puffing into the library armchair to think over his sins.

"Inspector."

He looked up to find the tall tutor, Perry, before him. "Well, what d'ya want, Mister?" growled Thumm.

Perry said quickly: "Permission to take the day off. I— these events have made me slightly—well, Inspector, yesterday was the day I usually have to myself, and since I wasn't permitted to leave the house and feel the need of fresh air . . ."

Thumm let the little burst of talk die away. Perry shifted

THE TRAGEDY OF Y   181

uneasily, but a spark appeared far within his deep eyes and the tart retort on Thumm's lips was never uttered. Instead he said in a kindlier tone: "I'm sorry, Perry, but that's impossible. Until we've touched bottom here somewhere, everyone will have to stay close to the house."

The spark died, Perry's shoulders drooped, and without a word he went wearily out of the library, through the corridor to the rear, and out into the garden. The sky threatened, and he hesitated. Then he caught sight of Barbara Hatter sitting under a large garden umbrella, reading quietly, and with springy steps he advanced across the grass . . .

*   *   *

It was remarkable how this case dawdled along, the Inspector thought as the afternoon dragged on. Something electric occurred, a touch of drama, an explosive event— and then nothing, absolutely nothing; a complete absence of positive action. There was something unnatural about the whole thing; it induced a feeling of helplessness and the wincing impression of a criminal inevitability, as if all this had been planned far in advance and was proceeding inexorably toward an invertible climax. But—what? What was the end?

During the afternoon Captain Trivett called, stumping along in his customary quiet manner, and mounted the stairs for one of his quaint visits to the deaf-dumb-and-blind woman, who was upstairs in Miss Smith's room resting in the complete vacuity of her isolation. A man came in to announce that the lawyer, Bigelow, was in the house; calling, presumably, on Jill Hatter. Gormly did not appear.

*   *   *

At four o'clock, while Thumm sat biting his nails in the library, one of his most trusted men entered quickly.

182 ACT II: SCENE 2

There was something portentous in the man's manner, and the Inspector came alive on the instant.

They whispered briefly together, and Thumm's eyes went brighter at each word. Finally he sprang to his feet, commanded the detective to station himself at the foot of the staircase, and lumbered up the two flights to the attic floor.

He knew his way about. The two doors at the rear, overlooking the garden, led to the bedrooms of the maid Virginia and of Edgar Perry. The room at the northeast corner was empty, and connected with it by a bathroom there was a storeroom at the southeast corner. The main room at the south was a large storeroom with adjoining bath—a storeroom now, but in the days of the Hatter house's Victorian glory, a guest bedroom. The entire western side of the attic floor was occupied by the Arbuckles.

The Inspector did not hesitate. He crossed the hall and tried the door of Edgar Perry's bedroom. It was unlocked. Quickly the Inspector went in, closing the door behind him. He ran to one of the windows overlooking the garden. Perry was seated beneath the umbrella, engaged in earnest conversation with Barbara.

The Inspector scowled with satisfaction and went to work.

It was a bare neat chamber—peculiarly like its tenant. A high bed, a dresser, a rug, a chair, and a large full bookcase. Everything seemed precisely in its place.

Very carefully and methodically Inspector Thumm searched the room. He seemed most interested in the contents of Perry's dresser. But this proved barren, and he tackled a small wardrobe closet, without shame going through the pockets of each article of clothing inside. . . . He raised the rug. He riffled the pages of books. He explored the empty spaces behind the tiers of books. He raised the mattress of the bed.

The Tragedy of Y 183

The net result of this expert and thorough investigation was nothing.

Thoughtfully he restored each touched article to its original place and went to the window. Perry was as deeply engrossed in his conversation with Barbara as before. Jill Hatter was now seated under a tree, idly ogling Chester Bigelow.

The Inspector went downstairs.

He made his way through the rear and descended by the short flight of wooden steps into the garden. There was a roll of thunder, and rain began to patter on the top of the umbrella. Neither Barbara nor Perry seemed aware of it. Bigelow and Jill, however, whose soft conversation had abruptly terminated with the appearance of Thumm, seemed glad of the elemental interruption and took the rain as an excuse to rise hastily and go back into the house. Bigelow nodded nervously as he passed the Inspector; and Jill darted a furious glance at him.

Thumm placed his hands together behind his back, grinned benevolently at the dark gray sky, and ambled across the grass toward the umbrella.

Barbara was saying, in her deep voice: "But my dear Mr. Perry, after all . . ."

"I insist that metaphysics has no place in poetry," Perry said tensely. His thin hand slapped the black cover of a thin book on the garden table between them; its title, Thumm saw, was *Feeble Concert,* and it bore the author's name of *Barbara Hatter*. "Oh, I grant you that you do it very well—there's the gloss of poetic delicacy and a strong imaginative quality——"

She laughed. "Gloss? Oh, thanks! At least that's honest criticism. It's refreshing to talk to someone who doesn't lap your feet."

"Well!" He blushed like a schoolboy and for the mo-

184   ACT II: SCENE 2

ment seemed at a loss for words. Neither of them noticed
Inspector Thumm pensively studying them in the rain.
"Now you take that third stanza in your poem, *'Pitch-
blende'*; the one that begins:

> *Mural mountains hung in——"*

"Ah," said Inspector Thumm, "excuse me."

They turned, startled, and the intensity drained out of
Perry's face. He rose awkwardly, his hand still on Barbara's book.

Barbara smiled and said: "Why, Inspector, it's raining!
Do join us under the umbrella."

"I think," said Perry abruptly, "I'll go in."

"No hurry, Mr. Perry," grinned the Inspector, sitting
down with a gentleman's lusty sigh. "As a matter of fact,
I was thinking I might like to talk to you."

"Oh!" said Barbara. "Then I think *I'll* go in."

"No, no," said the Inspector generously. "Not at all. This
is just a little nothing. Nothing at all. Matter of form. Sit
down, Perry, sit down. Dreary day, ain't it?"

The spirit of poesy, which had lighted up the man's
face a moment before, slunk off with drooping wings.
Perry tautened. He looked suddenly old, and Barbara
steadfastly kept her eyes averted from his face. The dark
and wet crept in under the umbrella where it had not been
before.

"Now, this business of your former employer," continued
the Inspector in the same genial voice.

Perry stiffened. "Yes?" he said in a harsh tone.

"How well did you know this James Liggett, who signed
your letter of recommendation?"

A slow flush. "How well . . . ?" faltered the tutor. "Why
—what you might expect—under the circumstances."

"I see." Thumm smiled. "Of course. That was a dumb

THE TRAGEDY OF Y 185

question. How long did you work for him, teaching his children?"

Perry was silent after a single convulsive start. He sat his chair rigidly, like an inexperienced rider. Then he said in a colorless voice: "I see you've found out."

"Yes, sir, we certainly have," replied Thumm, still smiling. "You see, Perry, there's never any use trying to put something over on the police. It was child's play to find out that there's no James Liggett and never was a James Liggett at the Park Avenue address in your references. Honestly, I feel hurt that you should think I'd be fooled by a dodge like that. . . ."

"Oh, for God's sake, stop!" cried Perry. "What do you want to do—arrest me? Then do so, and don't torture me this way!"

The grin faded from the Inspector's lips and he sat up very solidly. "Spill it, Perry. I want the truth."

Barbara Hatter did not even blink; she was staring at the cover of her book.

"Very well," said the tutor wearily. "It was foolish of me, I know. And my bad fortune to become involved in a murder investigation while working under false pretenses. Yes, I manufactured the references, Inspector."

"We," said Barbara Hatter sweetly.

Perry jumped as if he could not believe his ears. The Inspector's gaze narrowed. "What do you mean by that, Miss Hatter? This is a serious offense under the circumstances."

"I mean," replied Barbara in her deep clear voice, "precisely what I say. I knew Mr. Perry before he came here. He needed a job badly and—and would not accept financial assistance. I persuaded him, knowing my brother Conrad, to write the references, since he had none of his own. It's really my fault."

186 ACT II: SCENE 2

"Hmm," said the Inspector, wagging his head like the Rabbit. "I see, I see. Very nice, Miss Hatter. And very fortunate for you, Mr. Perry, to have such a loyal friend." Perry was as pale as Barbara's gown; he plucked at the lapel of his coat dazedly. "So you had no legitimate references of your own?"

The tutor cleared his dry throat. "I—well, I had no 'big' name to present. I did need the position, Inspector. . . . The—the salary was so generous, and then the opportunity to be near Miss"—he choked—"Miss Hatter, whose poetry has always been an inspiration to me. . . . I—the ruse worked, that's all."

Thumm glanced from Perry to Barbara and back again; Barbara was very still and Perry's confusion was embarrassing. "Okay," said Thumm. "Now, if you didn't have any high-toned references—that's understandable, and I'm a reasonable man, Perry—what references *did* you have? Who can vouch for you?"

Barbara rose suddenly. "Isn't my recommendation sufficient, Inspector Thumm?" There was ice in her voice and in her green eyes.

"Sure, sure, Miss Hatter. But I've got my job to do. Well?"

Perry fumbled with the book. "To tell the truth," he said slowly, "I never did tutor before, so I haven't any professional references to give you."

"Ah," said the Inspector. "Very interesting. How about personal references—aside from Miss Hatter, I mean?"

"I—nobody," stammered Perry. "I haven't any friends."

"By God," grinned Thumm, "you're a queer one, Perry. Imagine living out your life and not having two people who can vouch for you! Reminds me of the story of the feller who applied to the Naturalization Bureau for his

The Tragedy of Y 187

first citizenship papers after five years' residence in the U.S. When he was told he needed two American citizens as character witnesses he told the judge he didn't know two American citizens that well. Haw, haw! Judge refused his application—said if he could live in this country for five years . . ." Thumm shook his head sadly. "Well, I won't bore you. What college did you go to, Mr. Perry? Who're your family? Where do you come from? How long have you been in New York?"

"I believe," said Barbara Hatter coldly, "that you're reducing this to an absurdity, Inspector Thumm. Mr. Perry has committed no crime. Or has he? Then why don't you accuse him of it? Mr. Perry, you—you refuse to answer. I forbid you to. I think this has gone far enough!"

She swept out from under the umbrella, placed her hand on the tutor's arm and, oblivious of the rain, led him back across the lawn to the house. He moved like a man in a dream; and she held her head high. Neither looked back.

The Inspector sat there in the rain for a long time, smoking. His eyes were fixed on the door through which the poetess and Perry had disappeared. There was a malicious little grin in them.

He got to his feet, tramped across the lawn, went into the house, and bellowed imperiously for a detective.

Scene 3

The Library. Tuesday, June 7. 1 p.m.

On Tuesday, the seventh of June, the New York newspapers had a field day. There were two reportorial events

188   ACT II: SCENE 3

—the first the funeral of the murdered woman, Emily Hatter; the second the reading of the will.

Mrs. Hatter's body was released from the Morgue, sent to a funeral parlor, embalmed, and hurried to its last resting-place. This all occurred between Monday night and Tuesday morning; and by 10:30 Tuesday morning the funeral coaches were on their way to a Long Island cemetery. The Hatters, as might have been expected, seemed not too much impressed by the solemnity of the proceedings; their slightly unbalanced views on life and death precluded tears and the customary outward signs of mourning. With the exception of Barbara they were suspicious of each other, and wrangled all the way to Long Island. To the children, who refused to remain at home, it seemed a picnic; they had to be subdued by their mother constantly *en route,* and by the time the party reached the cemetery Martha Hatter was hot, tired, and irritable.

Mr. Drury Lane, for reasons of his own, was in attendance. He devoted his attention to the Hatters themselves, leaving the task of holding down the fort to the Inspector and District Attorney Bruno, who remained in the Hatter house. Lane was a silent observer, engrossed more and more with each passing moment in the Hatters, their history, their idiosyncrasies, their behavior, their gestures, their speech, and the nuances of their interrelationships.

A pack of reporters trailed the coaches, and poured out on the cemetery grounds. Cameras clicked, pencils scribbled, perspiring young men made earnest efforts to reach the family, who were surrounded by a cordon of police from the moment they set foot outside the cemetery gates until they reached the red pit in the earth into which Mrs. Hatter's bones were to be laid. Conrad Hatter became drunkenly officious, and tottered from group to group

THE TRAGEDY OF Y 189

swearing, yelling, ordering people about. . . . Ultimately, Barbara took him by the arm and led him away.

It was a queer ceremony. A coterie of the intelligentsia, friends and acquaintances of the poetess, had come out *en masse* to pay their respects not so much to the memory of the dead woman as to the grief of the living. The grave was surrounded by men and women famous in the artistic world.

Jill Hatter, on the other hand, was represented by an unruly mob of young and oldish gentlemen-about-town, all dressed very correctly, and all more concerned with catching Jill's eye or squeezing her hand than with observing the funeral ceremony.

It was, as has been said, a field day for the press. They ignored Edgar Perry, the Arbuckles, the maid. They snapped pictures of Louisa Campion and her nurse, Miss Smith. Special female writers wrote of "the tragic blankness" of Louisa's face, "her pitiful bewilderment," her "tears when the clods began to thump upon her mother's coffin, as if she could hear and each thump resounded in her heart."

Mr. Drury Lane observed everything with a kind but keen expression, like a physician listening to the heart of a sick patient.

* * *

The pack pursued the Hatters back to the City. In the Hatter cars there was a growing tension—a snapping of nerves, a feeling of excitement that had nothing to do with the clay left in the soil of Long Island. Chester Bigelow had been mysterious all morning; Conrad had tried with drunken subtlety to pump him. But Bigelow, basking in the warm sun of central interest, shook his head. "I can't say a thing until the formal reading, Mr. Hatter."

190 ACT II: SCENE 3

John Gormly, Conrad's partner, looked peaked this morning; he pulled Conrad away roughly.

Captain Trivett, who had attended the funeral attired in black, got out of the coach before the Hatter house, assisted Louisa to the sidewalk, pressed her hand, and turned away to go into his own house next door. Astonishingly, Chester Bigelow shouted to him to remain; and the old man, with an air of bewilderment, returned to Louisa's side. Gormly remained without invitation; there was a stubborn look about him as his eyes followed Jill.

* * *

A half hour after their return they were summoned by the lawyer's brisk young assistant to the library. Lane, standing with Inspector Thumm and Bruno at one side, watched the gathering of the clans with absorption. The children had been packed off to play in the garden, remanded to the custody of an unhappy detective; and Martha Hatter, stiff and straight, sat there, hands in her lap. Miss Smith, the Braille board and pieces ready, stood by Louisa Campion's chair.

Lane observed the others assemble, and more than ever was impressed by their abnormalities. The Hatters were all healthy enough appearing specimens; they were tall and sturdy; in fact Martha, not really a Hatter, was with Louisa—they were both of exactly the same height—the shortest of them all. But Lane noted everything—their nervous deportment, the slightly wild eyes of Jill and Conrad, the strange delicate intellectualism of Barbara— the utter callousness of the first two, at any rate, and their open relish to hear the will of their murdered mother read . . . all a vivid contrast to the semi-outsiders—Martha the crushed, and Louisa the human tomb.

Bigelow began crisply. "I want no interruptions, please.

The Tragedy of Y

The will is peculiar in some respects, and there must be no comment until I have concluded the reading." There was no sound. "I might explain before reading this testament that all bequests are based on an arbitrarily fixed estate of one million dollars after payment of legal debts. Actually, the estate will run to more than a million, but the arbitrary figure is necessary in order to simplify the distribution of the bequests, as will be seen in due course."

He took a long document from the hand of his assistant, threw back his shoulders, and commenced in a sonorous voice to read aloud the last will and testament of Emily Hatter.

From the first sentence the will struck an ominous note. After affirming that she was of sound mind, Mrs. Hatter proceeded in cold language to state that the primary purpose behind all provisions was to guarantee the future care of Louisa Campion, her daughter, after the demise of the testatrix, provided Louisa Campion was alive at the time of the will's reading.

Barbara Hatter, as the eldest child of Emily Hatter and York Hatter, was to be given initial choice of accepting responsibility for the future care and welfare of the helpless woman. Should Barbara consent to accept this responsibility, signifying her willingness to tend to the physical, mental, and moral well-being of Louisa for the rest of her natural life, the estate was to be apportioned as follows:

LOUISA (in trust with Barbara) $300,000
BARBARA (as her own inheritance) $300,000
CONRAD $300,000
JILL $100,000

Under this arrangement, Barbara was to hold Louisa's inheritance in trust. On Louisa's death this estate-in-trust

192 ACT II: SCENE 3

was to be divided equally among the three Hatter children, $100,000 going to each. This contingency did not in any way affect the original bequests to Barbara, Conrad, or Jill.

Bigelow paused for breath, and Jill, her face twisted with rage, shrilled: "I like that! Why should she give——"

The lawyer was flustered, but he summoned a reserve of dignity and said hurriedly: "Please, Miss Hatter, please! Please don't interrupt. It will expedite matters—ah—considerably." She flung herself back with a little sniff, glaring about her, and Bigelow with a sigh of relief continued.

Should Barbara *refuse,* the will went on, to assume the responsibility of caring for Louisa, Conrad, as next in line of seniority, was to be given the privilege of accepting the burden. In this event—that is, should Barbara refuse and Conrad consent, the apportionment was to be as follows:

LOUISA (in trust with Conrad) $300,000
CONRAD (as his own inheritance) $300,000
JILL $100,000
BARBARA (for her refusal) $50,000

The remainder of the estate, $250,000—deducted from the inheritance of Barbara Hatter—was to be used for the establishment of an institution to be named *The Louisa Campion Deaf-Dumb-and-Blind Home.* There followed long details pursuant to the foundation of this institution.

And, under this arrangement, on Louisa's death her $300,000 was to be divided between Conrad and Jill, Conrad receiving $200,000 of the whole, Jill $100,000. Nothing was to go to Barbara. . . .

There was a little silence, during which all eyes turned toward the poetess. She was relaxed in her chair, gazing steadily at Chester Bigelow's lips; she did not change ex-

The Tragedy of Y 193

pression. Conrad was staring at her with all his wild weak soul in his eyes.

"There's a picture for you," whispered Bruno to Lane; and although Bruno's voice was inaudible to Thumm next to him, Lane read the words on his lips and smiled sadly. "People's true colors always appear during the reading of a will. Watch Hatter; there's murder in his eyes. No matter what happens, Mr. Lane, there will be a contest, I'm sure. It's a crazy testament."

Bigelow licked his lips and went on. Should Conrad in his turn refuse to accept the responsibility of caring for Louisa, the apportionment was to be as follows:

BARBARA (for her refusal) $50,000
CONRAD (for refusal) $50,000
JILL (as before) $100,000
THE LOUISA CAMPION DEAF-DUMB-AND-BLIND
    HOME (as before) $250,000
LOUISA $500,000

There was a chorus of gasps. Five hundred thousand dollars! They looked furtively at the potential recipient of this fortune; they saw merely a plump little woman staring quietly at the wall.

Bigelow's voice jerked them back. What was he saying? ". . . and to Louisa the sum of five hundred thousand dollars, as stated above, to be held in trust for her by Captain Eli Trivett, who, I know, will be willing to accept the responsibility of caring for my unfortunate daughter, Louisa Campion. For his trouble, I bequeath to said Captain Trivett also an outright sum of fifty thousand dollars, should Barbara and Conrad refuse, and should Captain Trivett consent to care for Louisa. My daughter Jill has no choice."

ACT II: SCENE 3

In this last event, the lawyer continued, on Louisa's death, $100,000 of Louisa's half-million was to go to Jill as an additional inheritance; and the remainder, $400,000, was to be added to the $250,000 created for the Home's foundation fund. . . .

The silence was so thick that Bigelow hurried on without even looking up from the testament he was reading. To Mr. and Mrs. George Arbuckle, irrespective of other circumstances, the lawyer continued in a slightly shaking voice, the sum of $2500 in reward of faithful service. To Miss Angela Smith, nurse, the sum of $2500 in reward of faithful service. And should Miss Angela Smith consent to remain as Louisa Campion's nurse and companion after the death of the testatrix a fund was to be established out of which a salary of $75 per week was to be paid to the nurse for the duration of the service. Finally, to the maid Virginia, the sum of $500. . . .

Bigelow dropped the will and sat down. His assistant rose briskly and distributed copies of the testament. Each heir received the copy in silence.

No one spoke for some minutes. Conrad Hatter was turning the document over and over between his fingers, staring at the typewritten words with bleary eyes. Jill's pretty mouth was writhing in a grimace of pure hatred; her beautiful eyes slyly rolled toward Louisa Campion. Miss Smith insensibly moved near her charge.

Then Conrad exploded with a scream of rage. He sprang from his chair, flung the will on the floor, ground it under his heel in an ecstasy of hysteria. He babbled in a cracked voice, features crimsoned, advancing on Chester Bigelow so menacingly that the lawyer rose in alarm. Thumm hurled himself across the room and grasped the raving man's arm with granite fingers. "You fool!" he roared. "Control yourself!"

The Tragedy of Y

195

The red faded into pink, and the pink into dirty gray. Conrad shook his head slowly, like a man in a daze, as his insane fury drained away. Reason came back into his eyes. He turned to his sister Barbara and whispered: "You—what are you going to do about—her, Babs?"

Everyone sighed with relief. Barbara rose without replying, glided past her brother as if he did not exist, stooped over Louisa's chair to pat the deaf-dumb-and-blind woman's cheek, turned and said in her sweet deep voice: "Please excuse me," and departed. Conrad stared after her, imbecile-fingered.

Then it was Jill's turn, and she made the most of it. "Left out in the cold!" she shrieked. "Damn my mother's soul!" With the leap of a cat she was crouched before Louisa's chair. "You unspeakable *thing!*" she spat, and whirled to run out of the library.

Martha Hatter sat eying the Hatters with quiet contempt. Miss Smith was nervously manipulating the pieces on the Braille board for the information of Louisa; she was transferring the message of the will word for word by the metal pieces.

* * *

When the room had been cleared of all except Bigelow and his assistant, District Attorney Bruno said to Lane: "And what do you think of them now?"

"They're not only mad, Mr. Bruno, but vicious. So vicious, in fact," Lane continued quietly, "that I suspect it isn't their fault."

"What do you mean?"

"I mean that there is an evil stream in their blood. Undoubtedly a congenital weakness in the strain. The root of the evil must have been Mrs. Hatter—witness Louisa Campion, the most unfortunate victim of all."

"Victim and victor combined," said Bruno grimly. "No

196 ACT II: SCENE 3

matter what happens, she stands to lose nothing. A tidy fortune for a helpless woman, Mr. Lane."

"Too damned tidy," growled the Inspector. "She'll have to be watched like the U. S. Mint."

Bigelow was fumbling with the lock of his briefcase, and his assistant was fussing about the desk. Lane said: "Mr. Bigelow, how recent is this will?"

"Mrs. Hatter told me to draw up her new will on the day after the discovery of York Hatter's body in the Bay."

"What were the provisions of the old will?"

"York Hatter was left the entire estate, with the sole provision that he care for Louisa Campion for the rest of her life. On his death, his estate was to be apportioned according to his own testamentary judgment." Bigelow picked up his briefcase. "It was a simple document compared with this. She registered her confidence that her husband would make proper provision for the future of Louisa, if Louisa outlived him."

"And the family knew the provisions of this first will?"

"Oh, yes! Mrs. Hatter also told me that, should Louisa die before she herself did, she meant to divide her estate equally among Barbara, Jill, and Conrad."

"Thank you."

With a sigh of relief Bigelow hastily left the library, his assistant tagging after like a puppy.

* * *

"Louisa, Louisa," said Thumm irritably. "Always Louisa. She's the storm center of the whole mess. She'll be bumped off if we aren't careful."

"Just what is your opinion, Mr. Lane, of the case?" asked the District Attorney casually. "Thumm tells me you said yesterday that you wanted to give us some of your ideas today."

THE TRAGEDY OF Y

Mr. Drury Lane clutched his rattan stick firmly, and waved it in a little arc before him. "So I did," he murmured; his face was grave and strained. "And yet—I prefer not to say now, on second thought. I can't think here—the atmosphere is too disturbing."

The Inspector made an impolite sound; his temper was near the breaking point.

"I'm sorry, Inspector. I'm beginning to feel quite like the Hector in *Troilus and Cressida*—you know, the Shakespearean 'lame and impotent conclusion,' as Shakespeare himself said—although not about his own bad play! —which the Players are putting on in the City. Hector says: 'Modest doubt is call'd the beacon of the wise,' and I fear I shall have to echo him today." He sighed. "I'm going back to The Hamlet to resolve my doubts, if I can. . . . How long do you intend to besiege this unhappy Troy, Inspector?"

"Until I get me a nice wooden horse," grunted Thumm, with surprising erudition. "I'll be damned if I know what to do. They're beginning to ask questions in City Hall. All I know is this: I've got one lead."

"Really?"

"Perry."

Lane's eyes narrowed. "Perry? What about Perry?"

"Nothing yet. But—" Thumm added slyly, "maybe a lot soon. Mr. Edgar Perry—and I'll bet a dollar that's not his real name—forged his references to get in here—that's what!"

Lane seemed genuinely disturbed. The District Attorney leaned forward quickly. "If it's a real lead, Thumm," he said, "we can hold him on that charge, you know."

"Not so fast. Barbara Hatter stepped out and defended him—said she'd engineered the thing because Conrad wanted high-toned references and Perry didn't have any.

Boloney! But we've got to take her word for it. The interesting part of it is—he hasn't *any* references, by God, and he won't say anything about his past."

"So you are investigating him," said Lane slowly. "Well, that's wise, Inspector. Evidently you think Miss Hatter knows as little about him as we do."

"Evidently." Thumm grinned. "Nice gal, and all that, but I think she likes the guy—and they'll do anything when they're in love."

The District Attorney was thoughtful. "Then you've abandoned the Conrad theory?"

Thumm shrugged. "Nothing to abandon. Those shoe-prints on the rug upstairs—too pat, unless he was some woman's accomplice. And that business of the woman's cheek. . . . The hell with that. I'm going to work on Perry. I think I'll have something for you tomorrow."

"That will be splendid, Inspector." Lane buttoned his linen coat. "Perhaps you had better pay a visit to The Hamlet tomorrow afternoon. You can tell me all about the Perry affair, and I . . ."

"Go all the way out there?" muttered Thumm.

"Just a suggestion, Inspector," murmured Lane. "You'll come?"

"We'll come," said the District Attorney quickly.

"Excellent. You aren't relaxing vigilance, of course, Inspector? Be most careful to watch the house, and particularly the laboratory."

"And I'm keeping the poison expert Doc Schilling sent over on duty in the kitchen," said Thumm grimly. "Yes, I know all that. Sometimes, Mr. Lane, I get the feeling that you don't——"

Whatever the Inspector, in the general dissatisfaction of his temper at the moment, was about to say, was lost on

THE TRAGEDY OF Y 199

Mr. Drury Lane. For with a set smile Lane had waved, turned, and gone.

Thumm cracked his knuckles in despair. There was no use talking to a man who became deaf as soon as his back was turned.

Scene 4

THE HAMLET. WEDNESDAY, JUNE 8. 3 P.M.

Wednesday turned clear, but cold. The Hudson country was like a winter's sea; the swish and wash of the winds through the dense foliage was oceanic in its sound. There was June in the trees, and November in the air.

The police car negotiated the steep grades, the iron bridge, the gravel road, the clearing, the garden road in silence. Neither District Attorney Bruno nor Inspector Thumm felt inclined to talk.

Old Quacey, his upthrust hump as grotesque as ever, met them at the iron-hasped outer doors and conducted them through the main hall, with its rush-strewn floor, its vast candelabra, its knights in armor and mammoth masks of Comedy and Tragedy, to the little elevator concealed in the farther wall. A short ascent and they stepped out into Mr. Drury Lane's private apartments.

The old actor, in a brown velveteen jacket, was standing straight as a spear before the leaping flames of his fireplace. Even in the light, with its momentary changes of accent and its fluid running shadows, they saw the worry stamped on his face. He looked haggard, decidedly not himself. He greeted them, however, with his customary

ACT II: SCENE 4

courtesy, pulled a bell-cord and ordered little Falstaff to serve coffee and liqueurs, sent Quacey—who was sniffing about like an old hound—out of the room, and settled himself before the fire.

"First," he said quietly, "your news, Inspector, if there is any."

"Plenty. We've tracked down this Perry's record."

"Record?" Lane's eyebrows arched.

"Not a police record. I mean his past. You'll never guess who he is—what his real name is."

"I'm scarcely a seer, Inspector," said Lane with a faint smile. "He isn't the lost Dauphin, I trust?"

"The who? Listen, Mr. Lane, this is serious," growled the Inspector. "Edgar Perry's real name is Edgar *Campion!*"

Lane was quite still for a fleeting moment. "Edgar Campion," he said after a while. "Indeed. Not the son of Mrs. Hatter's first husband?"

"Yes! The lowdown is this: when Emily Hatter was Emily Campion, married to Tom Campion, who's dead now, Campion already had a son by a former wife. The son is Edgar Campion. He's therefore a half-brother to Louisa Campion—same father, different mothers."

"Hmm."

"What gets me," said the District Attorney in vast discontent, "is why Campion, or Perry, should pose as a tutor and come to live in the Hatter house. Thumm says that Barbara Hatter helped him get the job——"

"That's hooey," said the Inspector. "I knew it the minute she said it. She didn't know him before he got the job—I found *that* out. And what's more, it's a cinch she doesn't know who he really is. She's in love. *Love!*"

"Did Mrs. Hatter know that Edgar Perry was her stepson, Edgar Campion?" asked Lane thoughtfully.

THE TRAGEDY OF Y 201

"Nah—how could she, unless he told her? The trail showed that Perry was only six or seven years old when his father and Emily were divorced. She couldn't have recognized him as a man of forty-four."

"Have you spoken to him?"

"He won't open his yap, damn him."

"Thumm's placed him under arrest," remarked Bruno.

Lane stiffened, and then relaxed with a shake of his head. "My dear Inspector," he said, "that was rash, very rash. On what grounds can you hold him?"

"Don't like the idea, eh, Mr. Lane?" said Thumm with a grim smile. "Don't you worry about grounds; I've got him on a technical charge. No, sir, he's much too hot a prospect to leave running around free."

"You think he murdered Mrs. Hatter?" asked Lane dryly.

The Inspector shrugged. "Maybe, maybe not. Probably not, because I can't figure out a motive and, of course, I've no evidence. But he knows something, mark my words. A man doesn't disguise his identity and get a job in a house where murder is committed just like"—he snapped his fingers—"just like that, by God."

"And the smooth soft cheek, Inspector?"

"Pie. We've never eliminated the possibility of an accomplice, have we? Or else the deaf-mute was mistaken."

"Come, come," said the District Attorney impatiently. "We haven't made that long trip up from the City to hear *your* views, Thumm. Just what is it you had in mind, Mr. Lane?"

* * *

Lane did not speak for a long time. In the interim Falstaff plumped in bearing largesse, and Thumm drowned some of his ill-temper in a cup of steaming black coffee. When Falstaff had gone, Lane spoke.

ACT II: SCENE 4

202

"I have been reflecting on this problem, gentlemen," he said in the rich baritone that he handled so deftly, "ever since Sunday, and the result of my reflections has been rather—what shall I say?—disconcerting."

"What do you mean?" demanded Thumm.

"Certain issues are clear-cut—as clear-cut as certain issues were in the Longstreet affair, for example——"

"You mean you've *got* it?" said Bruno.

"No. No." Lane was silent again for a moment. "Don't misunderstand me. I am far—far from a solution. Because certain other issues are doubtful; and not only doubtful, gentlemen, but peculiar." His voice dropped to a whisper. *"Peculiar,"* he said, and they stared at him nervously.

He rose and began to patrol his rug before the fire. "I can't tell you how disturbed I am. Disturbed! I'm beginning to doubt the evidence of my senses—the four I have left." The two men looked at each other in bewilderment. "But enough of this," said Lane abruptly. "I can tell you now that I have reached a decision. There are two definitely marked lines of investigation open to me, and I intend to follow them. Neither has yet been touched."

"Leads?" broke in the Inspector irritably. "There he goes again! What the devil kind of leads that haven't been touched, as you say?"

Lane did not smile or cease his pacing. "The odor," he muttered, "the vanilla odor. That's one. Extraordinary—it has me baffled. I have a theory about it and I mean to follow it through. If it should please the gods to smile on me . . ." He shrugged. "The other I prefer not even to mention at this time. But it's so amazing, so incredible, and yet so logical . . ." He went on without giving either man a chance to interrupt with the questions he saw hovering on their lips. "Inspector, tell me what you believe, in

THE TRAGEDY OF Y   203

general, about this case. We may as well be frank with each other, and sometimes a meeting of minds accomplishes more than independent thinking."

"Now you're talking," said Thumm briskly. "Let's get together. To me it's plain; the poisoner sneaked into the bedroom last Saturday night, or rather in the early hours of Sunday morning, with the intention of poisoning the pear. The pear was meant for Louisa; the poisoner knew she would eat it in the morning. While the poisoner was in the room, Mrs. Hatter woke up, made a disturbance or cried out, and the poisoner lambasted her over the head in a panic. Probably didn't mean to kill her at all; just quiet her. The death of that old she-devil, I think, was an accident. Bruno agrees with me, and I don't see any reason to doubt it."

"In other words," murmured Mr. Drury Lane, "you and Mr. Bruno believe the murder of Mrs. Hatter to have been *un*premeditated, a crime of the moment under unforeseen circumstances?"

"Right," said Thumm.

"I thoroughly agree," said Bruno.

"Then, gentlemen," said Lane softly, *"you are both wrong."*

"I—what do you mean?" demanded Bruno, taken aback.

"I mean this. There is no question in my mind but that the murder of Mrs. Hatter *was* premeditated, that she was *intended* to be the victim before the murderer even stepped into that bedroom, and, furthermore, that *Louisa Campion was never meant to be poisoned at all!"*

*   *   *

They silently chewed upon this morsel, and there was confusion in both men's eyes, a suspension of judgment

ACT II: SCENE 4

that called for explanation. Lane provided it in his calm, deliberate way.

"We begin," he said, after seating himself before the fire and moistening his lips with a liqueur, "from Louisa Campion herself. What are the surface facts? From the hypodermic and the poisoned pear it would surely seem that the bichloride of mercury was aimed at Louisa—she loved fruit, whereas Mrs. Hatter, the only other person who ate fruit habitually from that bowl, did not care for fruit generally and detested pears particularly. A pear was poisoned. Then it would appear that the poisoner deliberately chose a fruit which he knew Louisa would eat and Mrs. Hatter would not. This apparently makes the attempt on Louisa's life the primary, motivating purpose, as you gentlemen maintain—in fact, the theory is strengthened by the circumstance that, two months before the second attempt, a first attempt had been made on her life, only to be frustrated at the last moment."

"Yes, sir," said the Inspector, "that's the way it looks to me. And if you can prove it's the other way around, you're a better man than I am."

"I can prove it, Inspector," replied Lane calmly. "Please follow me closely. If the poisoner expected Louisa Campion to eat that poisoned pear, then you are both right. But *did* he expect her to eat that poisoned pear?"

"Why, of course," said Bruno in bewilderment.

"I am sorry to contradict you, but he did not. For the following reasons: We may assume from the outset that the poisoner, whether a member of the household or not, at least is familiar with its intimate details. The assumption is soundly based; he knew, for example, that Louisa drinks an egg-nog at two-thirty every afternoon in the dining-room. He knew, for example, the house well enough

THE TRAGEDY OF Y   205

to have discovered something that apparently no one else knows—the secret of the chimney and fireplaces connecting laboratory and bedroom. He knew, for example, exactly where the mandolin was kept. He was familiar, surely, with the laboratory and its contents.

"Certainly these are sufficient to establish the contention that the culprit is thoroughly conversant with all details necessary to his plan. Now, if he knew these things, he certainly knew as well that Louisa is fastidious about her food and drink, and would therefore be aware that she does not eat spoiled or over-ripe fruit. Few people will, anyway *—particularly when there are ripe, fresh, unspoiled pieces of the identical fruit in the very bowl which contains the spoiled one.* And Dr. Schilling's analysis reported that the pear was spoiled *before* the injection of bichloride of mercury. Therefore, the poisoner deliberately poisoned a *spoiled pear.*"

They were listening with critical fascination. Lane smiled faintly. "Didn't that fact strike you as odd, gentlemen? To me it was extraordinary.

"Now, you may demur, you may say that this was an accident—in the darkness of the bedroom he might inadvertently have picked out of the bowl a rotting pear without realizing it. Even this is not entirely tenable, for it is easy to tell a spoiled piece of fruit even by touch; the fingers will slip on the rotted rind. But suppose we work on this theory—that the selection of the spoiled pear was sheer accident. I can prove that it wasn't.

"How? By the fact that Mrs. Arbuckle testified that she had put only two pears in the daily bowl the afternoon of the night the murder was committed; that Miss Smith had actually, at eleven-thirty that night, seen *only two* pears in that very bowl, and both of them were ripe, fresh, and un-

206 ACT II: SCENE 4

spoiled. Yet the morning after the crime we find *three* pears in the bowl. Conclusion: it was the poisoner who must have furnished the third—and spoiled—pear, since the two original pears we know by good testimony were fresh. Proof, then, that the poisoning of a spoiled pear was deliberate; so much so, that the poisoner provided *his own spoiled pear,* brought from outside.

"But why should a poisoner deliberately bring to the scene of his crime a spoiled piece of fruit when he knows that his intended victim will not eat a spoiled piece of fruit, fresh ones of the same variety being in the bowl? The only possible answer is: *He never intended her to eat it at all,* and I will stake my reputation on the infallible logic of the argument."

Neither listener said anything.

"In other words," continued Lane, "you are both wrong in assuming that the poisoner believed that Louisa Campion would eat the poisoned pear. He knew she would not; and since he also must have known that Mrs. Hatter, the only other partaker from that fruit-bowl, would not eat pears at all . . . then the entire incident of the poisoned pear must in all logic be considered a pure blind, a device on the part of the murderer to make the police *believe* Louisa was the intended victim."

"Just a moment," said the Inspector quickly. "If, as you say, this Campion woman wouldn't eat the fruit, how the devil did the poisoner expect to have this pretended poisoning of his *discovered at all?*"

"Good question, Thumm," said the District Attorney.

"Because, no matter what his motive was," Thumm went on, "his trick was useless unless somebody found it out. See what I mean?"

"I do," replied Lane, undisturbed. "A canny interpola-

THE TRAGEDY OF Y 207

tion, Inspector. You say that unless the plotter's pear were found by the police to have been poisoned, there was no point in his poisoning it at all. If no one found the pear to have been poisoned, no one would know that someone was apparently trying to poison Louisa—the effect the poisoner was attempting to achieve.

"Very well. There are three possible ways by which the poisoner might have expected to have his poisoning attempt become police knowledge—provided the murder of Mrs. Hatter was not foreseen, mind you, but an accident. First: by leaving the hypodermic in the room, as he did. This would arouse suspicion, of course, and cause an investigation, since there had been a previous poisoning attempt two months before. A possible hypothesis, but it's much more likely that the poisoner dropped the hypodermic in fright or panic.

"Second: by intentionally *adding* a pear—the poisoned pear—and *not* taking one away, making three in all, when several people knew there were supposed to be only two. But this is also improbable; it would be at best a long chance and most likely no one would notice an extra pear.

"Third: by *himself* calling attention, in some way, on some pretext, to the spoiled pear. This is by far the most likely of the three."

Thumm and Bruno nodded.

Lane shook his head. "But when I show you that the murder of Mrs. Hatter was *not* an accident, that it was deliberately schemed out to occur simultaneously with the false poisoning attempt, then you will see that none of the three possibilities I have given is necessary; that I have been setting up straw-men merely to knock them down.

"For, when our quarry planned to become not a poisoner

208   ACT II: SCENE 4

but a murderer, then *he knew in advance* that the poisoned
pear would be found. He could let matters take their natural course, could figure and depend on the official *murder*
investigation discovering the poisoned pear. No longer a
chance, then, but almost a certainty. The poisoning would
be accidentally discovered, the police would say that the
primary purpose of the crime was to poison Louisa, that
Mrs. Hatter had been killed by sheer accident; and the
murderer would in this way have accomplished his real
purpose: *to kill Mrs. Hatter and make the police search
for someone with motive to kill Louisa,* discounting the
old lady's murder altogether."

"I'll be eternally damned," muttered the Inspector.
"That's clever, if it's true."

"But it is true, Inspector. You remember that, even before we found the hypodermic syringe on the bed, you remarked that you would scout around to make sure nothing
was poisoned, working on the basis of the two-months-old
poisoning precedent. Which proves that the murderer had
anticipated the police reaction to a nicety. Even had we not
discovered the hypodermic—which I maintain from all
the facts was left by accident—even, in fact, if only two
pears had been found, you would probably have worked
on a poison theory and discovered the poisoned pear."

"That's right, Thumm," said the District Attorney.

Lane drew up his long thighs and stared into the fire.
"Now, to prove that Mrs. Hatter's murder was planned in
advance, was not an accident of the moment.

"One point is immediately apparent. The mandolin used
as the death-weapon was not part of the bedroom's equipment; its proper place was downstairs in the library under
a glass case, which was taboo to everyone and was never
touched. In fact, it was actually seen in its glass case down-

The Tragedy of Y

stairs by Conrad Hatter at one-thirty in the morning—two and a half hours before it snuffed out Mrs. Hatter's life; and had been seen that same evening by others.

"Then this much is certain: the murderer, of the household or not, was compelled to make a special trip to get hold of the mandolin, or else must have had to prepare himself with it in advance of his visit to the bedroom. . . ."

"Here, here," interrupted Bruno, drawing his brows together, "how do you figure that?"

Lane sighed. "If the murderer was one of the household, he had to come down from either the first floor or the attic floor to get it. If he was not of the household, he could not enter the house through the ground floor, because all doors and windows were locked; therefore he had to enter via the fire-escape to at least the first floor; or, just as likely, climbed the fire-escape to the roof and entered via the chimney. In any event, a trip downstairs for the mandolin was necessary. . . ."

"That follows," conceded Bruno, "but suppose it was somebody of the household who picked up the mandolin on his way upstairs, as he came in late from outside? There were a couple who did, you know."

"Very well," smiled Lane. "Suppose one of the late homecomers did arm himself with the mandolin on his or her way upstairs? Wouldn't that distinctly mean a plan, a preconceived purpose, a deliberately thought-out use for the mandolin?"

"Okay," said Thumm. "Shoot."

"Then the mandolin was brought into the bedroom by the murderer deliberately, for a special purpose. What could that purpose have been, gentlemen? Let's analyze and eliminate.

"First: the battered old mandolin might have been

210 ACT II: SCENE 4

brought into the bedroom for an indigenous purpose, which is to say, for use in its proper field, as a musical instrument. . . ." The Inspector snickered, and Bruno shook his head. "Naturally. Ridiculous, and doesn't even require discussion.

"Second: it might have been brought into the bedroom for the purpose of leaving a planted trail, a deliberately false clue implicating someone. But whom? There is only one person exclusively associated with the mandolin, the discovery of which would implicate him and him alone; that is, its owner, York Hatter. But York Hatter is dead. So our second surmise is wrong."

"Hold on, hold on," said the Inspector slowly. "Not so fast. Granted that York Hatter is dead, it's not impossible that whoever's committing these crimes isn't sure of it; or, if he is sure of it, he's trying to make us believe that York Hatter isn't dead because of the unsatisfactory circumstances surrounding the identification of the body. What d'ye say to that?"

"I say bravo, Inspector," chuckled Lane. "An intricate and ingenious thought. But I believe I can refute even that remote possibility. It would be a silly gesture on the plotter's part for two reasons: One, if the police are to be deluded into thinking that York Hatter is alive and that he accidentally left his own mandolin on the scene of his crime, then the deception must be acceptable to the police. But could the police be led to believe that Hatter would leave so obvious a clue to himself? Of course not; he would be the last person in the world to leave such an open and glaring trail to himself, and certainly the police would realize that it was a deception, not a genuine clue. Second: why such a weird object as a mandolin at all? It is the least conceivable object one associates with the spilling of

THE TRAGEDY OF Y 211

blood. The police, knowing that Hatter would not in all seriousness leave his own—peculiar!—property on the scene of his own crime, would reason that it was left by someone else to implicate Hatter, and therefore the plotter's purpose would be defeated.

"No, Inspector, there was no such ulterior purpose in our murderer's mind. The employment of the mandolin, strange as it appears, was legitimately connected with the murderer's own plot."

"Go on, Mr. Lane," said the District Attorney with an irritated glance at his colleague. "Thumm, you think of the most ridiculous things!"

"Don't scold the Inspector, Mr. Bruno," said Lane. "He is perfectly right to bring up far-fetched possibilities, or even impossibilities. Logic knows no law but its own.

"So, if the mandolin was not brought into the bedroom as a musical instrument, or as a false clue to York Hatter, what other conceivable purpose could the murderer have had? I challenge you to find more than one reasonable remaining motive: that is, *to use it as a weapon*."

"Damned funny weapon," muttered Thumm. "That's stuck in my craw since the beginning."

"I hardly blame you, Inspector," sighed Lane, "for adopting that attitude or posing that question. It *is* a queer weapon, as you say, and when we strike bottom in this case . . ." He paused, and something remarkably sad came into his eyes. Then he sat up straighter, and forged ahead in his deep voice. "Since we cannot answer the question now, let us forget it for the present. But certainly, whatever the reason is, the mandolin was brought to the bedroom for use as a weapon, and at the moment that is the nuclear consideration."

"Of course," said Bruno wearily, "if the mandolin was,

ACT II: SCENE 4

as you say, brought as a weapon, then its purpose from the beginning was offensive; that is, it was lugged along as an instrument of offense, or murder."

"Not by a long shot," growled Thumm before Lane could reply. "How do you know it was brought along as an offensive weapon? How do you know it wasn't brought as a *de*fensive weapon—no intention at all to assault the old witch, but taken along just in case it should be needed?"

"That's right, too," muttered Bruno.

"No," said Lane, "that's wrong. Here! Suppose, Inspector, as you say, the murderer merely anticipated the *possibility* of having to silence Mrs. Hatter, or even Louisa while he was poisoning the fruit; that is, that there was no original purpose to attack, but to defend. Now, we know that the marauder was well acquainted with the bedroom, and that in that bedroom there are half a dozen objects infinitely to be preferred as weapons—the iron fire-tools hanging at the fireplace; in fact, two heavy bookends lying on the night-table itself next to the victim's bed—any one of which would have struck a more effective blow than the comparatively light mandolin. Now, if the murderer made a special trip downstairs to get a weapon whose use was purely hypothetical, he was going to an extraordinary amount of trouble without cause, when there were even better bludgeons ready to his hand on the scene of his projected crime.

"Then logic dictates that the mandolin was not taken along as a weapon of defense; it was taken along as a weapon of offense. Not merely to be available if needed, but to be deliberately used. And no other weapon would do, please observe—only the mandolin."

"I see it now," confessed Thumm. "Go ahead, Mr. Lane."

"Very well. Now, if it was carried by the murderer to be

THE TRAGEDY OF Y   213

deliberately used in offense—against whom was it to be used? Against Louisa Campion? Surely not; I have pointed out that the poisoning was not meant to take effect, that the murderer did not want to poison her. And if he did not want to take her life with a poisoned pear, why should he want to take her life by striking her on the head with his strange weapon? No, the mandolin certainly could not have been meant for Louisa Campion. Then for whom else? Only Mrs. Hatter. Which is what I set out to prove, gentlemen: that it was never the murderer's intention to poison Louisa Campion, and that it was always his intention to murder Emily Hatter."

The actor stretched his legs and toasted his toes. "My throat! Retirement has softened me . . . Look here. When you consider the interrelationship of the fundamentals I shall mention, you will see that this entire line of reasoning is clarified and strengthened. First, a blind, a feint, a faked move, is generally a smoke screen to conceal a *real* purpose. Second: the poisoning attempt on Louisa was, as just shown, a blind. Third: despite the fact that it was a blind, a weapon was deliberately brought along by the criminal. Fourth: Mrs. Hatter was the only individual under the circumstances against whom the deliberately brought weapon could have had a real, or lethal, purpose."

In the silence that ensued the District Attorney and Inspector Thumm regarded each other with mingled expressions of admiration and mental turmoil. In Bruno's case the expression was even more subtle. Something insistent was struggling for recognition behind that keen mask; he took one look at Thumm and then dropped his glance to the floor, where he stubbornly kept it for a long time.

The Inspector was less upset. "It sure sounds like the right dope, Mr. Lane, much as I hate to admit it. We've

ACT II: SCENE 4

been on the wrong tack from the start. This changes the whole complexion of the investigation. We've got to keep our eyes peeled for different motive now—not motive against the Campion woman, but motive against Mrs. Hatter!"

Lane nodded; there was no satisfaction or triumph on his face. Despite the conclusiveness of his argument, he seemed disturbed by a sprouting emotional canker. Gloom settled upon him now that the glow of oration was fading; and from under his silky brows he kept watching District Attorney Bruno.

The Inspector was oblivious to this byplay; he was busy thinking aloud. "Motive against the old lady. That will business . . . Hell, they all stood to gain something by bumping off the old crow. . . . And where does that get you? Nowhere. For that matter, everybody stood to gain something by killing Louisa too—either money or the satisfaction of personal hatred. . . . Maybe we'll get somewhere when we see what Barbara Hatter does about Louisa."

"Ah—yes, yes," murmured Lane. "I beg your pardon, Inspector; I'm afraid that while my eyes registered what you said, my brain wasn't particularly attentive. . . . A more pressing problem. With the will's contents published and the testatrix dead, the previous *pretenses* at the poisoning of Louisa may very well turn into real attempts, now that the deaf-dumb-and-blind woman's death will benefit them all."

Thumm sat up, startled. "By God, I never thought of that! And there's another thing." He groaned. "We haven't any way of knowing who's who. If Louisa should be bumped off, it wouldn't necessarily mean that she was killed by the same one who killed her mother. Anybody, having

THE TRAGEDY OF Y

nothing to do with either the first poisoning attempt or the second plus the murder, would be in a swell position now to attempt Louisa's life, since he or she could be sure the police would pin it on the original poisoner and killer. What a mess!"

"Hmm. I agree with you, Inspector. Not only must Miss Campion be guarded night and day, but every single one of the Hatter household must be under constant surveillance, and the poison supply in the laboratory should be removed at once."

"You think so?" said Thumm slyly. "Not by a long shot. Oh, we'll watch the lab, all right, but the poisons stay there, what's left of 'em—and maybe somebody'll come snooping around for a bottleful!"

District Attorney Bruno raised his eyes to Mr. Drury Lane's. A spark kindled in them, and Lane crouched deeper in his chair, tension in all his muscles, as if he were setting himself for a blow.

There was quizzical triumph on Bruno's face. "Well!" he said. "I've been thinking things over, Mr. Lane."

"And you have concluded—?" asked Lane without expression.

Bruno grinned. "I hate to upset that beautiful analysis of yours, but I'm afraid I must. All through your reasoning you've assumed that the poisoner and murderer are *the same person* . . ." The tension dropped away from Lane, and he relaxed with a sigh. "Now, once before we discussed the possibility that poisoner and murderer were two people, not one, and that they did their separate jobs on the murder night at different times. . . ."

"Yes, yes."

"True," continued Bruno with a wave of his hand, "this leaves unexplained the motive of the *poisoner*, provided

ACT II: SCENE 4

there was an entirely separate murderer. But suppose his motive was merely to frighten the deaf-dumb-and-blind woman, scare her out of the house by these fake attacks on her life? Several have such motive, who might not stoop to murder. So, I say that you haven't taken into account the possibility of two separate criminals, a theory in which whoever killed Mrs. Hatter had nothing to do with the poisoning at all!"

"That night," added Thumm, with a look of astonishment at Bruno's perspicacity, "or two months ago, either. And man, how that jabs a needle into *your* analysis, Mr. Lane!"

Lane sat silent for a moment; and then his two guests were startled to hear him utter a cavernous chuckle. "Why, Mr. Bruno," he said, "I thought that was obvious."

"Obvious?" exclaimed both men.

"Of course. Isn't it?"

"Isn't what?"

"Oh, very well," chuckled Lane again. "Evidently my error in neglecting to point out what I thought was so perfectly apparent all the time. It's like you, Mr. Bruno, with your confoundedly tortuous legal mind, to propound a question like that. Popped at me, eh, as a sort of last-minute rebuttal?"

"I'd like to hear your explanation, anyway," said Bruno calmly.

"You shall." Lane composed himself and stared at his fire. "So you want to know why I assume that the poisoner and murderer are one and the same . . . ? The answer is: I do not assume it, I know it. I can provide mathematical proof."

"That's a tall order," said Inspector Thumm.

"I'm open to conviction," said the District Attorney.

THE TRAGEDY OF Y   217

"Perhaps, like 'the unanswerable tear in woman's eye,'" said Lane with a smile, "my argument will be too convincing. . . . I might begin by saying that most of the story was written on the floor of the bedroom."

"Floor of the bedroom?" echoed Thumm. "Showed one person, not—?"

"Pshaw, Inspector! I'm surprised at your lack of perspicacity. You will agree, won't you, that, if there were two people involved, not one, certainly then they must have come in at different times—since they admittedly had different purposes, one to poison the pear directed against Louisa, the other to murder Mrs. Hatter?"

Both men nodded.

"Very well, then. In what order did they visit the room?" Thumm and Bruno looked at each other. Bruno shrugged. "I don't see how you can say positively."

Lane shook his head. "Lack of coherent thought, Mr. Bruno. To place the poisoned pear on the night-table where we found it, the poisoner had to stand between the beds; that much is indubitable. To murder Mrs. Hatter the murderer also had to stand between the beds, as Dr. Schilling pointed out. Therefore, both, if there were two, walked over the same stretch of carpet—the rug between the beds. Yet there was only one set of footprints in the scattered powder on the rug at that place—we may discount Louisa Campion's, of course; for, if her testimony is to be impugned, we may as well surrender right now.

"Now, if the *first* invader had upset the powder, there would be *two* sets of footprints: the first set made by the first invader after he upset the powder, and the second set by the second invader inadvertently when he visited the room after the first was gone. But there is only one set of footprints. This means, plainly, that the powder must have

ACT II: SCENE 4

been upset by the second visitor, not the first, which would account for the fact that one visitor, necessarily the first, left no footprints at all. Fundamental.

"The problem logically set for us, then, is to discover whose prints we found—that is, who was the second visitor. The footprints in the powder were made by shoes which we found. On the toecap of the right shoe there was splattered liquid, asserted by the Medical Examiner to be bichloride of mercury, the same poison that was injected into the pear and that was found in the hypodermic. Obviously, then, the visitor who left the footprints in the powder—the second visitor—was the poisoner. This means that Number Two, having upset the box and walked in the talcum, was the poisoner; and, always provided there were two individuals involved, that Number One was the murderer. Do you follow so far?"

They nodded.

"Now, what does the mandolin, the weapon used by the murderer, or Number One, tell us about him, the first visitor? It tells this: It was the mandolin that knocked the powder-box off the night-table. How? There were blood lines on the cover of the powder box which could only have been placed there by contact with the bloody strings of the mandolin. Behind the spot on the table where the box had lain, before it was knocked over, we found a fresh dent made by some sharp edge. This dent, from its position and nature, we established to have been caused by the mandolin's edge striking the table; the mandolin, in confirmation, showing on one of its own edges at the lower end an abrasion corresponding to the table dent. Then the mandolin struck the table at that point, its strings touched the powder-box top, and hurled the box off the table.

"The mandolin could not wield itself. It was used to

The Tragedy of Y

batter the old lady's head. Then the blow which caused the box to fall must have been a result of the latter half of the swing exerted in striking Mrs. Hatter over the head right beside the table. This is really repetition; at the time we examined the scene of the crime we established these points beyond doubt."

Lane leaned forward and brandished a muscular fore-finger. "Now, we proved before that it was *the poisoner—Number Two*—who upset the powder-box. Yet at this moment it appears that Number One, the murderer, upset the powder-box. An insurmountable contradiction!" The actor smiled. "Another way of stating it: We discovered that the mandolin lay *on top of* a film of fallen powder. That means that the mandolin fell when the powder was already on the floor. And since in the first analysis the poisoner upset the powder, that means that the murderer must have come second. But if he came second, where in Heaven's name are his footprints, since the only footprints found are the poisoner's?

"And so if we have no murderer's footprints, there were not two people there *after the powder fell;* in other words, the murderer as a separate entity did not exist. Which is why I 'assumed,' as you say, from the beginning that both poisoner and murderer were one and the same individual!"

Scene 5

The Morgue. Thursday, June 9. 10:30 a.m.

Mr. Drury Lane mounted the steps of the grimy old City Morgue, a rather expectant expression on his face. Inside

ACT II: SCENE 5

he inquired for Dr. Leo Schilling, the Medical Examiner. After a short delay, he was conducted by an attendant to an autopsy-room.

His nose wrinkled at the strong odor of disinfectant, and he paused at the door. Dr. Schilling's chubby little figure was bent over an autopsy table, intent on exploring the vitals of a desiccated corpse. Lolling in a chair, watching the proceedings with a wholly indifferent air, was a short blondish man of middle age with fat features.

"Come in, Mr. Lane," said Dr. Schilling, without looking up from his gruesome work. *"Wunderlich,* Ingalls, how well preserved this pancreas is. . . . Sit down, Mr. Lane. Meet Dr. Ingalls, our toxicologist. I'll be through with this cadaver in a moment."

"Toxicologist?" asked Lane, shaking hands with the short middle-aged man. "A remarkable coincidence."

"How?" said Dr. Ingalls.

"He's the City man," said the Medical Examiner, busy with the vitals. "You've seen his name in the papers. A great one for publicity, Ingalls."

"Umm," said Dr. Ingalls.

Dr. Schilling yelled something unintelligible, and two men came in and carted off the corpse. "Well," he said, "now we can talk." He stripped off his rubber gloves and went to a basin. "What brings you to the Morgue, Mr. Lane?"

"A most unusual and futile errand, Doctor. I'm endeavoring to track down a smell."

Dr. Ingalls raised an eyebrow. "A smell, my dear sir?"

The Medical Examiner chuckled as he washed his hands. "You've come to the right place, Mr. Lane. The Morgue provides some very fancy smells indeed."

"Scarcely the kind of odor I'm after, Dr. Schilling,"

THE TRAGEDY OF Y

221

smiled Lane. "This is sweet and pleasant. It seemingly has no connection with crime, and yet it may be of major importance in the solution of a murder."

"What odor is it?" inquired Dr. Ingalls. "Perhaps I can help you."

"It's the odor of vanilla."

"Vanilla!" repeated both physicians. Dr. Schilling stared. "You've run across a vanilla odor in the Hatter case, Mr. Lane. That is strange, I must say."

"Yes, Louisa Campion maintains that in the instant of contact with the murderer," explained Lane patiently, "she detected an aroma which at first she described as 'piercing sweet,' and later identified through experiment as that of vanilla. Have you any suggestions?"

"Cosmetics, pastry, perfumes, cookery," said Ingalls rapidly. "A horde of others, none of them particularly interesting."

Lane waved his hand. "Naturally we've exhausted those. I tried to corral the common sources. Aside from those you have just mentioned. I got nowhere with such things as ice cream, candy, extracts, and so on. Nothing in that direction, I'm afraid."

"Flowers?" hazarded the Medical Examiner.

Lane shook his head. "The only trace in that connection is that there is a variety of orchid which exudes a vanilla odor. But that doesn't make sense, and we can find no trace of such a variety in the contemporary history of the case. I thought that you, Dr. Schilling, out of your knowledge of such things, might be able to suggest another source, perhaps more directly connected with the general concept of crime."

The two doctors exchanged glances, and Dr. Ingalls shrugged.

ACT II: SCENE 5

"How about chemicals?" ventured Dr. Schilling. "It seems to me——"

"My dear Doctor," said Lane with a faint smile, "that's why I'm here. I finally thought of the elusive vanilla as a possible chemical. It was natural for me not to consider vanilla in relation to chemistry at first, since the two conceptions are so utterly opposed in spirit, and my knowledge of the sciences is so abysmally small besides. Is there a poison, Dr. Ingalls, which smells like vanilla?"

The toxicologist shook his head. "I can't recall any off hand. Certainly it's no common toxin, or even toxicoid."

"You know," said Dr. Schilling thoughtfully, "vanilla itself has virtually no medicinal value. Oh yes, sometimes it's used as an aromatic stimulant in cases of hysteria or low fever, but . . ."

Lane cocked a suddenly interested eye. Dr. Ingalls looked startled, burst into a laugh, slapped his fat thigh, and rose to go to a desk in the corner. He scribbled a note, chuckling all the while. Then he went to the door. "McMurty!" he cried. An attendant ran up. "Take this to Scott's."

The man hurried off. "Just wait," grinned the toxicologist. "I think I've got something."

The Medical Examiner looked piqued. Lane sat quietly. "Do you know, Dr. Schilling," he said in a calm voice, as if the result of Dr. Ingalls's inspiration were of no interest to him, "I've been kicking myself from one end of The Hamlet to the other for not having thought of sniffing every bottle in York Hatter's laboratory."

"*Ach,* yes, the laboratory. You might have found it there."

"At least it was a chance. When I did think of it, the moment had passed; the fire had destroyed the room and most of the bottles had been smashed." He sighed. "How-

THE TRAGEDY OF Y 223

ever, Hatter's index is still intact, and I may ask you, Dr. Ingalls, to go over it with me and check every detail itemized in the man's files. You might get a lead there. I'm useless, naturally, for that kind of work."

"I don't believe," replied the toxicologist, "that such a procedure will be at all necessary, Mr. Lane."

"I sincerely hope not."

When the messenger returned, he was carrying a small white jar. Lane stood up abruptly as Dr. Ingalls unscrewed the aluminum cap, sniffed, smiled, and proffered the jar. Lane seized it. . . . It was filled with a harmless-looking substance of the general color and consistency of honey. He raised it to his nostrils. . . .

"I think," he said quietly, letting his arm fall, "that you have done us a great service, Dr. Ingalls. Unmistakably a vanilla odor. What is this stuff?"

The toxicologist lighted a cigarette. "It's called Balsam of Peru, Mr. Lane, and the astonishing part of this business is that you can find it in any pharmacy and in thousands of homes."

"Balsam of Peru . . ."

"Yes. A widely used viscid liquid, as you can see, employed chiefly in lotions and salves. Perfectly harmless, by the way."

"Lotion? Salve? For what purpose, Doctor?"

Dr. Schilling smote his forehead a mighty blow. *"Himmel!"* he cried in deep disgust. "What a jackass I am. I should have remembered, although it's years since I've had occasion to think of it. Balsam Peru is used as a base for lotions or salves applied in certain skin troubles. Very common, Mr. Lane."

Lane frowned. "Skin troubles . . . Strange. Is it used in its pure state?"

"Ja, sometimes. Although mostly with other ingredients."

224   ACT II: SCENE 6

"How does that help you?" asked Dr. Ingalls curiously.

"I confess that at the moment . . ." Mr. Drury Lane sat down and spent two minutes in protracted thought. When he looked up, there was doubt in his eyes. "Dr. Schilling, was anything wrong with Mrs. Hatter's skin? You performed the autopsy, and you must have noticed."

"The wrong tree," replied the Medical Examiner emphatically. "Absolutely. Mrs. Hatter's epidermis was as sound as her internal organs, aside from her heart."

"Oh, then she showed no evidences of disease internally?" asked Lane slowly, as if Schilling's response had awakened a forgotten chord in him.

Dr. Schilling looked puzzled. "I can't see . . . No. Autopsy revealed no pathological condition. Didn't run across anything . . . Just what do you mean?"

Lane regarded him steadily. A thoughtful squint came into the Medical Examiner's eye. "I see. No, Mr. Lane, nothing like that superficially. But, of course, I wasn't looking for such things. I wonder . . ."

Mr. Drury Lane shook hands with both physicians and left the autopsy-room. Dr. Schilling stared after him. Then he shrugged and said to the toxicologist: "A queer fellow, hey, Ingalls?"

Scene 6

DR. MERRIAM'S OFFICE. THURSDAY, JUNE 9. 11:45 A.M.

The car drew up twenty minutes later before an old sandstone three-story house on 11th Street between Fifth

THE TRAGEDY OF Y

and Sixth Avenues—a quiet aristocratic old neighborhood a few blocks from the Square. Mr. Drury Lane descended, looked up, caught the neat black-and-white placard in the first-floor window:

Y. MERRIAM, M.D.
VISITING HOURS
11-12 A.M.   6-7 P.M.

and slowly ascended the stone stoop.

He rang the outer bell and a colored maid in uniform opened the door.

"Dr. Merriam?"

"This way, sir."

The maid led him into a half-filled waiting-room directly off the front hall. There was a faintly medicinal smell about the house. The waiting-room contained half a dozen patients, and Lane took his place in a chair by the front window, patiently awaiting his turn.

After an empty hour of waiting a trim nurse opened the sliding doors at the rear of the room and approached him. "You haven't an appointment, have you?"

Lane fumbled for his card case. "No. But I think Dr. Merriam will see me."

He handed her one of his unpretentious personal cards, and her eyes widened. She hurried through the sliding doors and returned a moment later followed by old Dr. Merriam himself, spotless in a long surgical gown.

"Mr. Lane!" said the physician, hurrying forward. "Why didn't you announce yourself before? My nurse informs me you've been sitting here for an hour. Come in, come in."

Lane murmured: "No matter," and followed Dr. Merriam into a large office, from which an examining-room

226 ACT II: SCENE 6

could be seen. The office was like the waiting-room—neat and clean and old-fashioned.

"Sit down, Mr. Lane. What brings you here? Ah—you're not feeling well?"

Lane chuckled. "Not a personal call, Doctor. I'm always in disgustingly robust health. The only sign of senility I betray is that I insist on boasting about how far I can swim. . . ."

"All right, Miss Fulton," said Dr. Merriam abruptly, and the nurse went out, closing the sliding doors tight behind her. "Now, Mr. Lane." He managed, despite the tinge of amiability in his voice, to convey the impression that after all he was a professional man, whose every moment was precious.

"Yes." Lane clasped his hands on the head of his rattan. "Dr. Merriam, have you ever prescribed for any of the Hatter family, or for anyone connected with the Hatter family, a vanilla preparation?"

"Hmm," said the physician. He leaned back in his swivel-chair. "Still on the trail of that vanilla odor, I see. No, I have not."

"You're sure, Doctor? Perhaps you don't remember. Perhaps it was a case of hysteria, or of what I understand is called low fever."

"No!" Dr. Merriam's fingers traced patterns on the blotter before him.

"Then suppose you answer this question. Which of the Hatters received from you, probably within recent months, a prescription for a skin ailment which contained the pharmaceutical ingredient of Balsam Peru?"

Merriam started convulsively, red dyeing his face. Then he sank back again, wonder in his old blue eyes. "It's absolutely imposs——" he began, and stopped. He stood up

THE TRAGEDY OF Y

suddenly and said with anger: "I refuse to answer questions concerning my patients, Mr. Lane, and it's useless for you——"

"But you have answered it already, Doctor," said Lane gently. "It was York Hatter, I suppose?"

The old physician stood still by his desk, staring down at his blotter. "Very well," he said in a low forced voice. "Yes, it was York. About nine months ago. He came to me with a rash on his arms, above the wrists. It was a trifle, although he seemed very conscious of it. I prescribed a salve which contained Balsam of Peru—black balsam, it's also called. For some reason he insisted on my preserving secrecy—he was sensitive about it, he said, and asked me to tell no one, not even his family . . . Balsam Peru. I should have thought of it . . ."

"Yes," said Lane dryly. "So you should; we should have been saved considerable trouble. He never came to you again?"

"Not for that. He consulted me about—other things. I once asked him how his skin was getting along. He said it recurred periodically, and he applied the salve I had prescribed. Made his own prescriptions, I think—he had a pharmacy degree. And bandaged his arms himself, too."

"Himself?"

Dr. Merriam looked annoyed. "Well, he said that his daughter-in-law, Martha, had once walked in on him while he was applying the salve; and he was forced to tell her what was the matter with his arms. She was sympathetic, it seems, and after that she helped him bandage his arms once in a while."

"Interesting," murmured Lane. "There was no in-law problem as far as Hatter and Martha were concerned, then."

ACT II: SCENE 6

"I don't believe so. He didn't care if she knew, he told me; she was the only one in the house, he said, that he'd trust with a secret anyway."

"Hmm . . . Martha. He and she were really the only outsiders, in a sense, living in the house at that time." Lane stopped, and then said swiftly: "What caused York Hatter's skin ailment, Doctor?"

The physician blinked. "Blood condition. Really, Mr. Lane——"

"Would you mind giving me a duplicate of the original prescription?"

"Not at all," replied Merriam with relief. He reached for a pad of prescription blanks and wrote laboriously with a large blunt pen as old-fashioned as his office. When he had finished, Lane took the scribbled note from him and glanced over it. "Nothing poisonous, I fancy?"

"Of course not!"

"Merely a precautionary question, Doctor," murmured Lane, placing the prescription in his wallet. "And now, if you will let me see your record card on York Hatter . . ."

"Eh?" Dr. Merriam blinked again, very rapidly, and a tide of red surged into his waxen ears. "My record card?" he shouted. "This is outrageous! Asking me to disclose intimate details about my patients. . . . Why, I never heard of such a thing! I sh——"

"Dr. Merriam, let's understand each other. I thoroughly appreciate and commend your attitude. Still, you are aware that I'm here as an accredited representative of the law, that my purpose is only to apprehend a murderer."

"Yes, but I can't——"

"There may be other murders. It is within your province to assist the police, and you may have valuable facts at your command which we as yet do not know. Then where is your professional secrecy?"

THE TRAGEDY OF Y 229

"Can't do it," muttered the physician. "Against the ethics of the medical profession."

"Hang the ethics of the medical profession." Lane's smile dropped from him. "Shall I tell *you* why you can't tell *me?* Professional ethics! Do you think I'm as blind as I'm deaf?"

Something like alarm scurried into the old man's eyes and was hidden by the instant dropping of his veined lids. "What on earth . . ." he faltered. "What do you mean?"

"I mean precisely this. You refuse to open the Hatter case histories to me because you're afraid I will discover the pathological skeleton in the Hatter closet."

Dr. Merriam did not raise his eyelids.

Lane relaxed and the faint smile returned; not a smile of triumph, but of sadness. "Really, Doctor, it is all so hideously plain. Why Louisa Campion was born blind and dumb, and with a disposition toward deafness. . . ."

Dr. Merriam paled.

"Why Barbara Hatter is a genius. . . . Why Conrad Hatter is subject to maniacal rages, why he drinks and wastes his life away. . . . Why Jill Hatter is reckless and beautiful, but innately vicious, a harpy. . . ."

"Oh, stop, for God's sake," cried Dr. Merriam. "I've known them so long—seen them grow up—fought for them, for their right to live as decent human beings . . ."

"I know, Doctor," said Lane softly. "You've apotheosized the most Spartan virtues of your profession. At the same time, humanity itself dictates heroic measures. 'Diseases desperate grown,' as Claudius says, 'by desperate appliance are reliev'd.'"

Dr. Merriam shrank into his chair.

"It didn't take much," continued Lane in the same gentle voice. "I saw why they're all half mad, wild, eccentric; why poor York Hatter committed suicide. Of course, the

ACT II: SCENE 6

root of the trouble was Emily Hatter. I have no doubt now that she caused the death of her first husband, Thomas Campion, by infecting him before he grasped his danger; that she infected her second husband, Hatter, and transmitted the invidious germ to her children, and to her children's children. . . . It's horribly essential that we see eye to eye in this matter, Doctor, and forget for the period of the emergency all consideration of ethics."

"Yes."

Lane sighed. "Dr. Schilling found no traces of it in his autopsy, so I presume you approximated a cure?"

"When it was too late to save the others," muttered Merriam. He rose to his feet without another word and walked heavily to a locked cabinet in a corner of the office. Unlocking it, he searched a file and brought out a number of index cards of large size. These he handed silently to Lane and sat down again, shaken and pale; and during the entire period in which Lane read through the various cards he did not utter a sound.

The notes were voluminous, and all contained strikingly similar features. As Lane read, he nodded from time to time, the expression of sadness deepening on his smooth young face. Mrs. Hatter's case history traced her condition from the time when Dr. Merriam took her in charge, thirty years before, when Louisa Campion, Barbara, and Conrad Hatter had already been born, until the time of her death. The record was depressing, and Lane put it aside with a frown.

He riffled the cards until he came to York Hatter's. The record here was less detailed, and after a hasty glance through the bulk of the notes, Lane concentrated on the last entry, dated a month before Hatter's disappearance the previous year:

THE TRAGEDY OF Y

Age 67 . . . Wght 155, good . . . Hght 5′ 5″ . . .
Blood-pressure 190 . . . Cardiac cond. poor . . . Skin
clear . . . Wassermann—1 plus.

Louisa Campion's card, which Lane consulted next, bore
the date of May fourteenth of the current year at the last
notation:

Age 40 . . . Wght 148 (over) . . . Hght 5′ 4″ . . .
Incipient pectoris . . . Eyes, ears, larynx—no hope?
. . . Increasing neurosis . . . Wass.—neg. *Watch
heart* . . . Diet # 14 prescr.

Conrad Hatter's last visit to Dr. Merriam had been,
according to his card, on April eighteenth of the previous
year:

Age 31 . . . Wght 175 (bad) . . . Hght 5′ 10″ . . .
Gen. Cond. poor . . . Liver bad . . . Heart fatty . . .
Pronounced alcoholism . . . Wassermann—neg . . .
Worse than last visit . . . Quiet life prescr., altho
useless.

Barbara Hatter, from the last entry on her card, had
visited Dr. Merriam early in December last:

Age 36 . . . Wght 127 (under) . . . Hght 5′ 7½″ . . .
Anaemia worse . . . Prescr. liver . . . Gen. cond.
fair . . . Good if liv. relieves anae . . . Wassermann—
neg . . . Marriage would help.

Jill Hatter, February twenty-fourth, current year:

Age 25 . . . Wght 135 (sl. under) . . . Hght 5′ 5½″
. . . Cond. def. rundown . . . Try nerve tonic . . .
Incipient palpitation? . . . Slight alcoh . . . Wisdom
tooth abscess lower jaw, right—attend . . . Wass.—neg.

Act II: Scene 6

Jackie Hatter, May first, current year:

> Age 13 . . . Wght 80 . . . Hght 4′ 8″ . . . Watch carefully . . . Late puberty . . . Subnor. physic . . . Wass.—neg.

Billy Hatter, May first, current year:

> Age 4 . . . Wght 32 . . . Hght 2′ 10″ . . . Heart, lungs splendid . . . Seems normal, robust in all respects . . . *Watch.*

* * *

"Rather sad," remarked Mr. Drury Lane as he placed the cards together again and returned them to Dr. Merriam. "I see that you have no record of Martha Hatter."

"No," replied Merriam dully. "She was confined both times by another physician, and somehow never calls upon me, although it's true she brings the children to me for periodic examination."

"Then she knows?"

"Yes. Is it any wonder that she hates and despises her husband?" He rose; evidently the interview had been distasteful to him, and there was something determined now in the set of his old chin that caused Lane to rise also and pick up his hat.

"Have you any theory concerning the attempted poisonings of Louisa Campion and the murder of Mrs. Hatter, Doctor?"

"I should not be surprised if you discovered the murderer and poisoner to be any one of the Hatter family," Merriam said in a toneless voice. He plodded around his desk and placed his hand on the door. "You may be able to

The Tragedy of Y

233

catch, try, and convict the guilty one, Mr. Lane. But let me tell you this." They stared into each other's eyes for the space of a heart-beat. "No man of science or common sense would for an instant hold a single one of the Hatters morally responsible for the crime. Their brains have been twisted by a horrible physical inheritance. And they'll all come to a bad end."

"I sincerely trust not," said Mr. Drury Lane, and took his leave.

Scene 7

The Hatter House. Thursday, June 9. 3:00 p.m.

Lane spent the next two hours alone. He felt the need of solitude. He was irritated with himself. Why should he take this remarkable case so personally? he demanded of himself. After all, his duty, if he had a duty, was to the cause of law. Or was it? Perhaps justice demanded more of him than . . .

He heckled himself constantly as Dromio drove him uptown to the Friars' Club. His conscience would not let him alone. Even in the peace of his favorite corner at the Club, lunching by himself, mechanically acknowledging the salutations of friends, acquaintances, and ex-colleagues of the theater he could not bring himself to a state of mental ease. His face grew continually longer as he toyed with his food. Not even English mutton tasted good today.

After luncheon, as a moth is drawn to fire, Mr. Drury Lane commanded Dromio to drive him downtown to the Hatter house.

234　Act II: Scene 7

The house was quiet, for which he gave silent thanks. The loutish face of George Arbuckle, the houseman, glowered at him as he stepped through the vestibule into the hall.

"Is Inspector Thumm here?"

"Upstairs in Mr. Perry's room."

"Ask him to come to the laboratory."

Lane thoughtfully climbed the stairs. The door to the laboratory was open, and Detective Mosher was sitting limply on the work-bench near the windows.

Inspector Thumm's squashed nose appeared, and he grunted a greeting. Mosher jumped to his feet, but Thumm waved him aside and stood restless-eyed watching Lane, who was busy rummaging in the filing cabinet. He straightened up in a moment with the index file which contained the inventory of the laboratory's supplies.

"Ah," he said. "Here we are. One moment, Inspector."

He sat down in the half-charred swivel-chair by the old rolltop desk and began to examine the index cards. He gave each one a casual glance, and passed to the next with scarcely a pause. At the thirtieth card, however, he exclaimed softly and stopped.

Thumm leaned over his shoulder to see what had pleased him so. The card bore the characters: #30; and beneath the numbers the words Agar-Agar. But Lane seemed interested in the fact that through Agar-Agar a neat pen-line had been drawn, and beneath it the words Balsam Peru had been substituted.

"What the devil's that?" demanded Thumm.

"Patience, Inspector."

He rose and went to the corner of the room where the glass débris had been swept together after the explosion. He rooted about in the fragments, seeming absorbed in ex-

THE TRAGEDY OF Y

235

amining the bottles and jars which had been least damaged. Unsuccessful in his search, he proceeded to the flame-licked shelves and looked up at the middle section of the top one. Not a single bottle or jar remained standing there. He nodded, returned to the pile, selected several bottles and jars which were intact, and carefully arranged them in the center of the middle top section.

"Excellent," he said, brushing his hands, "excellent. And now, Inspector, may I send Mosher on an errand?"

"Sure."

"Mosher, fetch Martha Hatter."

Mosher bobbed up, all a-grin, and lumbered out of the laboratory. He returned promptly, preceded by Martha, closed the door behind him, and set his back against it in the approved sergeant-at-arms posture.

Martha Hatter stood hesitating before Thumm and Lane, searching both men's faces. She looked more wretched than ever, deep purple shadows under her eyes, her nose pinched, her lips tight, her complexion pale and pasty.

"Please sit down, Mrs. Hatter," said Lane pleasantly. "A matter of information . . . I understand that your father-in-law was afflicted with a certain skin ailment?"

She paused in the act of seating herself, startled. "Why—" Then she sank into the swivel-chair. "Yes, that's true. But how did you find out? I thought nobody——"

"You thought nobody but yourself, York Hatter, and Dr. Merriam knew. A simple matter . . . You helped Mr. Hatter secretly to apply his salve and bandage his arms?"

"What the devil is this?" muttered Thumm.

"I beg your pardon, Inspector. . . . Yes, Mrs. Hatter?"

"Yes, I did. Sometimes he called me in to help him."

"What was the name of the salve, Mrs. Hatter?"

"I really don't recall the name."

ACT II: SCENE 7

"Do you know where Mr. Hatter kept it?"

"Oh, yes! It was in one of the regular jars over there...." She rose and went quickly to the shelving. Standing before the middle section she reached on tiptoes and just managed to take down one of the jars which Lane had set on that part of the shelf not long before. Lane's eyes were fixed on her; he observed that she had taken the jar from the exact center of the section.

She handed him the jar, but he shook his head. "Please unscrew the cap and smell the contents of the jar, Mrs. Hatter."

She obeyed wonderingly. "Oh, no," she cried at once, as she sniffed. "This isn't the salve. It looked like loose honey, for one thing, and it smelled like——" There was dead instantaneous silence as she chopped the sentence in half. Her teeth appeared and bit deeply into her lower lip. An expression of appalling fear spread over her careworn face, and she dropped the jar. It shattered on the floor.

Thumm was staring at her intently. "Well, well?" he said hoarsely. "What did it smell like, Mrs. Hatter?"

"Yes, Mrs. Hatter?" said Lane softly.

She shook her head like a mechanical doll. "I don't . . . remember."

"Like vanilla, Mrs. Hatter?"

She began to back out of the room, keeping her fascinated gaze on Lane. He sighed, straightened up, patted her arm in a fatherly way, waved Mosher aside, and held the door open for her. She walked out with the slow step of a somnambulist.

"Jeeze!" shouted Thumm, leaping into motion. "Skin stuff—vanilla! This is hot, man, hot!"

Mr. Drury Lane went to the fireplace and stood in a stooped attitude, his back to the empty grate. "Yes," he

THE TRAGEDY OF Y 237

said thoughtfully, "I believe we have finally discovered the source of the odor Miss Campion testified to, Inspector."

Thumm was excited; he paced up and down, talking more to himself than to Lane. "Great! What a break . . . Come to think of it, this Perry business . . . Good God! Vanilla—and the salve . . . What do you think of it, Mr. Lane?"

"I think you were ill-advised to put Mr. Perry in prison, Inspector," smiled Lane.

"Oh, that! Yep, I'm beginning to think so, too. Yes, sir," Thumm went on with a crafty look in his eyes, "I'm beginning to see daylight."

"Eh?" said Lane sharply. "What's that?"

"Oh, no, you don't," grinned the Inspector. "You've had your inning, Mr. Lane, and I think I'm entitled to mine. Not givin' away anything yet. But for the first time in this blasted case I've got something real to do."

Lane considered him steadily. "You've formulated a theory?"

"In a way, in a way," chuckled Thumm. "Just hit me. One of those inspirations you read about, Mr. Lane. Swell! Cripes, if it's only possible . . ." He lumbered to the door. "Mosher," he said sternly, "you and Pink are responsible for this room. Understand?" He cast a glance at the windows; they had been boarded up. "Don't leave it for a second. Remember!"

"Okay, Inspector."

"I'll have your badge if you slip up. Going my way, Mr. Lane?"

"Not knowing which way yours is, Inspector, I think not. . . . By the way, before you go—have you a tape-measure?"

Thumm stopped short at the door and stared. "Tape-

238   ACT II: SCENE 7

measure? What the deuce do you want that for?" He produced a folding pocket-rule from his vest and handed it to Lane.

Smiling, Lane took it and once more approached the shelves. He flipped the rule open and measured the distance between the lower edge of the top shelf and the upper edge of the second shelf. "Hmm," he murmured. "Six inches . . . Good, good! And an inch for the thickness of the shelf . . ." He caressed his jaw, nodded, and then, with a peculiar expression of mingled gloom and satisfaction, folded the rule and returned it to Thumm.

Thumm's glee seemed to have departed all at once. "Come to think of it," he growled, "you said you had *two* leads yesterday. Vanilla stink was one—is this the second?"

"Eh? Oh, you mean this measuring? Scarcely." Lane shook his head absently. "I've still to investigate the other."

The Inspector hesitated, tottering on the brink of a question, then, shaking his head like a man who has decided to let well enough alone, he took his departure.

Mosher looked on indifferently.

Lane with lagging steps left the laboratory in Thumm's wake.

*   *   *

He peered into Miss Smith's bedroom next door; it was empty. Sauntering farther up the hall, he paused at a door in the southeast corner and knocked; no one came to the door.

He descended the stairs, met no one, and proceeded through the rear to the garden court. Despite the chill in the air, Miss Smith was seated there reading a book under the large umbrella beside Louisa Campion, who lay in a deck-chair, apparently asleep. Nearby, squatting in the grass and peering intently down, were Jackie and Billy,

THE TRAGEDY OF Y — 239

for once playing quietly; they were watching an ant colony, and both seemed fascinated by the busy scurryings of the insects.

"Miss Smith," said Lane, "can you tell me where I may find Miss Barbara Hatter?"

"Oh!" gasped Miss Smith, dropping her book. "I'm sorry; you startled me. I think Miss Hatter went out with the Inspector's permission, but I don't know where, or when she'll get back."

"I see." He looked down at a tug on his trousers; Billy, his fresh little face rosy, was craning up, shouting: "Gimme candy, gimme candy!"

"Hello, Billy," said Lane gravely.

"Babs went to the jail, Babs went to the jail to see Mr. Perry!" cried thirteen-year-old Jackie, pulling experimentally at the rattan.

"It's possible," said Miss Smith with a sniff.

Lane gently disengaged himself from the clutches of the boys—he seemed in no mood for play—and made his way through the alley around the house to Waverly Place. At the curb, where his car and Dromio waited, he turned about with a sick look in his eyes. Then he climbed heavily into the car.

Scene 8

BARBARA'S WORKROOM. FRIDAY, JUNE 10. 11:00 A.M.

The dangerous calm prevailing in the Mad Hatters' hutch still prevailed the next morning, when Mr. Drury Lane returned to the house. The Inspector was not there;

240   ACT II: SCENE 8

he had not been there, it seemed, since his departure the previous afternoon, according to the Arbuckles. Yes, Miss Barbara was at home.

"She's had breakfast served in her room," said Mrs. Arbuckle sourly. "Hasn't been down yet, and here it is eleven o'clock."

"Please ask her if I may see her."

Mrs. Arbuckle lifted an expressive eyebrow, but tramped upstairs obediently. When she returned, she said: "It's all right, she says. Go right up."

Lane found the poetess in the room at which he had knocked the previous afternoon. She was smoking a cigarette in a long jade holder; with legs drawn up she was perched on a window-seat overlooking the Park. "Come in, and please pardon my *déshabille*."

"It's charming."

Barbara was dressed in a silken mandarin robe, her faintly golden hair streaming over her shoulders. "Don't mind the condition of my room, Mr. Lane," she said smiling. "I'm a notoriously sloppy person, and it's not been tidied yet. Perhaps we'd better go into my workroom."

She led the way through half-open draperies to a tiny wing of the bedroom. It was eremitic in its furnishings— a large flat-topped desk, bookshelves helter-skelter about the walls, a typewriter, and a chair. "I've been scribbling all morning," she explained. "Do sit down in that chair, Mr. Lane. I'll perch on the desk."

"Thank you. A delightful room, Miss Hatter, and quite what I imagined."

"Really?" She laughed. "People say the most outrageous things about this house—and me. I've heard that my bedroom has mirrored walls, floor, and ceiling—a voluptuary's

THE TRAGEDY OF Y   241

refinement, you see! That I take a new lover every week; that I'm sexless; that I drink three quarts of black coffee and a gallon of gin a day. . . . Actually, as your very keen eyes can discern, Mr. Lane, I'm a most mediocre person. A poetess without a vice, despite the rumors!"

Lane sighed. "Miss Hatter, I've come to put a very peculiar question to you."

"Indeed?" The pleasure and serenity disappeared. "And what is that, Mr. Lane?" She picked up an enormous pencil sharpened to an enormous point and began to scribble meaninglessly on the desk.

"When I first met you, at the time of your little talk with Inspector Thumm, District Attorney Bruno, and myself, you mentioned something which has persisted in my brain almost without reason. For a long time now I have been intending to ask you more about it, Miss Hatter."

"Yes?" she said in a low voice.

Lane looked earnestly into her eyes. *"Did your father ever write a detective story?"*

She stared at him with the utmost astonishment, the cigarette drooping from her lips. The astonishment was genuine, he saw at once; it was as if she had expected almost with dread an entirely different question. "Why . . ." She laughed. "How amazing. Mr. Lane! You *are* like that lovable old Sherlock in whose adventures I used to wallow when I was a child. . . . Yes, father did. But how on earth did you know?"

Mr. Drury Lane stared a moment longer, and then he relaxed with a sibilant sigh. "So," he said slowly. "I was right." A world of inexplicable woe filled his eyes, and he dropped them quickly to conceal what was in them. She looked at him with a fading smile. "You said at that time that your father had dabbled in fiction. As for the partic-

ACT II: SCENE 8

ularity of my question—certain facts pointed to it as a rather fateful possibility."

She crushed her cigarette. "I'm afraid I don't quite understand," she said. "But I—I trust you, Mr. Lane. . . . Some time ago—in the early fall of last year—father came to me rather sheepishly and inquired if I could recommend a good literary agent. I suggested my own. I was rather astonished—was he writing something?"

She paused, and Lane muttered: "Go on, please."

"At first father was shy. But I urged him, and finally, when I promised to keep it secret, he confessed that he'd been trying his hand at planning a detective story."

"Planning?" asked Lane quickly.

"That's what he said, as I recall. He had prepared his ideas in outline form. He thought he had concocted something clever, and he wanted to consult someone in the book field to see what the chances were of disposing of it when it was finished."

"Yes, yes. I understand; everything clarifies. Did he say anything else, Miss Hatter?"

"No. Really, I wasn't too—too interested, Mr. Lane," she murmured, "and I'm ashamed of it now." She stared at her pencil. "Although I was rather amused at this sudden creative urge on the part of father, who always of course was severely scientific in his inclinations. That was the last I heard of it."

"Have you ever mentioned this to anyone?"

She shook her head. "The matter had entirely slipped my mind until you asked me the question a moment ago."

"Your father enjoined secrecy," remarked Lane. "Is it possible that he told your mother or the others about it?"

"I'm sure he did not. If he had, I should have heard about it." She sighed. "Jill, who is rather a rattle-brain, would have made it the butt of all her conversation, I

The Tragedy of Y 243

know, if she knew. Conrad would have sneered at it to the rest of us; and father, I'm certain, did not tell mother."

"Why are you so certain?"

She clenched her fist and stared at it. "Because father and mother hadn't been on more than speaking terms for years, Mr. Lane," she said in a low tone.

"I see. Pardon . . . Did you ever actually see a manuscript?"

"No. I don't believe there was one—merely a central idea in outline form, as I said."

"Have you a notion where he might have kept the outline?"

She shrugged helplessly. "Not the faintest, unless somewhere in that Paracelsian laboratory of his."

"And the idea itself—you say he remarked that it was clever. What was the idea, Miss Hatter?"

"I can't say. He told me nothing of the story."

"And did Mr. Hatter consult your agent about the detective story?"

"I'm sure he did not."

"How can you be sure?"

"I asked my agent if father had visited him, and he said no."

Mr. Drury Lane rose. "You've been of great assistance, Miss Hatter. Thank you."

Scene 9

The Laboratory. Friday, June 10. 3:30 p.m.

Hours later, when the house was deserted, Mr. Lane quietly mounted the stairs to the attic floor, climbed the

ACT II: SCENE 9

small flight leading to the trapdoor, pushed it up, and stepped out onto the slippery roof. A detective, wrapped in a slicker and holding an umbrella over his head, was miserably propped against the chimney. Lane greeted him pleasantly and, ignoring the rain on his clothes, peered into the darkness of the chimney orifice. He could see nothing, although he knew that with a flashlight he should be able to observe the top of the dividing wall between death-room and laboratory. He stood there thoughtfully for a moment, then waved farewell to the detective, and descended through the trapdoor by which he had come.

On the first floor he paused to look about. The doors to the bedrooms were all closed; the corridor was deserted. With a quick movement of his wrist he twisted the doorknob and entered the laboratory. Detective Mosher looked up from the newspaper he was reading.

"Well, well!" said Mosher heartily. "If it ain't Mr. Lane. Glad you came. This is the lousiest job I've ever been detailed to."

"No doubt," murmured Lane; his eyes were roving.

"It's good to see a decent human face, is what I say," went on Mosher confidentially. "It's been quiet as the grave here—haw, haw!"

"Indeed . . . Mosher, you may do something for me. Or rather for your colleague on the roof."

"Who—Krause?" demanded Mosher, mystified.

"I believe that is his name. Please join him on the roof. He seems sadly in need of companionship."

"Oh." Mosher shuffled his feet. "Well, now, I don't know, Mr. Lane. Chief's orders were strict—I'm not to leave this room."

"I'll relieve you of all responsibility, Mosher," said Lane with a trace of impatience. "Please now! And you might

THE TRAGEDY OF Y   245

be particularly watchful up there. For the next few minutes I want no interruption of any kind. If anyone attempts to explore the roof, scare him off. No hostile move, remember."

"Well," said Mosher doubtfully, "all right, Mr. Lane." He trudged out of the laboratory.

Lane's gray-green eyes glittered. He followed Mosher out into the corridor, waited until the man had disappeared upstairs, then opened the door to the death-room adjoining and went in. The room was empty. He crossed swiftly to the windows overlooking the garden, saw that they were closed and latched, returned to the door, set the bolt from the inside, ran out into the corridor, slammed the door shut and tried it. It was locked. Then he sprang back into the laboratory, bolted the door from the inside, peeled off his coat, rolled up his sleeves, and set to work.

At first the fireplace seemed to fascinate him. He touched the mantel, poked his head under the stone arch, withdrew, retreated. . . . He hesitated for a moment, and looked around. The rolltop desk was badly burnt. The steel filing cabinet he had examined before. The half-consumed dresser? Improbable.

His chin set, he stooped and without hesitation passed under the outer wall of the fireplace, straightening up inside between the outer wall and the firebrick wall which served as the back of the fireplace. This partition of ancient brick, black and smooth to the touch, ended almost on a level with Lane's head, and Lane was a trifle over six feet tall. He took a small pencil-flashlight from his vest pocket and sprayed its tiny ray about the bricks of the dividing wall. Whatever he hoped to discover by this cursory examination was fated to remain unfound; the bricks were divided all over the wall by sturdy lines. Nevertheless, he

246 ACT II: SCENE 9

tapped and prodded each brick, looking for signs of a loose one. At last, satisfied that on the laboratory side of the brick wall at least there was nothing to be found, he straightened up and measured the dividing wall with his eye.

Not insurmountable, he reflected, even to an aging gentleman. Whereupon he placed the pencil-flash on top of the wall, gripped the edge, and heaved himself up. The agility with which he clambered up and over to land on the bedroom side of the firebrick wall was remarkable. For all his sixty years, his muscles were as resilient as a young man's. . . . As he passed over the wall, he felt on his bare head and cheeks the soft rain coming down the chimney.

On the bedroom side he repeated his search for a loose brick, with as little success. By this time a frown had appeared to crease the skin between his eyes. He hoisted himself again to the top of the firebrick wall; but this time he sat there a-straddle, like a man on a horse, and flashed his light about.

Almost at once he stiffened, and the frown vanished. For there, about a foot above the top of the wall, in the side of the chimney itself, was one brick obviously loose: the mortar was chipped around it, and it projected from its neighbors slightly. Lane's fingers clamped on the small projection like iron, and he began to pull. He almost lost his balance and toppled to the floor; for the brick gave easily, emerging with a faint scraping sound. He placed the brick carefully on the top of the wall between his legs and focused his light inside the dark rectangular orifice left by the brick.

In the hole, which had been painfully chopped out and enlarged at its innermost end, something white glowed!

Lane's fingers dipped in. When they reappeared, there

THE TRAGEDY OF Y 247

was a wad of sooty, smudged, and yellow-white paper, folded many times, between them.

One rapid glance at the paper, and Lane had stowed it in his hip pocket and stooped to explore the interior of the hole again. Something glinted in the ray of the flashlight. He probed, and in an extra orifice chipped into the brick at the rear of the cache, he found a tiny test-tube tightly corked.

His eyes were dark as he took it out of the hole and examined it more closely. It was unlabeled and full of a whitish liquid. In the hole, too, as he was careful to ascertain, lay a rubber-capped liquid-dropper as well. But this he did not touch. Instead, without returning the loose brick to its place, he eased himself off the firebrick wall onto the laboratory floor of the fireplace, reached for the vial of white liquid and, stooping, crawled out in the laboratory.

His eyes were coldly green, more green than gray now, as if he were suffering pain.

Gloomy, grimed, he dropped the vial into one of the pockets of his discarded coat, went to one of the charred work-tables, took the wad of sooty paper out of his hip pocket and slowly unfolded it. . . . Unfolded, it turned out to be several sheets of thin cheap typewriter paper, covered with meticulous chirography. He began to read.

*   *   *

It was a notable moment in the investigation of the Hatter problem, as Lane was wont to point out long after. But from the expression on his face as he read the document, one would have said that he was more depressed than elated by his discovery. Certainly, as he read his face darkened; he nodded his head glumly from time to time, as if in confirmation of some already held conclusion; in one

ACT II: SCENE 9

place an expression of pure amazement swept over his features. But these temporary manifestations passed quickly, and when he had finished he seemed reluctant to make a movement, as if by sitting utterly still he could cheat time and events and the inevitable tragedy which loomed ahead of him. But then he blinked and, finding pencil and paper in the litter about him, began a swift writing. He wrote for a long time, painstakingly copying the words of the document he had found. When he had concluded his task, he rose, tucked both copy and original in his hip pockets, put on his coat, brushed the dirt off his trousers, and then opened the laboratory door. He looked out into the corridor. It was still silent and empty.

He stood waiting for long moments, quiet as death.

Finally he heard movement downstairs. He stirred and went to the railing of the staircase. Mrs. Arbuckle, he observed by peering between banister and floor, was waddling toward the kitchen.

"Mrs. Arbuckle," he called in a soft voice.

She started and looked up with a jerk. "Who— Oh, it's you! I didn't know you were still here. Yes, sir?"

"Would you be kind enough to fetch a bun and—yes, a glass of milk for me from your kitchen?" Lane asked pleasantly.

She stood stock-still, staring up at him. Then she nodded sulkily and waddled on out of sight. He waited in the same unnatural motionlessness. She returned shortly with a tray, on which were a jelly-bun and a cup of milk. She trudged up the stairs and handed the tray to him over the railing.

"Milk's getting low," she snapped. "Can't spare but a drop."

"It's quite sufficient, thank you." He picked up the cup and began to sip the milk slowly as she grunted down the

THE TRAGEDY OF Y 249

stairs with the same belligerent air. But the instant she reached the bottom of the staircase and disappeared in the corridor going toward the rear, Lane ceased his sipping and darted back into the laboratory, bolting the door securely behind him again.

Now he knew exactly what he wanted. He set the tray down on the work-table and searched in the floor closet beneath the shelves. Here less damage had been done, due to the protection of the closed doors and the nearness of closet to floor; and he very soon found what he was seeking. He straightened up with a tiny test-tube and cork, the duplicate of the one he had discovered in the hole. After washing it under the tap of one of the laboratory tables, he poured into the empty vial, with the utmost cautiousness, a quantity of milk from the cup equal to a minim to the quantity of white liquid in the test-tube from the hole.

When he was satisfied that the two vials looked alike, he stoppered the vialful of milk, poured the rest of the contents of the cup into the table sink, climbed back to straddle the firebrick wall in the fireplace, and thrust the vial of milk into the spot where he had found the original vial. He did not disturb the dropper in the hole. The yellowish, refolded wad of paper he then restored to its former position, replaced the loose brick as he had found it, and descended from his perch.

He brushed his hands together, distastefully. His features were set in etching-lines.

Suddenly, as if recalling something temporarily forgotten, he unlatched the laboratory door, returned, and climbed over the dividing wall of the fireplace again, dropping into the bedroom. Here he unlatched the bedroom door and went into the hall and through the now unlocked door back into the laboratory.

ACT II: SCENE 9

"Mosher!" he called guardedly up the chimney. "Mosher!"

The rain felt cool on his hot face.

"Yes, Mr. Lane?" came Mosher's muffled voice. Lane looked up and saw a blob dimly framed in the gray of the chimney opening.

"Come down at once. Krause is to remain on the roof."

"Sure!" said Mosher heartily, and his face disappeared. The man himself barged into the laboratory a few moments later. "Here I am," he said with an expansive smile. His suit was soaked with tiny beads of fine rain, but he did not seem to mind. "Get what you were after?"

"Ah—never mind that, Mosher," said Lane. He was standing in the center of the floor, feet solidly planted. "Did anyone try to get to the roof, the chimney?"

"Not a living soul. Nothin' stirring, Mr. Lane." Mosher's eyes goggled. For Lane's right hand appeared from behind his back and carried something to his mouth . . . It was, as Mosher perceived with astonishment, a bun, and Lane was thoughtfully munching on it just as if there were no such thing as poison in this Borgian household.

His left hand hidden in his coat pocket, however, tightly clutched the vial of white liquid.

ACT III

*"Let me embrace thee, sour adversity,
For wise men say it is the wisest course."*

Scene 1

PoLICE HEADQUARTERS. FRIDAY, JUNE 10. 5 P.M.

Mr. Drury Lane emerged from the Hatter house that cold rain-washed June afternoon looking ten years older than when he had gone in. Had Inspector Thumm been present, he doubtless would have wondered why Lane, apparently on the verge of success, should seem more upset than if he had met failure at every turn. It was not like him. He presented the appearance of a man of forty only because he had mastered himself early in life and sublimated the tendency to worry until it disappeared. Yet now he looked like one whose serenity, the faith of a long lifetime, had been irremediably shattered. He climbed into his car an old man.

Wearily he said to Dromio: "Police Headquarters," and sank back against the cushions. And all the way to the big gray building on Centre Street the expression of sadness and responsibility and a tragic realization of something immensely important did not leave his face.

Yet, because he was what he was, when he mounted the steps of Police Headquarters, he appeared the old Drury

ACT III: SCENE I

Lane, pleasant, gentle, unruffled, and quite confident and springy in his bearing. The lieutenant on duty at the desk recognized him and sent a sergeant with him as escort to Inspector Thumm's office.

It seemed to be a day for the doldrums, for he found the Inspector, ugly as life, sulking in his swivel-chair and regarding a dead cigar between his thick fingers. Something like pleasure illuminated the Inspector's face when he saw Lane. He squeezed Lane's hands earnestly. "I'm damned glad to see you. What's up, Mr. Lane?" Lane waved one hand and sat down with a sigh. "Any news? This place is deader than the Morgue."

Lane nodded. "News that should interest you and Mr. Bruno enormously."

"No kidding!" exclaimed Thumm. "Don't tell me you've found out that——" He stopped to eye Lane suspiciously. "You haven't run down the Perry trail, have you?"

"Perry trail?" Lane frowned. "I'm afraid I don't quite understand."

"That's a relief." The Inspector shoved the dead cigar into his mouth and chewed contemplatively. "We've uncovered something live this time. You know I had Perry released yesterday. Barbara Hatter was raising a fuss— she'd engaged a big lawyer—and after all . . . It didn't hurt, because he's being watched."

"For what reason? Are you still under the impression that Edgar Perry is connected with these crimes, Inspector?"

"What would you think? What would anyone think? Remember the set-up—Perry's real name is Campion, he's Louisa's half-brother, and his father was Emily Hatter's first husband. All right. When I spilled what I knew about him to the mug, he admitted it, but he shut up like a

THE TRAGEDY OF Y

clam. That's where I stood. But I didn't stop. I dug a little deeper. And what do you suppose I found out, Mr. Lane?"

"I haven't the faintest notion," smiled Lane.

"That Tom Campion, Perry's father and the old she-devil's first husband, died of——"

He stopped abruptly. Mr. Drury Lane's smile had faded, and a glint had appeared in the gray-green eyes.

"Then you knew," grumbled Thumm.

"Not from investigation, Inspector. But I was morally certain." Lane rested his head on the back of the chair. "I see your point. Mr. Edgar Perry Campion is now a very live issue, eh?"

"Well, why not?" said Thumm in an aggrieved tone. "That's the story, ain't it? Emily was responsible for Perry's dad's death—indirectly, sure, and probably not on purpose. But she killed him just as surely as if she'd stuck a knife into him. Nasty business all around. But now we've got motive, Mr. Lane—something we didn't have before."

"And it is . . . ?"

"Listen. You're a man of the world. When a man's father dies from an infection caused by a stepmother . . . well, I can understand that man wanting to get revenge on her if it takes the rest of his life to do it."

"Elementary psychology, Inspector, especially when so brutal a thing as this is involved. Of course." Lane sat musing. "I completely grasp your uneasiness. The man had motive and opportunity. And the intelligence to carry out a clever plan. But there's no proof."

"That's what we're up against."

"At the same time," remarked Lane, "I can't bring myself to think of Edgar Perry as a man of action. A man of plan, yes. But it seems to me that he would weaken and shrink from violence at the last moment."

ACT III: SCENE I

"Too deep for me," scoffed the Inspector. "Listen, Mr. Lane. Down here where we're just cops we don't worry about what a man *would* do. We're more concerned with what the facts show he *did* do."

"I must insist, Inspector," said Lane with calm emphasis. "Human conduct is merely the outgrowth of human psychology. Have you caught Mr. Edgar Perry Campion attempting to commit suicide?"

"Suicide, did you say? Hell, no! Why should he do a fool thing like that? Yes, if he's caught with the goods . . ."

Lane shook his head. "No, Inspector. Had Edgar Perry committed murder, being the man he is he would at once have taken his own life. You remember Hamlet? A man of indecision, of fluctuating emotions. Yet with the intelligence to conceive a plan. Hamlet wavers, torn between self-torment and self-incrimination, while violence and intrigue rage about him. But remember this: vacillating as he is, when he does go into action he runs amok, and afterwards promptly kills himself." Lane smiled sadly. "There I go again. But really, Inspector, examine into this suspect of yours. He's a sort of Hamlet who plays the drama out until the end of the fourth act. In the fifth—the action changes, and so does the comparison."

Thumm shifted restlessly. "Well, all right. Let it go at that. The point is—what do *you* think about the whole business?"

"I think," chuckled Lane suddenly, "that you're playing deep and dark, Inspector. How is it that you've taken up the Perry theory again? I thought you had discarded the tutor in favor of an inspiration, which you were careful not to divulge to me."

Thumm looked sheepish. "Make believe I never said anything about an inspiration. I did make some inquiries, but

THE TRAGEDY OF Y

255

nothing doing." He regarded Lane shrewdly. "You haven't answered my question, Mr. Lane."

It was Lane's turn to draw into his shell. A glimmer of the old weariness touched his face, and he quite lost his smile. "To tell the truth . . . I don't know what to think, Inspector."

"You mean you're sunk?"

"I mean that this is not the time to take any drastic steps whatever."

"Oh . . . Well, we've got a lot of confidence in you, Mr. Lane. You certainly proved your ability to get down to cases in the Longstreet business last year." The Inspector scrubbed his chin. "In a way," he said in some embarrassment, "Bruno and I are relying on you."

Lane leaped from his chair and began to pace the floor. "Please. Don't. Don't rely on me for anything." He was so openly upset that the Inspector's jaw dropped. "Proceed as if I hadn't appeared in the case at all, Inspector. Work out your own theories, please . . ."

Thumm's face darkened. "If that's the way you feel about it, damn it all . . ."

"Yesterday—that inspiration of yours—so there was no luck, eh?"

Thumm's suspicious glance did not waver. "Followed it up. Saw Merriam."

"Ah!" said Lane quickly. "That was good. Very good. And he told you . . . ?"

"Only what I already knew from you," replied Thumm rather stiffly. "That vanilla stuff York Hatter used on his arms. So you went to see the doc, too, hey?"

"Er—yes. Yes, of course." Lane subsided suddenly in the chair and shaded his eyes with his hand.

Thumm looked at him for a long time, puzzled, half

ACT III: SCENE 1

angry. Then he shrugged. "Well," he said with an effort at geniality, "you said you had news for Bruno and me. What is it?"

* * *

Lane raised his head. "I am going to give you a very important bit of information, Inspector. I must exact one promise—that you refrain from asking me where I got it."

"Well, what is it?" growled Thumm.

"This." He was speaking with superlative care, choosing each word as if it were precious. "Before York Hatter disappeared he was engaged in concocting the plot of a novel."

"A novel?" Thumm stared. "What of it?"

"But this was not a mere novel, Inspector," said Lane in barely audible tones. "It was a story which he was hoping some day to write and have published. A detective story."

For a moment Thumm sat glaring at Lane with a mesmeric stare, the cigar balanced on his lower lip, the vein in his right temple twitching like a live thing. Then he shot from his chair like a catapult, shouting: "A *detective* story!" The cigar fell to the floor. "Jeeze, that *is* news!"

"Yes," replied Lane heavily. "The outline of a story of murder and detection. . . . There is one thing more I should tell you."

Thumm was hardly listening; his eyes were glazed, and now he jerked them toward Lane with an effort at concentration.

"And that is . . ."

"Huh!" Thumm became keen and watchful again, after shaking his head from side to side in the familiar way. "What?"

"The background and characters of York Hatter's plot are *real*."

THE TRAGEDY OF Y

"Real?" muttered the Inspector. "Just how do you mean?"

"York Hatter took them directly from *his own family.*"

The Inspector's big body twitched once, as if an electric current had streaked through it. "No," he said hoarsely. "No, it can't be. It's too damned good. . . . I'll be——"

"Yes, Inspector," Lane said wearily. "Does that interest you? It should. A remarkable circumstance. A man creates a fiction story dealing with poisoning and murder. Then events begin to occur in his own household, in real life . . . *events coinciding in virtually every respect with the purely fictitious scenario of the novel.*"

Thumm drew a whistling breath, his piston of a chest falling and rising powerfully. "Do you mean to tell me," he said in his rich bass, "that everything that's been happening in the Hatter house—the two attempts to poison Louisa, the murder of Mrs. Hatter, the fire and explosion—are all written down on paper, made up out of Hatter's head and intended as a *story?* Cripes, it's unbelievable! I never heard of such a thing!"

"There are more things . . ." sighed Lane. "At any rate, there you are, Inspector. The sum and substance of my news."

He rose and gripped the knob of his stick in a sort of desperation, clinging to it. There was a helpless defeat in his eyes. Thumm paced the floor like a wild animal, exulting, muttering to himself, his brain buzzing, speculating, discarding, deciding. . . . Lane went to the door and paused. There was even a lack of the usual youthful co-ordination in his movements. He plodded, and his back— so straight and strong—was curved, sloped.

The Inspector stopped short. "Just a minute! You said you didn't want me to ask questions. Well, if you're keep-

258   ACT III: SCENE 2

ing something back, I suppose there's a good reason, and I won't be nosey. But tell me this. In every detective story there's a criminal. Whom did York Hatter make his criminal—in the story—if he was using characters out of his own family? Because it's a cinch that whoever was the criminal in the story can't be the criminal in real life—too dangerous. Well?"

Lane silently considered this, his hand on the door. "Yes," he said at last in a dead voice. "Certainly you're entitled to know that. . . . York Hatter's criminal in York Hatter's story of murder was—*York Hatter*."

Scene 2

THE HAMLET. FRIDAY, JUNE 10. 9 P.M.

Even The Hamlet, ordinarily the serenest and most soul-soothing of cloisters, was desolate that evening. The rain persisted, and with it came a creeping chill that penetrated clothing and raised gooseflesh. Perched high above the Hudson, rooted in the solid cliff-tops, The Hamlet took on the forbidding quality of a Poesque ruin, muffled as it was in gray folds of fog, with nothing below and the ghostly sky swirling about its head.

It was a night for fires, and old Quacey had prepared a Titan's conflagration in the huge fireplace in Lane's private quarters. It was warm there, toe-toasting, and Lane after a simple dinner flung himself on the raw-furry hearthrug and closed his eyes. The flames beat against his eyelids. The ancient hunchback pottered in and out of the room, anxiously, timidly. He was frightened half out of his sharp old

The Tragedy of Y

wits. He kept watching his master with screwed-up eyes, and blinked at every leap of the fire.

Once he crept to the hearthrug and touched his master's arm. The gray-green eyes, sleepless, full, filled with thought, instantly opened upon him. "Is anything the matter, Mr. Drury? Don't you feel well?"

"I'm quite all right."

After that Quacey retired to a chair in the corner and crouched motionless, his eyes never leaving the still figure outstretched before the flames.

At nine o'clock, after an hour of absolute stillness, the figure stirred and rose. "Quacey."

"Yes, Mr. Drury!" The old man was on his feet in an instant, eager, tongue-lolling, like a hound fawning upon his master.

"I am going into the study. I am not to be disturbed. You understand?"

"Yes, Mr. Drury."

"If Fritz Hof or Kropotkin should ask for me, I have retired. There is a play they are worried about. No matter. I will see them in the morning."

"Yes, Mr. Drury."

Lane patted the hunchback's bald pate, slapped his hump, and nudged him to the door. Old Quacey trudged out reluctantly. Lane locked the door behind him and with steady steps went into the adjoining room, his study.

He went to the carved old walnut desk, switched on a desk-lamp, and then opened a drawer. He drew out the wad of paper on which he had copied the contents of the yellowed manuscript he had found in the Hatter chimney cache.

Sinking into the leather chair before the desk, he spread the sheets out before him, his eyes dull, his face dark.

ACT III: SCENE 2

Then, slowly, with intense concentration, mulling over each word, he began to read over the copy of the outline he had scribbled so hastily in the afternoon. In the silence and the darkness, the words seemed to take on fresh significance. He absorbed them, bathed himself in them. . . .

Outline for Detective Story

Title (tentative): "The Vanilla Murder Mystery."

Author: Get pen-name. Miss Terry? H. York? Lewis Pastor?

Scene: N. Y. C. Gramercy Park? House like my own.

Time: Present.

Device: Written in first person. Myself as criminal.

Characters

York (myself). Y. Criminal. Husband of victim.

Emily. Victim. Old woman. Tyrant. (As is.)

Louisa. Deaf-dumb-blind daughter. (Not step-daughter of Y—helps motive.)

The Tragedy of Y 261

Conrad. Married son ⎫
Martha. His wife ⎬ no children, not necessary.

Barbara. Daughter. Eldest of Y and Emily. Keep her a writer. Psychological suspect?

Jill. Youngest of Y and Emily. Daughter.

Trivett. One-legged neighbor. Love interest for Louisa. (Too far-fetched?)

Gormly. Son's business partner.

Stock Characters

Nurse for Louisa, housekeeper, chauffeur, maid, family physician, family attorney, suitor for Jill?

Note!!! Get Fiction names for All above!!!

First Crime

Attempted poisoning of Louisa. Fact: Household has established custom; housekeeper makes up glass of egg-nog for Louisa and leaves it standing on dining-room table at 2:30 each afternoon.

Act III: Scene 2

Details: On certain day, Y (criminal) waits until housekeeper puts egg-nog on dining-room table; then, when no one is looking, Y sneaks into dining-room and drops Strychnin poison into egg-nog glass and hurries back to library, which is next to dining-room.

Y has got the Strychnin poison from Bottle No. 9 on his chemical laboratory shelves in his laboratory upstairs, taking three of the tablets from this bottle. No one knows this.

After putting poison into egg-nog, Y stays in library waiting for Louisa to come to drink egg-nog.

Just as Louisa is coming along, headed for the dining-room, Y comes out of library. Before Louisa can drink poisoned egg-nog, Y comes into dining-room, takes glass of egg-nog, says something is wrong with it, takes sip.

Immediately gets sick. (Y contrives to have others in immediate vicinity for suspects.)

Note: This makes everyone think somebody else is trying to poison Louisa; certainly not Y, because would a poisoner sip his own poison? And this also

THE TRAGEDY OF Y 263

prevents Louisa from being really poisoned—very important to plot.

Second Crime

Second "attempt" to poison Louisa, during which the old woman, Emily, Y's wife, is murdered. Time: 7 weeks after first poisoning attempt, to the day.

Details: During the night, about 4 o'clock in the morning, while everyone is asleep, and while Louisa and Emily are sleeping in their bedroom (mother and daughter sleep in the same room, twin beds), Y commits the 2nd crime.

The idea this time is to poison a pear and put it in the fruit-bowl on the night-table between Louisa's bed and the old woman's bed. A pear is used because everyone knows that old Emily never eats pears. Poisoning the pear will make it look as if Louisa was intended to be poisoned again, but Louisa will not eat the pear either, because Y, knowing she never eats spoiled or spotted fruit, purposely picks out (maybe steals one from kitchen) and brings into

ACT III: SCENE 2

room a squashy pear, which he poisons by jabbing pear with hypodermic filled with Bichloride of Mercury poison, taken from bottle in laboratory— Bottle No. 168.

Y has got the hypodermic from his steel filing cabinet in laboratory, where he has a case full of them.

Also before Y goes to Louisa's bedroom he has stolen a pair of Conrad's old white summer shoes. And at the time he fills up the hypodermic with Bichloride of Mercury in the laboratory (just before he goes to Louisa's room in the middle of the night), he purposely pours some of the poison (Bottle No. 168) on one of Conrad's white shoes.

Action: Y sneaks into Louisa's and Emily's bedroom. Goes to night-table and puts spoiled pear in fruit-bowl. Hits Emily over head with blunt instrument, killing her. (This is the Real Part of the Plot, but it will look as if Emily was killed by mistake, as if she woke up in the middle of the night and the murderer had to kill her to keep her quiet.)

THE TRAGEDY OF Y

Note: The killing of Emily is the main purpose behind the entire plot. The attempts to poison Louisa are just to make police think Louisa is the intended victim. So the police will suspect only those who would want to kill Louisa, not Emily. In the story Y will be very friendly with Louisa, so that he will not be suspected.

Explanation of False Trail: Y purposely spills bichloride on Conrad's shoe. He puts shoe back in Conrad's closet after he has come from bedroom. Police find shoe with poison on it, and this will make them suspect Conrad as the poisoner, who hates Louisa as everyone knows.

Clue which leads Police to Correct Solution: Louisa is deaf-dumb-and-blind. Idea is that while Y is killing Emily, Louisa awakens and smells the vanilla of Balsam Peru on Y's arms—smell being the best sense she has to furnish clue for police. She later testifies to vanilla odor, main detective follows trail, etc., etc., until he discovers truth, Y being the only character fitting vanilla odor.

Act III: Scene 2
The Fire

In the middle of the next night after the murder Y sets fire to the laboratory (where he sleeps also). He first leaves on one of his big laboratory tables a bottle of Carbon Bisulphide (from Bottle No. 256), which will explode at proximity of heat. He then strikes match and sets fire to his bed.

Purpose of Fire: Fire and subsequent explosion will seem like someone attempting to take Y's life, too. This will add still another false trail, making Y at least look innocent.

Third Crime

Two weeks after murder, Y makes another "attempt" to "poison" Louisa. This time he uses poison called Physostigmin, a white liquid from Bottle No. 220 on his laboratory shelves. Puts 15 drops with eye-dropper in Louisa's glass of buttermilk, which she drinks an hour after dinner each night. Again Y either calls attention to something

The Tragedy of Y

wrong with the buttermilk, or in some way Prevents Louisa from Drinking the Poisoned Buttermilk.

Purpose: The plot does not call for the death of Louisa at any time. This third attempt after the death of the old woman is just to continue making the police believe that the murderer still wants to kill Louisa, so that the police will look for those with motives against Louisa, not Emily.

General Notes

(1) Keep in mind that Y wears gloves all the time so that he never leaves fingerprints on anything in any of the crimes.

(2) Work out byplots.

(3) Work out how main detective finally reaches solution.

(4) Y's motive: Hatred of Emily—she ruined his career—his health—dominated and crushed him. . . . Real enough for a real crime!

This last comment, irrelevant and bitter, had been heavily penciled out of the manuscript (for Lane had ex-

ACT III: SCENE 2

actly copied what was in the original); but it had been legible. The outline concluded with two other notes.

(5) *Be sure disguise characters in book enough to make it look like fiction. If pen-name is used, good character names, no reason why public should recognize family. Perhaps change background to some other city, like Chicago or San Francisco.*

(6) *What is character of main detective? Doctor, because of vanilla and chemical stuff? Friend of Y? Not a regular detective. Make modus operandi deductive—intellectual detective; perhaps physical appearance of Sh. H., color of Poir., deductive methods of E. Q. . . . Bring laboratory prominently into investigation. . . . Work out a clue by means of numbers on bottles. This should not be difficult (?)*

* * *

Wearily Lane, his lean face taut, dropped the copy of York Hatter's amorphous detective story plot outline. He buried his head in his hands, thinking deeply in the strong silence. Fifteen minutes passed in this way, unbroken by any sound save the scarcely audible one of his own breathing.

Finally he sat up straight and stared across his desk at a calendar. His lips moved. Two weeks. . . .

The Tragedy of Y 269

He picked up a pencil and ringed the date June 18 with heavy, almost desperate, strokes.

Scene 3

The Morgue. Saturday, June 11. 11 a.m.

Something drove him on. Accustomed as he was to intense introspection and a sharp analysis of the world about him, he was nevertheless helpless in the grip of the viscous mood that enveloped him. Helpless either to analyze it completely or explain it away. Rationalization fled before it. It pressed on the nape of his neck like a lead weight.

And yet he could not stop. This thing must be searched out to the end—how bitter an end only he knew. What would happen then . . . Inwardly he shrank together, feeling his stomach contract in a spasm of pain and fear.

It was Saturday, and the sun shone hotly on the river, and here he was descending from the Lincoln, crossing the sidewalk, toiling up the battered stone steps of the Morgue. Why? Why not confess that he had entered upon an enterprise too conscienceless for a man of sensitive nature? At the height of his career on the stage he had met as much vituperation as praise. He had been called everything from "the world's foremost actor" to "an old has-been mumming a moth-eaten Shakespeare in the age of miracles." These he had accepted equably, meeting the sneers and the applause with dignity, as befitted an artist who knew the right way and the high place. Nothing the critics were able to say, out of the venom of the new young art, could shake his invincible purpose or the quiet conviction that he was

ACT III: SCENE 3

fulfilling a worthy destiny. Why had he not stopped there, at the peak of a full career? Why meddle? It was for the Thumms and the Brunos to ferret out and punish evil. Evil? There was no evil in the pure state; even Satan had been an angel. There were just ignorant or twisted people, or victims of a malicious fate.

Yet his lean legs carried him up the steps of the Morgue, bound on a new mission of exploration and confirmation, stubbornly refusing to heed the turmoil in his brain.

He found Dr. Ingalls, the City toxicologist, on the second floor of the building in a laboratory, lecturing to a class of young medical students. He waited dumbly, looking at the neat duplicate apparatus of glass and metal without really seeing it, lip-reading Ingalls's incisive words and watching the practiced movements of his hands without a quiver of sensory reaction.

When the class had been dismissed, Ingalls stripped off his rubber gloves and shook hands cordially. "Glad to see you, Mr. Lane. Another little problem in olfactory evidence?"

Mr. Drury Lane, shrunken within himself, looked about the deserted laboratory. This world of science, with its retorts and electrodes and glass jars full of chemicals! What was he doing here, after all, an outsider, an interloper, a bungler? He could not hope to cleanse the earth. . . . He sighed and said: "Can you give me any information about a poison called physostigmin, Doctor?"

"Physostigmin? Certainly!" beamed the toxicologist. "Right up our alley. It's a white, tasteless, toxic alkaloid—deadly poison, one of the papas of the alkaloid family. Chemically it's $C_{15}H_{21}N_3O_2$—derived from the Calabar bean."

"Calabar bean?" echoed Lane dully.

THE TRAGEDY OF Y

271

"*Physostigma venenosum*. Calabar bean's the highly poisonous seed of an African climbing vine of the bean family," explained Dr. Ingalls. "It's used medically in the treatment of certain nervous disorders, tetanus, epilepsy, and so on. The physostigmin is derived from this bean, and it's death on rats and just about everything else. Would you like to see a sample?"

"Scarcely necessary, Doctor." Lane took from his pocket a carefully wrapped and padded object. He stripped off the wrapping and padding. It was the stoppered vial of white fluid he had discovered in the chimney cache. "Is this physostigmin?"

"Hmm," said Ingalls, holding the vial up to the light. "Looks like it, all right. Just a moment, Mr. Lane. I'll make a couple of tests."

He worked intently, in silence; and Lane watched him without interrupting. "Certainly is," said the toxicologist at last. "Undoubtedly physostigmin, Mr. Lane, full strength. Where'd you get it?"

"In the Hatter house," replied Lane vaguely. He produced his wallet and fumbled inside until he found a small folded sheet of paper. "This," he said, "is the duplicate of a prescription, Dr. Ingalls. Will you look it over, please?"

The toxicologist took the prescription. "Hmm . . . Balsam Peru . . . I see! What do you want to know about this prescription, Mr. Lane?"

"Is it legitimate?"

"Oh! Certainly. Compounded salve used in the treatment of a skin ai——"

"Thank you," said Lane wearily. He did not bother to take back the prescription. "And now—will you do something for me, Doctor?"

"Just say the word."

ACT III: SCENE 4

"See that this vial is sent to Police Headquarters in my name, to be filed with the other exhibits of the Hatter case."

"It's done."

"It should," explained Lane heavily, "be preserved as a matter of official record. It is fatally important in the case. . . . Thank you for your courtesy, Doctor."

He shook Ingalls's hand and turned to the door. The toxicologist watched his slow departure with bewilderment.

Scene 4

INSPECTOR THUMM'S OFFICE. THURSDAY, JUNE 16. 10 A.M.

And there, it seemed, matters were fated to rest. From a case which had been born in attempted violence, sweeping the Mad Hatters in its path as it developed, darting from one manifestation of criminal activity to another without reason and yet with purpose, it suddenly came to a dead stop, as if gathering momentum over a long stretch it had unexpectedly crashed into an immovable barrier and fallen, shattered, to earth, never to move again.

It was a trying period. For six days after Lane's visit to the laboratory of Dr. Ingalls nothing whatever occurred. Inspector Thumm had blundered into a blind alley, and was going round and round on his heels in a frenzied activity that got nowhere. The Hatter house had returned to a semblance of routine, which is to say that its tenants resumed their eccentric mode of living, scarcely restrained further by the helpless police. The newspapers all week had been full of negative reports; the Mad Hatters, as one

The Tragedy of Y

paper expressed it, seemed to be coming out of "this latest escapade" unscathed. "Just another sickening example," darkly asserted an editorial, "of the growing tendency in American crime. Getting away with murder, among private citizens as among the racketeers, seems to be becoming fashionable—and safe."

Matters, then, were at an *impasse* until Thursday morning, a little less than two weeks after the murder of Mrs. Hatter, when Mr. Drury Lane chose to pay a visit to Police Headquarters.

Inspector Thumm showed the strain of the past week. He greeted Lane almost with doggy hope. "Greetings, brother!" he bellowed. "Where in God's name have you been? I've never been so glad to see anyone in my whole life! What's the good word?"

Lane shrugged. There were lines of resolution about his mouth, but he was still gloomy. "I'm singularly lacking in good words these days, Inspector."

"Huh! The old story," said Thumm, lapsing into saturnine contemplation of an old scar on the back of his hand. "Nobody knows anything."

"You've accomplished little, I understand."

"You're telling me?" snarled Thumm. "I've been playing that detective story angle to a fare-thee-well. Seemed to be just about the most important lead in the case. And where did it get me?" It was a rhetorical question that required no answer, but the Inspector supplied it nevertheless. "Nowhere, that's where!"

"Where did you expect it to get you, Inspector?" asked Lane quietly.

"Certainly I had a right to think it might lead to the murderer!" cried Thumm, rage boiling behind his eyes. "But I'll be damned if I can make head or tail of it. I'm

ACT III: SCENE 4

sick and tired of the whole rotten mess. Well!" He calmed. "No use getting all hopped up about it. . . . Look here. Let me tell you how I figure it . . ."

"Do."

"York Hatter writes a detective story, or as you say the outline of one. Bases it on characters in his own family, the same house, and so on. Not much originality, eh? But I'll admit he had damned good material to work with; it was a natural."

"I'm afraid I must charge Mr. Hatter with undervaluing his material," murmured Lane. "He didn't half begin to suspect the possibilities, Inspector. If he had known . . ."

"Yeah, but he didn't," growled Thumm. "So he sits there playing around with this fiction idea of his, and thinks: 'Swell! I'll be smart. I'll write this thing myself— author telling the story, and all that sort of hooey—and I'll make *myself* the criminal.' In the story, mind you . . ."

"Clever, Inspector."

"Well, if you go in for that sort of thing," grunted Thumm. "Now, look. After he's kicked the bucket himself —something *he* didn't figure when he set out to write a mystery story, I'll bet!—somebody comes along, finds his plot, and uses the plot of the *story* to guide him in the commission of a *real* murder. . . ."

"Precisely."

"Precisely your hat!" cried Thumm. "Damn it all, although that looks as if it means something, it doesn't mean anything at all! All you can squeeze out of it is that someone's been using York Hatter's idea as a steer. Might be anybody!"

"I believe you're understating the potentialities," said Lane.

"What d'ye mean?"

THE TRAGEDY OF Y

275

"Never mind."

"Well, maybe you're smarter than I am," grumbled the Inspector. "I claim that's why this is such a cockeyed crime. Following a detective story outline!" He whipped out a big handkerchief and honked his nose three times, violently. "It's a lousy detective story, I'll tell you that. But it helps in one way. There are lots of things in the real crime that just won't bear explanation. So I suppose whatever we can't explain we can blame on Hatter's punk plotting."

Lane said nothing.

Thumm added grumpily: "There's something else." He examined a fingernail minutely. "Y'know, last week when you told me about this outline business, I sort of respected your request not to ask questions. I don't mind telling you Bruno and I think a lot of your ability, Mr. Lane, get me straight—you've got something, I don't know what in hell it is, that neither Bruno nor I've got, and we know it. Otherwise we wouldn't let an outsider have his own way so much."

"I'm grateful, Inspector," murmured Lane.

"Yeah. But I'm not entirely dumb," went on the Inspector slowly. "And you can't expect my patience to last forever, either. Only one of three ways you could have found out about that outline. One is that you dug it up somewhere, and that doesn't seem likely, because we searched the house from top to bottom before you did. Two is—you got the information from the murderer himself. That's out, of course, for obvious reasons. Three—you're just guessing, following a hunch. But if that's the case, how do you know so exactly that the plot called for York Hatter to be the criminal? So that's out, too. I'll admit I'm stumped and, by God, I don't like the feeling!"

Mr. Drury Lane stirred, and sighed, and the torture in

ACT III: SCENE 4

his eyes belied the impatience with which he spoke. "Poor logic, Inspector, I'm sorry to say. But I simply cannot discuss it with you." He was silent for a moment, and then he said: "At the same time, I do owe you an explanation."

He rose as Thumm's eyes narrowed, and began to patrol the floor with hungry strides. "Inspector, this is the most unique crime in the history of your calling. When I became interested in criminology early last year, I read voluminously records of old cases, kept up with current ones, saturated myself in the subject. Believe me when I tell you that the whole history of criminal investigation has never recorded a more—what shall I say?—difficult, complex, and extraordinary crime."

"Maybe," growled Thumm. "All I know is—it's tough."

"You can't begin to comprehend its complexity," muttered Lane. "It concerns itself not only with matters of crime and punishment, Inspector. In the vortex of its elements are pathology, abnormal psychology, problems of sociology and ethics. . . ." He stopped, and bit his lip. "But let's stop this aimless talk. Have there been any developments at the Hatter house?"

"Everything's the same. Looks as if it's just petered out."

"Don't be deceived," cried Lane harshly. "It has not petered out. This is a hiatus, a lull in the hostilities. . . . Have there been further attempts at poisoning?"

"No. Dr. Dubin, the expert stationed in the house, is watching every drop of food and drink. Not a chance of that again."

"Louisa Campion. . . . Has Barbara Hatter decided?"

"Not yet. Conrad's showing his colors. He's been egging the poor girl on to pass up her chance—transparent as hell, he is, and of course Barbara sees through him. Know what that son-of-a-gun had the nerve to suggest?"

THE TRAGEDY OF Y

"Well?"

"He's propositioning Barbara! Says that if she'll refuse to take care of Louisa, he will, too, and then they'll both contest the will when old Cap Trivett takes over the job! Just a big-hearted brother. If she consented, he'd double-cross her and take the woman in himself. After all, control of three hundred grand isn't to be sneezed at."

"The others?"

"Jill Hatter's gone back to her old round of parties. Keeps on talking nasty about her old lady. Taken Gormly back on the string again, and ditched Bigelow; which," said Thumm grimly, "is one sweet break for Bigelow. He doesn't think so, though—he's sore as a pup—hasn't been near the house all week. And that's all. Hopeful, isn't it?"

Lane's eyes flickered. "Is Louisa Campion still sleeping in Miss Smith's room?"

"No, she's been sensible about it. Went back to her own bedroom. Place has been cleaned up. Miss Smith is sleeping there with her, occupying the old lady's bed. Didn't think she had the guts."

Lane ceased his pacing, confronting the Inspector squarely. "I have been endeavoring to muster sufficient courage, Inspector, to make still another demand on your patience and good nature."

Thumm rose, and they stood face to face—the large broad ugly man, and the tall slender muscular one. "I don't get you," said Thumm.

"I must ask you once more to do something for me without learning why."

"Depends," said Thumm.

"Very well. Your men are still stationed about and in the Hatter house?"

"Yes. What of it?"

278 ACT III: SCENE 4

Lane did not reply at once. He searched the Inspector's eyes, and in his own there was something child-like and pleading. "I want you," he said slowly, "to withdraw every policeman and detective on duty at the Hatter house."

* * *

Inspector Thumm, accustomed as he was to Mr. Drury Lane's vagaries, was scarcely prepared for such an astounding request as this.

"What!" he roared. "Leave the place absolutely unguarded?"

"Yes," said Lane in a low voice. "Absolutely unguarded, as you say. It's urgent, necessary."

"Dr. Dubin, too? Why, man, you don't know what you're asking. That will leave the poisoner a clear field!"

"Precisely what I aim to achieve."

"But my God," cried Thumm, "we can't do that! We're practically inviting another attack!"

Lane nodded quietly. "You've grasped the essence of the idea, Inspector."

"But," spluttered Thumm, "*somebody's* got to be on the premises to protect the family and nab the bastard!"

"Somebody will be there."

Thumm looked startled, as if he had suddenly begun to suspect the old actor's sanity. "But I thought you just said you didn't want us there."

"Correct."

"Eh?"

"I shall be there *myself*."

"Oh!" said Thumm in an altered tone. He became thoughtful instantly, and looked at Lane hard and long. "I get it. The old stunt, hey? They know you're one of us, though, unless——"

The Tragedy of Y

279

"Exactly what I intend to do," said Lane in a lifeless tone. "I shall not go as myself, but as someone else."

"Somebody they know, eh, and take for granted," muttered Thumm. "Not bad, not half bad, Mr. Lane. If you can fool 'em. After all, this isn't the stage. *Or* a detective story. Do you think you can make up—I mean, so well that . . . ?"

"A chance I shall have to take," said Lane. "Quacey is a genius. His art is brilliant because it is restrained. As for myself. . . . It won't be the first time I've played a part," he said bitterly. He checked himself. "Come, Inspector, we're losing valuable time. Will you grant my request or not?"

"Well, all right," said Thumm doubtfully. "Can't hurt, I guess, if you're extra careful. We'd have to be taking the boys away soon anyway. . . . Okay. What's the lay?"

Lane spoke crisply: "Where is Edgar Perry?"

"Back at the Hatter house. Released him and told him to stay there until we cleaned up."

"Call Mr. Perry at once and, on the pretext of questioning him again, have him come down here as soon as he can."

* * *

A half hour later Edgar Perry was sitting in Thumm's best chair, nervously glancing from Lane to the Inspector. The actor's mantle of distress had been cast off: he was quiet, but alert. He appraised the tutor with photographic eyes, measuring him, taking in every detail of gesture and appearance. Thumm sat by, fidgeting and scowling.

"Mr. Perry," said Lane at last, "you can be of inestimable service to the police."

"Ah—yes," said Perry vaguely, his student's dreamy eyes filled with apprehension.

ACT III: SCENE 4

"It is necessary to withdraw the police from the Hatter house."

Perry looked startled and eager. "Really?" he cried.

"Yes. At the same time we must have someone on the premises prepared for trouble." The tutor's eagerness fled, and the apprehension returned. "Someone, of course, who will have the freedom of the house and yet, while watching the occupants of the house, will move unsuspected among them. Do you understand?"

"Quite—quite."

"It goes without saying that a member of the police," continued Lane briskly, "will not do. I propose with your permission, Mr. Perry, to take your place in the Hatter house."

Perry blinked. "Take my place? I don't quite see . . ."

"I employ one of the greatest artists of make-up in the world. I select you because you are the only member of the household it is physically possible for me to impersonate with the least danger of unmasking. We are about the same physique and height, and we have not dissimilar features. At least there is nothing about you which Quacey's art cannot duplicate on me."

"Oh, yes. You're an actor," mumbled Perry.

"Do you agree?"

Perry did not reply at once. "Well . . ."

"You'd better," put in Inspector Thumm darkly. "Your pants aren't exactly clean in this business, Campion."

Anger flared into the soft eyes, and drained out. The tutor's shoulders sagged. "Very well," he muttered. "I consent."

*　　*　　*

Scene 5

The Hamlet. Friday, June 17. Afternoon.

In the morning Inspector Thumm arrived at The Hamlet in a small black car with Perry, explained that the Hatters were under the impression Perry was in for an all-day grilling, and immediately drove away.

Lane, now that he was on old ground, familiar with every step of the terrain, did not rush matters. He wandered about the estate with the tutor, chatting pleasantly of his theater, his books, his gardens—everything but the Hatters. Perry expanded under the spell of his extraordinarily beautiful surroundings, breathed deeply of the winy air, entered the re-created Mermaid Tavern with glistening eyes, reverently examined a glass-incased First Folio of Shakespeare in the sprawling quiet library, met Lane's incumbents, inspected his theater, discussed the modern drama with Kropotkin, Lane's Russian director—lost himself entirely. He seemed a new man.

Quietly Lane led him about, and his eyes were on the man's face, figure, and hands every minute of the morning. He studied the shape of Perry's mouth and the way he moved his lips, his posture, his walk, every nuance of gesture. At luncheon he watched Perry's eating mannerisms. Quacey tagged along, studying the tutor's head like a deformed little hawk, and vanished somewhere in the middle of the afternoon, mumbling excitedly to himself.

In the afternoon they continued their perambulations about the vast grounds; but now Lane adroitly led the conversation to Perry himself. In a little while it became personal. Lane discovered the man's tastes, prejudices, ideas,

281

ACT III: SCENE 5

the pith and core of his intellectual intercourse with Barbara Hatter, his relationships with the other members of the household, the extent of his tutoring of the two children. Here again Perry became animated, and told him where to find the books, and his methods of teaching each boy, and the routine of his daily life in the Hatter house.

*   *   *

In the evening after dinner the two men repaired to Quacey's little laboratory. It was a weird place, utterly unlike anything Perry had ever seen before. Despite its modern appurtenances it gave off an odor of antiquity. It looked like a medieval torture-room. On one wall hung a shelf on which were propped a row of heads—models of all races and types—Mongoloid, Caucasian, Negroid—in all expressions possible to the human countenance. Wigs—gray, black, brown, red, fuzzy, frilly, straight, dull, oily, curly—strewed the walls. Work-benches held a puzzling assortment of pigments, powders, creams, dyes, pastes, and small metal tools. An instrument like a sewing-machine, a huge many-faceted mirror, an enormous bulb-lamp, black shades. . . . From the moment he stepped across its threshold Perry's animation vanished, and his old fear and hesitating manner returned. The room seemed to depress him and bring him back to reality, for he became silent and moved about nervously. Lane watched him with sudden anxiety. Perry wandered about uneasily. His shadow, grotesquely elongated, kept pace with him on the blank wall.

"Mr. Perry, please undress," squeaked Quacey. He was busily propped up over a wooden model, putting the last touches to a remarkable wig of human hair.

Silently and slowly Perry obeyed. Lane stripped off his

THE TRAGEDY OF Y

own clothes quickly, and redressed in Perry's. They fitted; the two men were well matched physically.

Perry draped a dressing-gown about him and shivered.

Quacey fluttered about. The necessities of facial make-up, fortunately, were few. Lane seated himself in an oddly shaped chair before the mirrors and the old hunchback set to work. His gnarled fingers seemed imbued with uncanny intelligence. A slight adjustment to the nose and eyebrows, some wads to alter the shape of the cheeks and jawline; the eyes swiftly, deftly touched up, and the eyebrows dyed.

Perry looked on in silence. A glitter of determination crept into his eyes.

Quacey briskly motioned Perry to the bench, studied his hairline and head-shape, adjusted the wig to Lane's head, produced scissors. . . .

In two hours the transformation was complete. Mr. Drury Lane stood up, and Perry's eyes widened with horror. He was experiencing the remarkable, incredible sensation of gazing at himself. Lane opened his mouth, and out of it came Perry's own voice—the identical movements of the lips. . . .

"Oh, God!" cried Perry suddenly, his face contorted and crimson, "no! No, I say! I can't let you!"

The mask dropped, and it was Lane again, alarm in his eyes. "What do you mean?" he asked quietly.

"You're too perfect! The deception is too . . . I won't permit it, I tell you!" Perry sank to the bench, his shoulders quivering. "I—Barbara . . . To deceive her so . . ."

"You thought I might give myself away?" said Lane, with a pitying look in his eyes.

"Yes, yes. She would know I was forced. . . . But this way. No!" The tutor sprang to his feet, his jaw set. "If

ACT III: SCENE 5

you attempt to impersonate me, Mr. Lane, I shall be compelled to resort to violence. I shall not permit you to impose on the woman"—he paused and squared his chin—"the woman I love. Let me have my clothes, please."

He stripped off the dressing-gown and advanced one step toward Lane, defiance and the fire of determination in his eyes. Quacey, who had been looking on open-mouthed, screamed a warning, grabbed a heavy shears from the work-bench, and sprang forward like a monkey.

Lane stepped in his path and patted his shoulder gently. "No, Quacey. . . . You're right, Mr. Perry, perfectly right. Will you be my guest tonight?"

Perry stammered: "I'm sorry—I didn't mean to threaten. . . ."

"I have permitted my sense of values to become warped," said Lane steadily. "Unless we took Miss Hatter into our confidence. . . . No, it's better this way. Quacey, stop staring." He took off the wig with some difficulty and placed it in the old hunchback's astonished hand. "Keep this as a memento of my stupidity and the gallantry of a gentleman. . . ." And then, before Perry's eyes, a remarkable transformation came over Lane. The actor had stiffened, and blinked twice, and then smiled. "Would you care to visit my theater, Mr. Perry? Kropotkin is holding a dress rehearsal of our newest play."

*　　*　　*

When Perry had redressed and gone, escorted by Falstaff to Lane's theater, the actor dropped his mask of insouciance. "Quick, Quacey! Get Inspector Thumm on the wire!"

Quacey, alarmed, pattered to the wall and grasped a concealed telephone in his skinny talons. Lane paced behind

THE TRAGEDY OF Y 285

him impatiently. "Fast, old man. Fast. There's no time to lose."

There was difficulty locating the Inspector. He was not at Police Headquarters.

"Try his home."

The Inspector's wife answered the telephone. Quacey squealed urgently. The good lady was doubtful . . . the Inspector was snoring in an easy-chair, it seemed, and she hesitated to wake him.

"But it's Mr. Lane!" cried Quacey, in desperation. "Important!"

"Oh!" Peculiar sounds which had assailed Quacey's old ears with the regularity of a drumbeat suddenly ceased, and a moment later Thumm's familiar growl came over the wire.

"Ask him if his men have already left the Hatter house!"

Quacey stuttered the question, listened dutifully. "He says not yet. They were to go off as soon as you got there tonight."

"Luck! Tell the Inspector I've changed my mind. No impersonation of Perry. His men are to remain at the house until tomorrow. When I arrive some time during the forenoon, they are to leave at once."

Thumm's roar of inquiry made the receiver vibrate hoarsely. "He wants to know why, he says. He says he wants to know damned well why," reported the old hunchback.

"Can't explain now. Give the Inspector my undying affection and hang up on him."

*   *   *

Unconscious of the fact that he was striding about the

ACT III: SCENE 6

room clad only in athletic underwear, Mr. Drury Lane gesticulated wildly at the ancient and cried: "Now call the house of Dr. Merriam! You'll find him in the New York City directory."

Quacey wet a spatulate thumb and began to riffle pages. "Mer . . . Mer . . . Y. Merriam, M.D. That it?"

"Yes. Hurry!"

Quacey gave the number. After a moment a feminine voice answered. "Dr. Merriam, please," he said in his rusty squeak. "Mr. Drury Lane calling."

As he listened to the strident reply, his brown wrinkled face looked disappointed. "He's not home, she says. Went out of town this afternoon for the week-end, she says."

"Ah," said Mr. Drury Lane, sobering. "Week-end, eh? Perhaps it's just as well. . . . Hang up, Caliban. Hang up. This is growing complicated. Thank the lady and hang up."

"What now?" asked Quacey querulously, glaring at his master.

"I do believe," replied Mr. Drury Lane with a thoughtful smile, "that I have an even better idea."

Scene 6

THE DEATH-ROOM. SATURDAY, JUNE 18. 8:20 P.M.

At a few minutes to noon on Saturday morning, Mr. Drury Lane's limousine rolled up to the curb before the Hatter house and deposited Edgar Perry and his host on the sidewalk. Perry was pale, but determined; all the way

THE TRAGEDY OF Y 287

from Lanecliff he had been silent. Lane had not disturbed him.

A detective answered the bell. "Mornin', Mr. Lane. So you're back, Perry?" and winked to Lane as the tutor, without replying, rapidly walked down the corridor and disappeared up the stairs.

Lane strolled through the hall to the rear. He paused, then went into the kitchen.

When he reappeared a few moments later he made for the library. Conrad Hatter was there, writing at a desk. "Well, Mr. Hatter," said Lane heartily, "I hear your troubles are over."

"How? What's that?" exclaimed Hatter, looking up instantly. There were heavy rings under his eyes.

"I have been informed," went on Lane, sitting down, "that the ban is to be lifted this morning. The police are finally leaving."

Hatter muttered: "Oh! It's high time, too. Didn't accomplish anything worth a curse anyway. Just as far from finding out who killed my mother now as they were two weeks ago."

Lane grimaced. "We're not infallible, you know. . . . Yes, here they are. Good morning, Mosher."

"Morning, Mr. Lane," boomed Detective Mosher, advancing with elephantine tread into the library. "Well, sir, we're quitting, Mr. Hatter!"

"So Mr. Lane just said."

"Inspector's orders. Me and the boys are leaving—stroke of noon. Sorry, Mr. Hatter."

"Sorry?" echoed Hatter. He rose and stretched his arms voraciously. "Good riddance, damn all of you! Now we'll have some peace around here."

"And privacy," added a pettish voice. Jill Hatter stepped

288   ACT III: SCENE 6

into the room. "Of all the breaks, Connie. We're actually going to be let alone for a change."

The four men who had been stationed in the house—Mosher, Pinkussohn, Krause, and a dark young man, Dr. Dubin, the poison expert assigned to test the edibles—congregated in the doorway.

"Well, boys," said Pinkussohn, "let's be goin'. I gotta date. Haw, haw!" He began a long rolling laugh that shook the room. And then, in the midst of its reverberations he choked and the sound stopped as if by magic. He was staring at the chair in which Lane sat.

They all looked. Mr. Drury Lane was slumped on the back of his neck, his eyes closed, face drained of blood—unconscious.

*   *   *

Dr. Dubin sprang forward after that instant of stupefaction. Pinkussohn was gasping: "He stiffened up just like that! Got red in the face, choked a little bit, and passed out!"

The poison expert bumped to his knees beside the chair, tore open Lane's collar, bent to place his ear against Lane's chest, felt his pulse. His face was grave. "Water," he said in a low voice. "And whisky. At once."

Jill was pressed against the wall, staring. Conrad Hatter mumbled something, and produced a bottle of whisky from the cellaret. One of the detectives ran to the kitchen and returned quickly with a tumbler of water. Dr. Dubin forced Lane's mouth open and poured a generous amount of liquor down his throat. The detective, overzealous, flung the contents of the tumbler full into Lane's face.

The effect was electric. Lane spluttered, showed the whites of his eyes, rolled them wildly, coughed as the burning whisky coursed through his veins.

The Tragedy of Y 289

"You fool!" cried Dr. Dubin savagely. "What do you want to do—kill him? Here—lend a hand. . . . Mr. Hatter, where can we put him? I've got to get him to bed at once. Heart attack. . . ."

"You're sure it isn't poison?" gasped Jill. Barbara, Martha, the two children, Mrs. Arbuckle ran in, aroused by the commotion.

"Good heavens," said Barbara in a shocked voice. "What's happened to Mr. Lane?"

"Will somebody *please* lend a hand here?" panted Dr. Dubin, struggling to raise Lane's limp body from the chair.

There was a bellow from the hall, and those standing in the doorway were scattered as red-haired Dromio plunged in. . . .

Within fifteen minutes the house was quiet again. Lane's still form had been carried by Dr. Dubin and Dromio upstairs to the guest-room on the first floor. The three detectives had stood about, staring, uneasy, doubtful of the proper course to follow. Finally, in the absence of countermanding orders, they marched out of the house in a body, leaving Lane and the Hatters to their fate. After all, heart attacks did not come under the heading of homicide.

The others thronged about the closed door of the guest-room. There was no sound to be heard from behind the door. Suddenly it opened and Dromio's flaming head stuck out. "Doctor says you're all to get away from here and stop making noise!"

The door clicked shut.

So they slowly dispersed. A half hour later Dr. Dubin emerged and went downstairs. "Absolute quiet and rest," he informed them. "It's not serious. But he positively cannot be moved for a day or so. Please don't disturb him. His chauffeur is with him and will take care of him until

ACT III: SCENE 6

he can leave. I'll be back tomorrow—he'll feel better then."

* * *

At seven-thirty that evening Mr. Drury Lane set out to accomplish what his "heart-attack" had made possible. In obedience to the worthy Dr. Dubin's orders, no one had approached the "sick-room." True, Barbara Hatter had quietly telephoned the office of Dr. Merriam to enlist his services—disturbed perhaps by some vague feeling of uneasiness—but, when she learned that the physician was out of town, she made no further effort to interfere. Dromio, ensconced behind the closed door with a cigar and a magazine which he had with foresight tucked into his pocket, found the afternoon not unenjoyable; more enjoyable than his employer found it, to judge from the tension on Lane's face.

At six o'clock Barbara commanded Mrs. Arbuckle to make up a light tray and take it to the guest-room. Dromio accepted it with Gaelic gallantry, reported that Mr. Lane was resting comfortably, and shut the door in Mrs. Arbuckle's bitten face. Shortly thereafter Miss Smith, conscious that her profession demanded it, knocked on the door and asked whether she might be of service. Dromio discussed the matter with her for five minutes, at the end of which she found herself staring at the panels of the door, vaguely pleased, but nonetheless refused. She went away shaking her head.

At seven-thirty Mr. Drury Lane rose from his bed, spoke quietly to Dromio, and stood behind the door. Dromio opened it and looked out into the corridor. It was empty. Closing the door behind him, he strolled down the hall. The door to Miss Smith's room was open; the room was unoccupied. The laboratory and nursery doors were closed.

THE TRAGEDY OF Y

The door to Louisa Campion's room stood open; and Dromio, making sure that no one was inside, swiftly returned to the guest-room.

A moment later Mr. Drury Lane tiptoed down the corridor and hurried into the death-room.

Without hesitation he opened the door of the clothes closet and slipped inside. He brought the door to before him, and made sure that there was a crack wide enough to permit him to see into the room. The corridor, the whole floor, the room itself were entirely soundless. The room was rapidly growing dark, and the air in the closet was stifling. Nevertheless Lane burrowed more deeply into the nest of feminine clothing behind him, drew what breath he could, and composed himself for a long vigil.

The minutes passed. At times Dromio, crouched behind the door of the guest-room, heard voices from the corridor and fainter ones from downstairs; Lane had not even this awareness of the outside world. He was in complete darkness. No one entered the room in which he lay hidden.

At 7:50, as Lane saw by the radium-dial of his wristwatch, there came the first hint of action. He stiffened, put on guard by some primitive instinct. Without warning the room was flooded with light; he reflected that the electric switch was to the left of the closet, right by the door and therefore out of sight, which was why he had not seen the figure of the visitor. But he was not long kept in doubt. The portly figure of Miss Smith crossed his line of vision. With her heavy tread she walked across the rug and turned into the space between the twin beds. The room, Lane now saw in the brilliant light, had been thoroughly swept up, aired, and tidied; and all traces of the crime had been removed.

Miss Smith went to the night-table and picked up the

ACT III: SCENE 6

board and Braille pieces used by Louisa Campion. As she turned, Lane saw her face. She looked tired, and her large bosom heaved a sigh. Without touching anything further, she walked out of Lane's line of vision, going toward the door. A moment later the light disappeared and Lane was left in enveloping darkness.

He relaxed, and wiped his perspiring forehead.

At 8:05 the death-room received a second visitor. Again the light flared on, and Lane saw the tall drooping figure of Mrs. Arbuckle shuffle across the carpet. The woman was breathing rapidly from the exertion, Lane judged, of climbing the stairs. She carried a tray on which stood a tall glass of buttermilk and a platter of tiny cakes. Depositing the tray on the night-table, she scowled, rubbed the back of her neck, turned, and left the room.

This time, however—and Lane uttered a formless little prayer to all the gods of all the ages for the carelessness which had inspired Mrs. Arbuckle—the light remained on.

Almost at once things happened. It was exactly four minutes later, at 8:09, that Lane tensed with the consciousness that the blind of one of the windows across the room, which until that moment had been completely still, had fluttered. He crouched lower, set himself firmly, widened the crack in his door a trifle, and riveted his eyes on the window.

The drawn blind flew up very suddenly, and he made out the figure he had been awaiting perched on the ledge outside the window which ran around the first-floor outer wall overlooking the garden. It poised there for several seconds, then sprang lightly to the floor inside the room. The window, Lane saw, was now open, where before it had been closed.

THE TRAGEDY OF Y 293

Instantly the figure leaped across the room in the direction of the door, passing beyond Lane's vision. But he was certain that the visitor had closed the door of the room, since the figure returned in a twinkling and the lights remained on. The figure made at once for the fireplace, which Lane could barely see. It stooped a bit and disappeared, legs jerking upwards, out of sight. Lane waited with a pounding heart. Several seconds later the figure reappeared, carrying the vialful of white liquid and the dropper which Lane had left in the cache behind the loose brick.

The visitor ran across the room to the night-table. Eyes glistening, hand outstretched toward the glass of buttermilk. . . . Lane shivered in his hiding-place. A moment's hesitation. . . . Then, as if making up its mind, the figure uncorked the vial and dashed the entire contents into the glass of buttermilk Mrs. Arbuckle had left.

It moved so quickly. . . . A leap back to the window, a rapid look out into the garden, a scramble across the sill—and window and shade came down. The visitor had left the blind a little higher, Lane noticed, than it had been before. . . . He sighed and stretched his legs in the closet; his face was set hard as mortar.

The entire incident had not consumed more than three minutes. It was now, Lane saw on consulting his wrist-watch, exactly 8:12.

Interlude. . . . Nothing happened. The shade did not even flutter. Again Lane swabbed his forehead; the perspiration was trickling down his body beneath his clothing.

At 8:15 Lane was aroused once more. Two figures blotted out the light momentarily as they passed his line of sight —Louisa Campion, walking in slowly but confidently, as she walked all about the house and its premises, and Miss

ACT III: SCENE 6

Smith lagging behind. Louisa proceeded without hesitation to her own bed, sat down, crossed her legs, and mechanically, as if it were a nightly routine, reached forward to the night-table and grasped the glass of buttermilk. Miss Smith smiled rather wanly, patted her cheek, and went to the right—into the bathroom, Lane knew, remembering the geography of the room.

Lane was intent on watching, not Louisa, but the window through which the intruder had made exit. And as Louisa raised the glass to her lips, Lane saw a cautious shadowy blob, the specter of a face pressed hard against the window-pane in the space which the shade did not shield. The face was tense and pale, almost ghastly in its earnestness. . . .

And Louisa, calmly, with the blank and sweet expression on her face never changing, drained the glass of buttermilk, put it down, rose, and began to unbutton her dress.

This was the moment, and Lane's eyes pained with the intensity of his gaze. The face at the window, he was willing to swear, showed an incredible astonishment for a moment, followed by an expression of horrible disappointment.

And then it popped out of sight, like a toy.

While Miss Smith was still splashing in the bathroom, Lane cautiously stepped out of the closet and tiptoed from the room. Louisa Campion did not even turn her head in his direction.

Scene 7

THE LABORATORY. SUNDAY, JUNE 19. AFTERNOON.

Mr. Drury Lane felt much better Sunday morning—very much better. Nevertheless, Dromio reported to Barbara Hatter, the only member of the household who seemed concerned, that Mr. Drury would spend most of the morning and part of the afternoon in the guest-room resting, and would Miss Hatter be kind enough to see that he was not disturbed?

Miss Hatter would, and Mr. Drury Lane was not disturbed.

At 11:00 o'clock Dr. Dubin presented himself, closeted himself with the "patient," reappeared ten minutes later, reported the "patient" was virtually recovered from the attack, and departed.

Not long past noon Lane repeated his secret investigation of the preceding night. Had he really been taken ill he could not have looked worse. His face was haggard; he had passed a sleepless night. Dromio gave him the signal, and he slipped into the corridor with hurrying feet and bent shoulders.

This Sunday tour of reconnaissance, however, did not have the death-room for its object. Instead, he went quickly into the laboratory. He moved with the speed of predetermined plan, making at once for the clothes closet to the left of the door and leaving the door open in a crack which permitted excellent visibility. And again, grimly, he composed himself to wait.

It was on the surface so inane, so futile. This matter of

ACT III: SCENE 7

crouching in a dark, suffocating cubicle, barely breathing, dead ears helpless to catch the loudest sound, tiring eyes constantly on duty at the crack—waiting, waiting endlessly, for hours. Hours in which nothing whatever occurred, in which no one entered the laboratory, in which not the slightest movement came to his eyes.

The day lengthened, interminably.

Whatever his thoughts were, and they must have been furious and boiling and desperate, he did not allow his vigilance to relax for an instant. And finally, at 4:00 o'clock in the afternoon, his vigil ended.

The first he knew of it was a flashing figure darting across his line of vision, coming from the direction of the one door, which from his position could not be seen. Lane had not heard the door open or close, of course. The weariness of hours dropped from him at once, and he glued his eye to the crack.

It was the intruder of the night before.

The figure did not hesitate. It made at once for the left side of the room, near the shelving, pausing so closely to Lane that Lane could see the panting exhalations of breath. A hand shot up to a lower shelf—and took down one of the few remaining bottles. As the bottle descended Lane saw the red label with its white letters: POISON, prominently displayed.

The intruder paused now, quietly eying the booty; and then, after a slow survey of the room, proceeded to the pile of débris lying where it had been swept in the left corner of the room near the window, and dug out a little empty unbroken bottle. Without stopping to cleanse the bottle under the tap, the intruder filled it from the bottle of poison, stoppered it, replaced the poison bottle on the shelf, and cautiously tiptoed toward Lane. . . . For an in-

THE TRAGEDY OF Y

297

stant Lane looked full into those burning eyes . . . then they passed him, going toward the door.

Lane sat crouched in his fatiguing position for a long moment, and then, rising, quickly stepped out into the laboratory. The door was closed; the intruder was gone.

He did not even go to the shelves to see what poison it was that the marauder had stolen. He stood still, like an old man pressed down by the weight of a grave responsibility, dully considering the door.

Then the pain passed, and he was the old Lane, a little wan, a little bowed, as was consistent with a gentleman recovering from a heart attack. Leaving the room, and proceeding confidently if a trifle weakly, he followed the trail of its visitor.

* * *

POLICE HEADQUARTERS. *Evening.*

Headquarters was quiet. It was past the working day, and except for the police on night duty the corridors were deserted. District Attorney Bruno pounded down the hall and burst into the room on the door of which was lettered Inspector Thumm's name.

Thumm was sitting at his desk contemplating by the single light of a desk-lamp a set of Rogues' Gallery photographs.

"Well, Thumm?" cried Bruno.

Thumm did not raise his eyes. "Well—what?"

"Lane! Have you heard from him?"

"Not a word."

"I'm worried." Bruno scowled. "It was a crazy thing for you to permit, Thumm. It may have tragic consequences. Taking those people's protection away from them. . . ."

"Aw, go peddle your habeas corpuses," growled Thumm. "What the devil have we got to lose? Lane seems to know

298   ACT III: SCENE 8

what he's doing, and we're absolutely without an idea."
He flung the photographs aside and yawned. "You know
how he is—keeps his mouth shut till he's sure. Let him
alone."

Bruno shook his head. "I still think it was unwise. If anything should go wrong . . ."

"Hey, look here!" roared Thumm. His small eyes
gleamed fiercely. "Haven't I got enough to worry about
without listening to a lot of old woman's chat—?" He bit
his lip, startled. One of the telephones on his desk was
ringing insistently. Bruno stiffened.

Thumm snatched up the instrument.

"Hello," he said hoarsely.

An excited buzzing. . . . As Thumm listened, dark blood
congested the tiny blood-vessels of his face.

Then, without a word, he banged the receiver down and
plunged for the door.

Rather helplessly, Bruno ran after.

Scene 8

THE DINING-ROOM. SUNDAY, JUNE 19. 7 P.M.

It was an afternoon in which Mr. Drury Lane tottered
about the house, smiling feebly and engaging various
members of the household in conversation. Gormly had
called early, and for a time Lane had conversed with him
on matters of no importance. Captain Trivett had whiled
away the entire afternoon in the garden with Louisa Campion and Miss Smith. The others had wandered about, list-

THE TRAGEDY OF Y 299

less, seeming unable to concentrate on any normal course
of deportment, half afraid of each other still.

It was notable that not once did Lane sit down. He
moved constantly, eyes restless and desperately intent, following, watching. . . .

At a quarter to seven in the evening he managed to signal unseen to Dromio, his chauffeur. Dromio slipped to his
side, and they conversed in murmurs. Then Dromio drifted
out of the house. He returned five minutes later, grinning.

Seven o'clock found Lane sitting in the dining-room in
a corner, smiling benevolently. The table was set for dinner,
and the household were straggling into the room in the
same weary, deadly fashion. It was at this moment that
Inspector Thumm, accompanied by District Attorney
Bruno and a squad of detectives, burst into the house.

The smile faded as Lane rose to greet Thumm and
Bruno. For an instant no one moved: Louisa and Miss
Smith were seated at the table; Martha Hatter and the
children were just sitting down; Barbara was coming in
from the other doorway as Thumm entered; Conrad was
in the library next door, Thumm saw, at his usual business of pouring liquor down his throat. Jill was absent,
but Captain Trivett and John Gormly were present, standing at the moment behind Louisa's chair.

No one uttered a word until Lane murmured: "Ah,
Inspector." Then the startled looks faded away, and indifferently they proceeded to seat themselves.

Thumm growled a greeting. With Bruno at his heels he
strode over to Lane and nodded grimly. The three men
retreated to a corner. No one paid attention to them; those
at the dinner table unfolded napkins; Mrs. Arbuckle appeared; the maid Virginia came in staggering under a
heavy tray. . . .

ACT III: SCENE 8

"Well?" said Thumm, quietly enough.

The haggard look returned to Lane's face. "Well, Inspector." That was all he said, and for the moment they were silent.

Then the Inspector growled: "Your man—he just called me—told me you said you were through, all washed up."

Bruno said hoarsely: "You've failed?"

"Yes," whispered Lane, "I've failed. I'm giving up, gentlemen. The experiment . . . was not a success."

Neither Thumm nor Bruno uttered a word; they merely stared at him.

"I can't do anything more," continued Lane, his eyes fixed on something beyond Thumm's shoulder almost with pain. "I wanted you to know because I'm returning to The Hamlet. At the same time I didn't care to leave before you stationed your men in the house again—for the protection of the Hatters. . . ."

"Well," said Thumm harshly, for the second time. "So it's licked you, too."

"I'm afraid so. This afternoon I had high hopes. Now . . ." Lane shrugged. "I am beginning to believe, Inspector," he added with a wry smile, "that I overestimated my talents. In the Longstreet case last year I suppose I was lucky."

Bruno sighed. "No use crying over spilt milk, Mr. Lane. After all, we haven't done any better. You've no reason to feel so badly about it."

Thumm wagged his head ponderously. "Bruno's right. Don't take it so much to heart. You've the satisfaction of knowing that you've got company. . . ."

He stopped suddenly, wheeling like an overgrown cat. Lane was staring at something behind Thumm's back with a world of sick horror in his eyes.

The Tragedy of Y

It occurred so rapidly, so unpreventably, that before they could release their sucked-in breaths it was over. The thing was pure lightning, paralyzing, like the strike of a snake.

The petrified Hatters were seated at the table, with their guests. The boy, Jackie, who had been hammering on the table demanding more bread, had raised a glass of milk before him—there were several on the table: one before Jackie, one before Billy, and one before Louisa—and drained half the glass in a greedy gulp. And the glass fell from his fingers, suddenly nerveless. Shuddering once, as he made a gurgling sound in his throat, Jackie stiffened convulsively . . . and slumped in his chair, to drop an instant later with a thud to the floor.

And then the paralysis passed, and they sprang forward —Thumm and Lane together, with Bruno behind them. The others were stricken dumb with fear, sitting still with open mouths, forks poised between tablecloth and lips, hands outstretched for salt. . . . Mrs. Hatter shrieked and fell on her knees beside the still little figure.

"He's poisoned! He's poisoned! Oh, my God—Jackie, speak to me—speak to mother!"

Thumm shoved her roughly aside, grasped the boy's jaws, squeezed powerfully until they came apart, and stuck his finger down the boy's throat. A weak rattling sound . . . "Don't move, any of you!" shouted Thumm. "Call the doctor, Mosher! He's——"

The order died on his lips. The little figure in his arms leaped upward, once, and then relaxed quite like a sodden bundle of clothes.

It was apparent even to the distended eyes of his mother that the boy had expired.

*　　*　　*

ACT III: SCENE 8

THE SAME. 8 P.M.

Upstairs, in the nursery, Dr. Merriam paced the floor—Dr. Merriam, who fortunately had returned from his week-end trip only an hour before the tragedy. Mrs. Hatter wept hysterically, half demented, clutching the trembling figure of Billy, the youngster, to her. Billy was crying for his brother—frightened, clinging to his mother. The Hatters were grouped around the stiff little figure on the bed, silent and grim and not looking at one another. In the doorway stood detectives. . . .

Downstairs in the dining-room there were two people—Inspector Thumm and Drury Lane, his eyes filled with pain. He looked startlingly ill—an illness which not even his art could disguise.

They said nothing. Lane sat limply at the table, staring at the fallen glass of milk from which the dead boy had 'drained his last Socratic potion. Thumm thundered up and down, his face parboiled with rage, muttering to himself.

The door opened and the District Attorney stumbled in. "Just a mess," he was saying. "Just a mess. Just a mess."

Thumm shot a furious glance at Lane, who did not even look up, but sat plucking at the cloth.

"We'll never live this down, Thumm," groaned Bruno.

"The hell with that!" snarled the Inspector. "What riles me is that he wants to give up now. *Now.* Why, man, you *can't* give up now!"

"I must," said Lane simply. "I must, Inspector." He rose and stood stiffly by the table. "I no longer have a right to interfere. The death of the boy . . ." He licked his dry lips. "No. I should never have joined you at all. Please let me go."

"But Mr. Lane . . ." began Bruno tonelessly.

The Tragedy of Y

"There is nothing I can say now in self-justification. I've made the most horrible hash of things. The boy's death is my fault, and mine alone. No . . ."

"All right," muttered Thumm; the anger had left him. "It's your privilege to retire, Mr. Lane. If there's any blame attached to this thing, it will come down on me. If you want to duck out this way, without explaining, without giving us a hint of what you've been working on . . ."

"But I've told you," said Lane in a dead voice. "I've told you. I was wrong, that was all. Wrong."

"No," said Bruno. "You can't get off as easily as that, Mr. Lane. There's something deeper going on here. When you asked Thumm to take his men away and leave a clear field for you, you had something definite in mind. . . ."

"So I did." Lane's eyes were rimmed with purple, Bruno noticed suddenly with a sense of shock. "I thought I was capable of preventing a further attempt. I found I was not."

"All this hocus-pocus," growled Thumm. "You were so damned sure the poison business was a blind. Wasn't really meant. Not much!" He groaned and cupped his face in his hands. "I tell you this thing proves it's a wholesale butchery. The bunch of 'em, due to be wiped out. . . ."

Lane bowed his head miserably, began to say something, choked it back, and went to the door. He did not even take his hat. Outside he paused for a moment, hesitating as if he desired to look back; then, squaring his shoulders, he went out of the house. Dromio was waiting for him at the curb. In the semi-darkness a group of reporters sprang for him.

He shook them off, stepped into his car, and buried his face in his hands as the car shot away.

EPILOGUE

"Den Bösen sind sie los, die Bösen sind geblieben."

Two months pass.

The exit of Mr. Drury Lane from the Hatter house terminates his connection with the case. From The Hamlet there has been silence. Neither Inspector Thumm nor District Attorney Bruno has made further approach to Lane.

Newspaper criticism of the police has been excoriating. A passing mention of Lane's connection with the case has died of its own anæmia of facts. At the end of two months the inquiry is no more advanced than before. Despite Inspector Thumm's prediction, there have been no further developments of a criminal nature.

There has been, behind the closed doors of officialdom, an investigation. And while the Inspector has emerged from the mêlée scarred and bruised, the threat of demotion and disgrace has not materialized.

And so the police have been compelled to withdraw finally, and for all time, from the Hatter house—outwitted, as the press sarcastically comment, by the clever murderer. . . . It is not long after the burial of Jackie Hatter that the Hatters, held together for years by the iron hand of the old lady, fall out and

EPILOGUE

separate. . . . Jill Hatter disappears, leaving Gormly, Bigelow, her latest fiancé, and a horde of male worshipers at a loss to account for her desertion. . . . Martha, summoning the last vestiges of her self-respect in a pitiful determination, has left Conrad and lives with four-year-old Billy in a cheap apartment, pending a settlement. . . . Edgar Perry, under observation for weeks, has been released; he too disappears, only to bob up not long after as the husband of Barbara Hatter in a marriage that furnishes a journalistic and literary flurry which dies down quickly as the two quit America for England. . . . No one is left; the Hatter house is boarded up and offered for sale.

Captain Trivett potters about his garden, looking old and shrunken. Dr. Merriam continues his quiet, tight-lipped practice.

The case slips into limbo. Another unsolved crime added to the police records—one of New York's annual scores.

A single fact stands out, a circumstance which provides the newspapers with their last full measure of Hatterism. Three days before the marriage of Barbara Hatter and Edgar Perry, Louisa Campion has passed away in the middle of a siesta. The Medical Examiner agrees with Dr. Merriam that she has died of heart failure.

BEHIND THE SCENES

"View the whole scene, with critic judgment scan
And then deny him merit if you can."

Mr. Drury Lane was sprawled on the grass leaning over the stone lip of a pond, feeding breadcrumbs to his black swans, when old Quacey appeared in the path with Inspector Thumm and District Attorney Bruno behind him.

Both men looked sheepish and hung back. Quacey touched Lane's shoulder; Lane turned his head. He sprang to his feet at once with a look of immense surprise.

"Inspector! Mr. Bruno!" he cried.

"Glad to see you," muttered Thumm, shuffling forward like a schoolboy. "Come calling, Bruno and I."

"Er—hrrumph!—yes," said Bruno.

They stood as if they did not know what to do with themselves.

Lane studied them keenly. "You might help me sit on the grass," he said at last. He was dressed in shorts and a turtle-neck sweater, and his muscular brown legs were stained with the green of the grass. He folded his legs under him and sank into a squat, like an Indian.

Bruno shed his coat, unbuttoned his collar, and sat down

BEHIND THE SCENES

with a grateful sigh. The Inspector hesitated, and then flung himself earthward with the thunder of Olympus. They remained silent for a long moment. Lane was intent on his pond, and the amazing swoop of a long black swan's neck toward a crumb bobbing on the water.

"Well," said Thumm at last, "might's . . . Hey!" He reached forward and tapped Lane's arm; Lane looked at him. "I was talking, Mr. Lane!"

"Indeed," murmured Lane. "By all means proceed."

"I might as well tell you," said Thumm, blinking, "that we—that Bruno and I, that is—we're wanting to ask you something."

"If Louisa Campion died a natural death?"

They were startled, and looked at each other. Then Bruno leaned forward. "Yes," he said eagerly. "You've been reading the newspapers, I see. We're thinking of reopening the case. . . . What do you think?"

Thumm said nothing; he watched Lane from beneath his thick brows.

"I thought," murmured Lane, "that Dr. Schilling agreed with Dr. Merriam's verdict of heart failure."

"Yeah," said the Inspector slowly. "So he did. Merriam's always claimed the deaf-mute had a bum heart, anyway. His records bear it out, too. But we're not so sure. . . ."

"We think," said the District Attorney, "that some poison may have been used which leaves no trace, or else some form of injection that might have caused death without being suspicious."

"But I told you gentlemen two months ago," replied Lane mildly, tossing another handful of crumbs on the water, "that I was through."

"We know," said Bruno hastily, before Thumm could

THE TRAGEDY OF Y

309

growl a retort, "but we can't help feeling that you were always in possession of facts that——"

He stopped. Lane had turned his head aside. The gentle smile remained fixed on his lips, but his gray-green eyes brooded on the swans without seeing them. After a long time he sighed and turned back to his guests.

"You were correct," he said.

Thumm tore a fistful of grass from the sward and hurled it at his large feet. "I knew it!" he roared. "Bruno, what did I tell you? He's got something that we can use toward a——"

"The case is solved, Inspector," said Lane quietly.

They both started at that, and Thumm gripped Lane's arm so hard that Lane winced. "Solved?" he cried hoarsely. "Who? What? When? When, for God's sake—in the last week?"

"It was solved more than two months ago."

For a moment they could not find breath enough to speak. Then Bruno gasped aloud and went pale; and Thumm's upper lip trembled like a child's. "And you mean to say," whispered Thumm at last, "that for two months you've kept your mouth shut while the murderer's been at large?"

"The murderer is not at large."

They jumped to their feet like two puppets joined by the same pulleys. "You mean—?"

"I mean," said Lane in the saddest voice imaginable, "that the murderer is . . . dead."

One of the swans flapped sable wings, and sparkling water splashed over them.

"Sit down, please, both of you," said Lane. They obeyed mechanically. "In a way I'm glad you came today, and in a

310 BEHIND THE SCENES

way I'm not. I don't at this moment know whether I am doing right to tell you. . . ."

Thumm groaned.

"No, Inspector, I'm not tantalizing you out of sadistic delight in seeing you suffer," continued Lane somberly. "It's a very real problem."

"But why don't you tell us, man, for the love of Heaven?" cried Bruno.

"Because," said Lane, "you won't believe me."

A bead of sweat trickled down the Inspector's nose and dripped off his massive chin.

"It is so incredible," continued Lane quietly, "that I wouldn't blame either of you if, on hearing what I am about to say, you kicked me into the pond as a posturing liar, a romancer, a lunatic as mad"—his voice shook—"as mad as the Mad Hatters."

"*It was Louisa Campion,*" said the District Attorney slowly.

Lane's eyes bored into his. "No," he said.

Inspector Thumm waved his arm at the blue sky. "*It was York Hatter,*" he said harshly. "I knew it all the time."

"No." Mr. Drury Lane sighed and turned back to his swans. He tossed another handful of bread into the pond before they heard his voice again—low and clear and infinitely sorrowful. "No," he repeated. "It was—*Jackie.*"

*   *   *

It seemed as if all the world stood still. The breeze died down suddenly, and the swans glided away, the only moving things in their sight. Then old Quacey, somewhere far behind them, shouted in glee as he pursued a goldfish in the Ariel fountain, and the spell was broken.

Lane turned back. "You don't believe me," he said.

The Tragedy of Y

Thumm cleared his throat, tried to speak, failed, and cleared it again. "No," he said at last. "I don't believe you. I can't. . . ."

"It's impossible, Mr. Lane!" cried Bruno. "Absolute madness!"

Lane sighed. "Neither of you would be sane if you reacted otherwise," he murmured. "And yet, before I have finished, I shall have convinced both of you that it was thirteen-year-old Jackie Hatter—a child, a mere stripling touching on the fringe of adolescence, almost an infant as such things go—who three times set poison for Louisa Campion, who struck Mrs. Hatter over the head and caused her death, who . . ."

"Jackie Hatter," muttered Thumm. "Jackie Hatter," as if by repetition of the name he could garner some sense from the entire affair. "But how in the name of all that's holy could a skinny little mutt of thirteen years make up a plot like that and carry it off? Why, it's—it's nuts! Nobody would believe it!"

District Attorney Bruno thoughtfully shook his head. "Don't fly off the handle, Thumm. You're excited, or you'd know at least the answer to *that* one. It's not inconceivable for a boy of thirteen to *follow the outline of a crime all prepared for him.*"

Lane nodded lightly, and brooded at the grass.

The Inspector floundered like a dying fish. "York Hatter's outline!" he cried. "I see it all now. By God, yes! That devil of a brat . . . And I thought it was York Hatter— that he wasn't dead—tried to get on a dead man's trail. . . ." He shook with laughter that was made of bitterness and shame.

"It could never have been York Hatter," said Lane, "dead or alive, for, of course, there was always the possibility

BEHIND THE SCENES

that he *was* alive, identification not having been absolute. . . . No, gentlemen, it was Jackie Hatter, and from the beginning could only have been Jackie Hatter. Shall I tell you how—and why?"

They nodded dumbly. Mr. Drury Lane lay back on the grass, folded his hands beneath his head, and addressed his extraordinary story to the cloudless sky.

* * *

"I shall commence," he said, "at the investigation of the second crime—the murder of Emily Hatter. Remember, please, that I knew no more at the outset than either of you. I entered virgin territory with no preconceptions. What I saw, what I came to believe were purely the result of observation and analysis. Let me trace for you my reasoning from the facts—reasoning which convinced me that the boy was the prime mover in all the events, and which in turn led me to York Hatter's tragic outline. . . .

"The crime from the beginning presented extraordinary difficulties. We were faced with a murder to which there had actually been a witness, yet a witness who on the face of it might have been dead for all the assistance she promised. A deaf-dumb-and-blind woman . . . one who could not hear nor see and who, to complicate matters further, could not speak. Yet the problem was not insurmountable, for she did possess other senses which were alive. Taste, for one; touch, for another; and smell, for a third.

"Taste did not figure at all; we could not expect it to. But touch and smell did, and it was chiefly on the basis of clues derived from Louisa's having touched the murderer and smelled something about him that I got to the truth.

THE TRAGEDY OF Y

313

"I've already proved to you that the attempted poisoning of the pear in Louisa Campion's fruit-bowl and the murder of Mrs. Hatter in the next bed were the acts of a single person. I've also proved to you in former analyses that the poisoning of Louisa was never intended to be consummated, the only purpose of the plot being the death of Mrs. Hatter.

"Very well. Since poisoner and murderer were the same, then whomever Louisa touched that night in the darkness of the bedroom—the touch that caused her to faint—was our quarry. You will recall that Louisa had touched the nose and cheek of the murderer while she stood upright, her arm extended exactly parallel to the floor, shoulder high. You, Inspector, actually were on the track."

The Inspector blinked, and reddened.

"I don't see . . ." began Bruno slowly.

Lane, lying on his back, his eyes on the sky, did not see the movement of Bruno's lips. He continued quietly: "You said at once, Inspector, that the height of the murderer could be ascertained by figuring how tall a person would be if his nose and cheek were touched by a witness whose own height was known. Splendid! I thought then and there that you had got your teeth into the salient fact, and that the truth would soon come out, or what appeared to be the truth. But Mr. Bruno voiced an objection; he said: 'And how will you ever know that the murderer was not crouching at the time?'—a canny objection, to be sure, for if the murderer *were* crouching, his height depended upon the extent of his crouch, which naturally would be indeterminable. So, without examining into the facts further, both you and Mr. Bruno dropped this trail. Had you continued it—in fact, had you merely glanced down at the

BEHIND THE SCENES

floor—you would have had the truth at once, as I had it."

Bruno frowned, and Lane smiled sadly as he sat up and turned to face them. "Inspector, stand up."

"Eh?" said Thumm with bewilderment.

"Stand up, please."

Thumm obeyed wonderingly.

"Now, get on your tiptoes."

Awkwardly Thumm's heels left the grass, and he swayed on the tips of his toes.

"Now, still standing on tiptoe, crouch—and try to walk."

The Inspector bent at the knees clumsily, heels off the earth, and attempted to follow directions. He succeeded merely in waddling two steps and then lost his balance. Bruno chuckled—he looked like an overgrown duck.

Lane smiled again. "And what does your attempt prove, Inspector?"

Thumm bit off a blade of grass and scowled at Bruno. "Stop laughing, you hyena!" he growled. "Proves that it's damned hard to tiptoe in a crouching position."

"Very good!" said Lane crisply. "It is physically possible, of course, but we can certainly discard the possibility of a crouching walk on tiptoes when a murderer is leaving the immediate scene of his crime. Tiptoes, yes; but not tiptoes and a crouch. It is awkward, unnatural for a human being, and serves no purpose; in fact, retards speed. . . . In other words, if the murderer at the moment Louisa Campion touched him was tiptoeing from the room, we could discard at once the possibility that he was also crouching.

"The floor told a plain story. The footprints in the scattered talcum powder, you will recall, were only *toemarks* from the bed to the spot where Louisa touched the murderer—the spot, by the way, where the murderer changed direction and ran from the room, all the subsequent foot-

The Tragedy of Y   315

prints revealing not only toemarks but heelmarks as well, and much more widely spaced . . ."

"Toemarks," muttered Bruno. "Is it possible? But then I'm a dub at these things. I can't remember things photographically. *Were* they toemarks . . . ?"

"They were toemarks all right," growled Thumm. "Shut up, Bruno."

"Here," continued Lane calmly, "where there were only toemarks, there was the added fact that each toemark was only about four inches from the next one. Only one possible explanation—the murderer after turning from the bed at the point where he had bashed Mrs. Hatter's head, was leaving *on his toes*—no heelmarks. Was tiptoeing, further, because the successive marks were only four inches apart, the normal distance between steps while tiptoeing in a restricted area. . . . Then when Louisa Campion touched the murderer, he was standing erect—no crouch, remember—and on his tiptoes!

"But now," said Lane rapidly, "we *have* a basis on which to compute the murderer's height. Let me digress for a moment. We could see, of course, that Louisa Campion was of a certain height. At the time of the will-reading, when the entire family were together, it was also apparent that Louisa and Martha Hatter were both of the same height, and, moreover, that they were the shortest adults in the household. The height of Louisa I later established exactly when I visited Dr. Merriam and consulted her case card in his files: she was five feet four inches in height. But I myself did not require that exact height; I could see and approximate her height while she was telling her story. I estimated how tall she was at that time—as against my own height—and made a rapid calculation. Now follow, please, closely."

316 BEHIND THE SCENES

They watched him intently.

"How far from the top of a person's head is the top of his shoulder? Eh, Mr. Bruno?"

"Er—I haven't any idea," said Bruno. "I don't see how you can say exactly, anyhow."

"But you can," smiled Lane. "The measurements vary from individual to individual, and of course differ as between men and women. I happen to know vicariously; it is an item of information I picked up from Quacey, who knows more about the physical composition of the human head than anyone I've ever met. . . . The distance among women from top of head to top of shoulders is between nine and eleven inches—let's say ten inches for all women of average height, as you can verify by looking at any normal woman and estimating even with the eye.

"Very well, then! The tips of Louisa's fingers touching the cheek at a level with the murderer's nose told one thing at once—*that the murderer was shorter than Louisa.* For were he of the same height as she, she would have touched him at the top of his shoulder. Since she touched his nose and cheek, however, he must have been shorter than she.

"Could I get the murderer's height more exactly? Yes. Louisa was five feet four—64 inches tall. The distance from her outstretched arm to the floor being ten inches less than her full height, then the murderer's cheek where Louisa touched it was also ten inches less than her full height, or 54 inches from the floor. If the murderer's cheek near the nose were 54 inches from the floor, we merely have to estimate the proportionate distance from the murderer's nose to the top of his head to get his complete height. In the case of a person shorter than Louisa, roughly six inches. Total height of murderer, then, about 60 inches, or a flat

THE TRAGEDY OF Y

five feet tall. *But* the murderer was standing on tiptoes, so to get his real height you must subtract the distance a person rises in standing on tiptoe. I think you will find this to be about three inches. In other words, our murderer was roughly four feet nine inches tall!"

Bruno and Thumm looked dazed. "My God," groaned Thumm, "do we have to be mathematicians, too?"

Lane proceeded evenly. "Another way of computing the murderer's height: Had the murderer and Louisa been the same height, as I said a moment ago, she would have touched him shoulder-high, since her arm was rigidly outstretched shoulder-high. But she touched him at the nose and cheek. This means that his height equals her height minus the distance between his shoulder and nose. About four inches normally. Add three inches for being on the tips of his toes—seven in all. Then the murderer is seven inches shorter than Louisa, I said, who is five feet four. That made the murderer about four feet nine—a definite confirmation of my original calculations."

"Whew!" said Bruno. "That's going some. Getting such exact figures from a series of estimations by the eye!"

Lane shrugged. "You make it sound difficult, and no doubt my figures sound difficult, too. Yet it was ridiculously simple. . . . Let me give my argument leeway. Suppose Louisa's arm when extended was not exactly parallel to the floor—was a little lower than her shoulder, or a little higher. It could not be much either way, remember, for she is a blind person whose most accustomed gesture is the stiffly extended arm when walking; but we'll allow two inches higher or lower, certainly a liberal concession to the facts. That makes our murderer between four-seven and four-eleven. Still a very small person. . . . You may further object—I see the battle kindling in the Inspector's eye—

BEHIND THE SCENES

that my estimations of distances from the nose to the top of the head, or to the shoulder, are too exact. These you can test for yourself. But in any case, the very fact that Louisa touched the murderer's nose when he stood on tip-toe showed that he was considerably shorter than she—which in itself would have been sufficient for me to have said: It must have been Jackie Hatter she touched."

He stopped for breath, and Thumm sighed. It all seemed so simple when Lane explained it.

"Why Jackie Hatter?" continued Lane after a moment. "An elementary explanation enough. Since Louisa and Martha were *the shortest adults* in the family—she and Martha having been also of the same stature—as was apparent when they were all assembled together during the reading of the will, then the one she touched was no adult in the family. All other adults in the household are excluded too: Edgar Perry is tall, Mr. and Mrs. Arbuckle are tall, and so is Virginia. Outsiders, if this was a crime committed by someone not of the household? Well, Captain Trivett, John Gormly, Dr. Merriam—all tall. Chester Bigelow is of medium height, but medium height for a man is certainly not several inches less than five feet! The murderer could not have been a rank outsider, because from the other elements of the crimes the murderer proved himself to be on terms of familiarity with the house, the eating habits of its various tenants, topography, etcetera. . . ."

"I get it, I get it," said the Inspector glumly. "Right under our noses all the time."

"For once I must agree with you," said Lane with a chuckle. "Then the murderer could only have been Jackie Hatter, who my eye told me was just about the height my figures indicated—and this was confirmed with exactitude

THE TRAGEDY OF Y

319

when I read his case card at Dr. Merriam's and discovered that he was four feet eight inches tall—I was out one inch, that was all. . . . Naturally, it couldn't have been little Billy, his brother, aside from the palpable absurdity of the thought, because he is a tot, less than three feet tall. Another point: Louisa said she felt a smooth soft cheek. One thinks of a woman at once in this connection—as you did. *But a boy of thirteen has a smooth soft cheek, too.*"

"I'll be damned," said the Inspector.

"So, standing there in the bedroom learning Louisa's testimony, seeing her go through the experience of the night before—rapid computation—and there I was. Jackie Hatter, it seemed, was the prowler of the previous night, who had poisoned the pear intended for his aunt and had struck his grandmother over the head, causing her death."

Lane stopped for a moment to sigh and regard his swans. "Let me say at once that this seemed so absurd a conclusion that I discarded it immediately. That child the concoctor of an intricate plot requiring adult intelligence—and a murderer to boot? Ridiculous! I had precisely the same reaction then as you had a moment ago, Inspector; I laughed at myself. It was impossible. I must be wrong somewhere, or else there was an adult in the background who was directing the child. I even thought of an adult, whom I had never seen, lurking in the background—someone almost a midget—four feet eight or nine. But this was silly. I didn't know what to think.

"I kept my own counsel, of course. It would have been folly at the moment to have disclosed the result of my calculations to you. How could I expect you to believe when I myself did not believe?"

"I'm beginning to see—a lot of things," muttered Bruno.

"Indeed?" murmured Lane. "I don't think you see half

BEHIND THE SCENES

—one quarter—Mr. Bruno, with all respect for your perspicacity. . . . What happened? Louisa Campion claimed she smelled vanilla on the murderer. Vanilla! I said to myself; not incompatible with a child. I tried all the vanilla interpretations I could think of—candy, cake, flowers, and the rest, as you know. No progress. I searched the house alone for a possible connection, a clue. Still nothing. So ultimately I discarded the child theory in connection with vanilla and thought of vanilla as a chemical.

"I discovered from Dr. Ingalls that a certain base for salves used in various skin disorders, Balsam Peru, has a distinct vanilla odor. From Dr. Merriam I discovered that York Hatter had had a skin disorder on his arms and had actually used Balsam Peru as a healing agent. In the laboratory I found a record of a jar of this balsam . . . York Hatter! A dead man. Was it possible he was not dead?"

"That's where I went off," said Thumm gloomily.

Lane paid no attention. "Yes, it was possible. Identification had not been absolute. It was merely supposed that it was his body which had been picked up. . . . But—how about height? Your original account to me, Inspector, of the finding of the body did not mention its height; even if it were not York Hatter's body and he were planning a deception, he would have picked a corpse about his own stature, so that the height of the corpse would have helped me. But I did know York Hatter's height from his record card at Merriam's. It was five feet five inches. So it couldn't have been York Hatter Louisa touched—the murderer was a good deal shorter than Louisa, at the very least under five feet. . . .

"Then why that vanilla scent? The Balsam Peru logically must have been the source of the vanilla odor during the murder night; it was a chemical, it was in the laboratory

THE TRAGEDY OF Y 321

where the murderer selected his poisons, it was accessible on the shelves, and I had found trace of no other source of the vanilla odor. . . . Therefore, despite the fact that I felt Hatter could not have been responsible for the Balsam Peru odor on the night of the murder, I followed the trail hoping to uncover a reason why the balsam should have been used by someone else. The only reason I could ascribe to its use on the murder night was that the murderer deliberately left the trail hoping the police would find out that York Hatter had used Balsam Peru in the past. But this too seemed silly—York Hatter was dead. Or was he? The issue at that time was quite confused."

Lane sighed. "The next stop was the laboratory. You recall the disposition of the bottles and jars on the shelves? There were five shelves, each divided into three compartments, each compartment containing twenty receptacles, each receptacle numbered in order; Number One starting at the left side of the topmost shelf, first compartment. You recall, Inspector, that I pointed out the strychnine bottle, Number 9, as being almost in the center of the first section of the top shelf. And we found the prussic acid in Bottle Number 57, also on the top shelf, but in the third, or right-hand, partition. Had I not been present, and had you described this to me, I should have known that the order of the containers ran from left to right across the entire shelf, from first compartment to second to third. For Numbers 9 and 57 could not possibly be where they were unless this were the rotation. . . . So far, so good.

"Balsam Peru, by index, was in Jar Number 30—the jar was missing after the fire and explosion, but I could tell exactly where it had been standing from my knowledge of the order of containers. Since twenty containers filled one compartment, and there were no blank spaces, Number 30

322 BEHIND THE SCENES

must have stood virtually in dead center of the topmost middle shelf. . . . I had discovered that Martha Hatter was the only member of the household besides York himself who knew that the man suffered from a skin ailment. I called her and she confirmed this: yes, she had known he used a salve—she didn't recall the name—but she knew it smelled vanilla. When I asked her where the jar habitually stood—I had placed dummy bottles and jars in the central compartment of the top shelf—she walked over to the middle compartment and took down the jar which was standing where Number 30, the Balsam Peru, must have stood. . . . But then I discovered something important —something which had nothing to do with the nature of the *odor* at all!"

"What was that?" demanded Inspector Thumm. "I was there, and I didn't see anything remarkable happen."

"No?" smiled Lane. "But then you hadn't my advantages, Inspector. For how did Martha Hatter take down the jar? By standing on tiptoe; she barely reached the container. What did that mean? Simply that Martha Hatter, who was one of the two shortest adults in the household, had to stretch and stand on her toes in order to reach a jar on the top shelf. But the point was—she *could* reach the top shelf while standing on the floor!"

"But what's so illuminating about that, Mr. Lane?" frowned Bruno.

"You shall see." Lane's teeth flashed. "Do you recall that in our preliminary investigation of the laboratory—before the fire—we discovered two smudges on the edge of the shelving? Both were oval—obviously smudges left by fingertips. The first of them was on the edge of the second shelf directly under Bottle Number 69, the other on the edge of the second shelf directly under Bottle Number 90.

The Tragedy of Y

323

The smudges furthermore did not extend the entire depth of the edge, but only halfway up the edge. Now neither Bottle Number 90 nor Bottle Number 69 had any connection with the case—the first contained sulphuric acid, the second nitric acid. But there was another significance to the location of the smudges—Number 69, just above the first smudge, was directly under Bottle Number 9, one shelf below in other words; and Number 90, just above the second smudge, was directly under Jar Number 30—again one shelf below. And both Number 9 and Number 30 *had* figured in the case—9 containing the strychnine, which was used in the first poisoning attempt, in Louisa's egg-nog; 30 containing Balsam Peru, whose odor the murderer had given off the night of Mrs. Hatter's death. This could not have been a mere coincidence, obviously. . . . So my mind leaped to another circumstance at once. The three-legged stool, which by evidence of the three dustmarks stood normally between the work-tables, was actually found beneath the middle sections of the shelf. And the stool showed signs of disturbance—scratches and uneven dust smudges on its top. Certainly mere sitting could not have caused such an uneven dust effect, for sitting would have left either a smooth impression or would have wiped off most of the dust altogether. It could not cause scratches. . . . Now this stool, out of place, remember, was directly under Containers 30 and 90 in the middle section of the shelving. What could all this mean? Why had the stool been used? If not for sitting, then for what? Obviously for standing, which would explain both the nature of the scratches and the uneven dust smudges. But why standing? And then the story was plain.

"The finger smudges on the edge of the second shelf indicated that someone had tried to reach Containers Num-

324 BEHIND THE SCENES

ber 9 and 30 on the shelf above but had been unable to, the tips of the fingers reaching only to the edge of the second shelf. To get the bottles this person had to stand on something, and therefore used the stool. Presumably, of course, this latter attempt was successful, for we know the containers were used.

"Where did this take me? To this point: If someone had left a fingermark just below Bottles Number 69 and 90, then the distance from the shelf on which the smudges were to the floor must represent this person's height—not his real height, of course, but the height of his stretch, or reach. For if you try to get something which is just beyond your reach, you stretch to your full height, standing on your toes automatically, and extend your arm to its greatest vertical reach."

"I see," said the District Attorney slowly.

"Yes. For Martha Hatter had been able, standing not on the stool, but on the floor, to take a jar from the top shelf! This meant that every adult in the case could have reached the Balsam Peru on the top shelf without using the stool, while sanding on the floor, since Martha and Louisa were the shortest adults in the case. So the person who left the fingermarks on the edge of the second shelf and who then stood on the stool to reach the containers was that much shorter than Martha, and also was not an adult. . . . How much shorter? It was simple to compute. I borrowed your rule, Inspector, and measured the distance between the shelves, discovering that from the top shelf to the shelf below where the smudges were was exactly six inches. I also measured the depth of the shelfboard itself; it was one inch deep. Approximately, then, the smudge-maker was six inches plus one inch plus an added inch (for Martha reached an inch up the front of the jar)—which is to say,

The Tragedy of Y

325

about eight inches shorter than Martha. But since Martha is the same height as Louisa, and Louisa is five feet four, then the smudge-maker was about four feet eight inches tall!

"A remarkable and conclusive confirmation of my original deduction—again the trail of a fifty-six-inch murderer. Jackie once more!"

There was a little silence. "I can't get over it," muttered the Inspector. "I just can't."

"I scarcely blame you," replied Lane gravely. "I grew gloomier than before—damning confirmation of a theory I could not bring myself to believe. But this was too much. I could no longer shut my eyes to the truth. Jackie Hatter was not only the person who had poisoned the pear and hit Mrs. Hatter over the head, but he was also the one who had taken the strychnine for the egg-nog poisoning and had reached for the jar of Balsam Peru . . . all attributes of the murderer."

Lane paused and drew a deep breath. "I took stock. I had no doubt now that, mad as it seemed, thirteen-year-old Jackie was our *active* criminal. Fantastic, but unquestionable! Yet his plot was a complicated one—in a way clever, and undeniably mature and intelligent. It was absolutely inconceivable that this child of thirteen had thought it out himself, no matter how precocious. So this much I could say without further ado: There could be only two possible explanations. One was that he was merely the instrument of an adult intelligence who had worked out the plot and somehow got the child to carry it through. . . . But this was patently wrong. Would an adult use as his tool a child—the most undependable of creatures? Possible but not likely—the adult would run the enormous risk of the child's either disclosing his secret out of a

326 BEHIND THE SCENES

juvenile lack of values or from sheer mischief and bravado; or the child would crack under the first pressure of official interrogation and spill the whole story. Of course, it was possible that the child was being kept silent by threats of personal violence. But this did not seem likely either; children are transparent, and Jackie's behavior throughout was not that of a child being driven by fear."

"No argument from me on *that* point," grunted the Inspector.

"No," smiled Lane. "Now, even granting that an adult might have made the boy his tool, there were certain glaring inconsistencies in the execution of the plot to which an adult would never have subscribed—which an adult would never have permitted to occur—which were, as I shall point out in a moment, all indicative of a child-mind rather than a mature mind. On the basis of these inconsistencies I discarded the theory that an adult was directing Jackie's activities. Yet I could not but believe that the plot in its inception had been the product of an adult mind. So I was faced with this problem: How could an adult have conceived the plot and a child carried it out—and yet with no complicity between them? There was only one possible answer—my alternative—that the child was following a written plan which had been created by an adult, and that the adult knew nothing of the child's following of the plan (otherwise he would have revealed the plan to the police at once)."

"So that's how you got to the outline," said the District Attorney thoughtfully.

"Yes. I felt now that I was on the right track. Was there any indication of the adult creator of the plot? Yes. For one thing, the free and intelligent use of poisons certainly pointed to the chemist of the cast, York Hatter. For an-

THE TRAGEDY OF Y 327

other, Barbara Hatter had in her original testimony mentioned that her father had dabbled in fiction. This came back to me with force. Fiction! And then there was the Balsam Peru, which had been used exclusively by York Hatter. . . . The signs pointed to him, dead or alive."

Lane sighed, and stretched his arms. "You remember at one point I said I had two leads to follow, Inspector—and you were so amazed? The first was the vanilla odor, which I've described; the second was my visit to Barbara Hatter on the trail of the adult plotter. I was pleased to learn from her that my surmise that he had been working on a detective story was correct. For fiction dealing with crime is detective fiction, and I knew it must be that. She knew nothing more, except that Hatter had said he was *outlining* it. An outline, then, was possibly in existence! I was convinced that York Hatter, having at the very least outlined a murder plot with fictive intent, had inadvertently after his death furnished young Jackie with the blueprint instructions for a real-life crime.

"Jackie was following the outline. Had he destroyed it? Probably not; child psychology would dictate his hiding rather than destroying it. At least it was worth looking for. If he had hidden it, where could it be? Somewhere in the house, of course. Yet the house had been searched previously and nothing of the sort uncovered. Besides, I felt sure that a thirteen-year-old boy—in the pirate, cowboy-and-Indian, blood-and-thunder, Nick-Carter age—would choose a very romantic hiding-place for the outline. I had already discovered the boy's method of entry to the laboratory—the chimney and fireplaces. On the chance that this highly romantic method of ingress had dictated an equally romantic hiding-place for the outline, and since it seemed a likely place, I searched the interior of the chimney and

328 BEHIND THE SCENES

fireplaces and found above the dividing brick wall a loose brick, behind which was the outline. This was reasonable on another count, also; Jackie would be certain no one else knew of this fantastically appealing method of communication between the two rooms, and hiding the outline there would assure him that it would not be discovered by anyone.

"As far as the chimney is concerned, undoubtedly the child—mischievous, perverse, disobedient—in prowling about the house had deliberately tried to gain entrance to the laboratory just because he was forbidden to go there by his Gorgonish grandmother. As children will, amazingly sometimes, he must have ferreted in the fireplace on the bedroom side, seen that the wall did not extend all the way up, clambered up, and in this way found that he could get into the laboratory without having to use the door. Then he must have prowled about; and in the filing cabinet, in the one compartment we found empty, I suppose, he discovered the manuscript where Hatter had put it before committing suicide. Some time after, probably when he made up his mind to bring the fiction crime to life, he loosened the brick in the chimney—perhaps one was already loose and he merely took advantage of it as a hiding-place. . . . Another thing: Remember that he had a long time between the discovery of the outline and the first poisoning to mull over that fascinating murder plot, spelling out the hard words, getting the drift of it, no doubt not understanding half of it, but grasping enough to realize what to do. Remember, then, that this discovery of the outline was made before the first poisoning attempt but after the death of York Hatter."

"Just a kid," muttered the Inspector. "And all that . . ." He shook his head. "I— Hell, I don't know what to say."

THE TRAGEDY OF Y

"Then listen!" said Bruno savagely. "Go on, Mr. Lane."

"To get back to the outline itself," continued Lane, unsmiling now. "I could not take it away when I found it; Jackie would discover it was gone, and it suited my purpose to have him think he was gloriously successful as a plotter. So I copied it on the spot and replaced it. I found also a vial full of a white liquid I was sure was poison, and substituted milk for it to be on the safe side—and for another reason which will be apparent when you read the manuscript itself."

There was an old jacket lying on the grass nearby, and Lane reached for it. "I've been carrying it with me for weeks," he said quietly. "An amazing document. Suppose you gentlemen read it before I continue."

He produced from one of the jacket pockets the pencil copy of York Hatter's outline, and handed it to Bruno. The two visitors read it together, avidly. Lane waited in silence until they finished. Dawning intelligence was on both faces as they handed it back in the same silence.

"I said a moment ago," Lane went on when he had put the copy carefully away, "that there were certain glaring and childish inconsistencies in the *execution* of an otherwise maturely planned plot. I'll discuss them as they came up during the investigation.

"First, the poisoned pear. Forget for the moment that the intention was not to kill Louisa. At least the poisoner was going to poison the pear, no matter what his motive. Now we found the hypodermic used to inject the poison *in the room itself*. The pear, we knew, was not in the room to begin with: it had been brought in by the poisoner. In other words, the poisoner brought in an unpoisoned pear and proceeded to poison it on the scene of his crime. How ridiculous! In fact, how childish! Would an adult

330 BEHIND THE SCENES

have done this? A crime presupposes haste, the possibility of discovery or interruption. An adult intending to poison the pear would have poisoned it on the outside *before* coming into the room where he meant to leave it, so that there would be no necessity of standing and jabbing the needle into the piece of fruit at a time when every second was precious, when discovery was imminent at any moment.

"True, if the murderer had left the hypodermic in the room purposely, then I would not be able to conclude that the reason it was brought was to poison the pear *in* the room, for then I should not know whether the pear had been poisoned inside the room or out. But suppose for the moment I discuss the theory that the hypo was brought to be left in the room purposely. Why? Only one reasonable possibility: to bring attention to the fact that the pear *was* poisoned. But this was unnecessary; the murder of Mrs. Hatter, proved to be a premeditated crime, not an accident, and especially since it followed a previous poisoning attempt, would cause the discovery that the pear was poisoned, for the police would *look* for signs of poisoning —as, in fact, Inspector Thumm began to do. Then the probabilities pointed to the hypodermic's having been left by accident, and this meant that the only possible reason for bringing the hypodermic into the room at all was to use it in poisoning the pear in that room. . . . And this was confirmed when I read the outline."

He took the outline from the jacket pocket again and unfolded it. "Exactly what does the outline say? It says: 'The idea this time is to poison a pear and put it in fruit-bowl,' and so on. Then later it says: 'Y . . . brings into room a squashy pear, which is poisoned by jabbing pear with hypodermic,' etcetera. To a child's mind," continued Lane, tossing the sheets on the grass, "the outline was

THE TRAGEDY OF Y   331

ambiguous, did not specifically state whether the pear should be poisoned before coming into the room or after. Also it did not specify leaving the hypodermic in the room. Hatter took for granted, as any adult would, that the pear would be poisoned before it was brought to the scene of the crime.

"Therefore, whoever interpreted the outline's instructions interpreted them literally, poisoning the pear in the death-room. . . . I saw at once that this was a sign of the juvenile mind. In other words, the situation had been conceived by an adult but executed by a child—the execution showing how the juvenile mind operated when there were no specific orders."

"Damned if it isn't true," muttered the Inspector.

"Second inconsistency. You recall that the dust of the floor in the laboratory had many footprints, none of them whole or clear? Now the dust could not have had any-thing to do with Hatter's original plot. Obviously—since in that plot he himself would be living in the laboratory and there wouldn't be any dust at all. So the footmarks and anything else we derived from studying them applied to real-life events exclusively. We saw evidences that the user of the laboratory had scuffed away the outlines of all the clear footprints—ingenious, in a way, for a boy. Yet there was not a single footprint, scuffed or unscuffed, near the only door of the room! Now, an adult would not have neglected to leave traces of footprints near the door, because the real method of entry was through the chimney, and that was meant to be kept a secret. Footsteps near the door would have made the police believe the intruder had en-tered through the door, probably with a duplicate key. The lack of footprints near the door positively invited an in-vestigation of the fireplace. Again, as I say, the sign of an

332 BEHIND THE SCENES

immature mind, overlooking a most obvious loophole in his actions—a loophole which, since he *did* think of scuffing out the footprints, an adult would certainly not have left open."

"And that, too," said Thumm hoarsely. "God, I'm dumb!"

"Third inconsistency, and perhaps the most interesting of all." Lane's eyes sparkled momentarily. "You were both baffled—as I was—by the incredible weapon which killed Mrs. Hatter. Of all things, a mandolin! Why? Frankly, until I read the outline I hadn't the faintest idea why Jackie should have selected the mandolin as his weapon. I naturally assumed that whomever's plot he was following, the mandolin was specified for some peculiar reason. I even considered the possibility that it was used merely to implicate its owner, York. But that didn't make sense, either."

He picked up the outline again. "Consult the outline. What does it say? Not a word about a mandolin! It says just this: 'Hits Emily over head with *blunt instrument.*'"

Thumm's eyes widened, and Lane nodded. "I see you get the inference. Perfect indication of a childish interpretation. Ask the first thirteen-year-old child you meet what is meant by a 'blunt' instrument. The chances are a thousand to one against his knowing. Not another word in the outline refers to this blunt instrument of murder, York Hatter having put the phrase down automatically, knowing what any adult would know—a blunt instrument is a dull heavy weapon of some sort. Jackie reads it, and it is meaningless to him. He has to secure some outlandish thing called a 'blunt instrument' and hit his hated grandmother over the head with it. How does a child mind work? Instrument—it means only one thing to a child:

THE TRAGEDY OF Y

333

musical instrument. Blunt—well, he let it go at that; perhaps had never heard the word, or if he had, he didn't know what it meant. Or he may have looked it up in a dictionary and discovered that it was something broad, not pointed; dull rather than sharp. He must at once have thought of the mandolin—the *only* 'instrument' in the house, as Barbara Hatter said, having belonged besides to York Hatter, the criminal of the plot! This was positive proof of a child; only an adult idiot would have construed 'blunt instrument' that way."

"Amazing, amazing," was all Bruno could find to say.

"In a general way, I knew that Jackie had found the manuscript in the laboratory and was following it step for step to commit a real crime. Now consider the outline itself: it specifically states that York Hatter himself—of course, Hatter meant the character in his fiction story who represented himself—that York Hatter was meant to be the murderer. Suppose an adult found the outline and conceived the plan of following it in the execution of a real crime. He reads that York is to be the criminal in the story. But York is dead. Wouldn't an adult therefore discard any part of the written plot which leaves a trail to York? Naturally. Yet what did our murderer do? He used the business of the Balsam Peru, which was to lead back to York Hatter as the outline stated. York Hatter's use of it was clever: it was his 'smell' clue to lead back to the story's murderer, the clue by which he himself would be caught at the end of the tale. In real life, however, with Hatter dead, utilizing the vanilla odor to lead back to York Hatter is infantile. . . . Again what do we find? A mind blindly following printed instructions—an immature intelligence.

"A fourth inconsistency, or is it a fifth? In Hatter's story,

334   BEHIND THE SCENES

it is all right for him to be the criminal and to plant a clue which leads back to himself—the vanilla odor. In his story that is a *real* clue. But the clue of the shoes—Conrad's shoes—is a *false* clue, meant to be a false clue; as if the murderer were deliberately implicating Conrad to lead the police off the right trail.

"The situation changes, however, when it is no longer a story, but real life—someone following the fiction plot as a model for a genuine crime. The clue of the vanilla leading to York in this case becomes a *false* clue also! Because York is dead, not a factor in the plot now at all. Then why use two false clues leading to two different people, as the murderer did? Any adult in Jackie's place would have chosen the shoes of Conrad as his proper false trail and discarded the vanilla smell leading to the dead man—at least, would have chosen one of the two, not both indiscriminately. If he had chosen the shoes, he would not have felt the necessity of *wearing* them, too, as Jackie did. It was enough to splatter poison on one of the toecaps, then leave the shoes in Conrad's closet. But again Jackie, not being able to apply mature interpretation to the implied and specified instructions, actually wears the shoes when the outline didn't mean to have them worn at all. . . . The upsetting of the powder, not being called for by the outline, was sheer accident, proving that the shoes were not meant to be worn for the purpose of leaving footprints— the only possible excuse for wearing them. . . . All indications of a murderer without a sense of values, when confronted by a situation which requires only ordinary adult intelligence. Again, as I say, the earmarks of a child.

"And finally, the business of the fire. I was puzzled by the fire before I read the outline. Incidentally, too, before I read the outline many things puzzled me, because I was

The Tragedy of Y

335

trying to find reasons for everything, and there were none! things having been done blindly. . . . In the outline, the purpose of the fire is stated: to make it appear that York Hatter was being attacked by some outsider, and was therefore innocent. But with Hatter dead, the fire incident centering about his private room became purposeless, and any adult would either have discarded it entirely, or adapted it to his own use—that is, begun a fire in his own room or centered it in some way about himself. Probably an adult would have discarded it, because even in York's fiction story it is a poor device; not a particularly clever detective-story element.

"What have we, then? The outline of a fiction crime being followed with stupid blindness to the last detail— the follower showing by every action that calls for original or selective thinking that he is immature, a child. These things confirmed my belief that Jackie was the murderer, and will convince you, as they convinced me, that Jackie understood not one subtlety of the outline he was following so faithfully; that the only things he grasped were the clearly specified statements of *what was to be done*. The reasons for them he did not understand. The only mental hiatus his brain made was this: he saw by the outline that York was the criminal. He knew York was dead. He got the idea of himself being York, or the criminal. So wherever the outline said that York, or Y, had to do something, Jackie placed himself in York's position and did it. Even to the extent of following those instructions which York in his outline intended deliberately to be the undoing of himself, the criminal! And wherever Jackie did something on his own, or had to interpret something that was not specifically clear, he reacted characteristically and did the childish thing, giving himself away."

336 BEHIND THE SCENES

"That damned first poisoning attempt," said Thumm, clearing his throat. "I can't see . . ."

"Patience, Inspector. I was just coming to it. We had no way of knowing at that time whether the attempt was meant to be consummated or not. When we reasoned after the murder, however, that the second poisoning attempt was not meant to be consummated, it was fair to assume that the first had not been, either. Before I knew that the plot was York's, at the time when I felt Jackie to be the criminal, I said to myself: 'It was Jackie who, seemingly by accident, forestalled the poisoning attempt in the egg-nog incident. Is it possible that his drinking of the poisoned egg-nog was not an accident, but done deliberately? If so, why?' Well, if the second attempt was not meant, and the first attempt was not meant, how would the murderer plan to forestall Louisa's taking even a sip of the egg-nog, and yet at the same time bring to light the fact that the egg-nog was poisoned? After all, merely dosing the drink and spilling it as if by accident, for example, would not bring out the fact that it had been poisoned; the appearance of the puppy couldn't have been anything but an accident. So, if Louisa was not to drink it, and yet it must be known that it was poisoned, the murderer had to adopt heroic measures. The fact that Jackie himself drank some was *prima facie* evidence that he was following instructions of some sort—he could not have poisoned it himself and also conceived the idea of drinking it and getting sick —not child's reasoning at all. The fact that he went through with it at all confirmed my conviction that he was following a plot not his own.

"When I read the outline everything became clear. Y had intended in his story to poison the egg-nog, then sip a bit himself, getting slightly sick—accomplishing the triple end

The Tragedy of Y

337

of not harming Louisa, yet making it appear that someone was trying to harm her, and finally putting himself in the most innocent position of all—for would a poisoner deliberately fall into his own trap? A good plan on Hatter's part—for fiction; obviously, had he been creating a murder plot in real life, he would have balked at the thought of taking poison even as a blind."

Lane sighed. "Jackie reads the outline and sees that Y poisons the egg-nog and then sips it himself. Jackie knows he must do everything the outline says Y does; so he goes through with it as far as his courage—and the circumstances—permit him. The very fact that it was Jackie who drank the egg-nog in the first poisoning attempt, plus the fact that Jackie himself was the poisoner and murderer in the second case, was strong confirmation of his uncomprehending obedience to a fantastic and improbable plot which he certainly never understood in any of its implications."

"How about motive?" asked Thumm weakly. "I still can't get it through my nut why a kid should want to murder his grandmother."

"Baseball is one reason," said Bruno facetiously.

Thumm glared, and Bruno said: "After all, with a family like that it's easy enough to understand, Thumm. Eh, Mr. Lane?"

"Yes," said Lane with a sad smile. "You know the answer already, Inspector. You yourself know what the evil strain in this family was caused by. Although he was only thirteen, Jackie had in his veins the diseased blood of his father and grandmother. Probably at birth he was potentially a murderer—which is to say, he had the hereditary weakness of the Hatter strain, besides a predisposition to willfulness, mischief, and cruelty which all children, in a

338   BEHIND THE SCENES

measure, possess, but which he possessed in great measure.
... Do you remember his almost fanatic persecution of the
little fellow, Billy? His delight in destruction—trampling
flowers, trying to drown a cat—his absolute lack of discipline? Combine this with what I must vaguely guess at,
although it is probably true: there is no love lost anywhere
in the Hatter family and intra-family hatred is compatible
with the whole Hatter *mores*. She was always tanning the
boy's hide, in fact had whipped him only three weeks before
the crime for stealing a piece of Louisa's fruit; the boy
had overheard his mother, Martha, say: 'I wish you were
dead!' or something of the sort to the old lady—an accumu-
lation of boyish hatreds, fed by the evil in his brain, probably sparked into purpose when he read the outline and
saw that, of all people, his most pestiferous domestic enemy
and the enemy of his mother, 'Gran'ma Em'ly,' was scheduled to be murdered. ..."

The old haggard look that had so often appeared on
Lane's face returned to darken it now. "It is not hard to
understand then how this adolescent, warped by heredity
and environment, came to fall in with a plot which had
for its goal the death of his fancied enemy. And when he
took the first step—the attempted poisoning—and was not
found out, he saw no reason why he should not continue;
his criminal impulse fattened on success. ...

"Further complications of these confused crimes were introduced, as in most crimes, by accidents not planned by
York Hatter or anticipated by the little criminal: The upsetting of the powder-box on the night-table. The fact that
Jackie was touched by Louisa while he stood a-tiptoe.
The fingerprint smudges which confirmed the poisoner's
height."

The Tragedy of Y

Lane paused for breath, and Bruno hastened to ask: "Where does Perry, or Campion, fit in?"

"The Inspector has suggested the answer before," replied Lane. "Perry, stepson of Emily, nursing a hatred against her because she had been personally responsible for his father's horrid death—no doubt had something criminal in mind, else he wouldn't have changed his name and taken a job in the household. Nebulous or not, he wanted in some way to make Mrs. Hatter suffer. When the old lady was killed, however, he was in a precarious position. Yet he could not leave. Perhaps he abandoned his original intention long before the actual murder—he seemed much affected by Barbara's proximity. His actual intent will probably never be known."

For some time Inspector Thumm had been regarding Lane with a very queer sort of reflective attention. "Why," he asked, "were you so cagey all through the investigation? You say yourself that after the lab business you knew it was the kid. Why'd you make such a mystery of it? Wasn't quite fair to us, Mr. Lane."

Lane did not reply for a long time. When he did, it was in a subdued tone so full of unexpressed feeling that Thumm and Bruno were startled. "Let me give you a sketchy cross-section of my own emotions during the progress of the investigation. . . . When I knew that the child was the criminal, confirmation after confirmation banishing my last doubt, I was faced by a hideous problem.

"From every sociological standpoint that boy could not be considered morally responsible for his crime. He was a victim of his grandmother's sins. What was I to do? Reveal his guilt? What would your attitude have been if I had revealed it—you, sworn to uphold the law? Your

340   BEHIND THE SCENES

hands would have been tied. The child would have been
arrested. Perhaps sent to prison until he became legally of
age, and then tried for a murder which he had committed
at an age when he was morally irresponsible. Suppose he
were not convicted of murder, what then? The best he
could hope for would be acquittal on plea of insanity, and
he would spend the rest of his life in an asylum."

He sighed. "There I was, not sworn to uphold literal
justice, and feeling that, since the original sin was not the
boy's, since neither plot nor impulse was his, since he
was in the broadest sense the terrible victim of circumstances . . . he deserved his chance!"

Neither man said anything. Lane looked at the calm
ripples on the surface of the pond, and the black swans
gliding about. "From the beginning, even before I read
the outline, and while I worked on the assumption that the
plot had been conceived by an adult—I foresaw the possibility of another attempt on the life of Louisa. Why? Because, since the first two attempts had not really been
meant, since Mrs. Hatter's death was the prime purpose,
it seemed logical that the plotter had figured on one more
'attempt' against Louisa to strengthen the illusion that the
motive applied against her rather than her mother. . . . I
could not be sure that perhaps this third attempt might
even go through, providing the new plotter really wanted
to kill Louisa. At any rate, I felt certain another attempt
would be made.

"This theory was confirmed by the fact that in the cache
in the chimney wall I found a vialful of physostigmin, a
poison which had not yet been used in the plot. I substituted milk for the physostigmin for two reasons: to
forestall a slip, and to give Jackie his chance."

"I'm afraid I don't quite see how——" began Bruno.

The Tragedy of Y

341

"Which was why I couldn't tell you where I found the outline," retorted Lane. "You would never see until it was too late. You would have set a trap for him, caught him there, and arrested him. . . . In what way was I giving him a chance? In this way. The manuscript, when I found it, stated in more than one place that there was *no* intention, ever, to poison Louisa; repeated, as you read, that she was *not* to be killed. By placing a harmless fluid in the vial, I gave Jackie the opportunity of carrying out with no harmful results the last specific order of the outline—which was to make a third false poisoning attempt against Louisa. I felt sure he would follow the outline's instructions to the bitter end. . . . I asked myself: What will he do after he has poisoned the buttermilk, as the outline instructs him to do? The outline had not been worked out fully in this respect—Y merely says that he will either call attention to something wrong with the buttermilk, or in some other way prevent Louisa from drinking it. So I watched."

They were leaning forward, tense. "What did he do?" whispered the District Attorney.

"He slipped into the bedroom from the ledge, got his vial containing what he thought was poison. The outline, as I knew, called for fifteen drops in a glass of buttermilk. Jackie hesitated—and then poured *the entire contents of the vial* into the glass." Lane stopped, and winced at the sky. "This looked bad; it was the first time he had deliberately disobeyed the outline's instructions."

"And?" said Thumm harshly.

Lane looked at him with weariness. "Despite the fact that the plot instructed him to call attention to the poisoned milk before Louisa could drink, *he did not do so.* He allowed her to drink it; in fact, he watched from the ledge

BEHIND THE SCENES

outside the window, as I saw; and there was disappointment on his face when she drank the buttermilk and suffered no ill effects."

"Good God," said Bruno in a shocked voice.

"Not a very good God," said Lane heavily. "Not to that poor young creature. . . . Now my problem was: What would Jackie do? True, he had disobeyed the letter of the outline in several respects; but now that the outline was finished, would he let well enough alone? If he stopped there, if he made no further attempt to poison Louisa or anyone else, I meant firmly to say nothing at all about his guilt, to profess myself defeated, to step out of the drama. The boy would have his chance to correct the evil in him. . . ."

Inspector Thumm looked uncomfortable, and Bruno busied himself watching the mad pace of an ant hurrying hillward with a speck of dried leaf. "I watched the laboratory," came the lifeless voice. "The only place where Jackie could secure more poison—if he wanted it." A pause. "And he wanted it. I saw him steal into the room, deliberately take down a bottle marked POISON, and fill a little bottle. Then he left."

Lane jumped to his feet and toed a clump of earth. "Jackie had convicted himself, gentlemen. The lust for blood and murder had gone to his head. . . . Now he was using his own initiative, going beyond the prepared and specific instructions—in fact, disobeying the outline. I knew then that he was incorrigible, that if he lived on unsuspected he would be a lifelong menace to society. He was not fit to live. At the same time, if I denounced him, there would ensue the terrible spectacle of society revenging itself on a thirteen-year-old child for a crime which, in the last analysis, was society's own. . . ." Lane was silent.

THE TRAGEDY OF Y

343

When he spoke again, it was in a different tone. "The tragedy of the entire piece, as you might say, was properly the Tragedy of Y—as he called himself—York Hatter planning a crime in the spirit of fiction, and creating a Frankenstein monster in the mind of his own grandson, who took it up and carried it out to its gruesome conclusion—far beyond what Y had intended even in fiction. When the child died, I chose to act a part, as if I were shocked by the tragedy—rather than reveal his guilt. What good would it have done anyone? It was better for all concerned that the boy's guilt never be made public. Had I revealed his guilt then, at a time when your superiors and the press were clamoring for a solution, you would have been only human to publish the facts. . . ."

Thumm began to say something, but Lane forged on. "And there was Martha, Jackie's mother, to consider and, more important, the little fellow, Billy, who after all must have his chance, too. . . . At the same time, Inspector, I did not mean to see you suffer. Had you been demoted, for example, as a result of your failure to turn up the criminal, I should have felt constrained to come to you with the solution, so that you could get credit for it and save your position. That much I owed you, Inspector. . . ."

"Thanks," said Thumm in a dry voice.

"But when two months went by and the storm of protest died away, and you were as firmly entrenched as before, I no longer had reason to withhold the facts from either of you—as men, mind you, not officers of the law. My one hope is that you will understand from the human standpoint my motives in all this nasty business—and continue to keep Jackie Hatter's hideous story a secret."

Bruno and Thumm nodded heavily; both men were thoughtful and subdued. Thumm nodded several times to

Behind the Scenes

344

himself. . . . Suddenly he sat up in the grass and hugged his meaty knees to his big chest. "You know," he said casually, "there's something about the last phase of this business that I don't get." He plucked a blade of grass and began to chew on it. "How the devil did it happen that the kid made a mistake in that last attempt, so that he drank the poisoned milk he intended for the Campion woman? Eh, Mr. Lane?"

Lane did not reply. He turned his face slightly away from Thumm, and suddenly dipping his hand into his pocket and taking out a fistful of bread, he began to hurl pieces on the surface of the pond. The swans swam gracefully toward him and began to peck at the bread.

Thumm leaned forward and petulantly tapped Lane on the knee. "Hey, Mr. Lane? Didn't you hear what I said?"

District Attorney Bruno rose very suddenly. He punched Thumm's shoulder roughly and the Inspector, startled, looked up at him. Bruno's face was white, and his jawline was rigid.

Lane turned slowly around and looked at the two men with tortured eyes. Bruno said in a peculiar voice: "Come, Inspector. Mr. Lane is tired. We'd better be getting back to the City."

CURTAIN